They don't have dragons where half-faerie Sadie was born—not living ones, anyway—but in the Grove, everyone knows dragon eggs grow on trees like leaves and need Dreams to hatch. Without faerie Dreams, the dragons won't survive. And neither will anyone else.

Brash, boyish sixteen-year-old Sadie uses her half-human status to spy on the human monarchy, who've made it illegal to Dream. But spying is a risky business. Still, Sadie thought she was a pro until they sent a new human magistrate to the Grove. Evelyn.

Evelyn might be the most beautiful girl Sadie's ever seen, and Sadie might be betraying her family by falling in love with the ruthless leader who locks them up. But that's not even the biggest obstacle between the two: Evelyn is leading the charge against Dreaming, and there's something she doesn't know. Sadie can still Dream.

A NineStar Press Publication

Published by NineStar Press
P.O. Box 91792,
Albuquerque, New Mexico, 87199 USA.
www.ninestarpress.com

Lunav

Copyright © 2018 by Jenn Polish
Cover Art by Natasha Snow Copyright © 2018

This is a work of fiction. Names, characters, places, and incidents are either the product of the author's imagination or are used fictitiously. Any resemblance to actual persons living or dead, business establishments, events, or locales is entirely coincidental.

All rights reserved. No part of this publication may be reproduced in any material form, whether by printing, photocopying, scanning or otherwise without the written permission of the publisher. To request permission and all other inquiries, contact NineStar Press at the physical or web addresses above or at Contact@ninestarpress.com.

Printed in the USA
SunFire Press Imprint
First Edition
March, 2018

Print ISBN: 978-1-948608-33-6

Also available in eBook, ISBN: 978-1-948608-28-2

LUNAV

Jenn Polish

For Erika

PART ONE

PART ONE

Chapter One

THE NIGHT HANGS over us, in us, and I shiver a little in the cold. Even in the safety of my disguise, I swallow loudly. Lerian shoots me a look, pawing snow away from the packed dirt of the Tread with her front hoof. We both stare at the ground ahead of us, our ears straining for the signal that will indicate that we can proceed with our plan. We only have until the moon starts setting to infiltrate and sabotage the monarchy's weapons shipment. A small thumping ahead of us, in the clearing where the caravan has curled in on itself, gives us the sign we're waiting for.

"*No need to hang back anymore, you two,*" Osley tells us through the beating of quer paws. "*Sadie, the freeze spell worked. Come see.*"

Lerian meets my eyes before I reach down to receive permission from the grass for us to move forward. Her hooves and my feet barely make a sound as we slip across the thick layer of snow past the first wagon and the first pair of magically frozen guards. I pause to pat one lightly on the shoulder. He won't wake—not as long as my growns are holding their freeze spell on the encampment—but in this weather, the small dribble of drool on his chin will be stuck to his face when we're done here.

Osley stamps quer feet impatiently, quer long rabbit ears twitching with irritation, as Lerian bends way down to move the other guard's temporarily stiff fingers into a position that would for sure offend Mom.

"Do I seriously look like them?" I whisper.

"Yep. Spitting image. With your wings tucked away, Sadie, you look exactly like a non." I arch an eyebrow at the way she so casually refers to humans as nons: non-faeries, non-centaurs. Non-Grovian. Not like us. Except, I kind of am like nons, too. Ler pauses to consider me, running her fingers through her reddish hair. "Except probably you're uglier."

I roll my eyes and suppress a grin, not bothering to remind her that the front half of centaurs' bodies pretty much look like nons too.

Osley's thumps grow more insistent. "*Sadie, we're on a mission. Get Lerian over here.*"

"All right, all right, we're coming."

I give Lerian a sharp tug, and we follow Osley as que leaps toward the heart of the coiled wagons. The air itself is crystallized with particles of dirt and flakes of snow, all hanging suspended around us, like bubbles floating in the ocean. There's a fire pit in the middle of the encampment, but it, too, is still, with flames frozen in midcaress of the tree flesh it consumes, still midspark, midcrackle. The closer we get, the harder it is to breathe. The freeze spell has the Energies so deeply entangled it feels like walking through nectar. I limp even deeper than I usually do when I'm forced to walk.

A sharp smack from behind the fire pit makes our cautious steps turn into an awkward run and a graceful gallop. We round a bend in the encampment's wagons to see Mom and Mama, hovering over two chained faeries and their frozen non guards.

The faerie prisoners look like they're from the Samp, a marshy province a few days' journey from the Forest. The Sampians don't look much older than Lerian and me. They're nears, like us, but their wings are hidden away inside metal clamps, their necks connected by a piercing necklace. Their ankles and wrists, too, are chained together, and they've been propped up back to back, to sleep outside on the snow while most of the guards are around the fire or tucked into the relative warmth of their wagons.

One of the Sampians is flailing around, the chains from his wrists and ankles tugging on his fellow prisoner, threatening to both topple her over and whip her with their force. Mama's webbed hand is on her cheek. She looks like she's just gotten smacked—with flesh or metal, I can't tell. My stomach is as shaky as my bare fingers.

One of the prisoners is reaching out to Mama, apologizing for her partner-in-chains, crying softly, explaining that he can't help it, that it's not his fault.

Mama dodges another blow. Both of his eyelids are closed, relaxed, but his body is the opposite. Mom is trying to calm him, like she tries to calm me when I...My heart threatens to fall out of my throat. He's sleeping, yet he's moving about in his chains like...

I step closer, in a daze, my attention on nothing but the Sampian boy. His wings are in those clamps, so he can't move them except by thrashing his entire back around. To compensate, he's flapping his golden brown arms about, as much as his chains will let him, just like a sparrow does when she's taking flight. Soon enough, the motion of his arms evens out, like they're catching the wind underneath them, rising...

I don't realize I've stopped breathing until all my breath bursts out of me in one massive, cloudy white exhale, staying in the freeze spell instead of dissipating like it normally would. I step through the cloud so my attention doesn't have to leave the sight in front of me. My mouth is desert dry.

The imprisoned Sampian can Dream. Like me.

No wonder he's in chains.

Without even turning around, Mom calls back to me, "Sadie, don't." Don't act as if I've just found my kin. Don't act as if I've just seen, for the first time since I was a young one, another near, a nearly grown person, who sleeps as I do. Who hasn't been Sliced.

I grind my teeth at the thoughts of Slicings—when they cut into the skull of newly born faeries, nons, and centaurs, and inject dragon blood into our brains. Sometimes, it kills us right then and there from so-called complications. Always, it stops us from ever Dreaming. From ever forming the connections we need to with our hatchling trees and dragons. From ever connecting with any of the lives across Lunav beyond our own.

I clear my throat and bend over to help Mama twist the Energies, already so stiff around us from the freeze spell, to unlock the chains around the Sampian who's awake. When she notices me, she jolts back like she's been burned, her thin golden eyes wide with terror.

Mama grimaces and holds up her own hands, showing the Sampian girl the webbing between her fingers, the way she flies horizontally with her stomach facing the ground, instead of upright, like Grovians.

"Look, it's all right. I'm Sampian too. This is my daughter. She's Grovian. Her wings are hidden under her cloak," she says in Sampian faeric. The girl continues to stare at me. I look away. Lerian, shuffling behind us awkwardly, doesn't even scoff. For once.

Osley hops between the girl and me, thumping out a message urgently. *"Mara, these are the people I told you about on the Tread this sunup. These are the people the Grove has sent to help you sabotage the weapons shipment. To help you escape. It'll be all right."*

The girl—Mara—sighs and glances toward her companion. Mom's started to rouse him from his sleep, from his Dream. I wouldn't wish a bad Dream on anyone, but I hope it wasn't a great Dream, either. Waking from those is never exactly fun. Then again, it seems he was Dreaming some sort of bird, so compared to his chains... I look away and focus on Mara.

"Blame my moms. They made me tuck my wings away tonight so in case we got caught, I could pass as a non and maybe escape. I don't usually look this—" I glance over my shoulder at Lerian and grin. "—ugly."

Mara just bites the inside of her cheek. She turns to the boy and touches her webbed hands to the back of his neck, right above the chained collar. He jerks awake, eyes wide and pained. His breathing is ragged and shallow, and when his wild brown eyes find mine, he almost lets out a scream. Mama puts a gentle but urgent hand over his mouth.

"I'm sorry, so sorry, but you're safe, and so is your secret. This is my daughter; she's a faerie. We're resistance, and we're here to help." He twists his neck and finds Mara's eyes. She nods in the Sampian way, tilting her head all the way down to her right shoulder, confirming my mom's words. He closes his eyes again, and even though I don't know him, I can still tell what he's doing. He's willing himself back into the life of that bird. Willing himself to Dream again. But it won't come back. They never do on command. Dreams only come when we're in our deepest rest, when our Energies are most primed to be utterly synced with someone else, someone awake. After a moment, the boy sighs and opens his eyes again.

"You're here to help us sabotage the weapons, right?" He turns his gaze down to Osley. Que shakes quer hind legs at him in confirmation, and Mom and Mama set about twisting the Energies to ease Mara and the boy out of the rest of their chains. They clank to the ground and force soft tufts of freshly fallen snow up into the air. The clumps of white just hang there, suspended.

"H-how's it doing that?" the boy asks as he rubs his wrists, his neck, and sweeps his wings up eagerly, stretching them and sighing in relief.

"You never heard of a freeze spell?" Lerian asks as she tugs him to his feet, the boy's thick sunset-red wings still crumpled from the clamps.

He stares around at the still guards blankly expanding the gill flaps on his neck. "Wish we could do ourselves a freeze spell," he mutters to Mara. "How long will it last?"

Mom hovers in closer, seeming relieved that we can get started and do what we came here to do. "Long enough. But we're gonna have to get going. Can you conjure any magic?"

"We can't do anything like that freeze thing you did, but we can put some impurities into these weapons for sure," Mara says before grabbing the boy and pulling him in for a deep, hands-everywhere kiss.

I don't know whether to laugh or cry, so I study my feet intently. Lerian bends down to pack some snow into her fist, and Osley's long ears press down into quer gray-speckled white fur. Mom bows her head, touches her forehead to Mama's, and flies off toward one of the transport wagons, letting out a deep whistle into the disturbed Energies. That'll be the signal for the others surrounding the enclosure to come and help her sabotage her chosen wagon, full of palace weapons.

Mama gestures for the rest of us to accompany her into another wagon. She peeks inside its Izlanian buffalo-skin covering before nodding at us—no nons are sleeping in this wagon. It's just for weapons. Perfect.

I wiggle my fingers, preparing them to twist the already tensed Energies, which will work imperfections into the weapons they're shipping to the Samp. My stomach churns as the buffalo skin brushes my shoulders when we crowd into the wagon, swords and arrows and axes scattered around in skin bags, hanging from the skin walls. I catch eyes with the Sampian boy, who's slipped into the wagon behind me, still flexing his wings like he can't quite believe they're free of their clamps. I wonder if he's ever Dreamed an Izlanian buffalo.

I have.

I look away quickly so he won't see the question in my eyes. I know his secret. That doesn't mean he has to know mine.

"Know what to do, all?" Mama asks as she tenses her arms, conjuring a fire out of the freeze. It hovers in midair in front of her. Ler and I nod, and Os stamps quer feet on the dead tree floor. The Sampian boy just tilts his head and grabs a sword off the skin wall. He sticks it into the fire, warming it so we can magick invisible impurities into it.

I follow suit, tossing arrows from their quivers onto the floor for Osley. Que starts chewing away, making slight adjustments in the arrows that will make them snap under tension, downing them on release from their bows. A genius at this sort of thing, que is. Quer black eyes are steely as que works. I wonder if que's thinking of the non hunters who shot quer family with arrows like these.

"So name what yours is?" Lerian asks my fellow Dreamer in terrible Sampian faeric. She never was great at language learning pods.

"Leece," he tells us quietly. Lerian puts her forehead to Mama's before grabbing two swords at a time from the racks on the skin walls. I yank at the Energies to make a fire of my own, and Leece sticks a metal axe into it. We work in silence except for the crackling of the floating fires and the steady clicking of Osley's teeth on wooden arrows.

"So," Leece starts after a while, his attention carefully fixed on the axes he's holding, now one in each hand. They're glowing as red as his wings, and I'm sweating with the effort of pulling the Energies to magick impurities into the slightly melted parts. They'll still look sharp, but they'll be blunt and brittle in a battle. Or another massacre.

"You're half non, huh?"

I nod in the Sampian way, not taking my focus off the axes or the swirls of purple and blue haze flowing from my fingertips into the reddened metal. Lerian nudges me, gesturing for me to pass her another sword. I grab one off the rack next to me.

"Ever gotten with a non with your wings tucked away like that?" he asks.

I drop the sword. Lerian swears and reaches for it, but Mama stills it magically, yanking the Energies hard enough so the blade stops just above my thigh.

"Thanks," I breathe in relief, picking it up and passing it to Lerian. I look up at Leece, and the ghost of a playful grin is on his thin lips. I glance down at Osley with an arched eyebrow. Lerian's glowering at the Sampian boy, but Osley contents querself with a twitch of quer ears.

"If by 'gotten with' you mean gotten information out of them for the resistance, yeah. The one good thing my non looks have done for me," I tell him.

Mama smirks.

I change the subject. "So are you and Mara...a thing?"

Leece's wings flutter happily above him, and Mama sucks her teeth as she pushes his wings away from the sword racks. The gill flaps on his neck close, like Mama's do whenever Mom makes her blush.

"Mmhmm! I spent growing time in the Highlands, near the palace. I got sold away from my family, yes?"

Mama flinches. I know she's thinking about Mom. She glances at me. I dodge her gaze.

"Mara's growns are negotiators. They took her on one of their trips. An extended stay. A whole season. She spent most of her time in the kitchens with me." He's grinning, his eyes wide.

"But she how did end up... well... you with?" Lerian asks, balancing an axe in the flames for Mama to magick. Mangled grammar aside, we all know what she means. Captive.

I elbow her in the flank.

"What? It's the obvious question," she mutters to me in Forest faeric.

Leece's smile evaporates and Osley, below us, stops chewing at the arrows. "Her parents kept catching us together. At first, they thought she'd get over it. Move on. She didn't." His voice stays moss soft the whole time through, but it's injected with bitterness as he goes on. "They disowned her. Left her to be bought by the same nons that bought me. At least we've gotten to spend time together. But then the nons needed someone who knew the land, to ship these weapons. Sampians who've lived in servitude are apparently the best guides through the Grove, so...here we are."

I glance at Osley, who's gnawing away at the arrows again, but apologetically. I don't know what to say.

Mama clears her throat. "Faye—Sadie's other mother—was taken from the Grove when she was very young. Worked for a non man. He treated her like he owned her."

Lerian and I both freeze, but our immobility has nothing to do with my growns' Energy-twisting spell. I only ever hear this kind of hardness in my mother's voice when she talks about the non whose tree-flesh home I was born in. But I've never heard her be so direct about it.

I gulp uncomfortably. Lerian scrapes one of her hooves onto the wagon's dead-tree floor. Osley hops closer to me and lingers right near my feet, arrow between quer teeth. Quer body heat slows my heart rate.

Leece's eyes darken. His wings tense reflexively and his neck gills expand, refusing to blend into his skin, looking like the scales they are.

Mama touches his left wing with her blue one softly; their tips curl around each other eagerly, with a dexterity Forest faerie wings usually don't have. A look passes between them that's so intense I lower my eyes. Faeries tend to be big on nonverbal communication, but I can't tell what they're telling each other with their movements, their Energies. I don't think I want to know.

We all continue working, sweat beading on my forehead with the contained heat of the magicked fires, with the intensity of the twisting of the Energies needed to maintain both the fires and the freeze.

Purple, blue, and silver jets thread from my and Mama's russet-brown fingers to bleed themselves into the metals Lerian and Leece are holding, rendering the palace weapons useless. The strong silence is only broken by the sounds we make. The consistent chatter of Osley's teeth interacting with the dead-tree bits of the arrow shafts fills the wagon. The pauses as que artfully contemplates quer next maneuver ring out loudly. We whisper to each other without speech, passing deadly weapons between us as we transform them into props.

I lose track of time, focusing only on the axes Leece burns in front of me and melting them just enough for me to magick impurities into them. They will not work in battle, but they'll look and feel just fine.

I wonder which of the king's soldiers, his Hands, will use these weapons. Will they be killed when their swords inexplicably crack, when their arrows snap and collapse? If yes, are we different than the nons who kill us? Than the nons who planned the dragon massacres?

Am I a killer now too?

Sweat drops from my forehead into the fire and sizzles.

I yank at the Energies to pour impurities into the axes so hard that Leece stops rotating them to stare at me.

"Sorry," I mutter. I want to ask him about Dreaming. I don't.

Without warning, my mom gasps, her breath rattled and forced.

"Mama!"

Then I feel it too, and from the way Leece doubles over and almost singes his eyebrows on the magicked fire, I can tell it's having the same effect on him. The unwinding of the Energies is beginning.

Lerian and Osley look at the three of us, concern and confusion written all over their centaur and rabbit features. "I think the freeze spell is wearing off. We have to hurry," I tell them, and Mama tilts her head in a Sampian nod.

In a flurry of limbs and muttered apologies, we get the swords and axes back onto their racks and the arrows into their quivers. The buffalo-skin flap of a door bursts forward just as we're finishing, and a flurry of orange wings and pale sand skin tangles around Leece's body. His normal stance—his body hanging horizontally under his wings, facing the ground—is pushed upright as Mara yanks him into a deep embrace.

"Come on, you two," Mom's voice comes from behind them. Her Sampian accent is so perfect it reminds me how important it must have been to her to learn the language Mama grew up speaking. "You'll have plenty of time for this when we get you out of here."

She tugs them out of the wagon, looking askance at the enclosure's perimeter to make sure the soldiers guarding it aren't slipping out of the freeze yet.

"We're not going with you," Mara tells Mom, her face still pressed into Leece's bony shoulder.

"*What?*" Four voices ring out at once in as many languages.

Osley hops forward, slamming quer feet into the snow. "*We agreed that we would sabotage the weapons with you and then set you free. We agreed, and we will, we must. We can get you passage out of the Grove, we can—*"

Leece untangles himself from Mara's arms and hovers down low to the ground so he can run his hands over Osley's quivering fur.

"We have to stay, don't you get it? You have to lock us back up. If we escape, they'll know their weapons are compromised. We're so close to the Forest, they'll blame you and the Underlanders." He gestures up at Lerian. "They wanted guides to lead them to the Samp. We're going to lead them through our murkiest parts. Slow them down as much we can."

"But you—"

"Sadie." Leece flies up to my level now, which isn't that high since I'm grounded, my wings still hidden under my cloak. My left foot throbs beneath me, and my throat swells. "You can too, can't you?" He doesn't say it, but I know. We both do.

Dream.

I blink, my heart slamming hard. Is it that obvious?

"I saw the way you were looking at me when I woke. Like you knew. So you understand, don't you? Why we have to stay?"

Lerian steps forward, and I hold out a hand to stop her without breaking eye contact with Leece. Since I told her about my Dreaming in the aftermath of the attack that killed Jax's joiner, she's guarded the secret fiercely. But now's not the time.

I grind my teeth and glare up at Leece. He's right—of course I know. I've Dreamed the consequences of people being caught by the palace for lesser crimes than fleeing captivity. So has Leece. I nod and turn away.

The snowflakes floating statically in front of my foggy eyes move again. The guards will be waking soon.

I don't watch as Mom and Mama move forward to help Leece and Mara back into their chains. Mama whispers that she's magicked the chains so they won't hurt as much; Mom embraces Mara and cries. Even Lerian turns away at the sound of Mara and Leece kissing one more time before their wing clamps force them to face away from each other.

I can't take it. I can't.

He's like me, and he's locked up for it. He's like me, and he's probably going to get caught, to die. I start running.

"Sadie!" Lerian whisper-shouts, but she doesn't gallop after me.

Mama restrains her. "Let her run it off. She'll be safe enough with her wings tucked away."

I'm grateful for them letting me alone, and I relish the sprint up the Tread, toward the Lunavic River. The snowfall burns my exposed face like small, cold needle pricks. Even the burning in my foot is starting to feel good. Anything to get away from Leece and Mara letting themselves be locked back up so we don't get found out.

Anything to get away from a fellow Dreamer, in chains and in love.

I'm grateful for the space, for the air, for the pain.

Until the scream rents a hole into my chest and threatens to snap my bones into pieces. Until the scream that will change everything.

Chapter Two

I DON'T THINK. I just run faster. I don't even stop to ask permission from the creatures my feet are treading on. I try to step lightly. I don't know if I'm succeeding.

The screaming—which was one high-pitched cry at first but now is bleeding out into panicked uprisings of the throat—is coming from just off the Tread, on the side of the river where faeries aren't allowed to go unless we're in chains. I tear under branches and feel my way through the understory, pounding across a rickety old bridge until I find the source of the screams.

A non woman, draped in the snow-white uniform of a palace soldier is curled up on the ground, rocking herself around her bloodied forearm. The skin and muscles are ripped jaggedly, deeply. Bone is showing, whiter than the snow around her, which is rapidly reddening with her blood. A metal animal trap that Hands must have laid for hunting is tangled in her dangling flesh.

Trying my best not to vomit, I twist the Energies as hard as I can to try to hold what's left of this non soldier's arm together. Her screaming stops when she sees me and realizes what I'm trying to do, but she's still whimpering. Her breathing is still jagged.

My hands, freezing all night even with our magicked fires, are now warm. They're slippery now, slick with human blood. Since the attack, I've only seen this much blood in Dreams and at the Kinzemna massacre. I look wildly around for any other faerie, hopefully one who's better at healing than me, to help. But of course, there isn't anyone on this side of the rushing river. And if there were, they'd probably think I'm a non myself.

Suddenly, I'm not so grateful that they let me run off on my own.

My fingers brush the dead-tree club that all the king's Hands keep under their cloaks. I can just imagine what Lerian would say, seeing me helping a Hand or any non for that matter, like this. But then the Hand gasps as I take a particularly big pull on the Energies, her thin eyes wide with fear. I screw up my face and try to focus on what my mom would do, on how she talked to that scorched soldier that night all those harvests ago.

"Hey, you're okay, I've got you. What's your name, anyway?" I ask in Highlander non, the language I had to speak as a young one feeling foreign but also strangely comforting on my tongue.

"Ie...Iema," she chokes out, and I cock an eyebrow. Sounds like an Izlanian faeric name, even though she looks like she could be from around here. They never used to let Izlanians serve as Hands. Certainly not ones with faeric names. I wonder vaguely if she's hiding wings under her cloak too.

"All right, Iema, you're gonna be fine." I'm lying through my teeth— I'm not nearly the healer that Mom is, but I'm doing the best I can.

There's yelling in the distance, getting closer. Someone must have heard all that screaming.

"Have to...protect..." she mutters through gritted teeth.

"Uh-huh," I hum absently. She must be getting delirious from losing so much blood.

"I promised... lost track... need to find her," she coughs, which makes her whimper harder.

"Just try to stay still, yeah?" I'm sweating wildly now, and I don't know how to take the trap's teeth out of her muscles without hurting her more. Mom and Jax would know, but I can't take her to them. And I can't risk moving her anyway.

The footfalls in the snow are getting closer. I pull my wings as deeply as possible into the wing sleeves in my lower back. I try to wipe the sweat from my eyes with the back of my arm and only succeed in getting Iema's blood all over my face.

Thin green tendrils sweep out of my fingers and try to hold the remains of her flesh together. It worked better when I stitched the tender flesh of Zaylam's underbelly together during the Kinzemna massacre at the Flowing; but then, Zaylam's my hatchling dragon, so my magic, my Energies, are closely tugged to hers. This woman I've never met? She might die from this trap, and it might be in my arms.

Unless whoever's coming for her sees through my disguise. Then we both might die.

So much blood. And bone. Is that what my insides look like too? Lerian's? My little sibling, Aon's? I know it is—I watched quer tiny skull get cut open during quer Slicing, just a few sunups after que was born, the same night que lost all hope of ever having a hatchling dragon, since que hadn't Dreamed one before quer Slicing.

I'm dizzy again and my stomach heaves.

A pair of beady eyes watches us from the underbrush near the Tread. It's Osley. Que must have followed me here; quer gaze makes me feel safer somehow. I yank harder at the Energies as the shouting gets closer. More green tendrils emerge from my fingertips. The bleeding starts to slow. I let out a shaky breath. The Forest seems much quieter, and I realize it's because I'm no longer gasping for breath.

The shouts and approaching boot stomps are getting still louder. Whoever it is must be able to see us by now. Osley shrinks away farther into the underbrush. My breathing gets shakier again and my hands tremble so hard it's all I can do to keep the green waves of Energy flowing into Iema's wound to keep her from bleeding to death. Even if she is a Lunara-forsaken Hand.

And then Iema screams roughly. A low thwock accompanies a sudden, intense crunching to my face, and I'm a few flutters away, sprawled all akimbo in the snow. My jaw stings something wild and the world is spinning. I fumble for my cloak, making sure it's securely covering my wings. Every movement throbs. I can't tell if I'm bleeding or not because I'm already covered in Iema's insides.

"Stop it!" she shrieks, and I look up dazedly to see a newly arrived Hand, raising his club—I have enough of myself to be grateful it's not his sword—above his head with both hands. He's ready to strike me again, and he's grinning through his stiff gray beard and nearly snow-colored skin. "Stop it, she was trying to help me!"

He doesn't listen. His grin just gets broader. He prepares to strike. I prepare to roll away—I've been trained for exactly this—but find that I can't move. It's not the pain; it's something deeper, something in the Energies, something tugging, like it tugged when I stood over Leece while he was Dreaming. But I don't have time to wonder about the Energies.

I panic. I am about to die. Then—

"Reve!" Another voice cuts in, sharp and high and angry. The soldier's grin is replaced by a scowl. The protruding purple vein in his snow-pale forehead throbs.

"Leave her! Get over here and help me. Now." The soldier—Reve—spits down at me, right into my face. I lift a shoulder angrily to wipe the glob away. When I look up, the soldier is slipping his club back beneath his white cloak and trotting to where Iema lies a few flutters away. I stay on the ground, shaking and openmouthed, my jaw throbbing from where he hit me. But the Energies ease out as he creates some distance between us. I raise my head slightly.

A girl, looking like she's about my age-mate, is kneeling in the snow next to Iema, her chest heaving, running her gaze over her injury to assess the damage. The girl's tight black curls spill out of her hood as she yanks it down along her neck, somehow both urgent and graceful. Her lips are moving, but I can't hear her words as Reve looms over them both.

I stay down. I don't trust my ability to play non in front of this Reve character, not when there's blood melting through the snow. A fair stream of which might be mine.

"Tell the keepers of the inn at Lethe to prepare for an urgent patient. Use my name. Don't delay, and do not argue with me. Iema, this will sting. But you'll be all right soon enough. Here, squeeze my hand." She's weaving Energy bandages, much sturdier than mine, out of her wrist while Iema grabs at her other hand. Slices of Iema's flesh sizzle, but she stops leaking so much blood. The bandages the girl weaves have a rich golden color, like the mist of soul keepers that used to be so common around these parts. Until they, like Dreamers, started getting killed. Or worse, shipped off to the Pits. Mostly by light non men like the one who just clubbed me and spit in my face.

Reve drops to one knee and I hear him whisper-shouting at the girl in Highlander non, his voice harsh and urgent. I can't make out her words in response, but she sounds angry. His shoulders tense but he concedes, sweeping Iema into his arms like she weighs nothing. He sprints back to the Tread and up in the direction of the nearest non settlement, Lethe.

I know the inn she's talking about; I was there a few sunups ago to see about an antidote for the infections a lot of the dragons have been developing since the Kinzemna massacre. Mom and Jax are great healers, and the Forest learning pods are lucky to have them, but Highland healers have more resources in their poorest facilities than our best infirmaries are allowed to touch. And when I've got my wings tucked away, they'll talk to me like I'm one of their own.

Looking like the enemy makes for being a great spy.

I curse myself for not thinking to bring Iema there.

Reve's footsteps recede and leave me alone with the Forest, with the girl. Somewhere, I know that Osley is watching nearby, but que won't emerge with nons in the area. Que never does.

The girl's breaths are heavy and she's still on the ground, bloodied hands bracing her stomach on her thick thighs. She wheezes out something in what might be an Izlanian dialect. I recognize *thank* and Iema's name, but nothing else.

Not understanding the words, I try to read her body. I wonder if Izlanians communicate with their bodies like we do in the Grove. They hadn't mentioned it in our learning pod. Or maybe they did, and I was too busy fooling around with Lerian to notice.

Now, the girl tries to catch her breath; she must have sprinted to get here. She leans back, arching her back and tries to rub a stitch out of her full side, her expression tight with pain. She stays that way until her breathing regulates, her face ashy from the bite of the cold.

I don't move to lift my shoulders off the ground, even though the snow's already seeped through the back of my cloak and I'm starting to shiver. The girl looks at me then, without raising her head.

She stares at me for a moment and then takes a deep breath and switches to Highlander non. "You didn't understand a word I said, did you?"

My insides uncoil a little. She thinks I'm a non like her. Of course she does. I give a mock scoff and lean up on my elbows, lifting an unsteady hand to my smarting jaw. "I caught the gist."

She laughs softly, and it sounds like the wind on a sun season sunup, rushing through the skyflower trees in the Underland. "Sorry about that. After all this time, even with all the laws, sometimes I still forget to speak Highlander aloud."

I understand her words, but I'm still not completely sure what she's going on about. I just nod in the non way.

Leaning heavily on her thighs, the girl hoists herself up and brushes snow from her bloodstained cloak, gracefully and gingerly pulling her thick hood back over her halo of hair. She looks down at me. "I don't know you. I doubt Iema does either. But you helped her."

It's a statement but an uncertain one. Almost like a question. I drag myself off the ground unsteadily but don't go any closer to her. A blanket of bloodied snow lies between us.

"I was nearby, and she was hurt." She won't let me look away. She nods quietly before stepping gingerly around the steaming red snow toward me.

She's keeping one hand close to her belly, holding it limply from the wrist. A thick off-white bandage is protecting her knuckles. My lips part, but she speaks first.

"I'm Evelyn." She's looking into my eyes, but her functioning hand is reaching tentatively toward my bloodied jaw. She arches an eyebrow gently, and I nod. Immediately, I feel the Energies shift in front of me, within me, and healing warmth floods my jaw. Her gaze fixes on the spot where Reve clubbed me, leaving me free to take in the way her brown eyes have a small ring of amber in them, her wide nose, and full lips, painted purple.

My mouth runs dry as she exhales shakily into the space between us, the white cloud of her breath mingling with mine and with the golden tendrils of healing Energies she's magicking. I clear my throat.

"Evelyn," I repeat. "I'm uh..." I'm having trouble thinking straight, and for a moment, I can't even remember the name I use when I'm spying. And Sadie is a Highlander non name, anyway, like my wider-set shoulders and thinner wings—yet another thing to set me apart from Forest faeries.

Her stare drags up to mine at my hesitation, and all at once I feel a burning, like an unexplained but unchecked need, to give her my real name. "Sadie," I splutter. "Thanks for, uh..."

She shushes me, her attention refocusing on my wound. I stay as still as I can until she releases the Energies around us, done with her healing spells.

"And you have nothing to thank me for; it's quite the other way around." She locks her gaze into mine. "Sadie." I return her small grin and rub my hand over my jaw again. Not too much pain, but it's still slippery with Iema's blood.

Evelyn shudders. I look away from her then, overly conscious of how close we've been standing.

"So uh...your friend, she's gonna be okay, I think. They've got good healers in Lethe."

Evelyn nods, stepping back from me slightly and wrapping her arms around herself. I have the sudden impulse to replace her arms with mine, to warm her. To wash her friend's blood off her. I've been where she is—when I was drenched in Zaylam's golden insides—but I can't tell her that. She was probably sitting comfortably in some stone Highlander building while her people were slaughtering mine that day. I shift my weight off my left leg.

Evelyn swallows. "Yes, she'll be all right. Thanks to you." A pause. "What were you doing this close to the Forest anyway? I hear the faeric resistance is strong here."

There's disdain in her voice when she mentions my real people, and my heart sinks. "I could ask you the same question."

She stares at me, her head tilted off to one side. "I suppose you could say I needed to get away," she offers, her gaze so intense I almost step back. Almost.

"This is your idea of a getaway? Roaming the edges of the faeric Forest with two overeager soldiers?" I rub my jaw again absently.

She scoffs softly, her chin raised. Wind shakes the trees above us, and she pulls her cloak tighter around her body. "Iema's not overeager. Just Reve. And he has reason to be, he's been...they've both been...charged with my protection. You still haven't answered."

I shrug. "Wanted to just think, I guess. Your protection? They're not doing a good job of it, leaving you here like that."

Evelyn half smirks. "It's also their job to obey me."

"You some sort of dignitary? How many harvests have you got, anyway?"

"Nearly seventeen." Her shoulders straighten up even more, like she's offended that I asked her age. I grin.

"Same as me," I tell her, which isn't technically true. I haven't lived seventeen harvests—faerie young ones age much faster than nons until we become nears, when our growth evens out. I grew slower than most faeries, but faster than most nons. Which means we wouldn't have been age-mates as young ones, but since my growth has evened out in tune with hers, we are now.

I open my mouth, wanting to ask her what she means about needing protection. Does she imagine she needs protection from us, from faeries? I glance up and down at the deep white fur of her cloak and the shiny, almost slippery material I only remember from my young-one days in the Highlands; I'd have to patch it up for the woman who lived with the man we'd worked for. Evelyn must be from the Highlands Proper with such expensive clothes and promised protection from not one, but two soldiers.

I take a breath, but she beats me to it.

"I need to go," she tells me. "Check on Iema, make sure she's all right. But I..." I raise my eyebrows at her. She shifts her feet and looks up at me through hooded eyes.

The bottom of my stomach drops out. I don't have the wide-set eyes, the flattish ears, the pinched shoulders, and curved legs that most Grovian faeries have. So when other girls look at me, they only roll their eyes. They only whisper. They only laugh. Sometimes, they only spit at me, like Reve had done.

They never look at me like I could be...attractive.

My heart thuds a strange rhythm.

"I should be...around these parts more often in the coming seasons. Perhaps we could..." She wets her full lips. "Perhaps we could meet at the Lethean Inn, tomorrow after sundown? For a meal?"

I stare. She tumbles on, somehow with grace and confidence. "And I'm sure Iema will want to thank you, of course. For rescuing her from that Lunara-forsaken animal trap."

I hear Lerian's voice screaming in my ears, telling me to accept, to get all the information I can out of the prissy, spoiled non. To squeeze all the information I can out of her and then laugh about it later.

Arrogant non, she'd call her, even if she is Izlanian. She's still a non. And she's got the protection of non soldiers. Definitely has great info. *Go get it, faerie*, Lerian would tell me.

But Evelyn's eyes are wide and the white puffs of her breath are lingering with my own in the small space between our mouths. My throat catches, so I clear it and nod, *humanly*.

"Sure," I tell her. "You uh...you gonna be okay getting back there tonight? I can take you there now."

She smiles sadly, her eyes lowered. "Reve would hardly approve. I'll have to give him the slip tomorrow night." She purses her lips mischievously and I swallow, not knowing what to say.

"Thank you again...Sadie."

Without warning, the Energies tear around us, so hard I stumble off-balance. There's a low rumble, and she's gone.

A snap spell.

"Must have gone to one expensive learning pod," I mutter to the trees around me, none of whom I know personally. "They don't let us snap from place to place until we're basically elders."

"*Really?*" I hear being tapped out, muffled, on the snow behind me. "*That's the part of that conversation you're thinking about right now, Sadie? Not the parts where she's clearly a high-ranking Highlander and she wants to go on a date with some Grovian low-life that she thinks is human like her.*"

I turn and crouch in front of my quivering rabbit friend. "Careful, Osley. You're starting to sound like Lerian. And the Grove's only big enough for one of her."

Que lowers quer ears down to quer sides, and I sigh, heaving out a huge white cloud as I look around us. At the pool of bloodied snow that Iema left behind. At the footprints Evelyn made.

"Can she stay our little secret, Os? Just for now?"

Que stares up at me intently, quer nose twitching slightly. "*Can who stay our secret?*"

I grin and stand shakily. "Let's head back to the Plains. Everyone's probably back by now, probably flying out about where we are."

Osley thumps an affirmative and hops softly beside me as I limp in the direction of the Plains.

It takes us a long while, but we reach the protective, invisible barrier that surrounds the Plains without further incident. I glance down at Osley. "You ready?"

"*I'm not the one covered in human blood,*" que stamps out, nose twitching.

I stick my tongue out at quer but get quer point. I scrunch up my eyes and tug at the Energies, feeling Iema's blood dry and crust off of me almost instantly. Getting blood off my body—a spell I'm a little too good at.

Plenty of practice.

I grimace at Os and step forward through the barrier, letting it squeeze my lungs before releasing me into the secret home of the Grovian dragons and Lunavad trees.

A massive expanse of knotted Lunavad trees and a smattering of dragons—the survivors of the Kinzemna massacre—sift into view before the barrier's tugging of the Energies lets my eyes focus on the people closer by, in front of me. My growns hovering close together but just far enough apart so their wings don't interfere with each other. Mom's got her arms over her chest, and they're wearing the same facial expression, except for Mama's arched eyebrow.

Somehow, I feel the danger of being in trouble as much now as I had when Reve was standing over me, ready to hit me again.

Zaylam's hovering low over my growns, her massive magenta wings flapping lazily, just enough to keep her in the air. The long jagged scar on her furry underbelly is just visible, and I wonder if Iema's going to have a scar like that on her arm.

I can tell by the sparkle in my hatchling dragon's crystal eyes that she's both relieved and amused by my predicament. Her snout, which would be tucked all the way into triangular face if she were really upset, is slightly turned out with bemused curiosity at what my punishment will be for running off.

Beneath the three of them, Lerian stands on the ground, her hind horselike hooves pawing aimlessly at the snow.

I clench my jaw and rip off my cloak despite the cold, letting my midnight-colored, star-speckled wings free. I groan in relief as they expand themselves, and I crouch down, sitting back on my haunches. I stare up at my not-so-welcoming party as I stretch out my left foot, bending my toes all the painful way back.

"Well, you're kinda screwed this time, Sade," Lerian tells me unconcernedly, eyes darting between my mothers and me.

"Yeah, wouldn't have seen that coming," I deadpan, but my mind isn't on the Plains.

My mind is on Evelyn.

Chapter Three

"SOME HELP YOU were," I singsong up to Zaylam as we finally give my growns the slip, assuring them that yes, I'm fine (possibly true, though I haven't really sorted it all out in my head yet) and no, nothing significant happened (totally untrue, but they're the ones who let me lie so much with all this spying, so I'm not going to take blame for being good at it). I don't think Mama totally bought it, but with that high, soft voice of hers, she stemmed Mom's teary tirade about how could I run off alone like that, I could have just shared my feelings with them, on and on.

They all believed me when I waved off Lerian's invitation to come sleep near her in the Underlands, claiming to be too tired to go anywhere. That part's completely true.

As Zaylam and I fly up to get to our hatchling tree's canopy, I look out blearily over the Plains. No plant-life sprouts from the snowy, parched ground except the massive Lunavad trees, branchless most of the way up their knotted trunks until they bloom out into a circular, mushroom-shaped canopy. The dragons that aren't flying around—the only space in Lunav they can still do so freely—are hanging almost batlike from their hatchling trees' canopies, the elders singing melodies and the youngers chirping in harmony. Zaylam's the youngest of the youngers left in the Plains, though. Combine the Kinzemna massacre with the mandatory Slicings that destroy faeric Dreaming, and death meets an inability to be hatched in the first place.

At this rate, there won't be any more songs in the Plains. Because there won't be any more dragons.

I sigh and run a hand through my short hair as we fly, trying to see if I can trace one of Jorbam's limbs from the bumpy, root-patched ground all the way up her main body, where each of her roots joins with dozens of other tendrils to twist and coil, ropelike, to form her trunk.

My gaze flickers, and I wind up tracing a root back to Banion instead. Where a solitary dragon-hatchling bulb glows in purple fluorescence, hanging from his canopy. Banion is my little sibling Aon's hatchling tree, just like Jorbam is mine. But the dragon bulb won't hatch. Not now. Not since Aon's been Sliced. Not since they opened quer brain and ripped away quer ability to Dream.

My wings tense up and I lose height. Immediately, Zaylam swoops directly underneath me, extending her long, magenta neck up. She croons at me, eager for me to wrap my arms around her so she can take me the rest of the way to Jorbam. I concede; my wings are feeling pretty heavy. I let myself drop and settle with my legs straddling the spot where her shoulders slim out into her neck. I won't be able to do this when she gets older, so I take advantage of how she's still small.

For a dragon, anyway. Her face alone is still wider than my waist. She takes a steep, sudden drop, making me feel more weightless than I ever could with my own wings supporting me. I whoop loudly—she turns her face back to me and her snout is fully elongated with glee—and earn myself several scandalized glares from dragons like Harlenikal and Archa, who think the most resonant music is made exclusively by dragons. They don't look at me, exactly, though; more like they look past me. Only my hatchling dragon looks directly at me; everything else, all the songs and all the harmonizing, is always addressed to the Energies.

Zaylam glides somewhat ungracefully to a stop just under our hatchling tree's canopy. She lowers her neck so I can slide into a small gap between Jorbam's thick branches where her deep green, piney leaves don't grow. Zay slips her talons into her own special gap between the ropelike tendrils of Jorbam's trunk, and I nuzzle my face into her knotted bark, breathing in deeply.

"Is there anyone you haven't angered today, Sadie?" Jorbam's bark rumbles in a pattern I've understood since I first Dreamed her when I was a young one in the Highlands. The Dream forged the hatchling connection between us and allowed Zaylam to start growing in her sap. Some faeries Dream their hatchlings before their Slicing; people assume that's what happened with me. They're wrong.

I grin and run my fingers over the grooves in her bark, almost in a hickory-tree pattern, like the veins in Zaylam's wings. "You'd never be mad at me, Jorbam, though, right?" She takes her time processing the vibrations of my speech and eventually rumbles softly in response. Her laughter.

I cuddle closer into Jorbam's canopy, shifting my body so I'm firmly lodged between her trunk and two of her thickest branches. Harlenikal flies by, low, close to us. She doesn't know I can Dream. Mostly, nobody does. If they did, I'd be locked away in the Pits. Or dead. Or my whole family dead. My little sibling... I change the subject rapidly.

"Remember when you were hatched, Zay? Your bulb hung right there."

Zaylam hums and Jorbam rumbles softly, remembering with me.

It had been a fluorescent magenta, and when I was a young one—about a season after we started living in the Grove—it had swollen until even Jorbam's strong branches nearly couldn't hold it anymore.

What I didn't know then was that dragons don't break out of their bulbs and leave the shell behind. With dragons, their bulb shell becomes their wings.

I watched, a few branches away, my body moving in time with every motion the hatchling made. I'd been Dreaming her growth, and I knew she was ready to come out. We were already, through that Dreaming, synced. Without that connection, she couldn't have been born.

When the hatchling's body twitched left in her bulb, I twitched left into Jorbam's leaves. When she moved as though to try to flex her wings, even from inside them, mine stretched up and out. I hit my head on Jorbam's canopy a couple times because of it. And on and on, until finally—with a chorus of dragons singing above us—a body, small for dragons but already so much bigger than me, slipped unceremoniously out of the bottom of the bulb. The fine, mauve fur of her underbelly was slicked down with Jorbam's sap that nourished the hatchling inside the bulb, damp and shimmering like I imagine the fur of a baby dolphin in our ocean, the Flowing, or a gryphon in Izla would be.

Like most dragons, our hatchling emerged singing. There were no words yet—they would come later—but her quavering tones vibrated in every bone in my body. My wings took flight of their own accord and took me forward. I didn't know why, because I'd never seen a dragon hatched and no one had ever told me, but somehow I knew what to do. Probably all that Dreaming.

The little dragon, dripping with sap and kind of wrinkly in the places where she was more fleshy than scaly, was hanging from the remains of her bulb—of her wings. Seeing them stretched out with the sunlight shining through them, I realized with a tiny gasp that they had the same veiny patterns as Jorbam's hickory-style bark. All three of her eyelids were wide open. Her eyes were the color of the Flowing during sunup, and when they met mine, her voice stopped quavering.

I smiled tentatively. I'd never made eye contact with a dragon before. Her snout—hatched retracted all the way into her triangular head—elongated slightly, and then it came out so fast that she nearly hit me in the face. I backed up, but couldn't stop grinning.

"Zaaay. Lammm," she sang, proclaiming her name for the first time. She was still hanging from her massive wing sprouts, unable to give herself the upward thrust she needed to transform the bulb she was hanging by into her wings. I took a deep breath in and aimed my exhale at her wing sprouts, hoping I was faerie enough to give her the magic contained in fae breath.

I was.

Zaylam's body rose as she pulled down, and with a snap, she was soaring. Her bulb had separated into two magnificent wings, the rest of Jorbam's sap spilling to the earth far below. I wrapped my arms as far as I could around Jorbam's trunk; our hatchling had taken flight.

Now, the memory and the calm of both my hatchlings'—both tree and dragon—presence surrounds me and lulls me into relaxation.

Above us, dragons harmonize endlessly, and beneath us. I let my body relax. Usually we sleep in different trees, outside the Plains. Closer to the Gathering, where the Forest meets the Underland in a big clearing with most of our *public* communal spaces. Mom and Jax's infirmary is at the southernmost edge of the Gathering, so Mama, Aon, and I tend to sleep near there. So Mom has only a short flight to come home from after a long healing session. And, I think sometimes, even though neither of them says it, so Mama can keep an ear out for Mom while she works.

I let my body relax because, in the Plains, Mama doesn't have to tighten the Energies around me before I fall asleep to keep me from flailing around if I Dream. In the Plains—on the two nights for every six sunups that the Hands allow us to sleep here—I can rest without restraint, without the Energies tugging on me so tightly I almost always have trouble making magic in the early mornings.

In the Plains, Zaylam and Jorbam's bodies shield me from the view of any faeric traitors, like Tacon, that might be in the Plains and could give me away. And non patrols can't get into the Plains; not with the Lunavad trees' barrier around it, shielding it both from view and from entrance.

So I let my body relax; I let my ribcage expand so much more than it can when Mama's magic is holding my muscles tightly in place, all so I don't die. All so I don't lead to their deaths.

I let my eyes close, and I slip into sleep.

I don't Dream every night. Not every night is there a creature that passes through my exact Energy level. But tonight, there is. At some point in the early sunup, when my breathing has deepened enough for me to slip into complete unconsciousness, consciousness returns.

But it's not my consciousness that floods into my brain, into my body.

The me that is Sadie recedes into a fine, tiny point of light somewhere in the distance, and I become a different *I*, an *I* that is awake somewhere in Lunav. I am damp and slippery. I am crouched, curled into my powerful hind legs, my rubbery flesh blending in with the greenery around me. A mass of skin dangles down from my throat and fills with air, expanding bubble-like with every breath before contracting. It is my only movement.

I am waiting.

My heavy eyelids are rounded on top of my head, and some small part of me is dimly aware that that's not where I—she—Sadie—is used to having her eyes. A low buzzing from my right, and my tongue shoots out from the front of my mouth. I don't think about it—I don't have to—and then I am pulling a tiny fly back into my mouth and tossing it down my throat with my retreating tongue.

Two short croaks that are coarse and deep, a little like the horns the faeries use to call to each other, ring out a few leaps behind me. Without warning to anyone watching me, I launch myself into the brackish water, twisting my body away from the origin of that croak. I don't understand why the faeries and the rushes like to gather in such large groups; I'd prefer to distance myself from my fellow frogs, most of the time.

More croaking surrounds me, higher pitched this time. It's strange, sounding like a garden snake at first, and then bleeding into the sharper, staccato sounds of a crane.

Sss. Aay. Dee. Sss. Aay. Dee.

"Sadie. Sadie!"

She—I—I wake abruptly, trying to sit up at the urgency in my mom's tone. Instead, I catapult myself headlong into Jorbam's canopy, losing my coordination in her branches, her spiny leaves stinging my face.

"Sorry, Jorb," I croak as I try to untangle myself. I realized a little too late that in Dreaming that bullfrog, I'd contorted my body to be sitting on my own haunches, so that when I woke, my body wasn't lying as it was when I fell asleep. Trying to sit up was not such a great plan.

I blink a few times, struggling to switch my thoughts from the remnants of Sampian bullfrog languages to Grovian faeric. Jorbam rumbles her own apologies into my outstretched hand as Zaylam watches me intently. Mom runs her hands all over my body, checking for injuries like she always does when I toss myself around.

I squirm out of her way. "I'm fine," I snap, and she pulls her hands away like I've hit her. Jorbam rumbles harshly.

"Sadie," is all my hatchling tree's vibrations need to say. Zaylam's snout retreats all the way into the back of her face.

I sigh, hard. "I'm sorry." Mom just stares at me, cocks her eyebrow in a perfect imitation of Mama. I sigh again, softer this time. I let my body do my talking, because my spoken words are coming out all irritable. *"I'm sorry, Mom. Really. What's going on? You were calling me."* I really mean to say, *You woke me up from Dreaming while I'm in the one place left I can Dream safely*, but I hope she doesn't get that from my body language. One look at her face tells me she does.

"It's sunup, Sadie. Labor."

She slips her hand away from my knee and carefully slips the shiny, soft blue scarf she sleeps in away from her hair. She lets it hang loose over her shoulder as she starts undoing the twists in her hair, looking away from me, down across the Plains. "You might want to improve that mood before you traipse around the Forest with an axe."

I mutter a nonresponse and jump when the cannon that signals the final call for early morning labor booms in the distance. I shudder, then groan.

I hate when we have missions at night when the next day isn't a rest day. I try to drag sleep out of my eyes. It doesn't work. I let my head fall onto Zaylam's wing, groaning louder for good measure. Mom rolls her eyes and rubs my short hair before flying off.

"Make sure she gets to labor on time, Zaylam," she singsongs over her shoulder as she flies away under her hatchling dragon Gimla's shadow, hands checking her hair midflight.

Zaylam coos, and I glare halfheartedly, tugging on a fresh tunic from my little space between Jorbam's branches.

"Sadie!" A whinny from way below, near Jorbam's roots, jars me out of my depression.

"What are you doing up there, faerie? Didn't you hear the boom boom?"

I grin up into Zaylam's wide face and put my forehead gingerly against Jorbam's trunk. *"Duty calls."*

Jorbam rumbles, Zaylam hums, and I swoop down to an impatient Lerian, who's already strapped into her labor gear and holding out my faye-glass axe, handle first. "Come on, come on, do you see any other faeries left in the Plains?" She doesn't wait for me to answer. "What, no? Just dragons and trees? How could that be? What? Everyone's already left for labor? Really? Wow! How incredible!"

She's hit a gallop now, and I fly above her. I hold my breath as we pass through the barrier out into the Forest. "Good sunup to you too, Ler."

She cranes her neck up and grins at me broadly, even though she's already starting to sweat from the rough brown skin straps across her non-like shoulders, harnessing her deeply tanned, reddish body to the massive cart behind her.

Lerian will be hauling dead bodies all day. I'll be the one killing them.

At least the King's Registry lets us be labor partners. I don't know how I'd survive otherwise. Though I might not if we're much later than we already are.

We speed up, tearing across the Way, one of this season's centauric paths through the Forest, the fastest way to the Gathering to get today's assignment.

Lerian skids to a stop as soon as we reach the massive clearing between the Lunavic River and the Dropoff, where the Forest dips into the Underland. Where faeric life and centauric life are most connected. The Gathering is always a center of activity; it's lined around the edges with Growers' spaces, artist stages, learning pod clusters, Jax and Mom's infirmary, all hovering on magicked platforms just above the ground, so they don't kill the short layer of grass that coats the entire expanse. When I was a young one, the grass was taller than me, and the platforms only came close to the ground when they had to pick up centaurs or faeries that can't fly.

The non government cut the grass short the same night they cut Idrisim's life short.

Lerian stops so abruptly that my dangling legs almost slam into the back of her head. She swears audibly, but once people look and realize I'm with her, they turn right back around and act like we don't exist. Except to shift away from us.

I take in the sight before me and mirror her curse. The King's Registry—those faeric traitors who partner so willingly with the non government—always give us our labor assignments and grown lunch sacks in the Gathering, every sunup. It's always just a couple lines—one for the harvesters and one for the loggers, an informal kind of affair. To make sure we know what segment of the Forest we have to destroy that day.

But today? Today it seems like King Xavier's entire army has assembled to give us our daily orders. There are still lines. There are still murmured conversations and sunup greetings. There are still the beginning stirrings of preparations for Lunamez, our biggest Grovian holiday, always celebrated at the end of the frozen season.

But the Gathering is also crammed with the king's Hands, ones we've never seen before. Not the ones from Sachin's team of soldiers—a new deployment. With a lot more weapons.

"Forty-eight Hands. Looks like they've sent us a new Controller," a soft voice chimes somewhere a few flutters under my dangling feet.

Jax.

I fly lower to meet him on eye level. His angular jaw is jutted to the left slightly, like it always does when he's thinking hard. I put my forehead to his in greeting, and he takes his calloused hand off the wheel of his chair to touch the crook of my elbow. "I hear you weren't the most pleasant to your mother this morning," he says evenly.

I grunt and Lerian chuckles. "By which I mean to ask," his smooth voice continues, his eyes everywhere but my face as he keeps track of the movements of every single Hand in the Gathering, "are you feeling all right?"

"Always the healer," I tease him, flying sideways into his shoulder firmly enough to nudge him, but gently enough to avoid upsetting his chair. The silver merperson markings that swivel delicately up his neck, down his back, and across his broad chest glimmer, like they're dancing, the intricate, swirling patterns gleaming on his tawny skin. His flared nose twitches, but his mild gaze is serious when he looks at me briefly.

"I like to remind myself that life goes on, even when you're surrounded by soldiers," he muses in that rich, understated tone he gets when he doesn't want to be overheard.

"It doesn't seem like it's a response to last night's sabotage mission, but keep wary, Sadie. The more you try to keep your feelings about last night in, the harder it'll actually be to conceal your role in events if they're discovered." He's barely moving his lips, and our eyes don't meet as we both take in the invaded Gathering.

He raises his voice to a more typical volume now, his thick eyebrow arching at me. "And apologize to your mother after labor, would you? She's much harder to work with when she's taking out her anger at you on me." I strain my eyes toward the floating, open infirmary tent. Mom is bending over a patient, and her eyes catch mine. She grimaces at me and then gestures for Jax to come back to the platform. He nods and touches my arm and Lerian's flank.

"Don't enrage anyone too much today, if you can help it," he smirks as he spins his chair around and starts pushing himself toward the lowering infirmary platform.

"We make no promises, Jax," Lerian calls after him, and his deep, resonate chuckle makes me smile.

I look up at Lerian as I fly back to my preferred height, so my feet can dangle well above the ground.

"So I guess we've got a new Controller," she says like she's commenting on the weather. I grunt, and we shift to the end of the logger line. A path clears for us; it always does. I roll my eyes.

Lerian nudges me and jerks her head in the direction of the thickest cluster of Hands. I follow her gaze and almost fall out of the sky.

The new Controller is clearly recognizable in the typical pearly white uniform with the thick red stripe down both sides, with the palace-issued silver-tipped bow slung over the shoulder.

The new Controller is... I snap my mouth shut when I realize it's hanging open. Standing there in that dreaded white uniform is the girl from last night. The non who'd assumed I was one of her people, who asked me out because I saved her friend's life.

The new Controller is Evelyn.

Chapter Four

EVELYN'S GAZE IS skating around the Gathering as she nods passively, listening to the Hands chirping in both sides of her ears.

And then her stare falls to me.

Her lips purse in a delicately contained rage, and her eyes dart rapidly between my face and my wings. Like she's convincing herself that yes, I'm the one who saved her friend last night...and I'm a faerie. I watch the exquisite anger flit across her rounded features as she puts the pieces together and realizes, surely, that every breath I took in front of her had been a lie.

I almost fly down to her, ask to take her arm, pull her aside, desperately try to explain.

But the knuckles of her fully functioning hand are a shade lighter than the rest of her skin, they're gripping her sheathed sword so hard. And the amber ring in her eyes is almost fully golden, like her healing magic. Like she's summoning it all within herself.

Whether to calm herself or to kill me, I can't tell. Could be both.

I wrench my eyes away from her and fly down to Lerian's eye level. She nudges me in the ribs with her elbow and tilts her head Evelyn's way, muttering to me conspiratorially out of the side of her mouth.

"A girl! And looks like our age-mate too. And an Izlanian, what? Who'd've thought? I guess they're trying to get more Izlanians into the government now, with Xavier marrying one and all, huh? Conquer and mmphff," she makes a lewd gesture with her flank, "seems like the new strategy." She glances back at her, and my insides burn as I steal another peek myself, but Evelyn—no, the Controller, the Controller, her name can't matter anymore—is striding over to Tacon, the faeric Registrar and head of the King's Registry.

"Wonder how brutal she is to sweep this gig from under Sachin's feet, huh? An Izlanian near girl, Controller." Lerian says it like she's mulling it over, and she barks out a cruel laugh.

I grunt noncommittally. That's not too unusual. Lerian knows I don't much like crowds of faeries. They tend to part for me way too easily, and it always makes me want to hit something.

But today is not the day for me to randomly hit something. Evel—the new Controller—will probably latch onto any excuse to chuck me into the Pits.

"Next!"

That would be us. Lerian and I shift forward to the Hand who'd barked out the command. He's gazing over the shoulder of one of the Registry faeric traitors, onto the strip of dead tree flesh that holds today's labor assignments.

"You've both got the edge of the Forest today, near the eastern steam pools. You know the drill." He glances at me. "Chop quickly." He switches his bored gaze to Lerian. "Clear quickly. To the deposit slot where the river meets the Flowing." His cold stare swivel to Rada, a centauric elder, a grower with a shrewd eye and permanently melted skin on her right arm from the fires the night of the attack.

"Only give 'em the basics," the new Hand is telling her now, his Highlander non language cutting in comparison with our Grovian faeric vocabulary. "They're not working too hard today."

Rada tosses her thin brown hair off her neck and swishes her matching tail irritably. "I'm not sure how it works in the Highlands." My heart leaps nervously as she responds to him in Grovian faeric. She interrupts herself to lean down off the platform and squint at the Hand's ranking stripe. I suppress a laugh. There's nothing wrong with her eyesight. "Sir Underling," she emphasizes his low rank with barely disguised glee, "but in the Grove, when growing girls don't have enough to eat and spend all day chopping down trees and hauling their body parts around, they need more than just the basics to eat."

The Hand gulps visibly. His orders, probably, are to get us all to labor on time and without incident. Fighting with Rada would cause an incident. Not fighting with her could also cause an incident.

It strikes me that this nameless Hand isn't much older than me.

His eyes swivel to me and travel up and down my body. It's not lewd, just curious.

He's not the first non soldier to ever look at me like that. The first was covered in soot, sweat, and the blood of his joiner.

I WAS A young one, the age-mate of maybe a ten-harvest-old non. It was the night the Hands attacked the Forest, trying to break into the barrier around the Plains, just after Jax's screams had slammed into my bones even harder than the smoke of it all infiltrated my lungs. I'd watched as Tacon murdered Idrisim, Jax's joiner in the battle; as Jax broke and my growns had to protect both of us from Hand after Hand. There were two soldiers, though, who didn't try to attack us. One was holding the other, dragging his burned and bleeding body, cradling him in his arms as he begged us to save his friend, or maybe his joiner, in barely intelligible Grovian faeric.

Mom had gone to work healing the dying one immediately, and when she told Jax she needed his help, he'd nearly refused, red-eyed and shell-shocked. I can still hear the unwavering way she told him that *you don't leave people to die*. Jax's joiner was dead, and so were his eyes; but something about Mom saying that convinced Jax to help her save that non's life.

I think about that now, about not leaving people to die even if their people are trying to kill yours. I wonder if the Hand in charge of distributing our food is thinking something similar as he looks at me, so much like that Hand had during the attack when I'd spoken to him in Highlander, my wings not matching the shape of my face or the twang of my accent. Like he was curious, shocked, and thinking, maybe, that it was the first time he'd looked at a faerie and seen himself.

Before Mom and I fled the Highlands, I'd known that half faeries weren't terribly uncommon. But we were scorned, never quite belonging anywhere. This non, though? He just looked like I was some sort of strange miracle.

AND MAYBE I am. A half non, half faerie, living in the Grove. The only others like me I've ever met are in the Highlands. Not here. Not amongst the faeries. Not amongst the faeries to be looked at as a traitor by the faeries and a curious experiment by the nons.

Like the young non soldier, now, is looking at me. Somewhat bewildered by my human eyes and faeric wings, my human legs and faeric flight. Bewildered, but not repulsed.

I hold his gaze evenly, keeping my face deliberately mild. I know he's considered Rada's request to give us more food, and my calmness, or lack of it, can be the difference between being hungry all day and being able to feed the others.

Our daily supply of grown food—food that only growers can magick from the Energies, so we don't have to eat flesh—is strictly regulated by the type of labor we're assigned each sunup. And by how irritated the non Hands and Registry faeries happen to be at you.

Strictly, that is, if you lack a good relationship with growers. And Rada, one of the rare centauric growers, certainly has a good relationship with us.

The young Hand jerks his head at her granting her permission to give us extra food. He doesn't know we'll distribute it to those who are rationed less than we are, but Rada does.

So she winks at Lerian and me after nodding obediently to the Hand. She presses two steaming bowls of sunup stew into our hands and loops our bags of midday meals into my belt while I drink eagerly. I almost tilt over from the weight of the meal bags, and a ghost of a smile slips past Rada's lips. Her tail swishes softly as she paws at her low-hovering growing platform, where she twists the Energies all night, each night, preparing for the sunup distribution of grown rations.

I squint at her, wondering if she knows about our mission last night. Her lips curve more clearly—of course she does. Lerian might be a near now, but Rada's kept an eye on her since her growns were killed in the blood plague. And she's got her ears in the Centauric Council. She doesn't know I can Dream, but she's one of the few who know I'm a spy. One of the few who doesn't hate me.

"Don't scarf it all down in one sitting now, you two," she teases.

I grin and Lerian gives a soft whinny as we shift past Rada's growing platform toward the Forest.

The Controller's standing nearby, still listening to whatever Tacon's telling her, eyes still fixed on me. I tug at Lerian's arm.

"Labor time, Ler, c'mon."

We slip out of the Gathering into the throng of faeries and centaurs trudging to labor before Evelyn can do anything more extreme than glare at me.

"OH, GOOD SUNUP to you too, E'rix, how are you?" I roll my eyes as I fly above the Way—a system of paths through the Forest that the centaurs rotate each season to spare the plant life and confuse the Hands—and listen to Lerian's voice below me, oozing with false sincerity. I glance at E'rix, flying toward us, heading to harvest as we head to logging, the two major labor functions in the Grove.

Like pretty much everyone else, she avoids my eyes. Lerian is unimpressed.

"Yes, that's right, you know Sadie, we're all age-mates, we were in the language learning pod together when we were young ones," Ler continues overenthusiastically, twisting to say that last bit to the back of E'rix's retreating sapphire wings. I fly a little lower so I can grab Lerian's forearm, careful to avoid her permanent bruises from labor, and try to pull her forward, cart and all. No easy task when I'm trying not to slap her in the face with my wings.

"Come on, Ler, this is every sunup. Why're you always acting so surprised?" Her attention flits around furtively, and then without warning she pulls me nearly out of the air, so I'm practically riding her like nons ride horses. I squirm to get off, muttering wordless disclaimers to the offended-looking centaurs on the Way and to the faeries who are flying single-file through the thick network of trees and underbrush just off the path—anything to avoid interacting with someone like me. Flurries of soft snow burst down into our faces as faeries jostle branches to give me a wide berth. I touch each tree they bump into, muttering apologies for them. Lerian doesn't care about any of this. She's got me locked in her grip, and when she speaks, it's an urgent whisper straight into my ear.

"Look, I get the ones who don't like you 'cause you're all kinds of non-style ugly. Looking like the enemy and all. And I know you're all grateful to him, but Sachin didn't do you any social favors by not locking your somewhat faerie butt up when your moms tried to avoid Aon's Slicing." I glare hard. She ignores it and shoves me so my ear is even closer to her thin lips. "But E'rix's growns are resistance, she's one of the ones who knows you spy for us! You put your freaky neck out for us, Sade, even though you're dark enough to make it extra risky for you, and those ungrateful—"

The distinct crunch of skin boots on the snowy path just ahead, rising above the din of trotting centaur hooves, jolts us both. She lets me go with a backhanded shove and I fly wayward into a low hanging branch. Instead of trying to catch me, a few faeries flying nearby actually snicker. I glower as I wipe a small stinging cut off my cheek, twisting the Energies to heal it roughly, and tug my wings out of the bramble of leaves. Fingering the axe in my belt loop, I groan internally. The wearer of the skin boots is Tacon, his long skinny nose glistening in the sun and his permanent sneer widening with pleasure when he notices the blood on my face.

Lerian yanks me back toward our assigned labor spot, and we say nothing more.

We don't speak as we file into the small clearing just off the beach by the eastern steam pools and find a premarked tree to start murdering.

Mercifully, I do not know this one's name. As gushes of sap leak out of quer branches as I hack away, killing quer body limb by limb, I feel the Energies release like a coiled spring—this tree is ending quer own life, now, separating quer body from quer soul, so que doesn't have to endure the drawn-out, sharp death blows I am dealing, one branch at a time before the trunk.

This tree is sparing querself—sparing me—from the agony of the soul being tortured by my axe until it is wrenched forcibly out of the body. I almost vomit. I almost slam the axe down into my own body. I almost slam it into the nearest overseeing Hand. I almost scream.

I do not. The Hands have creative ways of making us comply. Making us kill each other.

Making the trees have to choose between ending their own lives or letting us end them, through hours of torture.

My growns say that when they were younger, if ever a tree needed to be chopped in some way—whether because of disease or some need of another being—soul keepers would come and host the soul of the tree until the pain of the body was done. The soul keepers would strengthen the soul and give it additional power, to heal the body when it returned.

But now, when this tree thrusts quer soul out of quer body, there is no soul keeper to host it until the pain is gone, to give it the strength to slip back into a newly healed body.

There is only me, and though I can Dream, I was not born with soul keeping abilities. There is only me, and I say nothing.

I say nothing throughout the day as I slam my axe into my assigned tree over and over and over again, taking only small comfort in the fact that que is no longer feeling any pain. I'm quiet as I sweat, as my faye glass axe's translucent, azure-speckled blade gathers sunlight and magnifies the heat on my face, giving me a small scrap of warmth amidst the snow. I grunt in time to the labor songs surrounding me, gathering the chopped flesh into my both frozen and sweating, calloused hands and loading them into the cart Lerian and the other centaurs have to strap themselves into every day. Throughout the day, the hum of faeric tunes rise to match, exactly, the rhythm of centaur hoof beats, everyone in the labor space working in time to each others' sounds. Even rests, we take musically, timing the collapse of our bodies into the muddied snow to sync in tiny gaps of silence between axe thuds, hoof beats, and the clatter of tree flesh into and out of the carts. We can at least send them to their factory graves in the Grovian way. But still, I say nothing.

My mouth stays sealed and my body refuses to talk as we break for lunch. I give the extra rations Rada had slipped us to Lerian, who passes them off to a young faeric near, Kashat, barely old enough to be at labor, as yet untainted by being kind to the two of us. He passes the extra grown food to his fellow first-time laborers, the ones who should be in their learning pods but instead are murdering trees under the threat of death.

More hacking, more threats from our Hand overseers follow. My muscles ripple but my mind stays controlled until the dusk cannon goes off, telling us all we can stop our government-mandated slaughter for the day. I follow along limply as Lerian and I set out for the Gathering.

I'm still quiet when a horde of faeries coming from harvest speed past us and completely bowl me over, knocking the wind and a wingful of blood of out me like I'm not even there. That kind of thing isn't too unusual. Lerian and I exchange furrowed glances, though, when a small stampede of centaurs flashes by us on the Way, also speeding toward the Gathering.

"What gives?" Lerian shouts after them.

"The new Controller... Dreamers!" is all I catch of a huffed, over-the-shoulder answer from one of the nears.

And Lerian's grip is viselike on my arm and Osley is on the ground beneath me, leaping up to tap my ankle and get my attention. I don't have to hear or smell what que is stomping out. Quer ears are flat against quer body, and que's primed to race us to the Gathering.

The pit in my stomach is as big as the Plains, but if something's happening in the Gathering to do with Dreamers, and everyone else is racing to see, the most suspicious thing I can do is avoid it. Better to act like the rest of them.

So the three of us race off after all the others, flying, leaping, and galloping through the snow until, winded, we skid to a stop at the edges of the Gathering, unable to go further. The crowd, both on the ground and in the air above, is too thick. There's an angry murmuring rising, and all I catch is words like Sampians and weapons and Izlanian and Dreamers.

The wind still whistling under my wings, I topple into Lerian's still carted shoulders and a pair of brown hands catches me, halting my tumble forward. Mama.

"Sade," she starts, in that mollifying tone, the one she uses when I'm about to see something I don't like.

I twist out of her grasp and fly up and over the crowd. I peer down beneath everyone, through the thick maze of faeric bodies. No one pays me any mind. For once, I'm grateful.

Below the crowd of spectating faeries, in the center of the Gathering, are two chained up Sampians, pink gashes on their faces. Evelyn is standing over them, her chin raised and her sword drawn, surrounded by a wingful of her smug-looking, pale-as-snow Hands.

They've captured Leece and Mara.

Chapter Five

"Faeries and centaurs of the Grove, you have traitors among you!" Evelyn's voice sounds nothing like it had when she was thanking me for saving Iema's life. Her face looks nothing like it had when we were standing so close that we were inhaling each other's exhales.

"We have been informed that last night, some among you assisted these two criminals, formerly employed in good faith by our righteous King Xavier, in sabotaging a caravan full of supplies vital to the assistance of hundreds of helpless Sampians, who are once again at risk of falling victim to the blood plague." Evelyn pauses and Mama settles into the air next to me, slipping her hand underneath my wings, at the base of my wing sprouts. My body relaxes somewhat. But my heart is still slamming so hard I think I might collapse at any moment.

"Though this is my first day serving as your Controller, I am confident that you are all aware of the dangers posed by faeric dissidents like these, who would have you all join them in refusing to allow their young ones to receive the blessing of Initiations, who would have you believe that Dreaming is worth more than your very lives, and the lives of all your families. Without Initiations, Lunavic life as we know it will cease to exist. If you insist on glorifying Dreaming, you insist on falling victim to the blood plague."

I grind my teeth and glare down at the Controller. *Initiations.* I scoff. The palace's euphemism for Slicings.

They made Slicings mandatory sometime after the first outbreak of the blood plague, harvests ago. They say the purpose is to cure the plague. Jax says if they stopped poisoning the Lunavic waters with their *development*, the plague would probably stop on its own. Slicings are really just to stop us from Dreaming.

"In a misguided, criminal attempt to withhold the curative Initiations from Sampians in need, these prisoners disrupted a palace caravan in ways that profoundly place all of Lunav at risk. They must therefore suffer the punishment."

Stirrings of whispers run through the Gathering, and I scowl at how everyone can understand her Highlander non; but if we tried speaking Grovian faeric in the Highlands, the nons wouldn't understand our words. I can't tell if people are agreeing, angry, or just excited to see some punishment. Jax says that kind of excitement's become more common since people stopped Dreaming. He says that other than preventing dragon hatches, that's exactly the point of the Slicings to begin with.

Nobody moves, except Mara, who tries to reach out for Leece's hand through their chains.

"But first we must weed out who assisted them last night in their attack. Hands, place the suspects under immediate arrest."

Without warning, Mama spins me around and slips her hand over my mouth, softly but firmly, encouraging my lips to open. She slips something past my teeth and a soft, nectar-flavored tablet starts dissolving on my tongue. She catches my eyes and removes her hand as quickly as she put it there, spinning me back around casually as she does so.

"From your other mother. Just keep calm, my love. You will be safe, I promise you. It's just in case," she whispers to me, her eyes wide and her jaw set.

Before I can open my mouth to ask her just in case of what, a pair of enchanted arrows attached to thick ropes lasso around me, pinning my wings painfully to my sides. Mama catches me as I fall and holds me as we both are pulled to the ground, where a group of centaurs rapidly parts for the tumbling pair of faeries careening their way.

P'Tal, loyal always to my growns, to me, doesn't move with the rest of them. As Lerian yells and screams somewhere out of my range of vision, P'Tal's arms close around my mom's, taking the weight of both of our falls.

"You'll be okay, Sadie," he whispers as they both release me, helpless, as the arrows twist around yet again and tug the ropes now binding my entire upper body forward. I crane my neck to look back at Mama, and her eyes are peeking out from P'Tal's disarrayed blonde hair. He's holding her close to him with one arm and catching a galloping Lerian with the other as she screams all kinds of curses and what she'll do if they don't let me go. P'Tal puts his hand on her mouth as Hands start surrounding her. His fingers start bleeding, but he holds her until she stops struggling enough to listen to whatever Mama is whispering in her ear. The wild look on Ler's face calms somewhat. She nudges at P'Tal's hand so that Mama can heal it, but she doesn't stop struggling to get away, to get to me.

I shake my shoulders at her as much as I can. *"Don't get yourself arrested, Ler,"* I tell her with my body as the Hands back off her, seeing she's gone down from tantruming to seething.

I wink at her. She glares at me. *"It's not funny."*

I swallow and turn back around, so I can face whatever it is they're arresting me for. *"I know."*

Low murmurs are rising rapidly above and behind me. I catch chaotic glimpses of shocked faces. A grim sense of satisfaction floods into me. Everyone seems shocked that I'm being arrested, that the Hands aren't doing me any favors because I look so much like a non. I almost roll my eyes, but I'm too busy being yanked along by enchanted ropes to have the energy to spare on sarcasm.

I find that I've been dragged in front of the Controller, and that she seems much taller when you're tied up and on your knees in front of her.

She looks down at me without lowering her chin, and there is barely contained fury in her face. I dare to glance left and right. Mara's next to me on one side, and we keep our expressions very clean, very not familiar. On my right, there's a row of assorted faeries and centaurs. Most of them I don't know by name. An elder grower or two, even a couple of young ones, one of whom is bleeding pretty heavily from her cheek. And that near that Lerian yelled at for ignoring me, just this sunup, E'rix. She meets my eyes apologetically, fearfully. There's a long, elegant cut under her thin eyes. I grimace at her. She grimaces back.

A rush of energy surges through me, and I spare a thought for the tablet Mama shoved into my mouth. I glance at Mom and Jax's infirmary. They're both on the edge of the open platform, watching. Aon is rocking in Mom's arms, and Jax is gripping the wheels of his chair, hard. He nods at me so subtly I almost think I'm imagining it. Mom does the same, even as she's cooing to soothe a crying Aon.

I swallow, but feel a little calmer. Somehow, whatever Mom gave Mama to give to me will keep me safe from... I glance left and right again. From whatever this is.

"I've heard that your former Controller was quite...lax...in his enforcement of the word of the good King Xavier. It is precisely this leniency that has allowed the blood plague to have a resurgence in the Samp, and even in the Highlands themselves. This ends today."

A murmur rushes up amongst the crowd; we haven't heard that anyone has fallen to the plague in the Highlands themselves lately. I stare up at Evelyn, and for a moment, I think there are tears in her eyes. I blink and they're gone. I flinch as a stream of dampness runs down my face.

Maybe the tears were mine.

"It is the belief of His Royal Majesty that only those who dare to hang onto faith in dangerous, deviant practices like Dreaming would join the rabble-rousing against his holy reign. We are going to test these suspects to ensure they have not resisted or subverted their Initiations. If they Dream during this test, we will know they are guilty of dissent against the palace, and they will be taken to the Pits along with these Sampian criminals."

Whispers spread around me, especially amongst the elders. Mama used to tell me stories of public tests to expose soul keepers. If they suspected a person of having the special ability to host another's soul inside them, they would kill someone close to the suspect; if the suspect saved their loved one with soul keeping, they'd be arrested or killed themselves. If they didn't, either because they weren't soul keepers or because they refused to reveal themselves, well...someone would be dead by the end of the test anyway. That is, unless a soul keeper in the crowd came forward to host the soul of the threatened person, to heal it through contact with their own soul, and put it back into the body, reviving the person. But then that soul keeper would be killed too. An impossible cycle.

Soul keepers used to be the perfect healers, rare and sought after for their powers all across Lunav. Until they were all hunted down by the palace. Like Dreamers, they threatened the palace's control. The tests for soul keepers haven't been done for a couple faerie generations, though. Everyone's either been caught or goes to great lengths to conceal their abilities. Like I do, with Dreaming.

But I've never heard of any tests for Dreaming. I'm nauseous.

An arrested young one down the line from me starts crying, in small little high-pitched gasps. I wonder if quer growns have told quer about the soul keeping tests too. I hold Lerian's wide eyes with mine and set my jaw.

Then, a single, soft but strong, voice breaks through the crowded Gathering. "If Dreaming really spreads the blood plague, why would you risk making them Dream in the middle of the Gathering?"

An audible gasp rises through us all, and I think it's Kashat, one of the nears on my labor shift. He's a bit of a heartthrob amongst the Lunamez learning pod this season, and I hear them quickly fly and gallop to close ranks around him.

Bows are strung and swords are drawn, but oddly, Evelyn just smiles softly. She holds up her arm and the Hands relax their weapons.

"My Grovian isn't as sharp as it could be yet, but I believe I was asked about the dangers of Dreaming. It's an important question. Please don't be alarmed, young man." I roll my eyes. He wasn't alarmed. He was challenging her logic. Either she doesn't get it or she's choosing to ignore it. I suspect the latter. "The suspects will be isolated by a magical barrier to prevent their contagion from spreading, should there be dissident Dreamers amongst them."

Her eyes shift and fall squarely on mine. She lowers her hand, and without further warning, the enchanted arrows holding all of our ropes in place slam down, splaying us all face first into the ground.

"I'm sorry," I mutter to the creatures beneath me, and I think they're rumbling a powerful response before I realize that no, that's just me, shaking.

Silence falls.

An air of expectancy settles in.

And then the pain begins.

It's not excruciating, but it's a low burning, like a deeply uncomfortable tingling, starting at my wing sprouts and moving out to my extremities. The Energies tighten around me; they must have magicked those barriers the Controller mentioned.

I try not to squirm with the discomfort, but it's hard not to when the Grovians around me are flinching, the young ones are crying openly, and E'rix down the line is thrashing.

Then the prisoners around me all go limp, eyes closed and slack jawed. I'm about to scream when I see Leece's chest rising up and down, slowly.

Grogginess starts to replace the burning, the pain, and I remember the tablet Mama made me eat, how it wakened my entire body.

They're forcing us to sleep. And when I sleep, I Dream.

But something's fighting the grogginess inside me, like a jittery burning. The tablet. My growns made sure I wouldn't sleep. It'll keep me awake, despite whatever spell they're twisting the Energies into.

But Mama also told me to keep calm. I have to pretend to sleep if I want to survive this. So I let my head fall forward, my body relax, my breathing even out. Which is rough, because my heart is slamming so hard against my chest that I'd be surprised if Evelyn couldn't hear it, let alone see it, standing over me like she is.

Heavy footsteps approach.

"Ma'am." Tacon's voice, in a horrible Highlander non accent, grates into my ears. It's clear from his tone that he never expected to be addressing a girl from Izla as a superior, no matter what he said to me this sunup about Controllers not bossing him around. "How long will it take to root out the Dreaming ones?" He sounds eager. Hungry. I fight not to pull my face into a glare.

"Not long, Registrar."

Skin boots crunch through the Gathering, observing us. Faint whispers and soft sobbing fills the air above me and behind me.

I wonder if my growns were able to slip Leece a tablet to keep him awake and resistant to whatever spell they put into the barriers around us. Because if they didn't... I want to open my eyes, I want to wiggle my fingers, at least, so I can twist the Energies around him, make sure he can't Dream. I'm close enough that I could at least try. But they're watching us for any movement. Especially her, I'd bet anything.

I have no doubts about why I'm in this lineup.

But Leece... I have to hope that my moms were able to get to him, to give him a tablet to keep him awake.

I start twitching my fingers slowly, just in case.

They didn't get to him. And I'm too slow. Too cowardly.

Because now there's movement to my left, crawling sounds—Leece might be Dreaming an insect—and gasps and screams erupt all around us. I am going to join all that screaming if I can't open my eyes, if I can't at least see what they'll do to him, now, what they'll do to me one day, because if this is how the new Controller is going to play things, I won't be able to hide my Dreaming forever.There is scuffling next to me, and someone kicks me in the gut. I grunt involuntarily and decide that, even if I were in an induced sleep, that kick would be enough to have me open my eyes, at least a little, at least groggily.

What I see is worse than what I could have imagined.

They're taking Leece's wings and forcing them into his wing sleeves, binding his entire torso in irons, not even clamping his wings outside his body. He is still trying to crawl. They pay no mind, because they're taking him quickly—quickly, because there are throngs of enraged faeries and centaurs ready to attack, to free us, behind him, behind us.

Immediately, weapons are on all of the prisoners, what looks like two Hands for each of us. A sword grazes my temple, and I close my inner eyelids. I swallow and try not to shake.

I thank Lunara that the others, at least, are sleeping through this living nightmare. Maybe somewhere else in Lunav, someone is Dreaming their sleep.

The crowd hushes. They won't storm the Hands with weapons at all our heads.

I clench my already rope-crunched wings deeper into my body, inviting the sharp pain. I focus on it. I breathe it in. The agony, somehow, keeps me conscious. Keeps me from screaming.

Part of me wishes Mama hadn't given me the tablet. At least then I wouldn't have to fake it like this. I could just be arrested, finally, for what I am. At least I wouldn't be lying anymore.

But Leece. They're going to kill Leece. Or lock him up in the Pits forever. Mara too, for helping him.

I'm the only one from the Grove in this lineup who actually helped sabotage the weapons caravan. They won't stop until they find us, and Evelyn must already suspect me.

I'm going to be hunted forever anyway. Might as well get the capture over with.

Sorry Zaylam, I think to myself, because somehow it's her agonized cry when she was almost killed in the Kinzemna massacre that rents through my mind.

I writhe out of my faked sleep, wrenching open both sets of my eyelids. They meet the Controller's eyes immediately.

But she doesn't move to arrest me, which would surely shock the Grovians who always assume I'm on the nons' side.

I'm confused momentarily, and chance a glimpse at everyone else in the lineup. They're all waking now too. It must just look like I was the first to come out of whatever spell they'd done. Sure enough, the Energies around me are reluctantly starting to unwind, and I can breathe a lot easier.

I swear internally at the same time as the pit in my stomach spasms with relief. I can't even turn myself in properly, and I'm glad of it.

Maybe I am as worthless, as non-like, as everyone seems to think.

Evelyn clears her throat as her Hands use their swords to none too gently cut us out of our enchanted binds. Or at least, they're none too gentle with the other prisoners. They very carefully cut me from my ropes. I must look a little too much like them for comfort.

I hear hissing behind me, and I know my fellow Grovians have noticed.

The pit comes back to my stomach, relief gone.

The Controller raises her voice to address the entire Gathering again. "As all of you can see, the instincts of His Esteemed Majesty are correct. One of the traitorous Sampians does, indeed, Dream. The other, his coconspirator in sabotaging the palace caravan, supported him in keeping his secret. They will both spend the rest of their short lives in the palace prisons."

I can't look at them. The Pits. Short lives. *They're in love.*

Leece's screams to let Mara go, to let her go because she passed the test, burn into my ears.

My eyes sting. I flex my crumpled, sore wings, ashamed that they exist. Ashamed that they're the most faeric things about my body. Ashamed that I'm staying quiet, that I'm letting Leece be punished for doing the same thing that I do every night. I just have a family to protect me. I just look like a non. That's the only difference between us.

Leece is still screaming, still trying to throw off his captors. The Controller, her face stone, nods at one of her Hands, giving a silent order. He obeys, winding up and striking Leece backhanded across the mouth. Blood spurts everywhere, and it's Mara's turn to scream.

The Controller nods again, and the Hand kicks Mara in the back of the knees before socking one of her eyes completely shut with the club he carries in his belt. When Leece tries to get to her, the Controller nods still again, and the Hand knocks him unconscious. He crumples to the ground and Mara writhes for him.

Enraged, horrified grumblings and gasps spread through the crowd behind me and above me, but the Controller gestures for her Hands to dig their weapons near into the prisoners' skins. I grit my teeth, E'rix lets out a single sob, and no one moves. The Controller drones on with a blank expression, like there isn't blood on her hands, like there isn't thick pink fluid pouring out of the faces of the two broken nears at her feet.

"Though none of the Grovians we tested today were found to Dream, we will not be ending our investigations. Someone assisted the Sampians in their criminal act of sabotage; we will be increasing our patrols and increasing our random Dream checks to ascertain who are the traitors among you." She lets her words hang over the stunned silence, interrupted only by Leece's sniffling and trembling next to Mara, whose steely eyes are breaking.

"You may all go about your evenings."

Murmurings arise and faeries and centaurs rush forward to their family and friends who were subjected to the test. I hear Lerian galloping toward me, and Mom is speeding through the crowd with little Aon wrapped in her arms. Before they reach me, someone takes me by the forearm.

A jolt of energy surges through me. I look down into the Controller's cold eyes.

"I know where you were last night. We'll see if you pass the next test."

I ignore her quip. I can't think about last night. I have Leece's blood spattered across my face, in my hair.

"How can you *do* this? Those Sampians, they're just nears. They're in love, for Lunara's sake. How can you send them off to die like that?" I don't know why I'm speaking. But even more, I don't know how to account for the contrast between the girl I met in the Forest and the cold-blooded Controller in front of my now. All I know is that my limbs are shaking and her eyes are on fire.

"How can you wish mass death on all of Lunav? Because that's what they're risking, the plague, with their pointless Dreaming. They don't deserve the mercy of the Pits."

"You're calling that torture hole mercy? You can't be serious, you conceited—"

"You don't want to finish that sentence. Watch yourself. Faerie."

She spits out the last word like it's poison in her mouth, and she releases my arm like my skin burned her hand. I blink as I try to respond. When I look up again, she's gone, and I'm surrounded by Lerian and my growns. I scoop Aon out of Mom's arms and put my forehead to quers.

"I never thought I'd say this, but I'm glad we got you Sliced, little one. You'll be safer this way," I mutter as Mom's hands flutter up and down my body, checking for injuries. Aon coos and drools a little, squirming in my arms. I don't tell quer—que wouldn't understand yet anyway—that quer hatchling dragon will probably never be hatched because que can't Dream.

But right now, I don't even care about that. All I care about is that when que gets older—in just a season or two—the Controller might put quer under this Dream test, and que needs to pass it.

My little sibling can't be dragged away in chains like they're dragging away Mara and Leece.

Tears streak down my growns' faces, and I know they're thinking the same thing.

I wonder if Mom's regretting faking my Slicing. I wonder if she's regretting subjecting me to being the only one. I wonder, and then I look at her steely eyes as Mama puts her lips to her temple.

They're inscrutable.

Chapter Six

WORD FROM THE shrubbery is that Leece and Mara are halfway to the Highlands proper by now. They're rumbling that the Mach met the regular soldiers who arrested them halfway along the Tread as soon as they left the non settlement in Lethe.

That's when we give up any hope of rescuing them en route. The Mach are the most elite of the king's forces, specially trained in massacre tactics. They're the ones who carried out the original occupation of Izla and the institution of nongovernmental control throughout the Grove and the Samp. They designed the massacres of the dragons and attempted to infiltrate the Plains barrier in the attack that killed Jax's joiner.

There's no overcoming the Mach. Their magic tears the Energies in ways most faeries refuse to do. So we can't beat them.

Mara and Leece are lost.

"What is it, Sadie?" Mom asks me one sunup, long after the Dreaming test. The labor canon won't go off for a while, and she's sitting between Mama's open legs on Banion, Aon's hatchling tree. My little sibling is bouncing around in Mom's lap as Mama undoes Mom's braids.

"What, what, Saaaadie," Aon babbles as que stretches quer wings tentatively, almost pitching querself off of Banion's canopy.

Mom leans down to catch quer and Mama jerks her hands away from Mom's head, narrowly avoiding yanking her hair at the sudden movement. Mama's eyes are on me, eyebrow raised, as Mom settles back into her with Aon. Mama's fingers pick up where they left off expertly.

I run my hand down Banion's trunk to ask if I can collapse onto one of his lower hanging branches. He rumbles a *"not now,"* so I spin in the air irritably, rolling myself around until I'm regarding my growns upside down, like Zaylam tends to do to me.

"It's nothing," I tell them with my body. I shake my shoulders and fly off, figuring I'll go for a morning fly with Zaylam before labor instead of hanging with the growns.

"Sadie," Mom calls again. It's her *you-better-talk-to-me-right-now* voice. My wings droop and I hover where I am, turning around cautiously. I catch Mom's waiting expression, and all at once everything is spilling out of my lips.

"You should never have let them lock themselves back up in that caravan! How could they possibly expect to lead those soldiers off course? They couldn't even do magic in those chains, they kept them from twisting the Energies or else they would have escaped without any help from us!"

I glance around us and switch to unspoken body language. *"And you knew he could Dream too, you knew, and you abandoned him! You made me lie next to him while they took him away, and he was like me! He was so like me, and you didn't even care!"*

Mom's eyes are full of tears, and Aon is just staring at me, quiet. Mama's hands have left Mom's hair, and are now bracing her waist, thumbs running up and down her skin.

"Are you done?" Mom's voice is full of gravel, and she says it like a statement. Something hot, like shame, comes rushing to the pit of my stomach.

"Faye." Mom ignores Mama, who takes a deep breath and looks away from both of us.

"Sadie, he was so heavily guarded from the moment they brought him here. We had no time to prepare, and we couldn't get to him, Sadie. Don't you think that kills me just as much as it does you? He grew up in non chains, so he was like me too, Sadie, in case you missed that bit."

A tear slips down Mom's cheek and breaks my heart along its path. Mama swallows and leans her head heavily onto Banion's trunk, her eyelids fluttering closed.

"You think..." My voice is all croaky now too, and I clear it and fly tentatively closer to my growns. Aon reaches quer pudgy arms around Mom's neck. I glance around again and switch to communicating with my body. *"You think it's better to get Sliced? To not Dream? Changed your mind now that one of your young ones can and one can't?"*

Mom says nothing, her eyes wide, but Mama shifts and her eyes flash. "Since when do you talk to your mother that way?"

I glower and just stare at Aon. Que reaches for something behind me, the bulb of quer hatchling dragon, hanging loosely from Banion's branches. Its fluorescent sunset orange glow, matching Aon's wings, is fading by the sunup. Because que can't Dream, the hatchling will never be born.

At least Aon Dreamed Banion in the short days after quer birth, before que was Sliced. A lot of newly borns don't even get to connect with their hatchling tree anymore. I sigh exaggeratedly, and I hear Banion rumbling something, though I can't feel it.

"He says you can come sit if you'd like," Mama says stiffly. "Though I don't know why." She directs this to Banion. I grimace as I scoot onto his branch with my growns and sibling, stroking my thanks into Banion's bark.

I lean around Mama to look at Mom. I take a deep breath.

"I'm sorry, Mom. Sometimes..." I toss up my hands helplessly and switch to using my body to talk. *"Sometimes I don't know if I'm sad for Aon or if I'm jealous of quer. For being Sliced. Because sure, I can't imagine life without Zay or Jorb, but..."*

I shudder and the anger fades from Mom's eyes. *"But you're always at risk of someone finding out."*

I shake my shoulders back and forth, and both my growns put one of their hands on mine.

"You were so alone in the Highlands, Sadie. We weren't really allowed to socialize with a lot of other faeries, and I...I wanted you to be connected to people. To faeric life, to your hatchlings." Mama rubs her shoulders and continues with her hair. Aon crawls over to me.

"I was younger, and I was alone, and I was probably stupid. Selfish. For putting you at risk like that."

I'm shaking my head now, and I'm hugging Aon to me like quer Mom. I nod my head toward Zaylam and Jorbam. "You're not selfish, Mom. I wouldn't have them if you didn't take that risk for me." I glance at the scar above her lip and shudder. "You lost a lot too."

Her face gets veiled, and she leans back closer into Mama. I can't look at her. I want to fly away. I can't. I don't.

"I know you felt connected to Leece, sherba."

I look at Mom over Aon's tightly coiled hair, rubbing my cheek into his sweet-smelling head. Mostly I'm too old for her to call me such a young-one-like endearment, but right now, I soak it up like water after a labor shift.

"It makes sense; you don't know other nears who can Dream. Another thing that's probably my fault." She holds up a hand to stop me before I protest. "And I'm so sorry they..." Her voice chokes and she pauses. I wait. "One day, sherba, they'll liberate the Pits and everyone there will be free. Leece too. All right?"

I don't believe her. But I pretend I do. For now, it feels nice to pretend that things will get better.

Aon's pudgy hands come up to clumsily touch my face, and I let quer have at it.

Que might be lonely without a hatchling dragon, but at least if que's ever forced into a Dreaming test like that, que will be something I'll never be.

Safe.

"YOU REALIZE THE Controller's first Slicing is coming up, right?"

I grunt in affirmation and heave my axe over my shoulder for another slam into the short tree I've been tasked with killing this sunup. Kashat opens his mouth to keep talking, but I grunt again, this time in warning. P'Tal and Lerian are approaching out of the corner of my eye, right behind him, and we can't talk about this in front of P'Tal.

Kashat follows my eyes and looks over his shoulder, alarmed, and we both swing our faye glass axes, hard, into the trees in front of us, carefully keeping time with the rhythms of the wordless labor songs.

"How's Lunamez prep coming, Kashat? You're getting your accounting performance together all right?" Lerian chimes, trying to change the subject as she passes behind us, hauling the pieces of tree bodies we and the others are chopping. She's been assigned one of the bigger carts today, so P'Tal is strapped in next to her, his torso dripping with sweat. The harnesses around his shoulders are digging into him and reddening his strained, pale skin. His hooves pull in time with hers, but his eyes are distant.

"Good, yeah," Kashat answers, his voice transparently overeager. "The Lunamez learning pod is being real sweet. Since I got old enough to do labor, they've been working with me after labor hours to get our performance together. Hazal's even teaching us how to make those whisp creations, you know, the ones she tells stories with, that get all scary sometimes but usually are pretty great." He nods at me when he says that. Mama *has* always been great at whisp art.

Kashat keeps on rambling about Lunamez, how excited he is for the holiday, and how it's the first time he's gotten to lead the performance. He's nervous because at the non equivalent of fourteen harvests old, he's the youngest to lead the accounting performance in a fair while.

While he babbles, I keep shooting P'Tal furtive glances. Kashat tries to engage me with the subject, to distract from what I know must be a deep pit of guilt in his belly for bringing up Slicings in front of the older centaur.

P'Tal, along with his joiners Aora and Zeel, are expecting a young one soon. The young one will be the first newly born under the new Controller. Zeel's been carrying their young one in quer belly for almost two full harvests and will be giving birth soon. With Sachin, our last Controller, there was always a chance of secretly avoiding a Slicing. Growns could disappear for a while and have a fake scar tattooed on the newly born's temple, and then return with false verification that they'd gotten it done elsewhere. Sort of like what Mom did with me when I was a young one.

But with Evelyn in charge, she's succeeding in warning everyone else what the consequences will be of interfering with palace operations. The public Dream test, dragging Mara and Leece away in front of everyone. Under her command, failure to Slice a newly born will have consequences.

I glance across the Forest at Aora, her long brown hair wrapped up in a scarf behind her broad back as she works. Until a few sunups ago, Zeel had done quer labor in the harvesting fields, with Mama, but so close to giving birth, que's now under mandatory rest, with nearly constant observation by the king's Registry. Not a lot of hope of galloping away with their newly born.

I check to make sure P'Tal, trudging along with Lerian, is out of listening range. "You heard that the—" I hack and grunt as I yank my axe out of tree flesh quickly, keeping in time with Kashat's pacing and sounds. "—Head Slicer is coming in tomorrow?"

Kashat grunts in the affirmative. He waits for the rhythm of the rest of the faeries to meet him, and swings his own axe in time to the melancholy but somehow soothing beat. P'Tal and Lerian are a safe distance away, dumping the contents of their cart in the assigned area, the tree flesh clattering in counterpoint with our axe strikes. I slam my axe down in keeping with the time for a while before taking a few heaving breaths, rubbing out the burning in my shoulders before shaking out my hands.

"Is it sick that I'm a little grateful? That maybe after the first Slicing goes off without a hitch, the new Controller will calm down a little bit and stop arresting us all randomly to check for Dreaming? Because—"

Lerian clears her throat loudly behind me. I jump and spin around. "P'Tal, I—"

He holds up his hands. "*Stop. I get it. Just stop.*"

I back away from the tree I've been assigned to kill and move toward him. His face is longer than usual. Tired. He repeats his hand gesture wearily, speaking with his body. "*You three were Sliced, right? You all can't Dream.*"

Ler glances at me, but says nothing, and neither do I. It's always seemed strange to me that Mama hasn't told P'Tal I can Dream; they've been so close ever since Mama first came to the Grove as a near. But I imagine it's for his safety. I feel guilty enough that I told Lerian and Osley when I was younger and stupider. I'm certainly not going to say anything to contradict Mama's decision to keep her friend safe.

P'Tal presses me, whispering aloud now. "So the little one will be fine. Que has to be, right? Even if que can't Dream. I can't Dream anymore, they Sliced me too. All of us. When we were older, of course, when they did all the growns, and I'm fine. We're fine."

"Everything all right over here?" We all straighten up, breaking rhythm with the rest of the laborers, as the crisp Highlander non words interrupt our conversation, accompanied by the sound of skin boots on the ground.

My stomach swirls. I know that voice.

I turn. A girl Hand—woman, I guess, but she's about my age-mate, so that feels odd saying—is staring right at me, with a challenge of a sparkle in her narrow eyes. Her jaw is set and her delicately manicured eyebrow is arched at me before I can even speak. There's a brown sling around her arm, offsetting her white uniform with dotted purple stripes along the sides. Her high ranking sends a shiver down my spine.

I know why I recognized her voice.

Iema. The girl I rescued the night I met Evelyn. She must have healed up enough in Lethe to come back on duty, protecting the Controller.

Her eyes glisten with recognition—probably she recognized me even before she approached and spoke to us—but her face registers no surprise at my wings. There's a warning in her stance, and I act as though I've never seen her before, as though she's never pleaded for her fellow soldier to stop hitting me because I was trying to save her life.

"Yes, ma'am," I stutter as my friends freeze.

She purses her thin lips and I remind myself to lower my gaze out of respect for her position.

"None of you seem to be working."

Lerian's tail swings around uncomfortably, and Kashat feigns extreme interest in the beetle climbing the grass under his dangling feet. P'Tal towers over Iema, standing at attention as though he were a Hand himself and she were his commander.

"You must all know by now how essential your work is here," Iema continues. "The entire Kingdom depends on this land being cleared so roads can connect the Forest and the Samp more easily to the Highlands. You know this is only going to help all of you, don't you?"

Kashat gulps, and I unfurl my wings enough to touch their tips to his chest. Only two seasons ago, he was a pre-choosing young one. Even though he's a near now, almost my age-mate, I feel extra protective of him. P'Tal too, extends his fingers toward Kashat's wing sprouts. His breathing slows at our touch.

I address this new Hand, this woman whose blood I was drenched in so recently. "One of P'Tal's joiners is due to give birth soon, ma'am. He was just wishing he and Aora could be home with quer, in case the young one begins to come. That's all."

Iema's eyebrows go up as she considers P'Tal, as though noticing him for the first time. "Is that what's happening, centaur? You're concerned about your wife?"

The side of his mouth twitches. Marriage is a non thing—faeries and centaurs have different forms of joining—and even if we did do marriage, wife wouldn't be the right word for Zeel, who at quer choosing declared querself beyond woman and man.

But P'Tal is smart. He nods in the human fashion, even widening his already wide eyes to look more pathetic. His narrow nose twitches in hope. I almost smirk.

A long silence where we all listen to the movement songs of the laboring Forest. Then, "Finish hauling the next few rounds of wood, then get one of the other centaurs to replace your cart. Then you and this...Aora? Can take the rest of the day to yourselves. Report to me before you leave so I can give you the proper documentation."

P'Tal bows his head, his shaggy hair flapping comically. "Many thanks, ma'am."

Iema shoots me a significant look before turning on her heel and walking off. We all glance at each other uneasily.

P'Tal beams at me while Lerian grins and hits me on the shoulder and Kashat thumps my wing sprouts. "Good save, faerie." I grin and push Lerian back, shaking off how unnerving seeing Iema was. Yet another Hand who surely has put together that I'm a spy.

"Yeah, you did great too, centaur. Loved the part where you said nothing at all." She and P'Tal give small whinnies in between the rhythmic thudding of axe blows. P'Tal shifts toward me and puts his forehead to mine before setting off.

As soon as they're out of range, Kashat shifts closer to me so that every time we raise our axes, we're in danger of smacking each other in the head with the blunt sides. He mutters to me in between swings, using the labor songs as cover to avoid being overheard.

"You caught how she deferred to you the whole time, right? Like you're all special and speak for the rest of us because you look kind of…"

"Like a non," I grunt wearily as I rear my axe up again, careful to avoid thwacking him. "And nope, I didn't notice exactly. But I see it now you mention it. I guess I'm just pretty used to it."

Kashat grunts and yanks his axe out of tree flesh with a whispered apology. He turns to me, wiping his face with the rapidly developing muscular ball of his shoulder. He shakes out his long, light brown fingers before pretending to examine his axe blade. He talks so softly now that I have to glance around us to make sure no one's watching. I lean really close into him then, so close I can smell the fruity oil in his hair. I lean down so it looks like I'm helping him check his axe for dents or imperfections.

"My growns have been working with Jax and some elders and a few newly post-choosing nears, like me." He's muttering quickly, his eyes darting across the area rapidly. "Jax figures, if we work with young ones whose growth has just slowed to a more non-like speed, and we try to actually induce Dreams, we might be able to restore Dreaming after Slicings. If we twist the Energies just right and put that twisting into medicine form, maybe we can get Dreaming back after Slicings take them away. We can have hatchling trees and dragons."

Kashat glances at my furrowed brow and grimaces apologetically. "He didn't tell you on account of you're too old, and he didn't want you to have another sneaky spy type thing to worry about." More likely, because I can already Dream, so there's not anything to restore. But I say nothing and nod him on. "And it makes your mom too sad to work on it. Anyway, point is, I've been in the infirmary a lot in between labor and Lunamez preparations. They're ready to try out a serum that might counteract the effects of the Slicing. But someone has to slip it into the head Slicer's equipment so we can try it in an actual Slicing. P'Tal, Aora, and Zeel knew and were excited, but it uh…it kind of stalled when this new Controller made it too risky to get to the head Slicer."

He widens his eyes at me, and I run my fingers over his blade as a pair of centaurs pass under us with their carts. "Jax would never let me go on another mission right now," I mutter back when they've passed by. "My growns would kill him, and he knows it. Not after what happened the other sunup. Too soon. They're worried about traumatizing me, or something."

Kashat inhales shakily, his eyes speeding around so quickly I'm worried he'll get a headache. And then his hand is in mine, and something shaped like a small vial, like the kind Mom and Jax keeps liquid medicines in, passes between us. I slip it into my pocket without looking at it. "Don't get me wrong, I care about you too, Sadie, but P'Tal's been really good to me on labor every day, and I'm not trying to be your grown." He winks at me.

"The head Slicer's coming in tomorrow. Which means he's probably staying at the Lethean Inn tonight," I whisper, a tingling rising in my forehead that always happens when I'm focusing extra hard.

Kashat nods as we pull apart from each other, slamming our axes extra hard for effect as another team of centaurs passes, hauling their cart. "And since this new Controller looks like she brought a whole new team of Hands along with her, it's super likely the head Slicer will be new too. He won't know what you look like at all."

I think about telling him no, that the risks of Dreaming aren't worth it.

The labor songs around us take up the rhythm of an old dragon hymn, and I nod at Kashat. I'll do it. It's worth it. It has to be.

How else will the future be full of dragon songs? How else will Zaylam not be the last of the dragons one day—unless by luck some younger faeries Dream both of their hatchling mates in the short period before their Slicings—when all her elders return to the Energies and none have hatched after her? I can't let her live through that.

I won't.

I swallow heavily as Iema patrols under us, her functioning arm drifting up to her cast absently. I hold her eyes for a long moment.

When she passes, I turn to Kashat and nod. "Cover for me with my growns tonight," I tell him. He grins and shakes his shoulders back and forth, a Grovian nod, conspiratorially.

Maybe P'Tal's young one does have some hope of Dreaming and having hatchlings mates, after all.

Chapter Seven

I FIDDLE WITH the vial, hidden in the pocket of my beige non-style trousers. I adjust the off-white, open-throated tunic, so similar to the one I normally wear, but without an opening for my wings. I twist my neck around as far as possible, making sure that the only thing making a dent in the shirt are my muscles, not my wings. The disguise is good; no one should notice a thing. But I toss a non-style cloak over my shoulders for good measure. I'm glad I brought it because even though the snow's been melting rapidly, it's still cool during the days and the nights are even colder. The white clouds of my breath aren't as defined as they were earlier in the season, but they're still there. I pull the cloak tighter around my body.

An amused thumping sound interrupts the calls of the nighttime Forest creatures and makes me jump and spin around. *"Trying to check yourself out? Hasn't the Controller been doing that enough for the both of you?"*

"Osley!" I whisper-shout, looking around us nervously. I drop to one knee in front of quer. *"What are you doing all the way out here? I thought you hated being this close to all those nons in Lethe,"* I ask quer with my body.

"You really think Kashat was going to send you on a mission without a scout? Without anyone to call for help if you fly into trouble?" I just stare at quer. *"Don't worry, I'm not planning to tell your moms. I haven't told them about Evelyn and Iema, have I? Even though that's what got you selected supposedly at random to go through that awful Dreaming test."*

"Shhh!" Even though que's not communicating in a language most nons would understand, sometimes trees and shrubs, let alone insects and birds, let alone groundlings, slip information to the wrong people.

Quer beady eyes look around, quer ears raised, alert. The left one twitches slightly. *"You've gotten so jumpy you might have some rabbit in you too, Sadie. And don't roll your eyes at me like that. It's a compliment."*

I sigh exaggeratedly and push my hands into my thighs, rising to my feet. *"All right, fine, come. But stay out of sight, yeah?"*

Osley's ears tilt back so far they almost touch quer body. I catch a whiff of quer bemused irritation when I breathe in. *"Did you even know I was following you? I'm good at staying out of sight, Sade."* And then, with sadder movements, a sadder scent. *"The only reason I'm still alive."*

My heart sinks and I grimace at quer. I didn't know Osley back when quer family was around, but I know que had a big one. Non hunters took them all out when the palace decided that eating grown food made it too reliant on fae magic. When they started to hunt.

Osley hops forward, nudging quer head into my ankle. *"Come on, then."* I nod in the human fashion, trying to get myself into formation.

We set off silently, continuing my path toward the edge of the Forest, where the Tread spills out into more open terrain at the border of the Grovian Forest and the non settlement of Lethe. We cross an old bridge carefully, the river rushing underneath us, Osley shivering as we go. The Lethean Inn, where I was supposed to have my dinner—meeting—date?—with Evelyn, isn't too far away. I can see its soft lights and the smoke from burning tree flesh spilling out of the two chimneys from the gaps between the last few Forest trees. The steady rush of the river behind us calms my nerves somewhat.

I sigh deeply and set my shoulders, making sure they have none of the pinchedness of most faeries. I wiggle my face around to wipe the tension off of it. I swing my arms back and forth, pumping my neck from side to side, like I'm getting ready to tackle some feat of great physical strength. Osley and I exchange glances. I nod at quer curtly.

"I don't know how long I'll be," I tell quer softly in the most widely used non dialect around these parts, adjusting easily to the accent I grew up with, that of the working people of the Highlands. When Mom and I first arrived in the Grove after we fled, that non accent was the first thing the other young ones noticed and hated about me. Then, it was the fact that I grew up so much slower than they did. The young ones I was agemates with when I got to the Grove went through their choosing and became nears before I had even moved on from their old learning pods. It was easier than it could have been, I guess, because Jax hadn't accepted another healing partner since Idrisim died, but he accepted Mom as his new co-healer. So the others had to accept it too. They didn't blame Mom for me. But they came to blame me for looking like a non, came to call me slow, stupid, ugly, because that's how I grew.

I sigh again and shake my head like I'm trying to get water out of my ears. Usually on spying missions, I know my moms are close by. Now, if Kashat did his job right, they're sleeping comfortably deep in the Forest, content with the lie that I'm helping him with Lunamez preparation and am going to be up all night in the Underland with him and Lerian.

Better to just jump in, like I do into the Flowing when the water is cold. Get the shock over with in one go.

"See you soon," I mutter to Osley, and, after receiving permission from the grass ahead of me, I limp out of the Forest and into Lethe, toward the inn. My fingers toy with the vial in my pocket, and I grind my teeth slightly.

I loosen my stride as I approach the inn, seeing a group of young non men standing around outside with flasks in their hands. They nod at me without seeming to really think about it. With my short hair and small chest, a lot of non men not only think I'm a non like them, but a man too. I nod back, eager to keep it that way, at least with these ones. They're all too young to be my mark, and dressed in typical Lethean laborer garb. Their trousers are stained from days of work, and their tunics are casual. The head Slicer certainly wouldn't be caught traveling in such unrefined clothing.

I yank open the door and pause as warmth, light, and scent from the inn's two tree flesh fireplaces hit me like a wall. My eyes swivel quickly around the room. It's a big place, with a three-sided bar in the center, surrounded by tree flesh tables and benches, and four exits, counting the one I'm walking into. One, I know from past experience, leads to the kitchens; one to the outside; and one to the rooms people can rent upstairs. The walls, all made of tree flesh, are supposed to give a homey feeling even though it seems to me like I've just walked into a den made of body parts. I remember growing up in buildings like these, though, and a small, ashamed part of me feels somewhat comforted.

No one really reacts to my entrance beyond a few scattered glances that quickly return to games of darts, conversations at full tables, or the bottoms of mugs. I scan the room and the pit in my stomach loosens a bit; this is too easy. A tall, reedy man who looks like he's never seen the sun in his life is sitting alone at a fully serviced table across from the quiet side of the bar. He's wearing a royal white robe with—my stomach swoops in relief—the orange stripes of the head Slicer. I shove my hands deep into my pockets and sidle over to the table next to him.

"Anyone sitting here?" I gruffly ask the two non girls at the other end of the tree flesh table I've chosen. They giggle and one looks me up and down. I cock an eyebrow.

"Go ahead," the one with reddish hair says, and I nod my thanks. I thrum my fingers on the tree flesh absently after I sit down, offering a silent apology to the trees whose lives were ended and bodies dismembered to make this table.

"What'll it be, sherba?" a soft voice asks. I almost jump at the Grovian faeric term of endearment, pressing my wings deeper into my wing sleeves. But I remind myself sternly that in Lethe especially, our languages influence each other. No matter how hard the palace tries to prevent it.

The barmaid, whose name I remember from my last mission is something like Ruth, is balancing an empty, circular tray on her fingertips in front of me, her eyebrows raised. Her red and white dress is super short and the top of it barely covers her chest. I swallow hard and nod my head toward the head Slicer at the next table.

"What he's got over there looks good," I tell her, my voice low-pitched but loud enough, hoping he'll hear it over the dart game on the other side of the bar. He does, and raises his steaming mug at me in acknowledgement. I grin at him, trying not to picture his hands covered in newly born blood.

Ruth chuckles, leaning her hips onto my table and bending over me conspiratorially. I force my eyes onto her face, which turns out not to be a problem; her eyes are a stormy kind of gray that proves nice to look at. "Sherba, are you even old enough to have what he's drinking?"

The Head Slicer chuckles, but not meanly. "Oh, get the kid some mulled mead, Ruth. Looks like he could use the warmth." He winks at me and I'm mildly surprised. Usually men of his rank take longer to warm up to me than this, probably because of my darker skin and my lower class accent. But who knows, maybe he's already been drinking a bunch of that brew. Maybe he thinks I'm a man and am trying to pick up the girls at my table, and he's trying to help me out, or pick me up himself. Or maybe I really do look cold and he's just not a bad person. Except for the fact that it's his job to slice open our newly borns' skulls.

But I don't think about that now. I can't. I grin up innocently at Ruth as the girls giggle beside me. Ruth screws her face into a mischievous grin and spins off to the bar to pour me a mug.

"He's right. You do look like you could use a little something to warm you up," one of the girls tells me. She has the greenest eyes I've ever seen. "Or someone," she throws in as an afterthought, and I hear the Head Slicer chuckle nearby.

"You volunteering?"

"Do you want me to be?"

I grin lopsidedly. The girl with the reddish hair rolls her eyes. "You two wanna be alone?"

I shake my head, but don't take my eyes off those green ones. "Nah. Just getting to know each other. What brings two beautiful ladies like yourselves out to an inn like this, huh?"

"Oh, nothing much. The chance of finding a man like you."

Part of me feels dirty and the other part is flying. They're nons and they think I am too. But being looked at like maybe I could be...attractive? It only happens when I'm spying and my wings are tucked away.

But they also think I'm a man. Evelyn knew I'm not, even with my wings tucked away. We were supposed to meet here for a date. Or something.

Because she looked at me like I could be attractive too.

It should disgust me, that thought. The Controller, of all people. And it does disgust me. For the most part.

But the small part of me that wonders what could have happened if she wasn't the Controller and I met her here like she'd asked me? That part of me sings, and I wish it were a limb so I could hack the traitorous feeling off of my body.

I swallow the thought down and slide over to the girls' side of the tree flesh table.

"So you're on the hunt for someone strong, sensitive, and dashingly good-looking?"

The head Slicer chuckles over at the next table. I let him catch my eye and he winks at me. I grin even as I swallow vomit.

Everything's going perfectly.

"On the hunt?" Green Eyes arches an eyebrow. "With that accent? What are you, one of those new hunting parties the king's putting together?"

I nod my thanks at Ruth as she puts a steaming mug in front of me. I drink deeply before I answer, and I sigh into the warmth flooding into me. "Maybe."

"Oh come on, he's playing us. He's too young to be on those squads. Look, he hasn't even started growing a beard yet."

The girl with reddish hair lifts her fingers to my face, and I can't help it. I jump a bit. It's too close for comfort. My knees slam into the underside of the tree flesh table, and Green Eye's drink tips over onto her dress.

"I'm sorry!" I stumble, trying to rise but making it worse. "I didn't mean to, I—"

"No, it's fine, it—"

"It's not fine, Maeve, you're drenched! Ugh, how could you look like a hunter but move like a filthy faerie?"

Maeve's friend drags her up and toward the bar to dry her dress off, glaring over her shoulder at me as she goes. I don't hear Maeve's protests even as her friend pulls her away, nor do I see the men on the other side of the bar laugh when she tells them the story of the loser with the smooth words but no moves to match. I don't feel anything except like I've flown top speed into one of Harlenikal's tail spikes. I just stay there, pathetically, half standing, my hands still pathetically half-outstretched. Mouth pathetically half-open.

Pathetically half-*human*.

Ruth bustles over with a rag in her hand and clicks her tongue at me. "No need to get your feet in a trap, sherba. It wasn't your fault. I keep telling my boss he's gotta get these damn tables raised."

I straighten up and nod, remembering Tamzel's training. I bring myself out of myself, out of Sadie, and into the person I become when I'm on a mission.

I let the head Slicer catch my gaze again and raise one shoulder at him.

"Doesn't look like it's your night," he says. He raises an eyebrow when he notices my limp, but doesn't comment on it.

I force an easy grin. "Just when I thought I'd found someone to talk to."

"Well, you can talk to me. Not as attractive as a pair of girls your age, I imagine, but I promise I won't storm off if you spill my mead. And hey, I'm the one who convinced Ruth to let you have it to begin with."

"Never forget a favor," I throw out a Lethean phrase as I raise my mug at him. I slip over to where he's sitting. "Sure you don't mind if I sit? I can't guarantee the safety of your drink."

The Head Slicer glances over my shoulder as I sit down. "As long as you can guarantee my safety from those girls—the redhead still looks like she wants to smack you—no, no, don't turn around—then we'll be fine."

"Thanks."

He waves me away like it's nothing. I take a deep breath. "You in the province for some palace business?" I nod toward his robes, trying to inject my voice with the undercurrent of awe that a lot of Highlander nons from outlying settlements like Lethe get when they talk to an official from the Highlands proper.

"How could you tell?"

I laugh a little, actively pushing down the swirling anger in my stomach. I don't want him to be funny and self-effacing. I don't want him to invite me to sit with him and say things that make me feel like less of a hybrid freak.

I want him to be terrible. I want him to be sadistic and evil. The job of framing him as the one who sabotages the Slicing, not me, will be much easier if he's a horrible person.

"I'm excited they sent me out here, actually," he goes on, gesturing for me to come sit directly across from him.

Good, I think. *He's probably excited because he loves hurting newly borns.*

"It's so much more peaceful out here. You can actually see the sky and smell the air rather than all those poisons they're pumping into everything these days."

Damn it all. Not because he loves hurting newly borns, then.

I nod. "Yeah, it is nice out here. Oh, uh, thanks Ruth." Her smile accompanies my refill and the head Slicer lifts his mug toward me once more. I do the same and we both drink deeply.

Too deeply. I cough slightly and squeeze my eyes shut, careful to close both eyelids so he doesn't notice my second pair. "Well," I wheeze, "that's one way to get rid of the chill." He laughs and half stands up so he can lean over and thump my back. My stomach seizes, but he touches me high enough up so he can't feel the slight bulge of my wing sprouts.

"So what brings you out here alone tonight...?"

"Jayden," I tell him smoothly, my fallback name for spying missions.

"Jayden," he repeats. "Artem."

I nod and hold my mug up to him again. "Thanks for the drink, Artem." We sip in silence for a few minutes, me turning on my tree flesh bench to watch the nears and growns on the louder side of the inn, across the bar. They're getting a bit raucous this late, dart games and the heady melodies from an old woman's lute joining with the mead to make everyone that much louder, that much braver, that much closer to each other.

"Looking for some quiet time in a not so quiet space," I finally answer his question, and he smiles indulgently.

"A near beyond your harvests, it seems," he says approvingly.

I shrug. He drinks deeply from his mug and signals Ruth for two more, and I'm grateful that I swiped a serum that suppresses intoxication before I left the Grove. "I have some business in the Forest in the next week or so, and I'm due to arrive tomorrow. An unpleasant matter, I'm afraid. So you're right. Some quiet time in a not so quiet space. Seems just right tonight."

I clench my toes together under the table, the only thing I can clench without him noticing me tensing up. "Unpleasant?"

"Mmmm. That's great, thank you, Ruth. You know about Initiations, of course." He gestures with his new mug at my Slicing scar. "I always feel terribly about those your age, the ones who were Initiated as children rather than as newly borns. I fear scalpels get scarier, not less frightening, with age." He sighs. "I've just been promoted to Head Initiator for the Grove, you see." He says it as a statement of fact, not as a matter of pride. "At least now, all the operations are on newly borns who don't know what to be scared of and won't remember the procedure once it's done."

Not true. Most of us do remember. Even that early, even eight sunups after we're born. Nons might not, but faeries definitely remember.

"Ah, still. It's for the best. Imagine Lunav back in the grips of that terrible plague! You know I hear the Forest only has two faye healers; so hard to get volunteers to learn since the plague wiped out so many of them."

I take a long swig of my warm mead. The spices more than the alcohol rush to my head. I keep quiet, just listening. I don't think about the way he'd never talk to me if he knew I was a faerie. I call to mind all my training and keep my face wiped clean, even sympathetic.

The head Slicer—Artem—clears his throat, looking away like he's embarrassed. "Ah, you came here for quiet, not to listen to the ramblings of some old man."

I try to protest that he's not old—and sure enough, with thick, graying brown hair and robust voice, he doesn't seem at all old to me—but he waves away my stammering.

"What about you, Jayden? Don't get enough quiet during your days?"

I grin and take a gulp of my mead. "No, sir. In the logging fields all day, sunup till sundown. The sound of those axes alone'll drive anyone away from direct noise." Non loggers are rarer—they like to use faeries for the hardest labor when possible—but by no means unheard of, especially in the poorer provinces like Lethe.

When I was younger, I learned that the easiest way to spy is to make up as few fake facts about myself as possible. I don't imagine Zaylam would appreciate having to fly out of the safety of the Plains, risking her life to cause the distraction I need to help me get away from growing suspicions at a gaping hole in my story. Again.

A strangely companionable silence falls between us. I swivel on the tree flesh bench between us to see what's causing the sudden commotion on the other side of the bar. An older man in a Hand's uniform is leading a younger one out of the inn by the scruff of his neck while the boy's friends hoot and carry on. I shift to make sure I'm not visible from the path to the door. I don't recognize the Hand, but that doesn't mean he's not one of the Controller's men.

I jump when Ruth appears at my side and puts a gentle hand on my shoulder. Thankfully, I don't knock anything over this time. She swaps our empty mugs for steaming full ones in an easy motion as she leans forward, her lips close to our tilted heads. I force myself to listen to her instead of soaking in the combination of her low-cut dress and breath of spiced ale.

"Seems the young one's father decided his performance in combat wasn't where it needs to be for him to deserve a night out with his friends," she tells us conspiratorially.

"Mmm. What'd the poor lad do?"

"According to him or according to his father?" We laugh. "Says he refused to arrest a mob of scum in the Samp. Gone all soft-like with them." She rests her elbows on the tree flesh, and I hold my breath to keep my face neutral. "He swears, of course, that he's just as tough on the slime as the rest. Just didn't get the orders right is all."

"Ruth! Another!" calls a voice from the bar.

She waves her rag in acknowledgment and lifts her tray back up.

"I'll be back." I return her wink, although there's a hole in my stomach.

Artem shakes his head at his mug. "Fathers," he mutters. "Have you got growns, Jayden?"

I think of Mama's comforting hands on Mom's shoulders and Mom's soft voice singing me to sleep each night when I was a young one in the Highlands.

I think of the light non man Mom worked for before I was born, who forced himself onto Mom and gave me my lighter skin shade and my slowed, almost non-rate growth, my rounded ears and straight legs. I remember when he caught me Dreaming one night—he'd never come to the storage closet where we slept before, Mom was always supposed to go to him—and I didn't know Mom had that much blood inside her. We were still running from him when we first met Mama.

After rescuing us from the Hands that chased us to the border of the Grove where we could claim sanctuary, Mama healed her. And me.

My growns.

"I guess everyone's got growns, huh?" Artem frowns with his mouth but grins with his eyes. He swishes his mead around in his mug before taking a swig and giving me a pointed look. As always when I'm Jayden, I move in part truths, part terrors.

"My mom's amazing. A healer, and not like one of those ones who just relies on faerie myths. She does the whole package. My dad's trash. Wish I could say I never met him, but what can you do, right?"

My heart tugs, calling that non family, not mentioning Mama, not bringing up Aon. But Jayden's heart swoops at the look of understanding in Artem's eyes, the way he runs his thumb over his growing chin stubble and nods at me sympathetically.

People don't look at me like this when I'm just Sadie. Not strangers, anyway.

Except Evelyn. I wonder, not for the first time, why I didn't use my spy name with her the first time we met.

"What about you, Artem? Family?"

The Head Slicer heaves a heavy sigh and signals Ruth for another round. I remind myself that he's not some nice person buying me mead. He'd never buy mead for me as Sadie—he'd just cut into my skull if he found out I haven't been Sliced.

"I had family. A big one. I suppose they're still my family, but..."

"But?" I brace myself for blood boiling.

"It was fine, if a little strained, as families can be. You know. But—oh, I guess it was what, ten harvests ago now—you'd have been no more than seven or so harvests, you probably won't even remember this—" I wasn't seven. I was just a newly born, but he can't know about my slightly faeric growth rate—"the king retaliated against the Grovian dragons for spreading the risk of blood plague infection. Good thing too, if unfortunate for the poor souls, because their blood, you know, is the key to granting immunity to the thing."

I watch him as he drinks deeply and fight off a smile. He leans in and points a casually uncoordinated finger at me.

"I have some of that lifesaving blood in a case in my room, just upstairs, you know. Funny, isn't it, how the lifeblood of such magnificent creatures can be the key to saving the lives of an entire civilization?"

He stares at me with big eyes, and I realize he wants an answer.

"Yeah." I think of Mama's hatchling dragon, Xamamlee. He was slaughtered in the so-called retaliation Artem's talking about. The first massacre. Zaylam's screams during the second send me deep into my mug for more mead even though it isn't affecting me.

Artem grins sadly at me. "I'm doing it again. You didn't ask me about dragons and blood! Growns! I have them. But they chose the wrong side of this whole thing. Good people, my growns. They just never understood the value of doing what needs to be done. Understand me, Jayden?"

"Yes, sir."

His smile reaches his eyes this time, and he reaches over to clap me on the shoulder.

"Sir is what they call me at my labor, Jayden. Artem. It's Artem."

I return his grin, hoping it doesn't look like a grimace.

"If that boy had sympathy for the faeries he was supposed to arrest, I understand. Initiations are hard. Especially that first round we had to do, of all the growns and young ones—we started with the humans, and then later mandated it for other creatures—growns had to submit to the surgeries, and wouldn't always accept the anasthetics." We both shudder. Mom hadn't. I don't know if Mama had—I never asked. Mom's muffled shrieks and tears were more than enough.

"I'm sure your mom gave you a great anesthetic, though. When you were a young one."

Artem's eyeing the Slicing scar on my right temple. I squirm, hoping he doesn't recognize it as a tattoo, faded white ink on light brown skin. Mom had done the tattoo herself—when I was a newly born, not a young one like Artem's imagining—when she convinced the man she worked for that she'd Slice me herself, being a healer and all.

"Yeah," I half lie. "She held my hand through the whole thing." Sort of. I was in her arms, anyway. A fully non newly born wouldn't remember something like that. I do.

I wonder if he knows that it's not only the older ones whose minds he's butchered, whose hatchling connections he's severed, that remember hearing his scalpel cut into tender flesh and newly formed bone.

I stand abruptly and, remembering myself, sway a little on the spot. Then I sway a lot.

Ruth, passing near me, lets out a throaty laugh. "Seems like you're too young to handle that mead after all."

I exaggerate another stagger, careful not to overdo it. I want to look young and in need of help, not pathetic in Artem's eyes. And sure enough, he steps around the edge of the table to me. "You all right, son?" His voice is concerned, but his eyes are mischievous. "Maybe we indulged too quickly, hm?" He puts his arm around my shoulders, and I'm glad for my thick layer of muscles carved out by labor. "Ruth! Can you get this nice young boy a room?"

I almost smirk at my own cleverness, but I just nod gratefully with a bemused grin on my face. "I've drank more than this before. Maybe 'cause I skipped dinner," I mutter in my own defense, but I've already won. I feel the vial Kashat took from Jax so acutely it's like the thing is burning in my pocket.

He supports me on my left side all the way up the rickety tree flesh stairs, winking at Ruth as she tells him which room to plop me in. I swallow my embarrassment as Maeve and her friend, now with the group playing darts on the other side of the bar, giggle at my retreating back. Artem takes on both the dead weight from my limp and the stumbling uncertainty of my fake intoxication surprisingly well; his reedy body doesn't look particularly well built, but I guess you have to be of a certain kind of strength to tug at the Energies like he must as a healer.

The Head Slicer leans me against his shoulder as he fiddles with a door just above the stairs to open it. It occurs to me that other than Jax and P'Tal, I've never had this much physical contact with a man before. It feels strange. I wonder if he'd be touching me any differently if he knew I was a woman. Or a faerie.

Artem looks around the empty room for a moment and stokes a small tree flesh flame in the fireplace before laying me gingerly onto the solitary mattress, stuffed with dried up plant carcasses.

"You rest here for a bit, and I'll have Ruth bring you up some water soon. She says you can have the room as long as you need, no charge. All right, Jayden?"

I let my neck wobble loosely like Lerian's did last Lunamez, when we smuggled some mead from Rada's stash and drank it deep into the nighttime celebrations. "Mmhmm." Artem chuckles and brushes a couple stray, curly hairs from my forehead before leaving the room, closing the door softly behind him.

The moment the door closes, I'm bolt upright on the mattress, my ears straining. I hear his footsteps thud down the stairs and back into the bar area, and I immediately crouch on my haunches, pressing my ear to the door, straining to hear any movement in the corridor.

I don't have much time.

Hearing nothing but the rustling from downstairs, I slip out of the room quietly and tiptoe to my left. The biggest room—the one reserved for the most esteemed passers-through—is in the left corner wing of the corridor.

I'm starting to sweat despite the chill in the air as I tug softly at the Energies around me, tugging and twisting until I hear a small click in the doorknob. The tree flesh door swings open with a slight creak and I flinch, frozen. But there's still no movement but my own.

I slip inside the room, hoping against hope that it's Artem's. I poke into a soft sack full of clothing, and sure enough, a change of Head Slicer clothing is folded neatly underneath some sleeping wear. I picked the right room.

He doesn't seem to have many possessions here. For a moment a swirl of panic flares up in my belly, but then I notice the hard case sticking out slightly from under the mattress. It looks like what Jax attaches to the back of his chair when he goes to heal someone who can't make it to the infirmary. A classic healer's case.

I lick my lips. This is it. I steady my hands so I can flip the catch of the case open. My eyes fall immediately on two vials. They're full of deep golden liquid, the color and consistency of Lunavad tree sap.

Dragon blood.

I shudder and wonder whose veins this blood used to run through. Before I was born, Mama's hatchling dragon, Xamamlee, died saving one of his friends in the massacre of the Plains. Mama says before the massacre, all Lunavic skies were always full of dragons and their songs. After Xamamlee and the others were killed, the Lunavad trees magicked the barrier around the Plains and with rare exception, the dragons don't leave their confines anymore.

I hope this blood is too new to be Xamamlee's. Mama still cries about him sometimes in the Plains with Baml, her hatchling tree, but only when she thinks I'm not watching.

My ears strain for movement in the corridor, but I can't hear anything beyond the cheers and shouts of the ever-rowdier crowd of Letheans downstairs. I slip the vial out of my pocket and remember what Kashat had told me— mixing its contents with the dragon blood will hopefully allow the Slicing to do whatever it supposedly does to prevent the plague, but will still allow the Sliced newly born to Dream.

My heart slams as there's rustling on the stairs. I freeze, helpless, but another door opens all the way down the other side of the corridor. I release the breath I didn't know I was holding and work faster.

I open the vial and twist off the stoppers for the dragon blood with my teeth, one at a time. I drop an equal amount of the liquid Kashat gave me into both vials before closing them up and giving them a swift shake. They glow for a moment, the whispy golden color of banned soul keeping magic, and then still. The blood looks the same as they did before I touched them, no trace of the sabotage I've attempted.

I wipe the vials carefully on my tunic to remove any smudges from my fingers or mouth and slip them back in the case, exhaling shakily as my eyes try to avoid looking at the carefully wrapped set of scalpels. I swallow vomit and seal the clasps of the case, placing it back against the wall in the same slanted position I'd found it in.

More movement on the stairs. I launch myself out of the room, silent as Osley, and slip into the room at the top of the stairs. I throw my body onto the mattress and remember to look intoxicated.

A soft knock at the door precedes a small sliver of light from the corridor glowing off my face. "Jayden," Ruth calls gently. "I brought you water."

I am absolutely alert, but force my body to move blearily, even with my heart beating wildly. I accept the water with a murmur of thanks and hold it with both hands as I drink it all hurriedly. Some slips down my chin onto my tunic. I don't care. I need something to do with my hands, my mouth, to keep my entire body from shaking.

Ruth's staring down at me with her head cocked to one side, her wide gray eyes narrowed as she looks down at me. "Want me to send for anyone to come get you?"

I shake my head and drag myself up, careful to stumble less than I had on the way up here. "No, no. But I uh...I should be getting back to town."

Ruth scoffs. "Town's a ways away. What're you gonna do, fly to get there?" She chuckles and I force a laugh.

"I'll be okay. Just needed to lie down a bit. Tell Artem uh...tell Artem thanks for the drinks. And the help."

Ruth sighs, her eyes looking at my face hard. Then she tosses up her hands slightly as the voices of young men yelling for more mead travel up the stairs.

"Duty calls," she tells me with a twisted smile. "You get home safe now, all right?"

I nod and wait until I hear drunken cheers rise up downstairs at her return. All eyes will be on her, I know. I descend the stairs at a crouch, my eyes seeking out Artem. He's staring thoughtfully into the bottom of his mug. I swing myself from the stairs to the back door and slip out into the night.

The cold air hits my sweaty skin like a sheet of ice, but Osley's bright eyes are waiting for me at the edge of the Forest. I force myself not to run, and I thank Lunara that the cold has forced the lingering men from earlier back into the inn.

"Mission accomplished, Os," I tell quer, bending down to stroke quer gray-white fur after seeking and receiving permission from the grass to step into the Forest again. Que nuzzles into my hands, and we both turn to look back at the inn.

I wonder if the people who were kind to me in there would have even hesitated to send for the king's Hands if they'd caught a glimpse of my wings.

I wonder what Artem would say if he knew the near he'd befriended tonight only talked to him to destroy his means of making a living. Because his means of making a living is destroying my life.

Chapter Eight

I'M TOO EXHAUSTED to make it to the Underland. I collapse in Jorbam's branches as the moon is just starting to disappear under the Forest's canopy, and Osley leaps away to tell a probably very anxious Kashat that I got back all right.

I'm asleep immediately after stripping out of the non clothes, before I can even answer Jorbam's rumbled inquires as to where in Lunav I've been.

I'm too wiped out to even Dream, but when the sun starts to invade my outer eyelids what seems like only moments after I've laid down, my groggy arm flails out as I shift to try to get away from the light. Zaylam grunts loudly—I've smacked her face as she sleeps perched on Jorbam's trunk just beneath me.

My outer eyelids drag open reluctantly, exhaustion heavy on my body like a weighty mist on and inside each of my limbs. The top layers of Zaylam's eyelids disappear into the top of her triangular head as they open immediately. Though I can't see her crystalline, Flowing green eyes with her bottom two layers of eyelids closed, I know she can see me. Her snout, circular and scaly, twitches back and forth sleepily when she recognizes my apologetic face staring down at her. I groan internally. — Zaylam likes her sleep.

"Sorry, Zay," I croak. "I guess I forgot you were down there." Her snout is twitching like she's trying not to elongate it. I narrow my bleary eyes at her. She's only pretending to be irritated. I don't have to pretend. I just want to go back to sleep. She raises her head and sings to me.

> *Faeries have such small remembrances*
> *With those small little bodies.*
> *Does the little one not remember*
> *Anything?*

I grin groggily, still after all these seasons getting used to having a dragon sing directly at me. Usually, they sing right out to the Energies, not to any one person in particular, but with their hatchlings, it's different.

"I'm tired," I moan, and she imitates me in singsong. I laugh at her antics despite myself.

My laugh turns into a cough, though, as I plummet deeper into Jorbam's branches. A strong wind pushes me forward, and the rush of wind from Zaylam's takeoff fills my ears. She's pumped her broad wings and flown herself away from Jorbam's canopy backwards, probably so she could watch me lose my balance from the force of her flapping.

She's roaring with laughter, and Jorbam rumbles with lethargic amusement.

And then Zaylam is shrieking.

I disengage myself, exhaustion abruptly gone. I scrape the side of my face on Jorbam's branches as I speed toward Zay, but Mom's hatchling dragon Gimla beats me to it; the Lunavad leaf-style spines that lie the center of his back are too sharp for him to catch anyone there, and as I turn I see him rolling over in midair so that he can break my screeching hatchling dragon's fall with his enormous, soft underbelly. His unfurled tail helps his wings slow their descent, and lifts straight up into the air, seemingly of its own accord.

I squint, and I realize that Harlenikal—with her earth-brown wings and body—has taken Gimla's tail into her toothless mouth, flapping her thick, smooth wings hard, holding up Gimla so he can slow down enough to avoid splattering spine-first onto the ground below. Semad and Kamid watch, silent for once, alongside a stunned-looking Archa. The entire Plains seems to be holding its breath.

The procession of falling dragons—Zaylam caught by Gimla, Harlenikal trying to hold them both—stops just before they splatter on the earth. Gimla rolls over gently, Zaylam's limp body slipping off of his belly and onto the ground. I land as Zay sprawls out, wings and limbs askew. I take a deep break and exhale onto her underbelly to comfort her. She groans. I ready myself to pull the Energies into Healing.

This has happened a lot since the Kinzemna massacre, when her underbelly was sliced through by the enchanted bones of fellow dragons and her air bladder was cut into shreds. For the most part, she's healing all right, but sometimes—like now—her scar crusts open and leaks thick blood.

Seasons-old screams from the massacre flood my mind. I shudder as I remember the sickening sounds of the palace's invisible, enchanted blades tearing through dragon flesh, cutting the wings off of some and puncturing the underbellies of others, like Zay. Each newly cut-off set of wings in turn came to life and sawed off flesh and bone from more dragons. So many were permanently sea dragons now—assuming they didn't bleed to death—and Zaylam, now, is permanently an air dragon. With her air bladder shredded as it was during the massacre, she'll never get to swim to Qathram on the Izlanian side of the Flowing. It's not something we really talk about, but I know it weighs heavily on her. I can feel it.

To distract myself as much as to distract her, I put on a horrible Highlander non accent while my hands work over her. "You are aware, are you not, dragon, that an injured specimen is not fit to serve the king? How very inconsiderate of you to just drop out of the sky like that. And at such an inconvenient hour!"

She laughs softly, deep in her long throat, and more golden blood leaks out of her scar. I twist the Energies harder.

> *And to think that dragonkind*
> *Has spent all this time*
> *Under the dreadful misimpression that*
> *We serve the king best when we're dead.*

She plays along, somehow affecting a Highlander accent into her dragon song. The ground under us rumbles. I drag my foot out from under my kneeling body so it rests behind me on one of Jorbam's roots, and the rumbling slows to a low tremble.

"I know," the swiping of my toes onto her roots tells Jorbam. "I got scared too."

> *Are the faye and the Lunavad singing*
> *About the dragon?*
> *I may have my eyelids closed*
> *But that doesn't mean I can't sense you.*

Zaylam reminds us, and I laugh aloud as Jorbam rumbles some more, this time humorously.

"How's it feel, Zay?" I ask her, mock Highlander accent gone. She opens her top two eyelid layers.

> *Like they cut out my air bladder*
> *And any hope for life in*
> *The Flowing*
> *That I had,*

she sings to me, her voice quavering. I put my forehead to her tail, furled near my lap. "I know," I murmur. "I know."

I tug on the Energies tighter, trying to heal her better than I did last time, wishing not for the first time that I had Mom's skills instead of my own. My paltry attempts at making stitches strong enough to hold together dragon flesh are definitely better than the first time I tried to conjure them.

But I look down at Zaylam's re-opened wound now and realize it didn't help enough. I yank at the Energies angrily, my hands shaking even harder than they had at the Lethean Inn last night.

I don't register the sound of small paws padding on dry ground until que stamps out quer words. *"Well you two are a dysfunctional burrowful of laughs. Are you going to spend the entire Rest day on the ground like this, after after after all your promises to spend the day preparing for Lunamez with the others?"*

"Morning, Osley," I singsong without looking up, and Zaylam fully opens her eyes. She lifts her head at the neck, keeping the rest of her curled up body perfectly still so I can continue restitching her wound, trying to remember everything I ever learned from Mom and from my too-short time in the healing learning pod.

> *The hatchling mates have had*
> *An eventful sunup.*
> *The faye woke the dragon*
> *By smacking her across the face*
> *And somehow came to land*
> *On this rather uncomfortable*
> *Earth.*
> *I cannot say I comprehend how*
> *Rabbitkind stays down here*
> *All the time.*

Gimla, circling low above us, hums with relief that Zaylam is strong enough to be singing full verses. He flies higher, his neck still craning down to monitor us.

Osley's nose twitches and que paws at me. *"You smacked Zaylam in the face? That seems more like something Tacon would do, now doesn't it?"*

I thrust my hands up from my ministrations to Zaylam's wound. "It was an accident!"

"You're still a danger to your hatchling mates," Jorbam chimes in with her rumbles. *"I would never smack you, Zay."*

"To be fair, you have no moveable limbs," Osley stamps out, and I smirk.

I finally release the Energies as the last magical stitch tugs through Zaylam's broken hide. "How's that?" I ask as she sighs deeply in relief.

"Hopefully better than your last attempts, since it keeps busting open. Sometimes it's hard to believe you're Faye's near," Osley interjects.

"How is that, *Zaylam*?" I ask again, with emphasis, glaring at a trilling Osley.

It isn't your fault that you are
Not the healer your mother is.

She pauses, letting the distant songs of the other dragons provide the music to bridge her own together.

Sorry to Osley:
My little faye's stitches
Saved my life
Even though it is fun to
Tease you,
Sadie.

I touch my forehead to hers, exhausted again, the rush of necessity sapped from my body. Osley's furry head nudges at my leg.

"Sadie, I know you're tired, but Kashat is eager to see you. He wants you to share sunup meal with him and Lerian in the Underland. And um...your moms realized you didn't spend the night in the Underland. Faye isn't too happy with you."

I groan loudly but lift my head, not sure if I'm more upset about Mom being upset with me or at Kashat's early-sunup eagerness to see me. If the roles were reversed, I know I'd be desperate to see him too. But I know coming to the Plains makes him miserable; he doesn't even have a hatchling tree, let alone a hatchling dragon, because he didn't Dream quer before his Slicing. That's probably why he's trying so hard to restore his ability to begin with.

"Will you be all right, Zay?" I ask with my body.

Zaylam hums wordlessly in reply, already drifting to sleep cuddled next to Jorbam's trunk, exhausted from the fall and all that bleeding. I sigh deeply and drag my body up. *"Os, Jor, take care of her, okay?"*

They promise to, and I set off for the Underlands drearily.

I fly around the outskirts of the Gathering, my wings so exhausted they can barely hold me up. I pause when I reach the Dropoff, the sharp Forest cliff that looks out over the Underland. Even though this was the spot where I hovered at the beginning of the massacre, I still love the way the soft, rolling hill of the Dropoff slips out before me, like someone had cleanly cut away the land with a giant hatchet. It's a dangerous cliff for groundlings that don't fly and don't expect it. Centaur young ones are taught never to gallop up the Dropoff, for fear that they'll get carried away and fall off the cliff. Lerian never used to listen to the centauric urgings to stay away. We used to get in so much trouble from the Underlandic Council.

The bottom of the Dropoff sharply enters the rolling Underland. More like the Gathering than the Forest, the Underland has open fields of exploding oranges, sun yellows, and the richest reds I've ever seen. It's open to the sun in ways the thick Forest isn't, and has more shades of green than most faeric dialects have expressions for.

The blooms of the short, squat skyflower trees open up into soft lilac petaled, star-shaped flowers. Each one is so enormous I can count their sharp petals and see their ripe, red fruit centers from all the way up here. Far ahead, the grasses grow longer and longer, until they stop completely. They open out into a short stretch of gleaming burnt-orange silt, lapped by the sparking blue Flowing.

A wave of dizziness tugs at me as I fight to keep my eyes open to take in the view. I blink heavily, the combination of lack of sleep last night and all that Energy twisting for Zaylam this morning convincing my eyes to stay closed. Convincing my wings to still.

I don't even flinch when I find myself crumpled on the ground. I'm just relieved to be curled up again, to have my eyes closed.

I jump when a calloused hand touches my shoulder, jarring me from what might have been a blink or a nightlong sleep. I twist around, my arms raised groggily, in attempt to be ready to call on the Energies and conjure a spell.

"Hey hey hey faerie, it's me. It's only me." Lerian. Both her hands are raised in mock surrender while I blink back rapidly, my eyelids still heavy. Her gaze is steady, her gray eyes soft. She keeps her hands up until I calm down. I grunt a little in acknowledgement. In thanks.

"How'd you know where I was?" I breathe out, shakily.

"Tamzel saw you fall out of the sky," Ler tells me, her voice deliberately casual. "Sorry it took me so long to get up here—had to take the long way, you know, through the tunnel. No wings to take the shortcuts you're all so fond of." She whispers in my ear. "Kashat says you went rogue to help P'Tal last night."

I grumble in the affirmative, whispering the story to her as we head back down the Dropoff and loop the long way around toward the Underland, where Kashat is playing with a bunch of centaur young ones. Instead of the enthusiasm I'm used to from her, Lerian's face stays neutral while I talk. She turns to me when I'm done with my story, her expression completely unmoved.

"You think forming a plan with someone who's barely even a near was such a good idea, Sade? You could have come to me, to your growns, come on. I mean, it sounds like you did all right, but it was a pretty easy-to-mess-up plan. Like, what if he didn't care that you were drunk? What if he did but he caught you snooping around his room? Don't do something stupid like that again, Sadie. I thought you were smarter than that."

"Ler, I—"

"Whatever, don't worry about it, we shouldn't talk about it here anyway. Look, Kashat wants to talk to you."

I look around the Underland for Kashat, but I don't find him amongst the playing centaurs or the faeries splashing each other in the Flowing's waves.

What I see is a small invasion force.

Soldiers.

Chapter Nine

KING'S HANDS, DOZENS of them, point their arrows toward a growing crowd of centaurs, but mostly all I see is an arrow less than a flutter away from the temple of a centauric young one, barely six harvests old. She must have been playing near the mouth of the tunnel when they emerged. My eyes search for Tamzel, the leader of the Centauric Council and another old friend of Mama's. She's standing next to P'Tal, who's got his arms completely folded around Kashat, keeping him from rushing at the Hands. Tamzel won't meet my gaze, looking more pained than surprised. I furrow my brow and wish I had my labor axe.

"The young one doesn't have to be harmed," announces a red-headed, bearded non. There's a solid, thin red stripe down the side of his uniform, marking him as the Controller's second-in-command.

"Faerie," Redhead continues, tossing his head at me before gesturing toward a wing-shaped metal contraption that a fellow Hand is holding. My stomach lurches. It's like the wing clamps they put Leece and Mara into. Redhead's thin pink lips curl like he's enjoying holding a weapon to a young one's face.

"The Controller requires your presence in the Gathering. Now. You can come with us without a struggle, or this..." He tightens the string of his already taut bow even more.

"All right, all right." I fly forward, my hands out in front of me, palms up.

"Sade," Lerian whispers, her voice strained. I lower myself to squeeze her arm as I flutter past her. Each movement feels mechanical, like I'm Dreaming myself, as if it were happening to someone else. I wish it was.

But no, it should be happening to me. I wonder how they found out about how I tampered with the vials so quickly. Maybe the Head Slicer realized something was up when I just left without saying goodbye. I curse myself for taking the easy way out.

Or, Evelyn could have told them I'm a spy. Or, someone could have tipped off the Hands that Mama had kept me awake during the Dreaming test, that I wasn't really asleep so the test wasn't true.

It could be anything.

I don't want to go off to the Pits. I won't survive. Other people do, sometimes. But me, I won't. Not with no light, not with no hope.

I'll be one of those sad stories who breaks, just from being there.

I swallow. They've still got drawn arrows pointed at people I care about.

I land in front of Redhead, turning so my back is facing him. For Grovian faeries, that gesture is typically to be a sign of respect, of trust. Of a willingness to be vulnerable.

Right now, it's just a plain old surrender.

Murmurs rise up amongst the centaurs, and Kashat whimpers. His eyes are so wide, so wild, that it threatens to break me to look at him. P'Tal's whispering in his ear, soothing him.

I scan around the crowd and find Tamzel, her strong shoulders hunched, head down, jet-black tail steady. Refusing to watch me get arrested. I do not scan the crowd for the rest of the Centauric Council members. A lot of them are part of the resistance. I do not, for now, want to know whether they endorse this, or whether they're being forced to endure it.

My eyes switch to Lerian's face as cold metal slips over my wrists, wrenched behind my back and bound together. It hurts. A lot. But the hardest part—the hardest part before they kill me, the wild part of my mind thinks desperately—is next, I know. Lerian knows it too; her eyes are wet, and I haven't seen her cry since the night we met, the night of the Attack.

Metal wing clamps creak open behind me, and I make sure not to move. Not to panic. Not to twist and resist and scream. Lerian holds my eyes like she's holding my body, and I am acutely aware that there are young ones staring at me. That Kashat is watching. I keep my face blank.

Redhead roughly gathers my wings into his fists. They crumple and I bite the inside of my lip until the soft flesh tears. Redhead stuffs my wings into the clamps, and every muscle in my body tightens, fully prepared for the metal clamps to close over my sensitive wing tips. I'm surprised when they don't.

But I'm dizzy without them fluttering freely behind me. If I'm in these clamps for much longer—and they only just snapped closed—I too will snap.

Lerian knows. She whinnies and surges forward.

Before I can even move, a thin thwack zips past my ear and Lerian's hot blood splatters onto my face.

An arrow is buried deep in her bare torso.

I don't make loud noises. I don't even really raise my voice to sing with the dragons in the Plains. But I yell now, her name, over and over, as the Hands make a wall with their bodies, pointing with their arrows between me and the centaurs and Kashat, between me and Lerian.

Kashat is screaming and P'Tal can't keep him from surging forward to her, because P'Tal too is now at Lerian's side, holding her up. Within seconds, his hands are thick with her blood.

A nearby Hand switches from bow to club, raising it above his head, preparing to strike at Kashat and P'Tal.

"Stop it!"

I recognize that scream, that very same plea.

Iema rushes forward, her back still arched with the exaggerated discipline of a Hand, but her face is a mess of emotions. My jaw tingles absently, my body remembering when she stopped that soldier, Reve, from beating me senseless.

But Lerian's already got a Palace arrow lodged in her torso, and Iema's eyes find mine briefly. I think there's an apology in them, but the next moment, her eyes are steely again, and her voice is commanding. "The Controller specifically instructed us not to harm any of them!"

Redhead leans into her way too close, leering. Her eyes snap straight ahead; the dotted purple lines running down the sides of her uniform remind everyone that she might be higher ranked than most of the other Hands, but Redhead is Evelyn's second-in-command, not her. If she wants to flinch away from his lips, not even a full flutter away from her ear, she does a good job at resisting.

He whispers to her, but he throws it loud enough so we can all hear him, even above Lerian's soft whimpers. "Can't be scared of a little centaur blood in a place like this, soldier. And the Controller's not here, now is she?"

"She is, as a matter of fact," Evelyn's voice rings out across the Underland.

I look around wildly, as much as I can in the wing clamps and cuffs. My eyes finally find the Controller, standing breathlessly at the mouth of the tunnel leading up to the Forest, her white cloak askew.

All the Hands stiffen into attention, and her eyes narrow once as she takes in the scene in front of her. Me in wing clamps and chains, Lerian with an arrow in her torso, a blood-covered P'Tal holding a still-struggling Kashat back from flying toward the Hands who are pointing arrows at the temples of three centauric young ones, who are all sniffling but standing straight up, their eyes fixed dead ahead like they're standing at attention too.

The Underland falls silent, like it's awaiting her judgment. The waves of the Flowing behind us mark the slow passage of time.

My mouth runs dry as I watch the Controller, and shame floods into my stomach, because I should hate her. No, I *do* hate her. Lerian's been shot. I'm being arrested. Both are her fault. Of course I hate her.

And yet, seeing her only fills my body with relief.

And I call myself a faerie. I blink slowly, and by the time I open my eyes, the Controller is in front of Lerian, her eyes liquid with concern.

Kashat yanks out of P'Tal's arms, placing his body in front of Lerian, his round face full of rage, full of defiance. His fingers are flexing at his sides; he's ready to use magic. "I won't let you hurt her." He doesn't even bother to use Highlander.

Evelyn rolls her eyes impatiently, moving Kashat aside with a sweep of her hand. He relents, looking bewildered. She leans in toward Lerian, and I struggle forward. She rolls her eyes at me too. "Save your strength, faerie." She disregards Kashat's use of faeric, responding in Highlander non.

She scrutinizes Lerian's bleeding torso while Lerian hisses through gritted teeth and my blood boils.

"She'll be fine, the wound is superficial. Take her to her healer, and mind you don't disobey me again or the arrow will be buried in your flesh, Richard. Do I make myself quite clear?"

She sweeps away and back up the tunnel without waiting for a response, her cloak whipping dramatically behind her. Redhead—or Richard, I guess—gives me a rough tug, following the Controller.

I keep trying to twist around to see Lerian, to see if she's all right, if the wound really is superficial. I hear her hooves trotting unsteadily behind me, and I content myself with that for now.

I focus on anything, everything, even the fact that the wing clamps are somehow dampening my ability to reach out to the Energies and use magic, except the tunnel as I'm marched up to the Gathering. The smallness of it makes my skin crawl. I try to move my wings in the clamps. No luck. I almost scream. I resist.

Barely.

Until we emerge into the Gathering.

Where there once was not only vast open space framed by our platforms, there is now a silver metal cage, crushing the creatures trying to grow and live below it, but not nearly big enough for the faeries within it to fly around.

Mama sits in the center of it, both ankles chained to each other and to the cage's bars. She is not wearing wing clamps, but she has a bloodstained wrapping on her forehead, and her neck gills are gunked in pink ooze.

Little Aon is in her lap.

Chapter Ten

SOMETHING DEEP IN the core of my body explodes. Mom, kneeling outside the cage, stares in at her joiner and young one with a look of deadened terror. She hasn't even noticed my arrival in the Gathering yet. Jax leans forward in his chair, one hand on Mom's back, the other stroking her wing sprouts softly, rhythmically.

Though the Gathering above me is full of hovering faeries, gawking at the cage like they can't quite believe it's even there, the murmur that accompanies my arrival—along with Hands and a procession of centaurs—is low, soft. It's enough to be noticeable, though, and Jax turns. Our eyes lock. He squeezes my mom's shoulders and starts wheeling toward me, his face contorted in anger, in the midst of all the murmuring.

I can't make out anything specific people say as Jax approaches me, surprisingly unhindered by Hands. I don't know whether they feel bad for me or if they're happy that the non-looking one finally stopped getting special treatment from the non government. I can't tell what their looks and whispers mean, and I don't care.

My eyes seek out the Controller wildly. She's standing outside of the cage next to Mom and Tacon, her bandaged hand resting on her stomach and her chin in the air defiantly.

The Controller smiles grimly when she sees me looking at her, and she steps forward, casting her voice so loudly that all the Gathering can hear her. As she speaks, Richard and Iema drag me forward, toward the Controller. Toward Jax and toward my caged family. The grip of Iema's usable arm is gentle and even steadying, especially compared to Richard's rough tugs.

"People of the Grove. I know that the presence of this temporary confinement home seems like a harsh and sudden imposition into your communal life." I'm so busy concentrating on letting my feet drag without walking or flying that it takes me a moment to realize, with a jolt, that Evelyn is addressing us in our own language. She continues, her voice level and her eyes never leaving mine.

"With Lunamez rapidly approaching, I know the temporary confinement home seems like a particular dampener of moods. However, in light of the upcoming Initiation for a soon-to-be newly born, it is my intention to ensure the safety of all Grovians. These two faeries will be held in confinement until after this first Initiation under my watch has passed without incident. I will not risk the blood plague returning in full force. Initiations will go uninterrupted, or this merciful form of preventative imprisonment will disappear, and the Pits will be the only option for dangerous dissidents."

She takes a long breath, but I only notice how shaky it is because by this point they've dragged me right in front of her. Up close, the Controller looks relieved, and I realize that she must have memorized those exact words in Grovian faeric.

"My little sibling is a dangerous dissident? Que can barely even fly!" My voice is raw, loud, and for once, I hear a murmur of agreement rise up from people in response to my words. Evelyn's eyes bore into mine and Richard shakes my upper arm roughly. I hear Iema tsk at him on my other side.

"The Controller represents King Xavier here, faye scum. You'll address her with respect." Richard certainly isn't bothering to sully his tongue with our language.

Mom flies forward behind Evelyn and Jax catches her ankle, holding her steady. He's staring har*d at the Controller, his gaze somehow at once furious and calm.

Evelyn addresses me like her second-in-command hasn't even spoken, softly now, so I have to lean in to hear her. "Your sibling may not be dangerous yet, Sadie, but I trust que will prove a good deterrent to dissident behavior."

"Are you locking up my daughter too, Controller? Why do you have her in those wing clamps?" Mom. Her hands are steady behind her back under her wing sprouts now, her brown eyes blazing.

"That depends, Faye. I have to ask her a few questions. Should she have nothing to hide, I'll be releasing her to you soon enough. Disperse these people," she tells Iema, who nods curtly.

What does she mean, she has a few questions for me?

If she brings in Artem, the Head Slicer, for any reason—if he's somewhere in the Gathering right now, watching all this—none of my lies will matter. He'll recognize me. I'd intended to keep a low profile until he went back to the Highlands after the Slicing.

So much for saving P'Tal's newly born from a Dreamless life, or for ever seeing my family free again. We'll probably all be shipped off to the Pits now. Jax's voice cuts into my panic.

"With respect, Controller, her wings shouldn't be in those clamps. She's still just a near, she—" Jax uncharacteristically stumbles over his words as Evelyn stares down at him, disdain clear on her face. She's a near too. In her position, I don't imagine she likes being reminded of that.

"You worry about her friend," Evelyn says, tossing her head behind me, toward Lerian. "She needs her healer." Jax just stares at her, incredulous. His merperson markings twitch with the muscles in his throat. After a moment, he nods in the human fashion and waves his arm at Lerian to go back to the infirmary platform with him. Ler's eyes are wide and red as she passes me. Jax grimaces at me and squeezes Mom's arm before following Lerian across the Gathering.

"Richard, the faerie can walk on her own from here. And Sadie, do walk. The better you cooperate, the easier this will be for all of us."

"Controller, please—" Mom starts to object.

"This community needs you, Faye. Don't leave everyone's health in only one person's hands." Mom glares harder than I've ever seen, but she says nothing. She flies up to me and Richard steels his grip on my arm, about to wrench me away from her. Evelyn holds up a hand to stay him, to dismiss him, and he releases me with a kind of backhand toss. He stomps away, and Evelyn watches him go with a slightly furrowed brow.

Mom says nothing, just smoothes a hand gently over my wing clamps, tears threatening to spill down her face. "You'll be all right, Sadie, —we all will. Your mom and Aon are just fine; I can keep an eye on them in there, all right? Everything's going to be fine."

I nod, not trusting my mouth to open.

The Controller clears her throat, and Mom chokes down a sob, turning away from me and flying off toward the cage, toward the infirmary.

"Mom!" I call after her. "I'm sorry I've been off lately." For lying last night. For snapping the other morning. She knows. She turns and her eyes twist up into a sad, horrible smile. She shakes her head and holds her hands over her heart, then throws them up in my direction.

"*No apologies, my love,*" she's saying. As everyone she loves is in chains around her.

My eyes swivel to Evelyn as Mom flies away. Iema must have done a good job clearing everyone out, because the air is much emptier now than it was; people have dispersed back to the Forest, the Underland, and those remaining in the area are in their learning pods, scattered across the outskirts of the Gathering on their different platforms.

In the center of everything, it's just the two of us.

And the cage she's brought to lock up my family.

I want to rage at her. I want to scream.

I don't. Maybe my words are stuck in the wing clamps she had them lock me in.

"Follow me," is all she says, in my language. I obey, my limp worse than usual on account of the chains and the dragging, my heart hammering away in my chest.

She says nothing as she strides into the Forest, her feet unsteady until we reach this season's centauric-formed Way.

It takes me far too long to realize where we're going: —the eastern steam pools near the Flowing, right on the Forest-Lethean border. For a wild moment, I wonder if she plans to kill me and let my body decay in the overly hot, massive black rock formations that join together and reach into the sky like vertical caves all across this part of the deserted beach.

She pauses when lush green Forest gives way to open sky and beige sand, bending to remove her shoes. It takes her a long time because she's only working with one hand. I almost go to help her.

Almost. Before I realize that both my hands are chained behind my back, and that it's her fault.

I take the opportunity, instead, to stare at the way her royal white uniform trousers flare out into a skirt in the back, highlighting every curve of her lower body. I've never seen that kind of clothing before, and I wonder vaguely if it's an Izlanian fashion or just the latest fad with royal women in the Highlands proper. Or both.

Evelyn turns to face me before I remember to stop staring. My face gets hot. She purses her lips, and I can't tell if she's pleased or angry. She holds both shoes dangling from the fingers of one hand and steps out onto the beach, gesturing with her head for me to follow her. I do.

She steps back when she reaches one of the smallest steam pool formations, bowing mockingly with a sweep of her hand for me to enter the tall cavern before her. I roll my eyes and step in, not caring that the ankle-deep level of water soaks the bottom of my trousers. After walking so long, the cavern-warmed water actually feels kind of good.

Water sloshes behind me. The Controller is holding the lower half of her outfit up above the water with the same hand that grips her shoes.

We stare at each other for a moment, the sunlight from the hole where the rock formations don't quite converge way up at the top of the steam pool shining in my eyes.

"You gonna shoot me like they shot Lerian if I sit?"

I take her frustrated glare as assent. There's a little outcropping in the rock behind me, and I sit gratefully, but only on the edge—it's not faeric habit to lean back like I've seen nons do, because of our wings. Especially not now with these clamps.

She doesn't wait for me to get comfortable. She doesn't wait for anything.

"Artem—don't get that look in your eyes, you know you know exactly who he is—caught a glimpse of you this sunup as you flew to the Underland. He informed me that a young man," she chuckles at this, "who looks, somehow, exactly like you, met him at the Lethean Inn last night."

Silence penetrates the cavern, punctuated by the echoed rushing of Flowing's waves surging through the gaps where different rocks making up the cavern meet, sloshing against their walls.

I don't know how long it is before I finally clear my throat. "That's...that's strange. I guess dashingly good looking is an in look with *humans* this season."

The Controller's eyes flash dangerously.

Her eyes scream the hurt anddisappointment that her pursed lips give no indication of. I tell myself it's good; the Controller's job is to dole out hurt and disappointment. So what if she feels it too?

"What were you doing there? Ah, no, and don't say grabbing a drink. I know your wings were tucked away, Sadie. I know you were spying, the same as you were the night we..." Waves, crashing, up, down. Ebb. Flow. "The night I met you in the Forest." Seagulls crying out overhead. The soft roar of an unusually big wave against the outside of the steam pool walls. "The night you saved Iema."

I lick my lips and taste the salt that saturates the air around us. Her eyes catch the movement before she looks away.

"So he says he recognized me. And you apparently believe him, since you're willing to lock up a young one to, what, prove a point? So what's your next trick? You going to lock me away now? Were you just lying to my mom about being able to see me soon? And you brought me here first to, what, tell me I'll never see my family again yourself? All nice and personal?"

She glares at me and I gulp. "Much as it displeases me, I owed you a debt for saving Iema. I convinced Artem to let me handle you, to send for new supplies but to not tell anyone else why." She must see the shock on my face and she chuckles humorlessly. "I have...friends...in high places." Something bitter flickers across her rounded features, and her face gets drawn, serious. Determined.

"Evelyn," I start into the rhythm of the sloshing water.

She looks daggers at me and I backfly. "Controller," I correct myself. Her body relaxes. Somewhat.

"Why'd you ask me to meet you at the inn?"

"Why did you lie about who you are?"

I narrow my eyes.

"You should have noticed, you being Izlanian and all, but in case you haven't made the connection, it's a lot easier looking like a *human* than it is looking like a faerie in Lunav these days." Her eyes sear into mine, and she doesn't even react when a particularly sharp wave splashes water all the way up to her thick thighs. I blink to make sure she doesn't think I'm staring.

"People around here don't exactly... I'm not quite everyone's favorite person. Even though they have to put up with me, because Mom's their healer."

The skin behind her eyes tightens like she's fighting some kind of battle with herself. "Surely you're not the only half faerie here."

I shake my head in the human fashion. "There are young ones from centaur and fae growns. But my...combination? I've only really ever met others in the Highlands. Unless they're all just passing as fully faeric."

A long pause. Ebb. Flow. Ebb.

"It's illegal."

"To be a non man and force yourself onto your faeric servant? No, it's not."

Evelyn's hurt hand convulses slightly, but she ignores it. When she speaks again, her voice is full of gravel. "To lie about your identity to a government official."

I scoff. "And how exactly was I supposed to know you had anything to do with the government? For all I knew you were just visiting from Izla and Iema and that creep were just your hired protection—"

"Enough! I won't quarrel with you as though we're on equal footing."

"Way I see it, we're on exactly equal footing. I lied, you lied."

"I didn't lie, you just assumed—"

"So did you!"

An impasse. We glare at each other for a long moment. She takes her eyes away first, and I don't suppress my victorious grin.

She notices. "Such arrogances for someone in chains! You might want to start taking me seriously—"

"You just locked up my family, I don't think taking you seriously is an issue—"

"I could have you all killed!"

"But you haven't. And I'm betting you won't. Now you tell me, huh, am I arrogant or am I right?"

She licks her lips, and I find myself wondering if they're as salty from the cavern air as mine are.

"All right, so you didn't know I work for the king. But Iema was wearing her uniform. You knew she was a Hand."

"Not when I first heard her screaming, I didn't."

The Controller's eyes flash. "So you would have let her bleed to death if you'd known?"

I shiver, even though the cavern is overly warm. "My mother—the one you didn't lock up—is a healer. You know that. It..." I can see the face of that young soldier, the one Mom and Jax saved all those harvests ago, burned and broken. His joiner's wild fear, his desperation to save his love. I repeat what Mom told Jax.

"You don't leave people to die."

For a moment, I can't tell if her eyes cloud up or if it's just some sort of effect of the cavern. But she blinks, and I'll never know.

"Fine. But know this, and know it well; I've used up my leniency with you, Sadie. I'm only protecting you right now because if you hadn't reached Iema when you did, she would have bled to death before I got there. Be grateful I'm imprisoning your family in the Gathering, not in the Pits. Because I'd be well within my rights to send all of you down there forever. My debt to you is repaid, in full. Do you understand me?"

Rise, fall. Ebb, flow. Up, down. Crash. Crash.

Crash.

I breathe in and out.

The Controller seethes, the ghosts of unspoken pains tugging at the skin behind her eyes.

"You're done doing favors for me, right. Does uh...does that mean you're gonna let me hobble back to the Gathering in these chains? Because I've gotta say, they're really starting to pinch..."

Evelyn spins halfway away from me, irritation and a tiny flash of amusement overtaking her features. The sudden movement of her feet splashes us both with water, and I grimace at her. She shakes her head, hard, and flicks her wrist chaotically, almost smacking me in the face with her shoes. My chains and wing clamps echo loudly as they clatter onto the outcropping.

Without meaning to, I close my eyes and groan loudly in relief, not knowing whether to rub my wing sprouts, wing tips, or wrists first.

When I open my eyes, I'm alone.

Chapter Eleven

"YOU SURE YOU should be training tonight, Ler?" Tamzel asks in Underlander, her brow furrowed and tail swishing uncertainly.

Lerian splashes her hooves in the water, her whinny bouncing off the walls of the cavernous steam pool. A massive one, not like the small one Evelyn had taken me into. "The Controller might be scum, but even I gotta admit, she's not a terrible healer," she offers, flexing her arms back and forth roughly as though to prove her point. Her torso still has an angry, puckered red wound, but it's only skin deep and the thick scab probably would have healed now if Lerian would just stop picking at it. I think she secretly wants it to scar; I'm pretty sure she thinks it makes her look tougher.

"Controller must've gone to one expensive learning pod," Ler mutters, nudging me conspiratorially with her elbow.

I chuckle and almost blurt out that I'd thought the same thing the first time I'd met her, but guilt swarms my stomach and tugs on my chest. That would require me to tell Lerian—and everyone else—that I met Evelyn before the non girl was the Controller. The enemy.

And I don't know if I'll ever be ready to have that conversation. Trying to explain away the fact that she'd questioned me without torturing me had been difficult enough; eventually the others accepted it as a scare tactic, a power show from a young, Izlanian Controller needing to assert her power.

Except what they don't want to admit is that it's working. With Mama and Aon imprisoned in the cage, everyone's given up on even a glimmer of hope that we can avoid the Slicing of P'Tal, Zeel, and Aora's newly born. Kashat assumes I was almost caught trying to contaminate the head Slicer's equipment, and I let him believe it.

But giving up on interfering with the Slicing doesn't mean the resistance is relaxing. Not exactly. Tamzel, Jax, and the other leaders are still insisting that we train to defend ourselves, our homes, our friends.

Mom's fiery argument with Jax—the first I've ever heard them have—is still ringing in my ears. Without Mama around for the past few sunups to put her hand below her wing sprouts, to whisper to her, to rub lotion into her skin when she needs to calm down and talk something through, Mom's been pretty on edge. Jax has been taking the brunt of it.

"Mom," I'd interfered with my body language when Jax looked ready to cave, "*none of the other faerie nears even look at me. The ones in the resistance do wild things like acknowledge my presence.*" She gave me a wet, sad smile at that. "*Let me go train with them. It'll be fun, it always is. I've done it before, right? Only difference now is that Mama and Aon are locked up. But no one's going to find out about the training, because even if anyone comes across us, it'll look like a bunch of nears just messing around, anyway.*"

Mom had closed her eyes, and I felt her resistance slipping away. "*We're healers, for Lunara's sake, Ja, how can we teach our near to hurt people like this? To risk being hurt?*"

Jax smiled softly at Mom calling me their near, and so did I. He took her hands into his lap, his muscles relaxed now that she'd calmed down. "She's at risk of being hurt by just flying around in her own skin, Faye. They'll be all right, Tamzel will take care of them. Let her go."

And she had.

So here I am, steam pool sand between my toes and lining my calves, trying to find the balance in a faye glass sword with a hand that's much more used to axes.

"Keep your wrist looser than that, Sade, you're gonna strain something." I roll my eyes at Kashat, who's balancing two swords, straight up in the air, on the tips of his fingers.

Lerian swipes her axe in front of Kashat, knocking both his swords out of balance.

"Hey!" he squeals, and Ler and I double over hysterically.

"You should've kept your wrists looser, Kash," I gasp through laughing. I raise my head slightly and almost bonk my forehead on Tamzel's imposing torso. I swallow my last bit of laughter and look up nervously at her face. Her hands are on her hips, and steam from the cavern's heated Flowing water rises behind her like she's in command of the air itself. Sweat and mist droplets work their way down her chiseled abdomen, and I lower my gaze immediately.

"You two need to take this more seriously," she scolds. "When the Mach invade again, they're not going to be laughing." She reaches over and jostles Kashat's hair with her long fingers. "They're not going to be, aimlessly balancing swords on their hands like Highland performers. They're going to be distracting you by yanking at the Energies, and taking advantage to put these swords right through you, using their magic to make you unhealable."

Kashat, Lerian, and I squirm like young ones. E'rix, the girl Lerian yelled at the other morning for ignoring me on the Way, averts her eyes, her sword poised in midbattle position. At least she's pretending not to listen to us get scolded. The other nears watch with hungry amusement. Lerian and I catch eyes, and I know we're thinking the same thing. Training to fight the palace is always more fun when P'Tal's around. But Zeel is due to start having her contractions any time now, so P'Tal is probably swishing his tail impatiently with Aora near the infirmary, waiting for their newly born to arrive.

"Sorry, Tamzel, we'll be more serious," Lerian mutters.

The corners of Tamzel's mouth twitch as she puts a sword back into Kashat's hand and murmurs something in his ear before trotting away to supervise the other faeries and centaurs, about twenty of us in all.

"What'd she tell you?" I ask him.

He grins lopsidedly. "She says I should save performing for Lunamez, and in the meantime, swipe upward."

He finishes his thought with a grunt as he swishes his sword chaotically, upward, right at me. I slam my wings into my sides, and they take me out of range. But I overshoot and bang my head on the cavern's rock face.

"Dammit, Tamzel!" I shout as Kashat and Lerian clap their hands and whoop in delight. She barely turns around from her instruction, but the smirk is written all over her body.

I grin in spite of myself, rubbing my head and blinking hard to get rid of the spots in front of my eyes. Lerian looks me over as I come back down to her eye level, putting her face into the back of my head. "Not bleeding, good. Can you see right?"

She's still grinning, but her eyes are worried. I respond by raising my sword to meet her axe. She parries and grits her teeth, thrusting forward so I have to pull my sword back and prepare for her strike.

Kashat attacks each of us in turn, so we both get the chance to fight off two people at once. E'rix comes to fight him one-on-one after a while, telling him he needs his own practice space. None of us mention that Kashat himself would never be on the front lines, that he's only here training because it's nighttime, and his growns are in the other corner of the cavern, and since Mama and Aon have gotten locked up, they barely let him go anywhere on his own, except the Gathering, to be with his Lunamez learning pod.

I think of Aon, who might be a tiny young one now, but is growing so fast que'll be Kashat's age-mate in less than a season, and I understand their feeling.

By the time the moon rises high enough to be angled away from the opening in the rock face at the top of the cavern, my limbs are shaking and my forearm is satisfyingly bloody from getting body slammed by an overly enthusiastic Lerian into an outcropping. She's still fussing over all the blood when we hand our swords and axes back to Kashat's growns, who fly them up to a storage space hewn into the rock, high up in the cavern.

Osley is waiting for us where the Forest meets the sand, eyes unmoving but quer ears twitching up a storm. Que isn't exactly enthusiastic about water. Or sand. Or exposed areas.

"Your mom and Jax asked if I'd get you safely back to the Gathering, Sade," que thumps out by way of explanation when I fly down low and look at quer questioningly. "I don't know if they think I'll be able to fight off a horde of Hands on my own if they try to arrest you again, but hey, I'm here."

I chuckle and run my hand over quer fur. "Ah ah ah!" que trills. "Bloody!"

I withdraw my arm apologetically and wipe the stream of blood off on my tunic.

"I can try to heal you, Sadie! We learned some basic healing spells in one of my learning pods," Kashat calls ahead from where he's hung back with E'rix, but I wave him off. Lerian can't be the only one who gets to look tough.

"Hey, Sadie, wait up!" Lerian scoffs and stamps away as E'rix approaches, Kashat behind her. She keeps glancing back at him, and he nudges her forward with his hand gestures.

"What?"

"I just...that Dreaming test they put us all through...it was scary. Getting arrested like that. Being...put to sleep like that in front of everyone. All that." She glances at Kashat again, and I look sideways at Lerian. "None of us thought they'd ever arrest you like that, put you through something like that, on account of...well, you know. Anyway, I'm sorry. And I'm sorry about your mom and sibling. Que's really cute. Que likes to fly to our learning pod before labor, and sometimes your mom lets me feed quer while she's busy with a patient."

She must realize she's rambling. She gulps and glances back at Kashat. He grins at her. "So um...right. I'm sorry."

I stare at her watery green eyes and don't really know what to say. Lerian spares me the trouble as a colossal, wet ball of sand flies through the air and lands right where E'rix's chest starts to rise out of her shirt. I avert my eyes and her face turns redder than Aon's wings.

"All right, all right, if you two are gonna make out or something, do it on your own time!" Lerian shouts, and I fly a flutter back from E'rix involuntarily.

"Lerian!"

"What? We get it, she's sorry she was a horrible person, but your super-cool-and-dangerous-spy value rose a ton when you got arrested twice in a row so you're all irresistible and she wants to be your best friend now! Can we all move on b—"

But the rest of her sentence is lost as E'rix launches her own glob of sand, right onto Lerian's face. Osley dashes for cover and Kashat screams in delight. I dive for my own fistful of sand and Lerian charges, intent on revenge as she swipes the glob off her face.

The other nears in our group catch on and join in, distinctly avoiding throwing sand at me at first, but once I hit a few of them right under their wing sprouts, I'm no exception and it's every faerie and centaur for themselves.

As I lean up against a tall, black rock to catch my breath, I look down and see Tamzel covering her face with her hand and shaking her head. She's probably thinking how hopeless the resistance is if these are the nears she's training to defend the Grove.

I drop a mess of sand on her head before flying away at breakneck speed.

By the time we all pour back into the Gathering, we're breathless, sweaty and riled up, shoving into each other and whooping, gritty sand and blood streaked across our limbs. Our shouts ring out about who won which round of sand fight, who will get revenge on who with snow fights when the cold season, fading rapidly now, rolls around again.

E'rix starts nudging us to hush as we fully emerge from the Forest, pointing with her head at three Hands on rest day patrol. We stop and stare, and they stiffen and stare back. As one, the Hands move as one to block our path, raising their swords at E'rix and Kashat's throats. I raise my chin up, doubled over with my hands on my thighs trying to catch my breath, and wait, entire body tensed. Ready.

I glance over the Hands' shoulders at Mama and Aon in the cage. Aon's sleeping, curled into quer own red wings like a dragon bulb in Mama's lap. Mama herself has gone rigid, her back completely straight, staring out at the brewing confrontation without blinking.

Rada gallops forward, the sound of her hooves on the grass the only sound in the Gathering aside from our heaving breath, her arms outstretched, palms up, in surrender. Even the crickets have stopped chirping and the birds have paused their songs.

"Hey, slow down there," she tells the Hands, her rounded stomach moving up and down rapidly as she catches her breath. My eyes fixate on the Hands' swords and stay there. "You give these nears one day a week to rest from labor, and you think they're not going to rough themselves around on the beach to let out some energy? They're just playing. It's almost Lunamez and they're just nears."

The lead Hand with his sword drawn at E'rix doesn't acknowledge Rada, but his eyes flicker at the sound of footsteps approaching.

"We're not afraid of rowdy nears on a rest day, now are we?" Iema asks the men she outranks, her voice light but her stance hard. Making her question an order. The Hand lowers his sword reluctantly, disdain clear on his face.

Whether his displeasure is about us or about the demand to lower his weapon, I can't tell. For now, I don't care. I grimace in pain from being so out of breath, so unable to move.

"They should be afraid, every last one of them," Kashat mutters, his eyes burning at the retreating backs of the Hands as they stiffly shift back to their posts on the perimeter of the Gathering.

"You'd think she'd have recruited people who know better, seeing as she's Izlanian," Lerian puts in, the hatred in her voice for the Controller making my eyes lower. I want to have the same hatred in my voice when I talk about her. But I can't. I don't.

As it is, she jostles me like I'm supposed to agree with her and come up with the next quip about the Controller. Lerian nudges me again and I grunt in falsely enthusiastic affirmation. She stares up at me like she can't quite make out whether she wants to hit me or ignore it, so she does nothing. I fly high enough to put my arm around her shoulders as we approach Rada's growing platform, and I tilt the side of my forehead to her temple. Lerian sighs hard, placated. For the moment.

Lerian's right, of course, about the Hand's, about everything. But I look down at my own non-looking legs, and can't tell if that means nons can't be a decent sort, once in a while.

My stomach roils in guilt, in worry that maybe, just maybe, deep down, I am the traitor that everyone always suspects me to be.

Chapter Twelve

M̲y̲ ̲w̲i̲n̲g̲s̲ ̲a̲r̲e̲ covered in feathers, and my voice comes out as a victorious shriek. The barest tilt of my body lets me ride up into the wind, riding it like a river current. I can see the tiniest rustlings of the tiniest creatures on the ground beneath me, even when I'm peering through gaps in the clouds.

A call reaches my ears, but it has a strange lilt to it; it's hollow, earth-low, compared to the cries that can pour out of my beak.

"Sade."

A sharp thumping joins the chorus of the strange word, the strange tones, and then I realize that I am not a hawk. I am not soaring above the Highland's mountains and valleys.

Lerian is calling me, shaking me. Osley is trying to tell me something.

I groan, and groan louder when the sound comes out in my own voice, not the majestic voice of that hawk.

Reluctantly, I blink a few times and take in the look on Lerian's face, leaning inches away from mine. Osley's thumping quer feet frantically near Ler's hooves.

"What?" My voice is groggy but my body's completely awake now, all traces of free flight gone.

"Rada," is all Lerian says, and she tears off into the tunnel, heading up into the Gathering.

I blink in the darkness and fly off after her, but I head up and over the Dropoff, meeting her where the tunnel lets out. Osley is on her heels, and I fly down as Lerian sprints forward. "What happened to her?"

"*They did another Dream test. Surprise. Extra creepy at night. They took Rada.*"

My wings give out and Ler has to double back and yank me up into the air by my arm.

Rada. They took Rada. Because she failed a Dream test.

Because Rada could Dream.

The Controller is nowhere to be seen, but the Gathering is interspersed with people who just woke to the news, flying or trotting around in shock. None of them seem to know what to do beyond milling about in the one place where we last saw Rada.

There's a developing convergence of people around her growing platform. Two Hands, one of whom I recognize as Richard, are dismantling it, taking apart the woven ground, the massive bowls that she would pour so much of her grown creations into before serving us all.

Confused murmurs are turning into angry murmurs, which are turning into shouts.

I look across the Gathering at Mama in her cage. Aon is sleeping, somehow, but Mama gestures for me to come toward the cage, away from the crowd at Rada's platform. But Lerian grabs my arm and Osley nips at my ankle, and I don't move.

I wish Mom and Jax were here, but they're both inside the infirmary, the tent closed to the chaos outside. Zeel must be giving birth.

Giving birth in the midst of all this.

Rada.

"Where did they take her?"

"The Pits..."

"The things they do to growers in the Pits..."

"Did you know she could Dream?"

I take in all the shouts; I don't know how people are shouting. I can't even remember how to open my mouth.

The Controller is nowhere in sight and Richard's neck muscles are tensing with each passing moment at the emerging yells, piece by piece gutting Rada's growing platform. The prominent vein in his forehead is pulsing, and now I'm terrified.

Because the Controller is nowhere in sight, and Richard let his Hands shoot Lerian the last time a lot of Grovians surrounded him.

But I'm too angry to let fear take over; fear, instead, buoys rage—Rada was a grower, one of the ones who helped make sure we don't have to kill anyone to stay alive; she was my friend—and I find myself surging forward with the rest of the centaurs and faeries, demanding to know if she's being taken to the Pits. We shout for her to be brought back to us.

Because Rada is tough, but no one is tough enough for the Pits.

My bones are on fire and my muscles are overheating. My fists are clenched and they are above my head.

I didn't know she could Dream. I'll never be able to ask her about it, now.

Across the Gathering, on the infirmary platform, Mom and Jax are helping Zeel give birth to a newly born.

On this side of the Gathering, lives are probably about to end.

I yell louder, the collective rage of all they've taken from us coursing through my bloodstream.

The shouts, the accusations, the pleas for them to leave Rada's platform alone don't you have any respect—like she's already dead, but yes, she might as well be—finally all cascade in the second-in-command's face.

"That's enough!" Richard screams in a tongue that's not ours, but none of us cede any ground.

I surge forward to try to stop a lower-ranking Hand from taking down the tapestries Rada liked to hang in the back of her platform. I grab his arm and pull.

Richard glances at a fellow Hand, who considers me for a moment. His eyes scan up and down my non features, and he raises his dead tree flesh club.

He doesn't strike me.

He strikes Lerian.

Her face streams with blood, as the Hand slams his dead tree flesh club into her temple. Twice.

Lerian collapses on top of me, and Osley trills in my ear, tearing away into the Forest. To get help.

And we'll need it, because now Richard has called all of his Hands. He is done humoring us. They emerge from different parts of the Gathering with chain mail covering their uniforms, some with clubs beating against their open palms, some with swords drawn, some with bows taut and loaded.

If we pause, we only pause momentarily. Rada has been taken. Lerian was struck for something I did. I look a little too much like them for their comfort.

My stomach lurches and my throat is sore from screams I didn't know I was making.

Rada has been taken. More will follow.

The last time we resisted like this, it was when labor was first mandated. Then, they killed dozens of us, and set fire to the part of the Forest we refused to cut down. Even more of us were shipped off to the Pits. I was a young one. And I hid the entire time, with Osley in one of quer bigger burrow holes.

Apparently I didn't need to, because —they wouldn't have hurt me, anyway.

I am not hiding this time. But perhaps I should be. Because it's my fault blood is pouring from Lerian's head onto my pinned-down body. That we are now being surrounded by armed Hands.

Someone tugs Lerian's unconscious form off of me—E'rix—and helps tug me up, out from under her. Together, we pull on Lerian's flank, trying to get her away from danger. We try to twist the Energies to help move her better, to heal her, but the Hands have such a strong grasp on them that I'm afraid if we pull them much harder, they'll snap and we'll all die.

Mama is banging on the edge of the cage, desperate to be out, to be something other than trapped, watching. Useless. A Hand, who's hung back to guard the cage, slams his club into the metal right near her face, and she collapses from the vibrations.

I yell but don't leave Lerian's side. I can't.

Aon is awake and wailing.

A club slams down on the shoulder of some centaur young one I don't know. Her blood is almost as dark as her skin, but it shines brightly on the Hand's pale fist.

Osley is back at my side. I put my forehead on quer's to feel what que's trying to tell me. No way I'd be able to hear quer over the sound of breaking bones.

E'rix is crying, hyperventilating, or maybe that's me, but she doesn't stop helping me get Lerian's limp body out of harm's way.

"I got the Controller," is I think what Osley is telling me. I stare at quer, and then everything stops. The Energies tense so tightly I would vomit if I could conjure up the strength. Without warning, the screaming, the slamming, the yelling, all freezes.

I look around wildly, and Evelyn is in the center of the Gathering, both of her hands raised above her head. Her face is contorted with effort, and her eyes sweep the scene with rage. Iema is next to her, her hands also raised.

"If the faeries and centaurs who are attacking my Hands do not withdraw immediately when I release the Energies, so help me, each of you present will join your comrade in the Pits. From here on in, each centaur and faerie will be subject to arrest and deportation to the Pits if you so much as step foot or wing into the Gathering in a mob at night. You will each be in your respective trees and other sleeping spaces within an hour after sundown each night. Those of you wandering through the Forest or the Underland, gathering in large groups and spreading fear and dissent, will be arrested, without question and without opportunity for protest."

She pauses and looks at each of her Hands in turn. "Each of you will use your training to Heal the faeries and centaurs you have wounded tonight; it seems the healers of this province are busy with a birth. Those faeries and centaurs that have gone through healing learning pods, you will assist in the healing of wounded Hands. When Iema and I release the Energies and you all can move around again, I suggest you do nothing to further provoke me. There will be consequences for anyone who disobeys."

Without even having to look at each other, Iema and Evelyn release the Energies in sync with one another, and everyone in the area lets out a deep gasp for breath.

A low murmuring rises as Hands begrudgingly move amongst those whose skulls they'd nearly cracked, casting filthy looks at the Controller all the while. Those of their victims who are conscious enough try to shift away from them, fear in their eyes.

But Evelyn's display of immense power to manipulate the Energies has put everyone into a submissive mood.

For now.

E'rix and I meet eyes over Lerian's limp form, and I notice for the first time a cut on her light beige cheek. "I'm no good at healing; you should go get that looked at."

Her eyes widen as she looks at something over my shoulder. I turn to see what's making her so scared. —Iema is picking her way through the dispersing crowd toward us, pink blood mixed with red soaked into her shoes and the bottom hem of her uniform trousers.

I turn back around and E'rix is gone. I can hardly say I blame her.

Osley's beady eyes reflect out of the outer edge of the Forest, and I take a deep breath before turning back around on my haunches to face the approaching Hand.

Iema kneels next to me, one knee on the ground getting drenched in Lerian's blood, the other a resting spot for her elbow. She asks me something in Izlanian non, I think; the only words I recognize are *she* and *do*. When I don't answer, Iema looks up at me like she's surprised I'm there.

"Sorry," she says in Highlander non. "What did she do that provoked this?"

Guilt roils in my stomach, and I don't say what I want to. *They should have hit me, I provoked them, not Lerian, this whole thing is my fault, but they hit her instead.* My voice is wild but somehow firm when I do speak. "They were taking apart Rada's growing platform, like she's dead—and she might as well be, sending her to the Pits like that!"

Iema ignores me as she bends at the hips to heal the wound on Lerian's face. The Energies tug inside me uncomfortably as silver threads weave their way out of her fingertips. *"The Controller had the centaur arrested for avoiding Initiation. I know your people are attached to Dreaming, but it can't really be worth risking the spread of the plague, can it?"*

I don't answer her. I just watch as she pours that silver magic into Lerian until the blood stops flowing out of her body, until her eyelids flutter and she starts to wake up.

Iema is gone before Lerian's eyes open.

Before I can thank her.

Chapter Thirteen

"And you're sure you're not hurt?"

I glance at her over the tops of my eyelids before returning my gaze to my little sibling's outstretched hands. "For the hundredth and last time, Mama, yes. I'm sure. You just pull on it, that's right, Aon, reach in with your mind. Focus on how the Energies can become a spark, just in this spot here—"

"You!"

"I told you this was a bad idea—"

I straighten up, Aon still flexing quer fingers, tongue between quer teeth, squinting at the Lunamez candle in my hand. I slip it behind my back as I spin around and spring to attention.

It's the Hand that hit Lerian a wingful of sunups ago. The Hand that hit Lerian when he should have hit me.

"What are you doing with the prisoners?"

I tighten my grip on the candle and jump when it starts to feel hot in my hands. I bring it out cautiously to the front of me so it doesn't singe my wings.

"Everyone's got to light one at the start of Lunamez season, sir. I was just making sure my little sibling here got a chance. Nice work, sherba," I mutter to quer, as the candle is glowing deep inside its fluorescent tube now, and not by my doing.

The Hand sighs visibly. He glances around the peripheries of the Gathering, where Kashat and the others of the Lunamez learning pod are getting the place ready for the season. Countless Lunamez candles float all across the treeline. The Gathering crackles pleasantly with the effort of keeping the candles afloat like bubbles in the Flowing, but the songs that usually accompany the floating are absent. Oncoming Slicings will do that.

"Go on," the Hand mutters, his eyes roving my distinctly non-like body. I give him a curt nod and fly off without a backward glance at Mama and Aon in the cage.

As I'm finding a place, an invisible groove in the Energies, to float Aon's candle, someone shoves me nearly clean out of the air. I turn, tensed, but it's just a pair of twins, older than me by a couple of harvests. They were in some learning pods with Lerian and me when we were young ones. Ler and I always called them Brute One and Brute Two. They used to tug on my wing sprouts to see if they were really part of me or just pasted on.

"Make sure you actually fly up and take the blame if the Hands don't like your candle placement, Highlander," One jeers.

I clench my jaw and instinctively look below me for Lerian. She's not there. Two against one aren't odds I want right now. Not when I know Aon's watching me from the cage, anyway. Not when the Head Slicer's on his way to strip Dreaming from P'Tal's newly born when the sun goes down tonight.

"Yeah, you're really into the Lunamez spirit, huh?"

"Well the way I see it, Highlander, is that the holiday is only for real Grovians. Not ones who play reckless then let real Grovians take the hits for them."

Aon watching be damned, I fly forward until a viselike grip catches my ankle.

"A newly born is getting Sliced tonight, you three; let's keep that the only tragedy of the day, why don't we? Get on your way, both of you." Jax gets to talk to the twins like that because Jax gets to talk to everyone like that, if he wants. Being our healer and all.

They fly off with two identical, cruel grins at me. I return them as best I can, but Jax is muscling me down to his eye level. "I tried ignoring them, Jax, they just—"

"Don't pick fights you can't win, Sadie. Not with a Slicing tonight." He releases my ankle and runs his fingers over a tired face. "P'Tal's a wreck. I have to get back to him. Just...keep it calm today."

I'm going to object, tell him it wasn't me who needed to be calm. But I just hang my head.

I have all day to stew, because no one speaks to me—and I don't open my mouth—until the Hands start combing the Forest after the evening labor canon. We are all required to be there, in the Gathering. For the Slicing.

It's been eight sunups since the uprising when they took Rada, since Zeel gave birth to quer, Aora, and P'Tal's newly born. Tonight, Blaze—that's what they named quer—will be Sliced. And we all have to watch.

I get brushed up against Lerian in the push toward the Gathering. She shakes her shoulders at me but otherwise says nothing. I'm excited when she grunts, thinking she's starting to say something to me, but I look around at her face and realize the grunt was one of pain.

"Hey," I say loudly to the Hand who pushed her roughly, to get her to move her faster as we trudge toward the Gathering.

"Calm down, faerie, you don't want to make them start beating down on us again," Lerian counters through gritted teeth. I splutter. E'rix glances at me furtively as she takes Lerian's arm and tugs her along so the rough Hands don't feel the need to. I grind my own teeth, jealousy flaring in the pit of my belly.

"Ler, I wasn't trying to—" But the rest of the half-formed thought dies on my lips, because she's not wrong. She got hit because of something I did, not her, and because they didn't want to hit someone with their bone structure, with their eyes. Lerian gives me a long, sad look as she splits in a different direction with E'rix.

I almost punch my fist into a nearby platform, but I hold my breath to restrain myself. When I feel calmer, I fly off toward the closed infirmary tent. As I slip inside, I think Artem, the Head Slicer, looks up from his preparations, from his position in the center of the Gathering, flanked on each side by two Hands. I think his eyes flicker with some emotion I can't identify as he catches my gaze.

When I look back at him, his gaze is keenly focused on his instruments of mutilation, my wings, my faeric filth, my betrayal, apparently forgotten.

Mom opens the flap of the infirmary tent wordlessly as she sees me approach through the small opening they're required to keep during the Slicing. I settle onto a cot next to Mom and in front of Jax.

"Lerian still angry?" Mom asks me. I grunt.

She puts her arm underneath my wing sprouts. "I'm sorry, Sadie," she says, putting her forehead to mine, and tears sting my eyes.

I catch a glimpse of Jax out of the corner of my eye. His chair is faced away from the opening of the tent, and he's doubled over with his elbows on his knees. I pull back and glance questioningly at Mom.

"Bad day," she explains with her body language.

I shake my shoulders back and forth. He has those pretty regularly. And today, I've contributed. I look down in guilt.

In the relative safety of the infirmary tent, I stare out at the Controller, standing next to Artem. Her stare is hard and glassy, and there are purple folds under her eyes. Her posture is more rigid than usual. Daring us to undermine her most sacred duty as Controller: —to oversee Slicings. Her gaze sweeps over the Gathering even though her body is still.

After everyone settles in and the Hands have tossed and thwacked the last of the centaurs and faeries into the Gathering, no one really moves.

With Blaze about to be under a knife, Mama and Aon in the cage, and the Hands out in force, if we think of using our numbers to surge at them, we resist. We won't be the cause of their deaths. Slicings are risky enough to begin with.

We only watch.

An unnatural silence falls on the Gathering. It's broken only by the youngest ones sobbing. Faeric and centaur young ones usually have sharper memories than non young ones, and most remember their own Slicings. Vividly.

The Head Slicer—Artem, Artem, I hate that he bought me drinks, that he was kind, that he called this unpleasant, that he wasn't excited about it, that he kind of talked about it how we talk about labor, all grim—is escorted from the edge of the Gathering to the space just below the infirmary platform, where Blaze will be held overnight to make sure que doesn't die from the intrusion into quer skull.

The Gathering takes a collective breath as a dozen Hands flank Artem, in an eerie reenactment of the tributes that we create with the centaurs to escort newly borns and their growns home after birth. Another set of Hands march Zeel, Aora, P'Tal, and Blaze, tiny and stumbling but moving quer hooves valiantly, from the edge of the Gathering to its center. Mom's grip on my knee tightens as the centaurs part sadly for them, their arms extended out to their sides to rest on the shoulders of their companions next to them, a communal centaur salute of mourning.

The procession of soldiers and growns pauses in front of the new center of the Gathering. It's now a public prison, a cage.

I glance at Mom, who's staring at Mama and Aon. Aon is squirming around; que's gotten so much bigger in the short time que's been imprisoned. I wonder what parts of quer growth we missed, that only Mama shared with quer.

I jump when Zeel tears quer throat with quer screams. The procession continues, reaching the space under the infirmary. Jax's head slumps against one of the arms of his chair, his merperson markings dull and lifeless against his skin. I look back down; Aora holds Zeel back, and P'Tal...P'Tal looks like I feel, like Jax looks dead inside. I look down at Blaze, at Artem picking quer up and placing quer onto the table they've set up, twisting the Energies to restrain quer small, flailing limbs. I keep looking and promptly regret it, as the Head Slicer's scalpel cuts into the newly born's flesh. There is no sound in the Gathering. Even the insects and birds are marking the atrocity with silence.

Hot red blood leaks out of Blaze's temple, and my stomach clenches as I glimpse the pure white of quer skull. Mom squeezes my hand so hard it feels like my fingers will fall off.

Artem sucks up thick, golden dragon blood out of the vial he's brought with him, into a vessel attached to a long, thin needle. As the blood harvested in massacres is pulled up the little tube, the head Slicer's eyes swivel up into the gap of the infirmary tent flap to meet mine. I can't read his face. But I don't look away.

I tear my eyes from Artem's, not wanting to watch as he plunges the needle directly into Blaze's brain. Infecting quer with the blood that will tear away quer ability to Dream. —The dragon blood that would prevent quer, were que a faerie, from ever having a hatchling tree and dragon. I'm glad, at least, that centaurs like Blaze don't have that to lose.

Aon is crying in the cage, in Mama's arms. I can't look at quer face. It's shining with tears, but wide-eyed. Learning.

The Slicing continues.

My eyes sting.

And then it's over. The Slicing is done—little Blaze will never Dream again—and the Controller is thanking the Head Slicer, bright newly born blood dripping from his hands. She is thanking the Grovian *citizens* for supporting Aora, Zeel, and P'Tal in their decision to help keep Lunav free of a horrible plague.

Decision.

It would be funny if it weren't so brutal. Forcing growns to watch someone open the skull of a newly born they helped bring to life. Violating quer body, forever changing it, without quer consent.

Decision.

Jax jolts out of his stupor, like he's just realizing where he is. "She has to release Hazal and Aon now," he says, his voice scratchy. He sits straight in his chair and flares open the infirmary tent flap, lowering the platform to the ground so P'Tal and the others can come stay with their newly born while he completes quer post-Slicing care.

I nod at him and fly out of the infirmary into the dispersing crowd of mourning Grovians, Mom's hand locked in mine. I can't look at P'Tal's face as we pass him. I don't even think he notices us. He's holding Blaze like he's never seen someone so tiny before, like if que jostles quer even a little bit, que will never wake up.

Before I process where my wings are taking me, Mom and I are directly in front of the Controller. A breeze makes her light cloak stir along with her flowing locks, and I refuse to speak. She knows that she promised to release my family if her first Slicing proceeds without further interference.

"I could argue that the little riot against my Hands last week constitutes interference with the Slicing," the Controller says with false levity in heavily accented Grovian faeric.

I just stare. Mom flies even closer to Evelyn. "Let them go, Controller, or I swear, last week's uprising will look like—"

"You don't want to finish that sentence," the Controller deadpans before inclining her chin toward the cage, her eyes locking into mine. I hold her gaze—which is hard and blazing with an emotion and intensity I can't identify or explain—until a small body slams into my side. Aon's arms are all over my torso, and I wrench my eyes away to greet quer, laughing at quer's warmth and fervor. I grin crookedly as Mama kisses Mom with deep ferocity, both of their hands everywhere at once. Lerian whinnies loudly and suggestively behind me, and I laugh as Mom and Mama startle apart in response. Aon doesn't look so sure that que knows what's funny, but que joins in the laughter until que starts to cry.

Part Two

Chapter Fourteen

LUNAMEZ IS FINALLY upon us.

I haven't even seen Kashat except during labor, where he doesn't waste any energy communicating. The past few sunups, he's been up all night, every night, leading his learning pod in preparation. The floating candles they put up around the Gathering earlier in the season have been replaced floating lanterns, the candles having burned so long they're now down to their charred cores. The lanterns, in their stead, rotate the colors they fluoresce into the nights. I think Kashat is trying to recreate the effect of dragon bulbs hanging from Lunavad trees. And he's succeeding.

The Lunamez buzz is all around us, seasonal songs rising up irrepressibly, at unexpected intervals.

Even during labor. We adjust the slamming of our axes to fit the tunes of our songs giving thanks to Lunav, to Lunara.

Even the Forest's fireflies are preparing, often blinking in time with our melodies.

With the cold season that marked Evelyn's arrival in the Grove almost passed, Aon is already the age-mate of a twelve- or thirteen-harvest-old non—and already causing that much trouble.

I grimace into the buzzing Lunamez songs around us as Zaylam flaps her wings over the bright blue bruise on my side. Jorbam rumbles softly under my sore back as I hang my head backwards off her branches.

"You'd think you'd want to leave the beating to the Hands, huh?" I cough, and Zaylam's snout twitches back and forth slightly.

"We're really sorry, Sadie! We didn't see you there!" Blaze is calling up from way below, quer little hooves shifting back and forth on the parched ground of the Plains, as Aon hovers around my shoulder, his hands braced on a branch to help keep pressure off of his wings.

"Can we do anything, Sade?"

I wink at Zaylam, but Aon's too distressed to notice. "Yeah, it hurts real bad. Maybe you can go get Mom, ask her to come take a look at me?"

I bite my lip so I don't break out laughing as Aon starts to sweat, his half-webbed, brown fingers gripping at Jorbam tighter. "Uh, well, maybe Jax? Or maybe I can try to Heal you? And Zaylam, her wing wind helps, right? Mom's really stressed, you know, with those elders getting shipped off to the Pits, and that news about all those faye dying in that explosion in the Izlanian mines. And I heard on the way here that they executed another near in the Samp because she was just swimming home from her Learning Pod alone, so Mom's bound to be busy comforting Mama about that, right? So we probably shouldn't—"

"You're seriously using the 'people are going to prison and getting killed' excuse so I won't get you in trouble with Mom?" I ask him, sitting up with disbelief, all the amusement gone from my face.

"Uh, well, you seem to be feeling better, hm, so I'm just gonna—"

"Aon!" I call, but he's already gone, Blaze galloping away underneath his flight path. Zaylam hooks a talon over my waist to keep me where I am. I sigh heavily and go back to lying down with my head dangling from Jor's branches.

"Were we like that, Zay? Are we like that?"

> *Are you asking about the part*
> *Where he and Blaze fly and gallop into*
> *Everything and everyone*
> *All the time*
> *Or the part where*
> *He made use of death*
> *To get out of a small bit*
> *Of trouble?*

I lock eyes with her. *"The second one."*

She lets a lot of air out of her snout, fully retracted now, blowing my head and hair back.

> *He doesn't Dream,*
> *And neither do his young friends.*

I sigh again. "But we did a lot of that first one, huh?"

Zaylam's snout elongates, and I grin too. "Remember when we flew into Gimla and knocked him right out of the air?"

Whoever knew that we could
Be so powerful?

Jorbam's trunk rumbles hard, and she produces some sap for us. Zaylam's tongue, longer than almost my whole leg, worms across my body to taste it. I scoop my finger through the sap and lick it thoughtfully. I feel what Jorbam's saying in the textures and tangs of the thick liquid.

I trace her bark with my fingers, smiling. "We were just always really careful not to fly into you, Jor. It's not because you're not special! It's on account of we love you!"

Zaylam flaps her wings in assent. Jorbam ruffles her leaves, satisfied.

"You know, I've been thinking—"

I'm interrupted by two short screams. They sound an awful lot like Aon and Blaze, just outside the barrier.

Bruise be damned, I take off at top speed, pulling up short just before bursting through the barrier, because what I see makes me need to vomit. Urgently.

Aon is hovering in front of Blaze, who's staring up at Richard, the Controller's second-in-command, and a short scruffy Hand whose name I don't know. Or care about.

And Richard is putting his bow into Aon's pudgy hands, muttering to him about how to load an arrow, how to find your target. How to shoot.

How to hunt.

And Aon looks fascinated, his sunset red wings curled at the tips in eagerness.

"See," Scruffy is saying, "I told you we didn't want to hurt you. We're not the bad guys here. Don't you want to learn how to get your own food?"

"Growers give us all the food we need," Blaze protests, but quer Flowing green eyes too, are wide and fixated on the bow. Quer beige, poker-straight tail swishes in anticipation, and quer objection is halfhearted.

"But think of the power you could have by getting your own food. What if you didn't have to rely on an elite of growers?" Richard says to them. Then he mutters to Scruffy as he takes an arrow from his quiver and helps Aon fit it into the bow, "This is why they need us here, see? Even those related to the basically *human* one need our help."

I grind my teeth and Zaylam, hovering above, looks down at me, her snout retracted so hard it must hurt.

"But what would we shoot? Rabbits? They're not food, they're people."

My stomach churns, thinking of Osley. Aon rotates on his right foot with the loaded bow, taller than his whole body. His arms shake with the effort, and the non men hold in the laughter Aon can't see, wouldn't understand. My little brother is looking for prey, but the Hands have already found theirs.

"Aon!" I call out, about to fly through the barrier and reveal myself.

But Zaylam's talons loop around me, holding me back, because another voice has called out too. Iema.

"Richard, sir! Why are you giving these young ones weapons?"

Aon squeals and drops the bow and arrow, which flies forward a little before clattering listlessly onto the plant-softened ground. He takes off, Blaze galloping as well as que can through the underbrush to keep up with him. I linger only long enough to hear Iema scoff at Richard's angry explanation that he was just having a little fun, that she has no right to interfere with a superior's entertainment, before I tear off after Blaze and Aon, dipping into the Forest as soon as I'm out of sight of the shouting Hands.

When Blaze crashes onto an old Way path, Aon swoops down and half flies, his wings pumping while he holds onto quer shoulders. Even though Aon's a few shades darker than me and Blaze is a few shades lighter and with different undertones than Lerian, they remind me forcibly of Ler and me when we were young ones. I breathe roughly as I fly behind them too speechless to want to reveal myself yet.

They tumble out of the Forest onto the beach by the eastern steam pools, and, as one creature, careen into someone's stomach.

That someone is none other than Evelyn.

"Of course," I mutter under my breath. I slip sideways behind a tree I don't know, asking permission with my fingertips to stay there for a while. The tree rumbles—even without tasting his sap, I know he's amused. He seems willing to let me stay.

I peer around the trunk tentatively, holding my breath and waiting for Evelyn to arrest Blaze, to send Aon back to the cage that made him incapable of flying steadily on his own in the first place.

Aon and Blaze have both frozen, only their heaving chests and rigid spines testifying to their alertness. They back away from the Controller, trembling with heads nodded into a partial bow and muttering apologies in all the languages they've studied in their learning pods so far. The tips of Blaze's ears are growing redder by the moment.

Evelyn's hand is on her stomach, and she's doubled over slightly, clearly winded and in pain from their impact. I know what that feels like; my own bruise throbs.

Aon starts to shake as the Controller raises her head enough to look at them. Her other hand lifts, extends toward them, like she's either going to hit them or embrace them. I flex my fingers.

"Please Controller ma'am," Blaze stammers in Highlander non, "we were just excited, and Aon can't fly too good, his wings—"

Evelyn stops her with a furrowed brow. "His?" she says in Underlander. "You've made your Choosing, then?" she asks Aon in Grovian faeric.

He nods in the human fashion. "I'm a boy," he says in a small voice. He's still shaking—this woman imprisoned him—but I can't help grinning at his simple declaration, and neither, it seems, can Evelyn.

The Controller nods like she's in the palace and she's acknowledging a young dignitary. "A fine choice," she says. Her eyes glisten as they dart across the deserted beach around them. I pull my head back behind the tree and make sure my wings are pulled in tight to my body.

"Shouldn't you two be in your learning pods?" she whispers conspiratorially, still in a Grovian tongue.

"It's boring today. We want to learn how to be soul keepers, not the history of the whole Grove! They don't even give Aon spell impressions, so he can't learn how to twist the Energies yet!"

I run a frustrated hand over my face at Blaze's response. Evelyn's leaning forward so she's at eye level with them, her hands bracing her upper body on her thighs. The bodice of her white dress runs dangerously low across her chest, and heat swirls in my belly. Face. Her face. I focus on her face. Which looks thoughtful, her full lips puckering in consideration.

"Soul keeping isn't something you can teach with spell impressions or Energy twistings," she tells them like it's her turn to instruct a learning pod. Blaze looks rapt, and Aon's even stopped shaking a little. "You have to be born with the ability. But, you can't go around talking to other Hands about soul keeping, all right? You'll get yourselves in more trouble than you could already have from, how do I say it, a *certain bruise* I'm sure I'll have," she teases, her fingers caressing her rounded stomach again.

I tilt my head, wondering when her Grovian languages got so good. I can't figure it out, nor why she's not locking the young ones up for recklessness or something. Worse, watching them is making my heart warm instead of making my skin crawl.

Aon flies backward at that, but Evelyn laughs, shaking her head. "Don't worry, little one. It was a joke. A bad one. But I'm not going to hurt you, all right?" He hovers where he is, looking wary. Blaze shifts so she's standing between them, and I find myself admiring the young one.

Evelyn and Aon just stare at each other for a long while. The Controller's eyes get misty for a moment before she reaches into a hidden pocket in her dress. "Here," she says, holding her hand out in front of her. "Grown candy." Aon and Blaze approach slowly, cautiously.

"Go on, take it. For Lunamez." They snatch the grown candy from her hand, their relatively tiny fingers quick and sticky, and dash off in the opposite direction, along the beach toward the Underland.

She watches them go, shaking her head. A small, sad smile lingers on her face.

I fly away, back into the depths of the Forest, toward the Plains, before she realizes there was a witness to that strange affair.

BACK IN THE Plains, I let my eyes droop closed, soaking in the sounds of Lunamez approaching, only a few sunups away now. The dragons too are harmonizing with our hymns, and Jorbam rumbles in time beneath me.

A cool twilight breeze is growing, and out of nowhere, I have no wings.

I am human. I look down at my hands. He is—I am—covered in chain mail armor. My ears are full of dozens of thundering centaurs trotting across a beach all at once. I look down again. The man I am Dreaming is not surrounded by centaurs; he is surrounded by horses, and by human soldiers riding them. His—my—heart is racing, and I become aware, as his memories sync into mine, of this being his first assignment out of the Highlands. My chest aches, my lower back stiff from riding so long, and I wonder what will happen to my joiner back at home if this first assignment is my last.

I grip the reins too tightly, and the horse I am commanding grunts angrily.

"Relax, kid, this'll be a breeze. The centaurs don't have magic. We'll take them by surprise, and anyway, the Grovian Controller's apparently something to look at." My fellow soldier, riding alongside me, nudges me with the backside of his sharpened axe, the symbol of the Mach clearly visible on the handle, matching the design on his helmet. I try to grin my thanks at him, but my own metal helmet covers most of my face. I grunt instead.

"Maybe if you fight well enough you can earn a private audience with her, huh?" The Mach soldier laughs at his own words and makes a lewd gesture with his hands and hips, carelessly jostling the horse he's riding. I don't mention my joiner. I force a chuckle and reposition the axe in my belt.

I feel the sweat dripping down his face like it's my own.

My own. This is not my reality.

I jerk awake, and I am choking.

"Zaylam!" I shout.

She swoops down from the clouds and lands with her face on my level. She grasps her talons around her usual spot to keep herself in place without blowing me over with her wing wind.

I look around wildly, fly forward slightly, and whisper directly into her ear. No one can hear how I know what I know. What I've seen.

"I just Dreamed..." I try to call moisture into my dry mouth. "I just Dreamed a soldier, a Mach soldier, the Mach, the king's special kill unit, they were—they're going—right now—Lerian!—Zay, are my growns with Jax?—Zay, we have to warn them—"

I flail upwards and start flying, but she expands her wings and blocks my way.

> *Sadie,*
> *You need to breathe*
> *And tell me what—*

"The Mach are about to invade the Underland, Zay."

She stares at me, her snout pulled so deeply into her face it looks like she's got a hole in it.

And then she wails into the evening sky, letting the other dragons and trees know, without mentioning my Dream, of course. As the message spreads, she doesn't hesitate or heed the fact that her wound from the massacre only recently stopped spontaneously bleeding. She ignores the dangers of a dragon traveling out of the Plains, alone and unallowed. Not when they're about to attack the same place where so many fought to save her life.

She flies instead. We both do.

We soar as one creature. I dart through the myriad obstacles beneath the Forest understory, and Zaylam, way too big for that, flies high above the treetops. We don't need to speak or sing to each other. We are perfectly in sync. When I rise to avoid a bramble, I feel Zaylam rise higher above the trees. When I swerve to swoop beside an errant branch, Zaylam loops in the sky above me. When she darts down lower to avoid being spotted by a Hand, my toes skim the Forest ground, often hitching on a branch, on a bush, forcing my wings to course correct as I yell apologies over my shoulder. When I do, she waits above me.

I'm about to break out of the Forest and fly down the Dropoff into the Underland. I feel Zaylam's shadow coming over me. Beneath us, heading into the Underland along the Flowing's beach, is a massive deployment of Mach soldiers—one of whose lives I've just been Dreaming—marching and riding horses in military formation.

I have no plan, but I hear other faeries flying above me, exclaiming about Zaylam, about the Mach—apparently the news of the invasion has already spread.

And then everything vanishes. There's a very vague but very loud thump on the side of my head as someone, something, slams into my skull. My wings seize up. I free fall off the Dropoff. I remember nothing else.

Chapter Fifteen

ZAYLAM'S QUICK. THAT'S my first groggy thought upon waking. I'm sprawled out on her smooth scaled, hickory-patterned wing, like a vast magenta blanket curled around me protectively. She must have caught me. The tip of her massive tailfin is stroking my legs—I'm glad to know I can feel them—but the rest of her body is stock-still. With tension.

The Underland! I remember vaguely. My Dream. Another invasion.

I try to sit up. My throbbing head and subtle pressure from Zaylam's tail makes clear what an absurd idea that is. I crack both sets of eyelids open again, slower this time. Even the moonlight hurts. I close my outer eyelids quickly.

My ears start working again, sorting out specific sounds from the dull ringing. Lots of faeries hovering, wings fluttering but tense. Zaylam's triple heartbeat in her broad chest, thin underbelly fur slick with sweat. I touch my forehead and my hand drips with the dark pink heat of my own blood.

The rustle of skyflower petals, poised to resist axes and fire. The Controller's voice, dignified and firm.

Evelyn's voice.

I pull myself up, more carefully this time, bit by bit, so I can see over the curve of Zay's wing. Evelyn is standing in front of an entire deployment of heavily armed soldiers: the Mach, all covered in chain mail like I Dreamed.

I have to blink several times to interpret what the Mach are doing, to make sure it's not my bleeding head making me see things. No. It's true. The Mach have their magic-enhancing weaponry drawn and raised at...Evelyn.

It can't be.

And then I realize with a dull jolt that she is standing just flutters in front of us, directly between the invading force and Zaylam's curled-up body.

Their weapons, then, are raised at Zay. At me. At the lone dragon, impulsive where her elders were restrained, flown out of the forced shelter of the Plains to protect the Underland.

Yet the Controller has positioned herself between us and a small army. Her back is poker straight, and I imagine the look on her face. Steely. Dignified. Calm.

I see her silhouette through half-opened eyes as her full form radiates in the moonlight. She is without hesitation. Chin raised, her hands are distinctly away from her bow. Her white skirt sways in contrast with the stiff uniforms of even her own soldiers, who are scattered behind her, surrounding us. The nearest Hands look distinctly uncomfortable, glancing sidelong at Zaylam with a combination of fear, curiosity, and hatred. They are the dividing line between us and the crowd of centaurs caught between both forces. Many of their bows are drawn at the faeries hovering above our heads.

Most of her own Hands seem unsure if they will actually defend their Controller; by the tilt of their bows, the flexing of their fingers, and the hatred in their gazes, they seem more ready to attack the resting dragon, the wide-eyed faeries, the unarmed centaurs, than they are to defend their Controller against the Mach soldiers she is holding back with only her posture.

All except Iema, arm healed by now, who walks steadily in the midst of the growing silence to stand near Evelyn, knuckles purple on the hilt of her sword. Ready to protect the Controller. And, by extension, me and Zay.

I blink rapidly, trying to focus enough to actually interpret what she's saying, the Highlander non harsh on my buzzing ears. "I can't understand how engaging in military operations in a Grovian province without the approval or foreknowledge of the Controller of the Grove can bear any productive fruit for the king."

An angry whisper goes through the Hands, who are looking more and more ready to cross her and join the regiment with their weapons poised at her chest. Even I can see that with my pounding eyesight. Only Iema doesn't flinch at her words, and my heart twists a little.

My dragging eyes find Lerian in the crowd of people, between the shoulders of two Hands. She looks ready to fight. She glances at me briefly and nods sharply. She looks back at the horses many of the Mach are riding. The four-legged newcomers look ashamed to be bridled. Lerian lowers her eyes and flexes her shoulder muscles, her jaw set.

"You dare question the orders of the good King Xavier?" an unpleasantly thick voice rings out. "You've been trained better than this, Evelyn." My breath catches and I duck down behind Zaylam's flesh dizzyingly. I know that condescending voice, that sneer, that gray beard and deathly white skin.

The Commander of the Mach is—Reve, the man in the Forest with Evelyn the night I saved Iema. The one who clubbed me, who was charged with protecting Evelyn.

"You misunderstand me, Commander," Evelyn retorts calmly. "I am not questioning His Majesty's orders, simply your sloppy protocol." A few amused gasps rise up amongst some centaurs and faeries. They are shushed immediately. "When you return with the proper verification that the good King Xavier has commanded you to route this place, I will gladly allow you to proceed and will make security arrangements accordingly. But as it stands, you come bearing no documentation of His Majesty's orders, which all of his Hands, Mach or otherwise, as you well know, are required to carry at all times."

A small rumble goes up amongst the Hands at that. My jaw drops slightly. She's talked them into a corner where the action perceived as most loyal to the king right now is to defend the Underland. "Well played," I mutter, and Zaylam's heat patch glows.

I can't see what's happening now, because I can't risk Reve spotting me, but I hear the trotting of a horse, right up to where Evelyn is standing. A strange tugging on the Energies carves its way into the pit of my stomach the closer the horse gets, and it feels vaguely familiar, from the night Reve hit me. I strain my ears to hear.

"Don't think Xavier won't be informed about this, Evelyn. You will regret these actions, mark my words." He's speaking softly, but not soft enough. Maybe no one's ever told him that faeric hearing is much better than nons'.

"Controller," Evelyn says, projecting for us all to hear as though Commander Reve weren't standing right in front of her. "At my current station, my title is the Controller of the Grovian Provinces, Commander. Do well not to forget that again if you return with those authentications from the king. You'd do well to remember too that I serve the king, not any man who marches into the provinces that the king himself appointed me to keep safe from rebel activity. Come back with King Xavier's seal and you shall receive my full cooperation." A pause. "You've been dismissed, Commander."

I almost laugh out loud. I slam my fist into my mouth to stem the sound, and more blood pours from my head. I slide down Zaylam's underbelly, unbearably woozy again.

I hear Reve's angry, poorly whispering voice again, but can't make out his words. A low thundering rises up, and it must be the Mach turning their horses around and retreating. Some scattered centaurs and faeries whoop alongside the even more victorious cries from birds and insects and groundlings of the Forest and the Underland, who must too have been excellently concealed, poised to fight. My moms' voices approach me like we're under the Flowing's waters, and there is nothing else.

THE FAINT LIGHT of Lunamez's floating lanterns seeps under my outer eyelids. I blink once, twice, three times. Groggily. Painfully.

The inside of the infirmary tent swoops in and out of focus. The medicinal lanterns hanging from three parts of the roof burn softly, dimly, at this time of night. Jax's low workbench, Mom's higher one, both full of their healing styles. Mom's is ordered and sensible, not a vial out of place; Jax's is chaotic and messily strewn, not a vial in place. Jax is awake and puttering quietly with some salve or other at his bench. If he's realized I'm awake, he doesn't let on.

Mom's steady breathing nearby lets me know she's fallen asleep on the platform floor next to my cot. I realize groggily that her hand is reaching up even in her rest, still locked with my fingers. I smile faintly and turn my head carefully to the cot next to mine.

I gasp and almost sit bolt upright, but my throbbing wound keeps me in place. Evelyn starts speaking immediately.

"It wasn't one of mine that hit you." I blink rapidly, trying to make my thoughts clearer somehow. She uncrosses her legs with a soft hiss of pain, like she's been sitting there so long her foot's fallen asleep. I glance wildly at Jax. He doesn't turn to look at me. What they discussed, if anything, while I was unconscious, I will never know. Because I won't ask. But I do wonder vaguely if Mom is feigning sleep or if she really is out.

Evelyn continues through my confusion. "I confronted him before he rode away. He claims that he was thinking you were going to attack, because you were flying so fast, and there was a dragon above you." I'm pretty sure she rolls her eyes, but my head is still stiff and throbbing, so I can't be sure. I am sure, though, that she's speaking in my own language, which might be more confusing than her being in the infirmary in the first place. "Most of you fly quickly. His ignorance of your habits could have cost you your life. Though I will say, flying out of the Plains with your dragon in tow was perhaps not the wisest idea."

I try to sit up again, and she reaches out a hand to stop me, pausing just before her skin touches mine. "Your dragon flew away safely." My entire body relaxes.

She stares at me, her eyes flickering to the thick wrapping on my head. Is she trying to ask how I'm feeling? Apologize for the pain I'm in?

"If they do return with true orders from the king, I won't stop them." Is that preemptive regret in her voice? A warning? A threat? An apology? My head swims. Jax keeps his eyes fixed on his work, but his hands are still. I wonder why the Controller seems so much older than she is. I shut my eyes to try to focus.

She's gone when I look back up. I turn to Jax, opening my mouth to ask him for water and an explanation for what is happening to my life, but a rough voice cuts into my thoughts as the infirmary tent flap is thrust open again.

"What, the Controller's giving you house calls now? Must be nice, being ugly enough to attract her so much."

Lerian calling me ugly has never, ever hurt before.

Until right now.

"Lerian," Jax says in his warning voice, and Mom sits bolt upright on the floor, squeezing my hand before letting it go and flying up to Lerian's eye level.

"I'm sorry Jax, Faye, but Sadie needs to hear a few things." Mom hesitates, but relents after putting her forehead to my cheek, zipping out of the tent into the night. I would feel abandoned, but I actually feel grateful. I don't want her to hear what I know Lerian's about to say, and somehow I think she knows that too. Jax wheels protectively but quietly over to my cot, his expression neutral, checking the bandages on my head.

"Ler, I'm sorry I got you hit when they took Rada, but hey, look, we're even now." I grin crookedly and point to my forehead. My stomach is so knotted I don't think it'll ever come undone. Lerian just scoffs.

"You think I'm mad because I got hit? I'd get hit for you any day, Sade. I took an arrow for you, didn't I? And what, you think it's funny? You think it was fun for me seeing you drop out of the sky like that today? Who do you think... You know what, just..." She sighs deeply, like she's steeling herself for something, and I brace myself, lips pursed and breath held.

"You used to be one of us. You used to only be like them when you were risking your neck for us. And then the new Controller came, and sure, I know she's arrested you twice, but you've gotten reckless, like being arrested makes you special, like it gives you some kind of credibility. But she didn't put you in that cage, Sadie, and she didn't ship you to the Pits. Because you...she... You've been taking risks that you can get away with on account of you look like them, but it's like you don't even care anymore how it affects the rest of us. Did you stop to think what would happen to the rest of us when you went after that Hand the night they took Rada?"

"I didn't go after—"

"It doesn't matter, they were just dying for an excuse, any excuse, and you gave it to them when you knew they wouldn't take it out on you, not on the Controller's little non pet!"

I start to sit up, and Jax, his eyes anywhere but my face, pushes me back down gently.

"The Controller just saved the Underland—"

Lerian lets out a harsh laugh, and her fists open and close rapidly like a washed up fish gaping, trying not to suffocate, on the beach.

"You can't seriously be defending her? To me? You think nons like her can save us, Sadie? Is that what you've been trying to do this whole time, save us with your dashing non looks?"

Every word penetrates my skin like burning knives laced with acid. Hot droplets run down my face, and I know they're not blood.

"Your precious Controller said it herself; she was only waiting to get proper orders from her damn king. She was protecting herself, not us, just like she was protecting herself when she Healed me, because she wants to be obeyed. She needs to be obeyed, or don't you remember that her own people are being killed by the palace occupation every single day too? She should know better, she should fight with us, but instead she's scrambling for whatever ounce of palace-approved power she can get, and who cares, but I spent all these harvests thinking you were different, that you wouldn't be tempted by... I defended you, I—"

She's spitting now, and her stormy gray eyes are about to pour. Jax studies his fingers carefully.

"You're my best friend, Sadie, but this woman is gonna let my home be destroyed. My home, my people. I thought we were your people too, but you keep defending her. You've picked your side." Lerian's face has hardened now, a mask of all our memories together frozen in time. "Let me know when you remember who your real people are."

She turns on her back hooves and tosses the flap of the infirmary tent aside.

"Lerian!" I call after her, but I can't move beyond following her with my eyes. The subtle but firm pressure of Jax's hands won't let me do anything else. I screw up my face, closing both sets of eyelids. I try to breathe.

"She carried you here, you know, Sade. She insisted. She loves you."

I crack open my outer eyelids and stare up at him. "You sure I'm not too non for her?"

Jax sighs heavily and releases me. He leans forward, elbows on his widespread knees. His fingers trace the merperson markings on his neck thoughtfully. "She loves you. She's just scared you won't always love her."

I try to sit up and he pushes me back down by my shoulders firmly. I grimace. "That's ridiculous, why wouldn't I—"

"She has eyes, you know. So do we all. Life passing as a non in the Highlands with someone with the Controller's kind of power would be a lot easier than life as a faerie here."

He starts to wheel away, but I make a clumsy grab for his chair. It's ineffective, but he sees the motion and stops.

"Jax, I wouldn't abandon my family. And you guys are my family as much as my moms and Aon."

He smiles sadly at me, leaning over to ladle some steaming tonic out of his creation bowl. He passes it to me and I drink. "I know, sherba. I know. I'm just not the one who needs convincing. No, no arguments! I don't want to hear how ridiculous and irrational she's being. I want to hear you breathing deeply, not talking. Asleep. Now, Sadie."

I give him a lopsided grin that is sincerely trying to be a glare, but whatever tonic he gave me takes over my body.

I sleep.

When I wake up, daylight is creeping into the infirmary, and there's a small, warm body lying on my stomach.

"Os," I croak, to let quer know I'm. See if que's awake too. Que is. So is Mom. She's half lying on the cot Evelyn sat on last night, watching over Osley and me while she rubs skyflower fruit oil onto Mama's skin. Mama has her own hands full with Aon, who's grumbling halfheartedly as she twists his hair into short braids.

"You wanted it like this, don't complain," she tells him with a small grin. He glares, but it's got a smile underneath it.

"Hi, Sadie!" he enthuses. I grunt at him. "Mom, why can't you just fully heal Sadie's head?"

"The Energies can only fix so much, Aon. Only soul keepers can heal certain injuries completely without rest time—you know that."

He narrows his eyes. "I do know. That's why I want to be one."

Osley trills in mild amusement.

"So Jax tells me you had an active night, Sade," Mama ventures, glancing at me as she shifts so Mom can reach her knees with the oil.

Memory crashes over me. Evelyn. Lerian. Lerian. Evelyn.

Lerian.

Unexpected tears flood my eyes and my vision fogs. "You don't think I'm some heartless non traitor, do you?"

Osley rubs quer head against my stomach, and Aon's eyes widen sadly. Mom flutters over to my cot, putting her forehead to my arm. "Sherba, no, you..." She glances over her shoulder at Mama, whose fingers relent from Aon's hair.

"Sade, you and the Controller just—"

But I don't find out what Mama thinks about me and the Controller, because Mom and Jax's names are being shouted from across the Gathering. Mom darts up and out of the infirmary, thrusting its door flap open wide, wide. I flinch and close my eyes away from the growing light. Mama puts her hand in front of my face to block most of it, and Osley leaps down from my stomach as Mom twists the Energies to lower the platform for Jax to come in from where he sleeps nearby. To let their new patient come in.

Aon zips to the edge of the tent behind Mom, trying to see who would be calling so desperately for a healer.

He lets out a gnarled scream as he speeds past Mom toward the sounds.

And with a jolt, I recognize the voices. Mama does too; I see it in her eyes. "Stay here, stay still," she tells me, and flies even faster than Aon out of the infirmary.

Toward P'Tal. Toward P'Tal and Aora and Zeel, because they're galloping, fast, toward us, shouting. Their hoof steps get louder and louder the closer they get. Osley crouches down next to me, quer body tensed.

My eyes widen as half a dozen figures fill the door flap of the infirmary tent. Aon is still screaming, shouting, a name, a name, over and over again.

Blaze.

Que is dangling in Zeel and Aora's arms, Mom leaning over quer, mostly blocking quer body from my view. P'Tal's upper torso has collapsed against Mama's arms, and she's cooing to him, quieting him as he gasps, trying to explain what's happened.

I hear the rolling sound of Jax wheeling onto the platform and into the tent, and his eyes catch mine briefly. They're wide and disarrayed, his entire body rigid. I haven't seen his face like this since he watched Idrisim die.

I start shaking without knowing quite why. Aon hovers low and grabs desperately at my tunic, putting his forehead on my chest and heaving deep sobs.

"Aon, what—"

And then Mom shifts as she, Zeel, and Aora successfully maneuver Blaze's body onto a cot specifically designed for small centaurs. I get my first real glimpse of quer injuries.

But they're not injuries. Blaze's limbs are twitching uncontrollably, and que is covered in raised, angry welts that are oozing yellow pus and thick red blood, everywhere from quer non-like torso to quer horselike flank. Quer tiny, vestigial skyflower orange wings have flopped down off the cot liked wilted lettuce, and quer hooves, when they're not twitching, are hanging down like they're not attached by any bones.

Blaze has the blood plague.

Chapter Sixteen

"Why did they still set up the nestling? Why aren't they canceling Lunamez?" Aon demands angrily, of no one in particular.

Mama, her hand being squeezed by P'Tal on her left, leans over to put her forehead on Aon's shoulder. A droplet of clear liquid slips down his arm, and though it's gotten warm in the infirmary with so many people and so many medicinal brews on the make, I know it's not sweat.

Zeel raises quer deep brown eyes and runs a hand over quer nearly bald head and down quer face, stopping to fiddle distractedly with the silver ring poking out of the expanse of quer broad, flat nose. Quer thick chest muscles twitch as the vein in quer neck throbs. "We can't stop all of Lunav moving, Ay," Zeel says, quer thick, deep voice rumbling over us all, even as Blaze takes a rattling, half-conscious breath. P'Tal flinches and Mama lifts her head from Aon's shoulder so she can lean closer to him. Aora observes their closeness with a small furrow of her brow, her eyes flickering back to her young one almost immediately.

Aon's eyes are wide as he nods, though he's clearly unsatisfied with the answer. When Zeel looks away, he turns to me. *"Why not?"* his body asks me.

I know what he means.

"Que was just playing in the Forest... that redheaded Hand, the second-in-command, brought quer to us... que was just playing, and then que just... started developing the pustules..."

Aora had repeated the story of how the Hand, Richard, had found Blaze. There was no warning, no prior sickness. No explanation except the constant risk of the plague, the constant risk of its resurgence. And if que'd played near anything that someone from the Samp had passed through, the Samp where they'd had a small outbreak lately...

Aora's numb processing, over and over again, of how this could have happened, rings out in my ears, as the final preparations for Lunamez rise around us outside. Shouts of "good season, good Lunamez" and the squeals of young ones tumbling through the Gathering meld with her disbelief, her trying to convince herself that it's true. Her young one is dying, with no hope of a cure.

I listen to all of it, numb as the Growers outside twist the Energies to conjure up the ingredients for Lunamez stew into massive bronze pots over enormous, floating pits of fire. In the midst of all this jovial chaos, the eight of us hold vigil with a rapidly weakening Blaze inside.

Zeel and Aora; P'Tal won't let go of Mama's hand, and it has me wondering just how close they were when they were nears; Mom and Jax; Aon, because he refuses to leave as much as we try to remind him that Blaze wouldn't want him to miss his first Lunamez; and me, because my family is here and because I'm stuck until my head stops spinning when I sit up.

The flap to the infirmary tent opens slightly, tentatively, and we all turn to stare at the newcomer. I grin faintly.

"Shouldn't you be getting ready, Kashat? Big day for you tomorrow." Jax glances up from his feverish mixing of herbs and Energies that should help ease some of Blaze's agony.

"It is, yeah." But Kashat isn't looking at Jax. His eyes have fallen on Blaze's lopsided form and won't let go. I reach a hand out over my head to touch his hovering knee. He starts and stares down at me like he's trying to remember something.

"Jax, Faye, is Sadie all right to come outside for a little bit? I'll help her fly. I...I need her help with something." Mom and Jax exchange a long look.

"She's going to insist she can fly, and she can't, Kash, so hold her at all times," Mom tells him. I mutter wordlessly under my breath, and though Aon's eyes are locked on Blaze's oblivious form, the corners of his lips twitch upward slightly. A good sign, I think. I hope.

I try to drag myself up. Mom gives me a pointed look and I mutter some more as I let Kashat help drag me off my cot.

A hushed murmur rises up when we flutter outside of the tent, with faeries, centaurs, and Hands alike giving us a wide berth. I raise my eyebrows at Kashat, and he shakes his shoulders back and forth as much as he can while supporting most of my weight, his arm under my wing sprouts and mine tightly under his. "They know the plague only spreads after...death...but you know, the palace is all about how exposing Dreamers to un-Sliced young ones can spread the plague. Don't know how that's supposed to make sense, but I guess it's getting people nervous." He raises his voice, half shouting, to no one in particular, and to everyone, who are backing away as we fly together. "Even though the palace's lies make no kind of sense!"

I smirk because it's something Lerian would do, even as the muttering around us increases.

"Where are we going?"

Kashat just grins sideways at me. "Up," he says, and starts ascending from our low hover. I gasp as I realize that he's taking me to the nestling.

Every season at Lunamez, the Lunamez learning pod is tasked with performing at the accounting, passing on their own understanding of our history, our faith, through the story they put together. Kashat has been working hard at it this season, and it shows through the nestling.

A woven stage for the performance, the nestling is enchanted to float amongst the treetops on the southernmost edge of the Gathering. It has a long, sturdy platform so the centaur performers can be elevated with the faeries, but that's not the impressive part. This season, Kashat and the others designed it as deep orange, bucket-shaped, with tendrils emerging from the ends, wrapping the performance space in a sealike embrace.

And that's where we're heading.

When Kashat approaches, the faeries that are twisting the Energies to make sure it stays afloat during the accounting flitter away somberly. I furrow my brow. "They know your family is close to P'Tal's. They know you're...mourning."

I grunt. "No one else seems to care. Everyone else seems to just care about catching the plague." I wiggle my fingers grotesquely, and Kashat sighs.

"Yeah, but my learning pod doesn't fall into the palace lies." I arch an eyebrow at him. "You'll see."

"Do you actually need my help with anything, Kash?" He settles me into a little nook in the deepest part of the basketlike structure. Probably no one can see us from here. A dull curiosity grows in me.

Kashat's eyes sweep around before he asks wordlessly, moving his body rather than his lips, *"Have Jax and your mom talked to you yet?"*

"About?"

A pause, and I can't tell if he's being dramatic or cautious.

"Your Dreaming."

I almost jump up, but the wave of dizziness that sweeps over me keeps me in place.

"They told you?" I whisper-shout. He clamps a hand over my mouth and shakes his shoulders back and forth.

"Last night when you were unconscious, the Controller came to the infirmary with the head Slicer about Blaze. They were both furious about the infection. Anyway, point is that your growns are worried that because the Controller and Head Slicer are both obviously powerfully connected to the Energies, they'll sense the barrier your mom puts around you when you sleep so you don't move around when you Dream."

I blink. They really did tell him everything. Talking about all this with someone other than Lerian is surreal. And cleansing. I'm almost giddy. And terrified. My head spins, and I'm not sure if it's the wound or the casual way he's talking about my Dreaming.

I think, unbidden, of Leece, the despair in his eyes when they arrested him. When they took Mara to the Pits alongside him.

"Since you're going to have to stay in the infirmary for the next few sunups, and you'll be all exposed while you're sleeping, I have to tell you our plan. Remember I told you I was working with Jax and some others to restore Dreaming?" I nod. How could I forget? *"They want me to teach you a technique we've been using to shield our efforts from manifesting physically. Jax has been meaning to teach you himself, but with everything that's going on..."*

I nod again, numbly. Will I finally be able to sleep outside of the Plains without Mama's barrier holding me tightly in place?

"It's pretty easy, really. I just have to give you the impression of the spell." He pauses, waiting for my consent. I give it.

A warm, almost overwhelmingly hot sensation floods my body, tickling each of my limbs, shuttling back and forth across my core. Then the heat turns to ice, and I shudder, but somehow don't feel unpleasantly cold after the first moment. My head feels remarkably clear, and I wonder if somehow this spell can help my wound too. I dimly make a note to tell Jax about its potential healing properties.

A wave of thin, purple strands of Energy seeps out of Kashat's steady fingertips and into mine. I feel them swimming through my bloodstream like small, wriggling worms, splitting at my shoulders so some go up my neck through to my head, and some go down through my chest, my legs, my toes. I try not to squirm at the extremely odd sensation. I fail.

Kashat watches almost hungrily. After a few moments, the heat, the cold, the wormlike Energy strands, all fade into memory. My body relaxes, and the throbbing returns to my head at full force. I groan. So much for healing properties.

"Did it work?"

"I uh...I think so. I'll just...I'll just call that up before I sleep, right?" He nods, looking me up and down like he's examining his prize work.

"All right, let's get you back." He gestures around him proudly. "Still have some work to do!"

He half assists, half carries me back down to the infirmary platform. My mind is spinning. If his spell works, I'll be able to sleep wherever I want, my Dreams undetected. If his spell works, I'm safe. Forever. Maybe. Everything makes sense and nothing makes sense. I decide to think about it later, when my head is spinning less.

No one, it seems, has moved in the infirmary; everyone is still attending to a mostly unconscious Blaze. Mom's wiping the new pustules of blood appearing on quer face, using a small vial to drop sizzling, clear liquid onto them. She glances up when Kashat opens the infirmary flap and helps me back into my cot.

"Is it done?" she asks, and Jax looks up from his spell work too.

Kashat nods solemnly, Mama runs a relieved and gentle hand over my cheek, and I fall fast asleep.

"SADIE," MAMA IS whispering. "Sadie, sherba, come. Your mother and Jax say it's all right to take you outside for the threading, as long as you don't try to fly alone."

I breathe deeply and try to crack open my heavy eyes. "It's Lunamez already?"

I hear her smile more than I see it. "You fell asleep, sherba."

"How's Blaze?"

No response. I open my eyes wildly and look across the infirmary. Que's still there, still with quer chest rising and falling. Still with quer breath rattling. At least we can all be around quer. Que won't be contagious until after que dies. One strange blessing of the plague: people don't have to die alone and untouched, at least.

I sigh and let Mama and Mom, who's hovered over, help me sit up. I look at her questioningly. "Jax is going to stay with Blaze. I want to spend Lunamez with my daughter. I'll be right outside if he needs me."

"Aon?"

Mom and Mama exchange a glance. "Blaze woke up at sunup, wanting to know what day it is. Que told Aon in no uncertain terms that he's to attend the ceremonies." Mom sighs. "He's outside, brooding."

I nod painfully and my growns help me up. Jax grimaces at us as we leave. "Good season," he calls so softly I almost don't hear him, his rich voice tinged with tired bitterness.

I blink rapidly as we emerge into the day. The air is still thick with sunup moisture, but it's also thick with faeries, with calls for a good season, with squeals of joy and flutterings of anticipation; and with Hands, backs straight and muscles tensed, eyes everywhere and nowhere at once. Their uniforms look freshly cleaned, almost sparkling white, but their faces are all stone.

By instinct, I almost try to guide Mom and Mama—both of whom have firm arms under my wing spouts, Mama basically supporting me from underneath because of the way Sampians tend to fly—over to Rada's platform. Her grown Lunamez breads and stew are always the best.

My heart lurches when I realize she's not there. When I remember that they dismantled her platform, even after we tried to not let them. Even after I got Lerian a slam in the face that probably made her head spin like mine is doing now.

I wonder if Rada's seen Leece and Mara in the Pits, or if they keep everyone alone. I wonder if she has track of the time; if she knows it's Lunamez. If she's asleep right now and Dreaming one of us and getting to celebrate that way.

I wonder if she's alive to be Dreaming.

As Mom and Mama fly me toward Aon, people give us a wide berth, parting in the sky for us with wide eyes and soft mutterings. Mama and Mom ignore them expertly.

We find Aon, sitting on the grass, leaning against the cage he was once imprisoned in. This space, the center of the Gathering, is usually reserved for the faeries that can't fly, or can't fly for long; everyone keeps a clear a path in the sky between this spot and the nestling. This harvest, we're among a few elders, growns, and young ones, using the imposition of the cage as an advantage, as something to lean against. Aon's face is impassive, but both his eyelids are open wide, drinking in everything like medicine.

I put my forehead to his shoulder as our growns get permission from the grass below to sit me down next to him. He tilts his head to rest it on mine, delicately avoiding my now closed but still throbbing wound. Affection for my little sibling—well, now, my little brother—surges inside me.

Mom and Mama fly off to get us grown breakfast, and as soon as they disappear into the crowd, the Controller steps out from the mix. She looks down at Aon and me for a beat, and none of us speak. When Aon's body goes completely stiff, the skin behind her eyes tighten. "How is your friend?" she asks him in our language.

"Dying," Aon deadpans, and the Controller closes her eyes and sighs.

"How is que, Sadie? And how's your head?" she tries instead.

I blink up at her. "Am I supposed to believe you care? About my head or about Blaze? What do you care if que dies of the blood plague? *Humans* are the reason the plague exists anyway; bet you'd be happy if we all just dropped dead from it."

The Controller looks like I smacked her across the face for a long, long moment. Aon's still little body tenses near me and I ready myself to shift in front of him in case she retaliates physically. She doesn't. She just speaks, in an unfamiliar, far off kind of voice, Grovian gone, replaced by cold Highlander non.

"Isn't Lunamez supposed to be about new beginnings for your people?"

I scoff and refuse to look at her, steel myself against the open, soft look on her face. I won't let her convince me that she gives a damn about us. I can't. "Kinda hard to have a new beginning with someone who's locking away your people, wouldn't you think?"

Mom and Mama return just as Evelyn opens her mouth to respond.

"Our young ones have quite enough going on right now, Controller. Maybe save the interrogations for later?" Mama scathes.

"I wasn't—" Evelyn objects before she seems to realize that the Controller, even an Izlanian one, doesn't need to justify herself to a grieving family of mere faeries. She raises her chin with dignity and sweeps away after sending one last, unreadable look at me.

As she goes, Mama mutters a swear that has Aon giggling and Mom saying, "Hazal, it's Lunamez!" But the corners of her mouth are twitching.

By the time they return and we bite into the sweetened Lunamez breads, a silence rises in the Gathering.

The grass, sliced short by the king's Registry though it's been, waves about in anticipation. I lower my fingers to caress the grassy shoots nearest me, and they tingle gently in response. I sigh and burrow deeper into Aon's shoulder, my eyes, like everyone else's, fixed on the spot where the tunnel to the Underland opens up in the Forest.

"What's everyone waiting for?" he asks me. I just hold up a finger.

"Wait for it." I don't tell him that Rada used to lead this part of the celebration, calling her people from the Underland into the Gathering. Today, it's Tamzel, trotting over to the edge of the Gathering along with an elder faerie with curly black hair streaked with gray; que sweeps the hair out of quer face and shakes quer shoulders at Tamzel as a hush falls over all the faeries.

Tamzel stamps her hind legs four times and gives a loud whinny; at the same moment, the elder faerie twists the Energies to conjure orange and green sparks into the sky. In response to these calls, an enormous thunder arises as the centaurs storm up the tunnel and spill out of the Forest's edge into the Gathering. Lerian leads the charge of unranked centaurs behind the Council leaders, bursting into the Gathering with her eyes bright and her face nearly covered in delicately patterned silt from the Flowing. Her gaze finds mine as cheers arise and young ones from music learning pods strike up songs and weave intricate melodies into our bones.

I can't dance—Jax and Mom would never allow it—but I push Aon up and away from me as Mom and Mama extend their hands to pull him up into the celebration. In true Grovian fashion, there is no preamble to the movement; it just begins. All around me, other faeries that can't fly are joining hands with centaurs and with low-flying faeries, moving whatever parts of their bodies they can, if only their eyes, in tune with the rhythm of the bodies, of the songs. Usually, I dance with Jax. Usually, I dance with Lerian. This harvest, my heart sinks. Lerian's fingers are linked with other centaur nears, with E'rix.

My fingers feel empty.

I lean my head against the bars of the cage behind me as Grovians blaze patterns along with the songs rising up from all the edges of the Gathering. All around me, faeries and centaurs twirl and twist and sing. Even Aon is smiling reluctantly now as Mama moves ridiculously in front of him. They flow like one liquid creature around the cage the Controller placed in the center of us all.

My swiveling gaze finds the infirmary tent; Jax has thrust open the flap, and repositioned Blaze's cot so que can see out into the Gathering without moving much. Quer first Lunamez.

And quer last.

I blink hard, and my face feels wet.

As the dancing crescendos into a veritable mess of bodies, of young ones' yelps and growns' laughter, centaur calls rise. Lerian even dances her way toward me, her eyes hard but sparkling. Aon looks nervous, and I gesture for him to pull me to my feet. He grabs one hand, and Lerian lets a hand down to grab my other one. Aon and I both look up at her, bewildered, and she shrugs as she yanks me up.

"It's Lunamez." Her tone is softer than usual, even though she's shouting to be heard above the din. "And it's time to call them!"

I grin and nudge Aon. "Here goes," I tell him and his gaze shifts to the infirmary.

As the centaur calls rise higher and higher, all the faeries who can twist the Energies become still in response. Most of our eyes flutter closed, and Lerian flinches slightly as she prepares for so many of us to summon the Energies at once. The Hands tense, but it looks like they've been warned about this part of the celebrations, because they do nothing.

My own eyes finally drift closed as the message starts to build in the core of feeling underneath my belly, my insides glowing. I feel distinctly every Energy wave in my body, can trace the ways the other faeries are summoning an identical spell to mine, radiating out from our middles. I curl in on myself as I concentrate the melding of the Energies into the enchanted message we're all building to the dragons. I send up a silent prayer to Lunara that she'll keep them safe, that this Lunamez will be noteworthy for nothing more than being a great holiday.

It is, after all, the dragons' holiday as much as it is ours. Maybe even more so.

Like a frozen wave bursting out of its shell after a long and deep cold, warm and soothing magic shoots through my insides. My tightly muscled arms shudder a bit right before midday yellow and sunset orange waves of contorted Energies billow out of my fingertips. They ripple, along with those being sent up by the faeries around me, up into the cloudless sky and explode in fluorescent aquas and lavenders.

A hushed silence falls on the Gathering as even the youngest of the young ones simply watch the signal we've sent above us; or, more accurately, watch for the response to the signal we've sent.

And sure enough, within minutes, shouts rise up amongst those flying higher than others, those with the best sight.

"Hands!" comes Richard's clipped voice above the excited tumult. "Dragons approaching!" At his warning, nearly every Hand in the Gathering loads their bows and point them at the sky.

They are preparing for another massacre.

Chapter Seventeen

BUT BEFORE WE can all surge forward, Evelyn emerges from who-knows-where, and she's at Richard's side next to the cage, calling off his attack.

"And just what did you expect when I briefed you as to the nature of these celebrations? We trained for it. And we agreed to let the Grovians have their holiday unimpeded unless a greater threat was presented."

He does not let down his bow, and somehow, though she's talking softly, everyone in the Gathering is bristling, keenly aware of their conversation.

"With respect, ma'am, no one agreed, just you and that girl—"

"Iema outranks everyone here except you, and I outrank you tenfold, Richard. Now put down your weapon, or so help me—"

"What? You'll tell your *joiner* on us?"

My stomach lurches and Evelyn's eyes flash dangerously.

"I have no *joiner*," she says, deathly soft. "Disarm. Now. This is not a suggestion."

He hesitates for only one more moment and then releases the tension in his bow, slinging his arrow messily back into its quiver.

"Stand down!" Evelyn calls to the other Hands. "Let them come." Her other soldiers obey her reluctantly.

Just in time too.

Because the dragons are casting shadows directly above the Gathering now, flying in traditional Lunamez formation, with the youngest dragons, like Zaylam and Semad, ensconced in the middle of an undulating wave of elder and grown dragons, like Archa, Harlenikal, and Gimla. They sweep patterns around each other, their tails unfurling into the fins they become in the Flowing, as the lower half of the dragons move their bodies like dolphins, swimming through the air, while the upper half swoop like hawks, cutting through the air with powerful wings and deep harmonies to the melodies of the lower dragons. They sift between each other seamlessly, so that each dragon takes on each role. I try to track Zaylam with my eyes, but keep losing her relatively tiny body in the midst of all the others.

Lerian nudges me and jerks her head towards Aon. His eyes are narrow and hard, watching faeries and their dragons spinning in their hatchling greetings. Without warning, he wrenches his hand from mine, leaving Lerian's arms alone to support me. He flies up and away from the reverie, his arms locked tightly around his torso.

"Aon!" The effort of shouting after him makes my head throb.

"Let him go." Lerian sighs. "Of course he's gonna be jealous. Angry. He should be."

Aon slips into the infirmary tent with Blaze, and judging from his glowering expression, it looks like it's hit him that without Dreaming, he and Banion will never have their hatchling dragon.

He's not the only one in our family who aren't exactly thrilled to see the dragons. Even as Mom speeds toward her hatchling dragon, Gimla, and even as Zaylam sings down to me, I reach out for Mama's hand, trying to catch her downcast eyes with mine. Her hatchling dragon, Xamamlee, was killed in the first massacre. Mama doesn't look at me, and I swipe my thumb across the back of her hand. She squeezes slightly.

Then a single, solemn deer call erupts from the southwest edge of the Gathering. The dancing, the singing, and the hatchling greetings all fade to a stop. The dragons, of course, are the last to quiet their songs, gradually tapering out into low hums in the bases of their throats.

When the last of their humming finally peters out, I open my eyes—I didn't realize I'd closed them—and find Lerian's hand still in mine, and Mama's. They both help me move as everyone in the Gathering flutters, trots, slithers, crawls, and wheels into formation. We never coordinate this part of our Lunamez celebration, but even the Forest creatures come out for it, and it always seems to come together. Sure enough, Osley leaps up to rub against my ankle. Together.

The threading.

When we account for all we've grown and lost since the last Lunamez celebration.

Zaylam and the other dragons fly so high above the Gathering that I wonder if the nons can distinguish who is who. An assortment of other winged creatures are swarming out of the Forest, so many that the

Hands again try to raise their bows before the Controller gestures for them to stay their shots. The air is thick with the rustling of wings of all stripes: leathery, feathery, thin and translucent, wide and narrow and everything in between. We faeries wait for the Forest birds to settle into endless formations between the dragons and the treetops surrounding the Gathering—then we follow. Mom has cajoled Aon out of the infirmary, and Lerian gives Mom my hand so she and Mama can help fly me up with the others. Below, groundlings like Lerian and Osley shuffle into their own positions on the Gathering grounds. I don't have to look down to know that Os will arrange querself below me, but I do check to see where Lerian is. She's below me too, giving me an irritated look that says, *"Whatever, it's Lunamez. You're still a traitor."*

My heart rises and sinks at the same time.

An anticipatory humming fills the air. I look up at a winged friend of mine, Zaem, who sometimes plays lookout for me on my spy missions. Her little wings are keeping her steady near my right wingtip. She offers a chirp, and I raise the side of my mouth at her. We wait.

It's too dangerous for the dragons to extend the thin, ropelike, sunup colored threads of Energies directly into the Plains, as they would in Lunamezes past. Now, the nons would surely try to trace the connections to locate their hidden home, to dismantle the Barrier. So they send their threads, emanating from the tips of their wings and their furry underbellies, down to the canopies of local Forest trees, who extend them back through their roots across the entire Forest and Underland, through into the Plains.

Already, there are gaps in the Energies that the threading bends, trees we've been forced to chop down since last Lunamez, those who have evacuated their souls from their bodies preemptively, to avoid the torture of the axe. We wait for the threads to pass through us.

Undulating soundlessly through the air, an Energy thread that tastes like Zaylam's songs swims into my chest. I welcome it. I'm both warm and freezing in my core where it joins me, as it makes its way through my wings before spreading out of the tips into those I love best. More pass through me and more are spread. I keenly feel Mama and Aon connecting to my threads, and the sharp, bitter taste of my current connection with Lerian. Osley's thread slips up through my left foot and I grin.

The entire air above the Gathering is crisscrossed with golds and reds and fire oranges as threads made of woven ropes of the Energies pass through more and more of us, in more and more combinations. When mine connects with P'Tal, I almost fall out of the sky from the depth of his sadness. Mom and Mama increase their grip on me. When I connect with Blaze, it feels almost too weak to notice, too faint to exist. Que is fading. I push more effort into my thread with quer.

We all hold each other through the connections. The threading part of Lunamez makes physical the connections we've forged with each other since last Lunamez, and I'm reminded uncomfortably of that now as E'rix extends an orange thread my way. It reminds us—makes sure we don't forget—those lost by anger, by death, by betrayal. Because those we hate send threads through us too; my tug on Tacon is pretty strong and tastes like decay. But it also tastes like sorrow; I wonder if he's sending that to me.

Because that's the other thing the threading does. It allows us to communicate feelings unspoken, connections otherwise forgotten, otherwise sidelined, otherwise dismissed as uncomplicated.

All of us are bathed in the glow of the threads we've made; they extend way out into the rest of the Grove and into the Flowing, I know, but I'm not flying high enough to see them dip into the waves. I know Zaylam is, and I am eager for her to tell me what it looks like. I glance over at Kashat, hovering near the nestling; his eyes are fixed on the breakages in the threads, the places where death has left them with no soul to latch on to. His face is made of steel. I tug on the thread I have running through his chest, and he looks at me and winks. I grimace and wonder why he's so nervous about the Accounting.

When the dragons sing again, we let go of the threads. They become thinner and thinner, dimmer and dimmer, until they are restored to the usual translucence of the Energies. The threading doesn't create things that weren't already there; it just makes visible things we tend to forget in our daily lives.

As most of the birds and insects, and all manner of groundlings, flit and scamper back to their goings on. They usually don't share our traditions, but the threading draws them in because we are all, after all, creatures of Lunav. Watching them scatter, Mom and Mama fly with Aon and me, back to the infirmary, where I can lie with Blaze and get a good, head-safe view of the nestling.

Centaurs and faeries across the Gathering settle in for Kashat and the others' accounting performance. The dragons have slipped back to the Plains under the cover of the swarms of creatures returning to the Forest and Underland.

Jax puts a gentle hand behind my head as my growns lay me down on my cot, positioning me so that I, like Blaze—who seems to be awake now, but barely—can look out in the Gathering and have a good view of the nestling. We can't actually see the performers from our spots; the bucket-like edges just allow us to see what they want us to. As the anticipatory hush rises across the Gathering, I get a glimpse of Kashat's wings, fluttering their tips up above the nestling as he helps the younger faeries and centaurs manage their magic and puppets. I settle back and feel Mom's hand running through my hair. Blaze coughs and Aon sniffs.

Kashat's voice, booming with the help of whatever spell he's twisted the Energies into, makes me jump slightly.

The accounting has begun.

"The beginnings of Lunav," he proclaims. A large puppet of a Lunavad tree rises from the nestling—I can't tell which centaur is controlling the puppet, but I don't have time to think about it because one of the faeries then conjures up a misty, green map of Lunav's connected lands, above and around the tree puppet. More whispy images overlay the map and interact with the puppets the centaurs are operating, weaving the origin story the Accounting always gives. Kashat's voice settles in over the tale they're painting in the air.

"It is said that on the eve of the birth of Lunav, a single tree—a Dragon Spawn sapling, a sapling of who we today call Lunavad trees—burst forth from the first tear of rain, emerging so excitedly that the tree's roots split the ground of Lunav into the many regions that now make up our cracked land." A roar like thunder booms from the nestling as the misted map of Lunav is ripped asunder, one round landmass breaking out into a few smaller ones.

"This tree towered over all of Lunav, so high that the vast expanse of its flattened canopy covered all of the land in dark, impenetrable shadow, covering the entire land, even beyond the edges of Lunav itself." A deep gloom settles over the entire Gathering, and I meet Jax's eye and grin. Kashat's outdoing himself.

"The tree, known by the name of our land itself—Lunav, Lunav, Lunav—absorbed all the sun and rain que needed, but the land remained parched and lifeless underneath quer." A new narrator, an elder whose voice I vaguely recognize but can't place, carries on the story.

"Lunav wanted companionship, for the richness of many lives, but knew the permanently sheltered land could not bear more life. From quer spindly, tactile leaves, que wove and breathed life into a single, giant spider—Lunara—and explained to her quer idea."

From the leaves of the vast tree puppet itself weaves a smoky figure, jet-black with orange tips on each of her eight spindly legs. Her eight unblinking eyes glisten through the shadows the performers have created. She flexes her sharply bent, tall legs experimentally like she's a real being just emerged from the depths of pre-life. As vast as Lunav's circular canopy, their puppet version of Lunara looks uncannily alive. A small swarm of flies and bees who've stayed for the performance fly backward, away from the nestling. Blaze raises a shaky hand toward the outside, inviting the flies and bees to play.

"Born knowing of webs and of weaving, Lunara contemplated Lunav's request. As Lunav asked, Lunara took the tree's soul into her own body. The first soul keeper." Aon and Blaze exchange an excited look at that, and for a moment, it's like que's not sick at all. Like que's not dying.

I remember pleading for my growns to call a soul keeper after Idrisim died. I wonder if Aon will do the same when Blaze's rattled breath stops. It won't be long now.

Jax catches me staring at the two of them and shakes his head slightly at me. Mom's rhythmic fingers continue massaging my head. I swivel my gaze back to the performance.

"The spider glowed"—sure enough, an intense golden glow emanates from the nestling—"with the essence of two lives inside her, her own and the tree's, as she unwound the intricate connections of what had been Lunav's body into millions and millions of life-giving tendrils." The tree puppet is being unspun, like unweaving a length of rope, splitting into smaller threads as the elder speaks. I think about Jorbam's trunk being unwoven like that and shudder.

"These tendrils, Lunara scattered about the various lands of Lunav, and made sure to sow the tree's tender leaves and strong trunk branches into the trenches that are now rivers across the lands. A strong wind blew—" And, right on cue, a mighty gust rushes through the Gathering, ticking my face with the scent of the grasses beneath us—"and most of the leaves were carried to the northwest, where today lies the impenetrable wall of soft, lush greenery that borders all of Lunav's limits." The Borderland's unapproachable moss of forestry whisps into being on the map of Lunav above the nestling. "Blown herself by this wind, Lunara overbalanced, letting the biggest, strongest threat of Lunav's trunk fall to the south, cracking open several lands, expanding the trenches that have become today's ocean—the Flowing—and all its provinces." Salty water rains down on the Gathering in a soft mist as the wispy map of Lunav splits according to the narration. Murmurs and shouts of approval flutter through the Gathering. I glance at the Controller, and she looks equal parts bewildered and absorbed. I grin in spite of myself.

Kashat picks up the tale. "The tree no longer standing, but scattered in pieces across the land, Lunav the tree had given life to Lunav the land. The rivers and oceans began to fill. Lunara laughed heartily as the earth below warmed and seemed to glow with pleasure, anticipating what would happen next. Lunara, the first soul keeper, tenderly breathed out, the luminescence that was Lunav's soul inside her leaving her body." The enchanted spider figure flexes her jointed, arched legs as Lunara's earth-colored soul undulates out of her pincers, mixed intimately with the golden tendrils of her soul keeping magic.

"Lunav's soul spread across Lunav's land, touching every piece of quer body that Lunara had unspun. At each touch, new life arose; from the smallest insects to the largest dragons, and groundlings of all kinds, life sparkled across Lunav, from Lunav. Lunara watched Lunav's soul giving life to all on, above, and below ground. The world as we know it had begun."

The chiming of faerie wings gently meeting another person's wings starts ringing out immediately, along with centauric whinnies and whoops, signaling our appreciation of the Accounting, of the work and artistry put in by those in this harvest's Lunamez learning pod. But the noises simmer down when the realization sweeps across the Gathering that the performers are not finished. Mom's hand stills on my head, and her body tenses. Mama's head lifts from P'Tal's shoulder, and Aora rises from Zeel's lap. Blaze and Aon exchange a look, and Jax wheels all the way to the edge of the platform to see outside better. A confused buzz rises up throughout the entire Gathering, but quickly subdues as it becomes clear that Kashat isn't done speaking, the enchanted, wispy images still forming above the nestling basket.

My eyes seek out Evelyn in the crowd below us and her lips are open slightly as her eyes take in the confusion around her. Her body, though, remains calm, remains dignified, like nothing can ruffle her, like nothing surprises her.

"And so it was that the trees made their first sacrifice to animal forms, and so it was that began the dominance of animal creatures. So it was that we began the legacy of the terrors we inflict today, and so it is that we still reenact Lunara's birth. But so it must be that we do not celebrate her birth to reinforce our dominance, but to recognize our origins as treely peoples, as planted-based peoples." There's a stirring across the Gathering from the Hands, from Tacon and his King's Registry cronies. Mom's fingers have migrated from my head to my shoulder, and she squeezes. The Controller lifts two fingers gently by her side, but it's enough. Richard looks furious, but he does not raise his weapon. If Kashat notices the Hands gripping their weapons tightly from his place in the nestling, his voice remains steady, and he doesn't let on.

"So we pray today, on this day of days, that we will not be uncritical of the places we come from."

A young one's voice rises to replace Kashat's, speaking in Underlandic centaur. "Lunav asked Lunara to sacrifice quer for the good of the land, but today we ask—should Lunara have acquiesced? Yes, Lunav's soul is now within us all, but what is the cost of our lives? To be born of deadly sacrifice, even willingly made—was it willingly?—is to be borne of blood."

"Blood." It's Kashat's voice again, but he, too, uses the centauric tongue. The map of Lunav fades and is replaced by flashing smoky images, wisps of color and chaotic patterns, forming images of Dreams, of Slicings, of the palace's injustices. Of a beautiful young non woman in soft blue riding gear bonding with a young spotted horse. Of that non dying of the plague.

Of the massacres. Of Lerian getting shot. Of Leece and Mara being dragged away. Of Rada.

Gasps jump through the Gathering and I tear my eyes away from Kashat and the others' display to watch Evelyn. Something hard has settled into her eyes and she, now, is gripping her bow, her arm extended back toward her quiver. Her chin is raised, her healed hand steady. Iema is at her side, whispering urgently in her ear.

Kashat does not stop. He and the others weave intricate portraits of our souls through the sky. As he weaves, people—not in the Lunamez learning pod, just people, faeries and centaurs from the crowd, begin shouting out.

"How are we supposed to live without our hatchling dragons?"

"Or hatchling trees?"

"The young ones don't know what it's like to connect to the rest of Lunavic life anymore– "

"They don't understand why we don't eat flesh, they don't want grown food anymore!"

"And they're not thinking of labor as murder!"

"Murder!"

"Settle down, Grovians," a Hand interjects.

"And what about the dragons? They'll be extinct if we can't Dream any more hatchlings!"

"That's enough, you've had enough warning!" Richard is clearly losing patience, but Evelyn has yet to give any attack signals.

The whisp images continue as Kashat's voice cuts back into the chaos. "We are treely peoples, and we are being killed. Like Lunav before us. Consider this, people of the Grove, when you next take up your axes and scythes for labor. But if Lunav, the tree, could find a reason to celebrate—could find a reason for quer soul to glow that golden glow just as que was about to die—we, too, must celebrate, this day. Celebrate, because Lunav's soul contains that kind of strength. Lunav's soul contains that kind of power. And so do we all. Good season, good Lunamez."

Kashat ends the accounting just as Evelyn is loading her bow, looking both reluctant and steady. Iema keeps whispering. The wisps, the images, fade, and all that remains is the descending nestling, the mutterings and gasps of the faeries and the centaurs, the eager buzzing of the surrounding insects.

As slowly as she raised it, Evelyn lowers her bow. Some of her men start toward the nestling, and she holds up a hand to stop them, her head still tilted toward Iema's lips.

"Good season, good Lunamez." The murmur starts with those standing near Tamzel, and spreads through the Gathering, through the lips of all the faeries and centaurs. Through my own lips, through Aon's, even Blaze's, though softly and bloodily. Whinnies and sparks and faerie wing chiming spread throughout the Gathering as the shocked crowd recovers itself. The sounds build and build, until the cheers and the chiming far outweigh the disgruntled complaints of Tacon, the angry arguments of Richard. Evelyn looks like she issues a short series of orders and slips away from the center of the Gathering, out of my range of vision.

Mom and Mama squeeze my shoulders as they hover up and out of the infirmary tent. "Your friend sure has some courage," Mom says mildly.

"Mmmm."

"Is it time for Lunamez stew?" Blaze coughs softly, quer voice choked with the chunks of blood lining quer throat.

Her growns laugh until tears leak out of their eyes.

"Yes, sherba, Hazal and I are going to bring back enough for everyone," Mom tells quer in Underlandic centaur.

"Even Aon?" que asks. I grin and Aon nudges quer gently, like Lerian does—used to do—to me.

"Yes, even enough for Aon's fifteen stomachs," Mama assures quer. Jax grimaces a smile as they fly out into the throngs of Grovians waiting to be served Lunamez stew from the various bubbling pots that the Growers have conjured around the edges of the Gathering.

Shouts of good seasons and whispers of Kashat's bold performance drift up to the platform on the breeze of the growing evening, the growing celebration.

Chapter Eighteen

I CLOSE MY eyes and before I know it, it's the dead of night. Though the sounds of Lunamez merriment still ring in the distance, Aon is curled up sleeping at the foot of Blaze's cot. Mama has her arms around him; the scarf she's wrapped around her hair lopsided from the way his wings keep fluttering against her as he shifts restlessly.

There's a soft rustling at the entrance to the infirmary platform. I blink rapidly and squint at the spot. My pulse drops. It's the Controller.

Aon doesn't stir as Evelyn enters, and for a moment I envy him his obliviousness, because now my body is completely awake.

Mom rises defensively and Jax stiffens. The Controller holds her hands up, palms facing them, as she approaches Blaze's cot wordlessly. The young one's eyes open with difficulty as que stares up at Evelyn, quer bloodstained face glistening in the flickering light of the infirmary lanterns.

Evelyn stands, looking down at quer for a moment, and all eyes are on her, but nobody, not even Blaze's growns, move. Aon rolls over in his sleep and Mama, in hers, grasps him tighter. Mom adjusts Mama's scarf absentmindedly so it doesn't slip off completely, but her eyes are glued to the Controller's face.

In the silence in which only Blaze's pained, rattled breath can be heard, Evelyn reaches deep into the pocket of her light cloak and pulls out a small, carved box with a fae glass circle on top. I squint and shift to sit up on my elbows to see better. Evelyn's gaze shifts in my direction at my movement, but she doesn't actually look at me; she's back to looking at Blaze before I can even be sure she's registered my presence.

Blaze tries to move forward too, but Aora's fingertips on quer blood-crusted flank stills quer. Evelyn leans down to Blaze's level, like she did the day que and Aon careened into her stomach by the steam pools, holding the box out in front of her so Blaze can see better. Jax leans over to turn up the flame of the lanterns a little, and after blinking in the newly adjusted light, I let out a small gasp at the same time as Blaze does. It sets quer off into a coughing fit, but once the blood is wiped away, everyone awake in the infirmary takes in the beauty of the box Evelyn's brought out.

It's a delicate little thing, a little bigger than my fist. Laced with gold and Flowing themed, the box is carved with waves on its side, complete with dolphins and mers swimming intricate patterns around each other fluidly in the fae glass globe that tops the box elegantly. The Controller smiles softly as Blaze tries to reach out for it. She pulls it back slightly and shakes her head.

"That's not all," she whispers, and reaches her thumb and first finger under the box, twisting something that must be sticking out from the bottom. The sound of metal winding into itself clicks through the infirmary, and, the moment Evelyn pulls her hand away, an ethereal serenade floods into our ears. I can't make out the words—I think it's Izlanian—and my heart flutters when I realize that the song is as layered, if not more so, than the most complex of dragon songs.

"It's a music box from my home," Evelyn tells an enraptured Blaze. Even though quer whole left ear and some of quer right ear are covered in pus-filled blisters, the rich tones are clearly reaching quer.

When que smiles, a small stream of blood trickles down quer cracked lips; but que reaches, again, for the box anyway. This time, Evelyn presses it gently into quer hands, and then, softly, tenderly even, wipes away the blood that is now leaking down Blaze's chin. I wonder what happened to the ruthless woman who's worn the Controller's uniform so well since she got here.

The growns in the infirmary take a collective breath of shock, and I lick my lips, forgetting how to breathe for a moment. Mom shakes Mama's shoulder a little, and Mama opens her eyes immediately and processes the scene in front of her. She swallows and cranes her neck up without moving Aon to exchange an incredulous look with Mom. They both look at me, then, and I close my mouth and try to focus, not on Evelyn, but on Blaze.

For quer part, Blaze's now puffy, stiff fingers struggle to re-wind the music box as its song peters out into silence. Que squirms angrily when quer fingers can't make it, but Evelyn just smiles that soft smile again, the one that I'm starting to associate with her looking at young ones. She asks with her eyes if she can take the music box back, and Blaze lets her with a frustrated huff. "Would you like me to enchant it so that it keeps playing?" she asks in Blaze's home language.

The frustration on Blaze's face dissolves somewhat, and que assents. Evelyn makes a big show of letting Blaze see all the golden bands of light that flow from her elegant brown fingertips to the music box. Something clicks inside of it, and we all know it will play until...

Until someone can no longer bear it, because Blaze will be gone.

Evelyn's curls cover part of her face as she bends over Blaze to give quer back the music box, to make sure it's positioned right so Blaze can hold it without too much trouble.

"Enjoy it, sherba," she whispers into the harmonizing box, and straightens up slowly, all but forgotten by the fascinated young one. P'Tal leans over to help quer shift the box around so que can see it, see the globe with the swimming mers and dolphins, from all angles. He glances up at the Controller.

"Why?" he asks simply.

There's a long pause, but somehow we all seem content to soak in the Izlanian melodies while we wait for Evelyn to compose an answer.

"Because Blaze is a young one, and I know quer Initiation was successful. This is not any of your faults, and it is certainly not quer's." Another pause. Jax stares at her quizzically. She sighs slightly.

"You want me to explain the things you don't like, you want me to explain the things you do. Is there anything I can do in your presence that you won't demand an explanation for?"

There's a hesitation before a soft bark of laughter chokes its way out of my lips. Jax is next, then my growns, and, finally, P'Tal's. Blaze querself is oblivious to all but the music box, but the laughter, finally, wakes Aon. He blinks both sets of eyelids in turn, rapidly, stretching and almost punching Mama in the face.

"What's funny? What—" He splutters when he notices the Controller and shrinks back into Mama.

Evelyn grows somber at his response, and turns her eyes to Jax. "How is que?"

Jax just shakes his head. Evelyn nods, pursing her lips hard.

"Shall I send for Artem?"

"The man who Sliced quer? I don't think—"

"You know he's been unsuccessful finding a cure, but perhaps he can help now with pain reduction," Evelyn whispers as though she didn't hear Aora's outburst.

"He might have some medicines we don't have access to, Aora," Mom whispers, fluttering over to her, hand slipping onto the spot on her back where her earthy brown flank meets her skin.

"You want us to trust him? Now?" she asks Mom, staring around at P'Tal and Zeel, and finally, at me.

I just stare at the music box that Aon and Blaze are examining together. Aora falls silent and nods curtly. I mirror the nod at Evelyn, and flutter my fingers outward at her. A Grovian faeric thank you.

Evelyn nods and waves her own wrist out toward me, our way of saying there is no need for thanks. Her dress rustles as she gingerly drops off of the low-flying platform and walks away quickly.

We wait together in silence, broken only by the soothing sounds flooding out of the music box.

Broken only by Blaze's breathing, growing more rattled by the minute.

P'Tal has streaks of his young one's blood on his face, from where he hastily wiped a tear from his eye after holding quer hand.

Jax starts to boil pine leaves. He's putting more and more into a large, metal bowl, methodically, sullenly.

He does this when hope is lost. The scent comforts him, and, often, those who are sick. Dying.

But I doubt Blaze can smell it. At this point, Aon has to hold the music box almost right up to quer ear for quer to hear anything. His eyes are wild, but won't leave quer face.

So maybe the pine leaves boiling are just really for quer growns. For Aon.

No one looks up except me when the head Slicer walks back in with Evelyn. It's clear she woke him; it's clear she made him sprint back with her. Her hands rest on her thighs, her mouth open slightly, her gaze penetrating the small crowd around Blaze, seeking only the young one's face.

For my part, I shuffle off my cot and huddle myself into the corner of the infirmary, on the floor of the platform. Artem follows me with his eyes, and he stares for a moment or two at my wings as he, too, catches his breath. He takes something out of his carrying case, which looks similar to what I sabotaged in the Lethean Inn.

It feels like a lifetime ago, when Blaze was more an idea than a person, when P'Tal was worried the Slicing would kill quer.

I keep Artem's gaze evenly until it makes my head swim, but I don't blink. I don't look away. He retreats first, bending over Jax, whispering something to him as he passes him a vial and jerks his head in my direction. Jax nods wordlessly, absently. He pockets the vial and keeps stirring his boiling pine leaves. Mom takes the vial out of his pocket and puts it neatly in place on her own workspace. He doesn't seem to notice.

The Head Slicer now mutters something to Evelyn, and she nods her assent. He looks over Blaze as Aora shifts over for him skeptically.

"Que won't feel the pain of passing quite as much if we can get quer to drink this," he tells quer growns, who glare at him for vocalizing the inevitable, the about-to-happen.

But Zeel grabs the green vial from his open hand and turns, more gently, to Blaze. "Sherba, hey, you've got to swallow this now, just a little bit."

Que turns quer head, and blood leaks out of quer ears. I shift deeper into my corner and Aon's own lip starts to bleed from biting it so hard. P'Tal's body starts to wrack with barely contained tears and Zeel is clenching quer fist behind quer back so hard it's making the veins in quer corded forearms all stand out.

"What is it?" Blaze croaks, and the words are so garbled I can barely make them out.

There's a long pause. Jax wheels forward into Blaze's range of vision. "Something to help you hear the music better, sherba." His voice cracks. "You'll hear the music better."

Blaze stares at him solemnly, clear droplets now dripping alongside the red ones out of quer eyes.

"Will it hurt?"

Evelyn chokes down a sob and turns away. Artem looks down.

Mama takes P'Tal by the shoulders as Mom slips hers under Aon's wing sprouts.

"Not even a little bit, Blaze," Aon answers in a voice that's not quite his own. Que grimaces up at him and each of quer parents reach to wipe the blood away from quer lips. Evelyn's eyes are squeezed shut and her lips are pursed so hard it's a wonder she's not bleeding too. She wraps her arms around herself, but shrugs away from Artem's offered touch.

I think about getting up and approaching her, but my body decides it likes the corner I've made my own.

Zeel helps guide the vial into Blaze's lips, and P'Tal holds quer hand while Aora helps quer move quer head back to swallow.

Que smiles blearily as the liquid goes down.

"It does sound stronger," que rattles.

We wait. There is nothing else to do.

Blaze knows. "I'm scared."

We wait. There is nothing else to do.

We try to let the Izlanian melodies sweep us away.

Jax keeps boiling more and more pine leaves.

As the moon rises even higher into the night, the infuriatingly joyful Lunamez calls now mercifully diminishing, Artem slips out of the infirmary, knowing he's done all he can with that vial. He motions to Jax, then to Mom's workspace, then to me, before he steps off the platform. Jax nods without making eye contact. Whatever medicine Artem gave him to give to me, it can wait.

Everything can wait, because there is nothing else that matters.

The Controller remains when the Head Slicer leaves, stock-still. She stands away from the family. I stay in my corner, my knees drawn up to my chest, my wings wilted, my elbows dangling my forearms off my legs.

My fists, like the one Zeel still holds behind quer back, are clenched.

Small moans are coming from Blaze's little mouth, now, and Mom's knuckles are purple as she holds my brother up by his waist, his wings crumpled, wilted. I think about flying over there, being with him.

My body won't move.

It doesn't matter anyway.

My eyes sting, but they're dry. At least I think they are. I can't quite tell. Jax's and Evelyn's aren't. Evelyn's long nails are digging into her skin as her arms wrap even tighter around herself, like's she's trying to hold her body in one piece. She's been like that for I don't know how long, and must be bleeding by now. But there's blood on all of us at this point.

Blaze's blood.

I do not wonder why she's here. Why she cares. I don't have the energy.

I can't look at P'Tal, Aora, or Zeel. I can't look at Aon, or my growns. I can't move any part of my body. Not even my eyes. They leave Evelyn's nails, her skin, and drop to a spot on the platform ground between us. They stay there. Imagining them moving is...unimaginable. Why does it matter if I move my eyes? If I do anything but sit here? Ever?

My eyes are too heavy to look up. My head is pounding and I can't bring myself to care. Nothing matters. Because the wracked sobs and the choked out goodbyes that are filling my ears…there will never be another noise. I think vaguely of Zaylam, and wonder how she can possibly be anywhere but here. I wonder how anyone can possibly be doing anything else, thinking about anything else. A breeze rustles the infirmary tent, and I want to scream at it. Punch it. How dare it. How dare anything, anyone, do anything but mourn this young one. Que is younger than me, younger than Aon. And que's dying.

So I don't understand why the world still exists.

It happens only a little while later. There are no profound last words. No lingering comfort. Just a last gasp. It sounds more like surprise than it does like pain. Then, the most horrible sounds I've ever heard, pouring out of the throats of Blaze's growns, of my little brother. All the screams they'd kept inside while Blaze was here, while quer soul was in quer body.

Aon is sobbing something, some words, something about being sorry he can't be a soul keeper, quer soul keeper. But even soul keepers couldn't stop the plague.

Doesn't he know it's useless? P'Tal, Zeel, and Aora cling to each other, to Mama, so hard I don't know how they're not breaking each other's bones. Zeel starts screaming, clutching at quer chiseled stomach, beating into it with quer fists. P'Tal grabs at them, holding them steady, but he's wailing too. Aora turns and wretches.

I force my eyes up to where Evelyn's been standing. She's gone. My burning eyes find Jax, now, as my numb ears register Evelyn's music box playing Blaze's life away.

Jax does not wheel over to the growns, does not acknowledge the agony around him. I know he knows that soon, he will have to set Blaze's body on fire to stop the spread of the plague. He will have to rip P'Tal away from quer body, as P'Tal once had to rip him away from Idrisim's. And I know he cannot face it yet. He's crushing pine needles with his bare hands, not even bothering to pull out the splinters that are surely sticking right into his flesh. Hard. Clear droplets, falling off his face, sizzle when they hit the boiling water he's putting the pine needles into.

I force myself to breathe deeply, through my mouth. It helps a little. But not much. Nothing will. Not ever.

Aon weeps and wails with his head on Blaze's cot. He shifts, eventually—shuffles on his knees to put his head in Mom's lap—and he stays like that, his limp wings, his limp body, dead looking when they aren't wracking violently with sobs.

I do not move toward him. I can't.

I haven't flown without assistance for many sunups. Too many. I drag myself up, drag my heavy body to Mom's workspace. Jax does not stop me. Neither does Mom or Mama, when they catch my deadened eyes with their wet ones. I uncap the vial Artem told Jax was meant for me and chug it down. Almost instantly, my head clears.

Damn the Highlanders and the medicines they keep from us.

I wipe my mouth so roughly with the back of my hand that it feels like I've smacked myself. It feels good.

I take one last look at Blaze, knowing that quer body will be ashes by the time I return. No sign of the young one whose Slicing I tried to sabotage remains; no trace of my little brother's best friend, who galloped with him when he needed someone most, when he needed someone who didn't care that his sister looked like a traitor. No trace except for the grief que's left in quer wake.

I leave the tent, limp out to the edge of the low-hovering platform, and launch myself into the humid night sky, where sporadic shouts of good Lunamez make me want to light the entire Forest on fire.

Chapter Nineteen

SUNUP MOCKS ME. A whole cacophony of birds greeting the sky. I open my eyes a crack and peer through the leaves of a sympathetic tree who'd let me collapse in his branches before I fell asleep. The sky is burnt orange and cloudless, and the air is crisp. On another day, it might be beautiful. It's not. I don't care. Why would anyone care?

Blaze will never see another sunup.

Guilt stabs at my gut—I am alive, again—and I twitch, hard, almost rolling myself off of the branch I'm on. Instinct catches me, not conscious effort. I let my arms fall off the branch carelessly and my fingertips skim the layer of leaves beneath me.

A soft, persistent thumping from below invades my consciousness. I drag my head down, let it hang loose. Osley's beady eyes are staring up into mine.

"Quer service is soon. Your moms sent me to bring you."

Que doesn't ask how I am, and I'm grateful.

I can't move. But how dare I mope for the death of a centaur young one when every day I help kill so many people at labor? And I bet P'Tal and the others aren't just lying there, useless.

I lean over the other side of the branch, away from Osley, and throw up violently.

I hear quer scamper away as I finish. I don't even wipe my mouth. I just continue to lie there, arms and legs dangling like dead weights.

Dead. Like Blaze. Like all of us, one day. I think of Evelyn, of Lerian, and my body twitches again of its own accord.

"Hey, What's Your Name."

This time, my body doesn't react at all. Not even to Tacon's grating voice. I don't wonder what he's doing here, but it dimly makes sense why Osley leapt off only after I was done throwing up. My body doesn't panic like it usually does when he approaches. I don't feel anything. Not even curiosity about why Tacon is flying up to my eye level right now. Not even humiliation that he probably just saw me vomit.

I stare at him. I wait. He stares back. There's something different than usual about his face. He's even paler than he normally is. Like he hasn't slept. Like he might be having feelings other than hatred.

"You'll be late for the service," he singsongs, and I wonder vaguely as his silver wings flutter when the last time was that I saw him actually fly this high.

I exhale. Loudly. He gets my meaning. *"What do you want, Tacon?"*

He gestures like he's creating lethal magic toward the nearest cluster of birds and nods toward me. Despite myself, I raise an eyebrow. He usually rejects our nonverbal languages, like the nons do. But, out of practice though he may be, he's being quite clear. The birds still have celebratory Lunamez songs rolling out of their beaks. *"I just want to kill all those birds for singing about a good season this sunup, don't you?"*

I stare at him wearily and hope he understands. *"Because there's not enough death already?"*

He goes on like he didn't get what I said, but I know he did. And the infuriating thing is, that despite what I said, I agree with him. He knows. *"And the sun. For shining. Life has such gall, doesn't it, to go on after a young one dies?"*

I furrow my brow at him. He scoffs.

"I'm not heartless, What's Your Name. I know you think I am. But I'm not. And Blaze was a good young one." A long pause, and I wonder if his eyes were always that blue or if I've just never noticed. "The service will do you good, What's Your Name. And then labor. Lying around all day won't help it go away."

"I hate labor," I mutter thickly, out loud. "I'm not a killer, like you."

I regret it the moment it comes out of my mouth. Of all the emotions I've ever seen on Tacon's face, sheer pain has never been one of them. Until now. He pauses. "I know what you think. Poor martyred Idrisim and sainted Jax. And you, parading around like you're better than everyone else because even though you look *human*, you hate them. You don't know—your sanctimonious people don't talk about it—" He looks like he's searching for words, his thin face contorting, scrunching up around his nose. He gives up. "You don't know."

I sit up now, still feeling heavy and my head spinning a bit. But I'm finally disturbed enough to be curious.

"What don't I know, Tacon?"

We have another staring contest, and I get the distinct feeling he's measuring me up for something. Apparently, I don't have whatever he's looking for, because his face goes blank again, and he says, "Go to the service. Go to labor. It'll feel better than lying around alone all day."

He flies off without another word.

I expect Osley to emerge from wherever que hopped off to as soon as he leaves, but que doesn't. I shrug and keep hanging off the branch. The tree rumbles to me that maybe I should go, that I might regret it if I don't. I ignore him.

I ignore everyone.

I don't go to the service. The buzz around me is that it was beautiful. I don't understand what could be beautiful about the eight people closest to Blaze rising into the air with quer burning body to help quer soul reintegrate with the Energies.

I don't understand what could be beautiful about that at all.

I close my eyes.

Somehow, the next thing I know is that we're lying together in the Plains, aimlessly, on the parched ground under his hatchling tree, Banion.

No one tries to stop us, either.

Eventually, Zaylam swoops over and curls herself around us, Banion rumbles with his roots under us, and Gimla flies low every so often to check on us. Even Harlenikal seems concerned.

The sun comes up and back down, and no one pushes me into going to labor or Aon into his learning pod. Somehow, Mama gets permission to leave her labor at some point each day to make sure we eat, that she and Mom take turns holding us to them each night. They keep exchanging worried looks over our heads. Aon keeps grinding his teeth and muttering Blaze's name. Zaylam flies low constantly, singing to us and soothing us with her wing wind. Jorbam and Banion are rumbling to each other about us, but they take care to not let us decipher what, exactly, they're saying.

Looking at Aon's broken eyes, no spark in them at all, rebreaks me every time I look at him.

Whenever the sun is high, soon after Mama makes us eat grown food—never as good as Rada's—soon after she leaves, Osley cuddles into my side and doesn't move until sundown. In the beginning, que doesn't say anything except to Zaylam.

After this ritual has gone by a few sunups and Aon and I are still inert, que starts thumping incessant information to me. Que tells me that the Controller is nowhere to be seen; after the ceremony of the dead—the ceremony of Blaze—she retreated into her dwelling and hasn't emerged since. Que tells me that for the last few sunups, que's seen Iema slipping in and out of the Controller's dwelling, coming in with food and coming out with still full plates, and with orders for the Hands. Unpleasant heat pools in my stomach, and I grunt and roll over, away from quer.

"Just trying to pique your interest, Sadie," que thumps out apologetically, but also a little affronted, a little frustrated. I grunt again and Aon shifts so his head is on my ribcage. I run my fingers through his thick hair the way Mom ran her fingers through mine, just a few sunups ago, when Blaze was alive. When the world wasn't over.

I'm not sure how exactly many times the sun rises and falls, but then there are strong arms around Aon, pulling him from me.

He struggles and then he realizes who it is. I gasp and scramble to sit up on my elbows. P'Tal is cradling Aon in his arms like he's still a pre-choosing young one.

"Your mother tells me you haven't been flying, sherba, or going to your learning pod," he says mildly, his voice low and thick.

I glance over P'Tal's shoulder and see Aora and Zeel standing at the edge of the Plains, with downcast eyes and arms looped over each other's flanks.

"I'm sorry, P'Tal. You..." Aon glances back at me, and I mouth the unfamiliar words to him. He nods and looks back up at P'Tal, repeating them shakily. "May you feel your lost one in the Energies, so that que may be found." A traditional Underlander offering of consolation. I swallow the lump in my throat, grateful that Aon's never had to use it before.

P'Tal smiles softly, tears shining in his eyes. He loops his hands under Aon's wing sprouts, so he can support his entire weight. He presses my little brother to his bare chest, and Aon starts to shake. And shake, and shake, and shake. P'Tal presses his lips to Aon's hair, beige skin all over brown, P'Tal's hands securing my brother in his wild tears.

I look away and glance at Zaylam, at Osley. Banion, Aon's hatchling tree, rumbles his roots under my legs. *"He'll be all right, Sadie. He's releasing it to the Energies, now. What about you?"*

I run my fingers wordlessly over his roots, my lips clamped shut. Osley rubs quer head onto my ankle, and Zaylam gets up to hover over Aon and P'Tal, offering them her soothing wing wind.

When Aon's howls simmer down to soft sniffling, P'Tal lifts his chin up so they're looking each other in the eyes.

"You can mourn, sherba, and you should. B..." P'Tal closes his eyes, sets his jaw. "Blaze would want you to miss quer." He chuckles. "A lot." Aon gives a watery smile. "A lot, but not...not so much that you can't breathe. You too, Sadie. I know you're sad for your brother, I know you've never seen a young one... Your brother will be all right. And so will you."

I open my mouth to object. "And so will I." He pauses, glancing around cautiously, taking the opportunity to dry his eyes on the bulging muscle of his shoulder. "Thank you. For what you tried to do for Blaze. Kashat told us." He glances back at Zeel and Aora, who both bow slightly at me. I bow back, my forehead almost touching my knees.

"Have a meal with us, Aon. Tacon excused you from your learning pod and your sister from her labor. I know, I was as surprised as anyone. If you'd like, we know you have a lot of Blaze stories, that we wish we could know, that we wish you could share with us. We could share ours too." P'Tal's wet smile is agonized, but also real. Aon shakes his shoulders back and forth and follows P'Tal toward Blaze's other growns. His wings are too wilted for him to fly, so he trudges along, his feet dragging next to P'Tal's hooves. I hover awkwardly, waiting for them to invite me. They don't.

P'Tal turns to me, then, like he can read my thoughts, his eyes full to the brim. "Labor's almost over, Sadie. Kashat said he'd meet you here. He has something to show you."

I bow again, and they're gone.

I have nothing to do but wait for Kashat. I flop back down onto the ground, cheek pressing uncomfortably against the parched earth. Osley hops onto my lower back and settles in just under my wing sprouts. Zaylam fans me with her wings. Her wing wind helps, but only just.

How can I be so weak? P'Tal just lost his own young one, and he came all the way out to the Plains to find Aon, to find his young one's best friend, so that he could comfort him. We should all be comforting P'Tal. How weak must I be that I flew away from Leece being locked up again, that I let Lerian get hit instead of me and let myself fall apart when P'Tal,

P'Tal of all people, is out there functioning, trying to comfort my little brother, something I couldn't even do properly, because I flew away from that too?

Lerian's right.

I only fly on impulse. I don't think about how my actions impact people with actual hardships. Just me. Selfish. Weak.

Lerian's right.

I miss Lerian.

My eyes drift close. Sleep feels nice.

Until Kashat is tapping on my face, tugging at my shoulder, chiming his wing against mine. "Sade, come on, Sadie!"

"What could you possibly want, Kashat?" I grumble. Banion rumbles under me hopefully, and I groan.

"Hush, Banion, just because I'm snapping at people doesn't mean I feel any better."

"According to Jorbam, snapping at people is kind of how you let the world know you're awake every morning, Sadie, so perhaps—"

"Why? Why are all the people in my life who are supposed to love me so irritating?"

"And you're trying to make an argument that Banion doesn't have a point there, Sade?"

I fix Kashat with a deathly glare as I drag myself up from the ground, feeling Osley hop off me and hearing Zaylam hum in amusement. I point a groggy finger up at her. "I don't want to hear it from you, Zay."

She hums louder. I close my eyes and hold my breath, trying to calm myself down. They think I'm joking around.

They're wrong.

I sigh deeply, letting the breath out through my mouth like Mama taught me. It doesn't help much, so I suck in another big breath and hold it again. Longer this time. Thankfully, Kashat just hovers there, waiting, not interrupting.

When my head starts getting hazy, I let out a massive exhale.

"What?" I ask him again.

He gestures upward with his head, and we fly up into Banion's branches, leaving Osley watching with quer ears craned up after us.

"Are you all right?" he asks me without preamble when we're safely above Banion's canopy, Zaylam hovering nearby.

"Yeah, grand. Why wouldn't I be?"

"Oh, I don't know. You haven't left the Plains for sunups on end because it was just Lunamez but instead of celebrating all night, you watched helplessly while your little brother's best friend, the young one of your mom's best friend, who you tried to save from quer Slicing but couldn't and your family was arrested for your efforts, died right in front of you, and your own best friend isn't talking to you in all this because you're in love with the Controller."

It's only the last thing that wipes the boredom off my face. "I'm not in love with—"

Kashat laughs, a deep, rich belly laugh, and I wonder how many harvests the stress of all of these events have put on him.

"I'm not in love with anyone," I insist. Zaylam hums in amusement and I glare at her again. Kashat waves me off, and I try to shove him in the gut. He flies backward, out of my range and into Zaylam's underbelly.

"Kashat!" He just laughs again.

"Listen Sade, say what you want, that's all right. But look, I... did Osley tell you the Controller's locked herself up since Blaze's ceremony?"

I nod in the human fashion.

Kashat glances around furtively, and Zaylam flies closer to us.

"Blaze wasn't the first person she knew to die of the blood plague, Sadie."

I shrug, numb. "Lots of nons must have known people from when they were little."

"No, I mean..." He looks around again. "So you know I'm trying to learn how to remember my Dreams from before my Slicing, so maybe it could reconnect me to the Energies so I can Dream again?"

I nod irritably, my brow furrowed.

"It worked. I've been working on it extra hard since Blaze, you know..." He clears his throat, trying again. "Can I show you? Give you the impression of my Dream? One I had before I was Sliced?"

"Why would I need to see—"

"Sadie, please."

I shrug. I have nothing else to do, and he's at least made me curious. It feels almost pointless, the curiosity, but at least it's something to distract from the pain.

"Go for it. Same like when you gave me that spell? Just take in the impression?"

He shakes his shoulders back and forth, and I motion for him to follow me. Jorbam is a bigger tree than Banion, older, and has better leaf cover. If we're going to be doing something like share old Dreams, we should be hidden better than Banion could hide us in his sparse canopy.

We settle into the cover of Jorbam's leaves, and I put my forehead to her bark, breathing in her sun-soaked scent.

"Aon will be all right, Sadie, and absolutely none of this is your fault, nor a weakness of some kind. And I hear rumblings that Lerian's been asking about you. That she sent Kashat to help you feel better. She's angry, but she's worried, Sadie. She's worried about you."

I pull back and glare. "Why do you always know what's on my mind?"

"I don't always. But you are my hatchling. And you don't have much of an impassive face."

I put my forehead to her bark again wearily, and Kashat waits, swinging his legs irritatingly off her branches. His kicking interrupts my numbed peace, and I sit bolt upright, glaring.

"All right all right, what? Just show me what you want to show me."

Kashat looks unfazed. "Remember how I conjured an image of a non girl with a horse during the accounting?"

I nod.

He asks with his arched eyebrow if I'm ready to receive the impression of his Dream.

I still don't understand why he's so eager to share this Dream with me. It'll be a few seasons old by now, since he didn't become a near that long ago. I can't see how any of this matters. But he looks so eager, almost pained.

And it'll be nice to be someone else for a while.

I consent, and with a whoosh, I am no longer in the Plains.

Stone walls surround me, the stone floor resonating, echoing, under the rapid clanking of my heeled shoes. They pinch my feet slightly, but I keep moving. She needs her journal. She wants to write things down before...

She needs her journal. I ignore the scandalized look from the uniformed soldier keeping guard outside the shifting entrance to the kitchens. I burst in and call out an apology in stilted Highlander faeric, so that the head of the kitchen, an elder faerie with little patience for anyone interrupting his schedule, doesn't give me too much of a problem.

"Fiora needs..." I rifle through the small corner of the preparation room off the kitchen, overturning a blanket and a sack of flour. "I'm sorry...her journal..." I look up at the indignant Grovian, but his eyes are softer than usual.

"Has she reached the final stage?"

My hands stop their search, and I nod helplessly.

He reaches into his robe, with his berry-stained fingers, and slips Fi's journal into my shaking grasp. "I was keeping it safe, Madam. Please tell her...Tell her she will not be forgotten."

I bow my thanks before remembering my station. He looks shocked, and I turn to leave. He grabs my shoulder. We meet eyes.

"She's not the only reason you're welcome here."

I nod again, and sprint, almost slamming the heavy wooden door in the face of the soldier nearby, doubly scandalized this time. I can't bring myself to care if the soldier reports it to his superiors.

I know nothing but the path to the stables, where she stubbornly refused to leave, even when the worst of the pustules started overtaking her.

My stable girl, until the end.

Someone will have to clean up all her blood.

I run faster.

"Fiora!" I burst through the heavy doors, my shoes sticking in the hay, in the dirt. At her impromptu bedside, I rest my hands on my thighs, catching my breath, her journal between my fingers.

When she smiles at me, blood creeps out of her mouth, her nose. I wipe it with my fingers, and glance up at the surrounding horses, at the wary-looking healer. She shakes her head at me, and the horses, especially Balthazar, look away in despair, pawing at the ground in pain.

I gulp and stroke her face, speaking in Highlander non. "I brought your journal, love. You wanted to write, remember? You...you wanted to write, love."

Fiora laughs softly, which turns into a monstrous cough. Her blood spurts onto my face, but I barely notice. I caress her forehead, link my fingers through her stiff, puffy ones. Once the most beautiful earthen brown, her skin is gray now, still beautiful, but sickened, only visible in the spots where it's not covered in blood, in pus, in crusted wounds.

She reaches a hand out for Balthazar, who trots forward and bows his head so she can pat his face. "Don't forget, Evy, you understand me? You go after what..." Another cough, more of her blood makes my hand slippery. Balthazar nudges the left side of her face with his own, and his warm breath coats mine as I lean forward, pressing my cheek against her blood. "You go after what you need. Don't let him... Don't let him run your life, Evelyn. You promise me?" Her breath rattles, and her chest quakes.

"Fi—"

"Promise me, huh? It's rude to keep a dying girl waiting, don't you think?"

"Don't say that, Fi, don't—"

"It's all right, Evy. It'll be all right. I...I love..."

"I love you, Fiora, I love you, I love you I love you I love you."

She dies with a small smile on her face, my words washing over her as much as they wash over me, convinced that the more I say them, the more they could protect her, the more she would feel it, the more...but it doesn't matter. Nothing does. Balthazar lets out an agonized whinny and I think I do too, as I run her blood dripping from my hands, from my clothes, from my face, and I ignore the calls of her horse friends, I ignore the calls of the healer, I ignore the sound of my shoe's heel snapping off in the cobbled stone path between the open air of the stable and the stale air of the sterile stone walls, I ignore the calls of the soldiers stationed outside each door, to keep an eye out for nothing, to keep an eye out for me, I ignore everything until I come to my own reflection, in my own mirror, in the room he gave me when he brought me to this Lunara forsaken place.

My wild, swollen eyes stare back at me, Fiora's blood on my face, in the hair she twisted out for me just last week, her blood dripping down the lips that she once kissed, and I hate myself for not having kissed her one last time, for not—

And then there is no more reflection. There is no more mirror.

There is only a loud shattering sound and the scream that must have come from my mouth. There is only my blood, now, dripping down my crushed knuckles, joining in my veins with Fiora's blood, dripping onto the shards of glass that my fist has sent all across this beautiful room, this beautiful prison.

The door bursts open, and Iema is standing there, mouth agape, breathless and wide-eyed.

"Oh, Evelyn," she breathes with tears in her throat as she takes in the broken mirror, my broken hand, my broken heart.

She approaches me, her hands out, tentatively. I'm doubled over my destroyed hand, panting in pain, the tears finally threatening to take over my body, but I won't let her heal me. I need this pain. I need it. Iema opens her mouth, and she says my name again and again, as she gathers my broken form into her much smaller arms.

"Sadie, Sadie, Sadie." The voice is at once too deep and too young to be Iema's. I jolt awake, holding my right hand out in front of me. It's my own shade of brown, now, rougher than the hand in the Dream, veinier, but unbroken, bloodless, the knuckles all aligned in the usual way.

But the ghost of the pain remains.

I look up at Kashat, at Zaylam. I look back at my hand. My chest is heaving like I'd just sprinted as much as the woman I'd Dreamed.

"What in Lunara... Kashat, what was that?"

"You didn't recognize her?"

I fight to get enough air into my body, rubbing my left hand over my right, rocking back and forth slightly.

"Kashat, what—"

"It was the Controller, Sadie. Come on, I know you recognized her in that mirror. I Dreamed the Controller before I was Sliced."

I just look at him, and my eyes must be wild. Kashat swallows, the growing ball in his throat bobbing up and down. His eyes search mine curiously. "I didn't realize until... Throughout my time in the experiments with Jax and the others, I only caught snippets, but the last few sunups, with Blaze..." He trails off for a moment. "Everyone's miserable, Sade, and the rebellion is fracturing, people thinking it's worth it to be Sliced just to avoid deaths like this, even after my accounting performance, people aren't listening, they're not getting it, I figure if I can just prove to them once and for all that the palace lies aren't true, that it's not Dreaming that leaves us vulnerable to the plague...so I tried and tried, until I got it. I restored the Dream. And I thought, especially because the Controller's locked herself away since the service...I thought you'd want to know."

I furrow my brow, clinging to one last hope that he won't force me to face this. *"Why me?"*

Kashat sighs like he's one of my growns. "Lerian knows you, Sade. If she thinks you're being disloyal, there's gotta be a reason." I bristle, and he throws up his hands, palms up. "I'm not calling you a traitor. I'm saying, you love our people. You're a faerie, no matter what you look like."

"Yeah, and?"

"And..."

"You must have some reason to defend her as much as you have been, Sadie," Jorbam finishes for him. Kashat exhales his thank you awkwardly.

I throw up my hands, tears stinging my eyes for some reason I don't quite understand.

"All right, so now, what? The Controller had servants, and one of them...one of them worked in the stables, right, and she died of the plague?"

"Even though she never should have gotten the plague, because everyone had been Sliced by then. By the time I Dreamed it, everyone around her should have been Sliced, immune. But the girl she loved, that Fiora girl, she got sick anyway."

"And?"

"Just like Blaze. And the rumor is, the Controller's all cut up about Blaze's death. I just thought you'd want to know."

"Why? What am I supposed to—"

But Kashat's sped off before I can even finish.

I slump back into Jorbam's branches and stare aimlessly at Zaylam's serious face.

Evelyn was in love with another non near. A Highlander servant, it seems like. And she died... Fiora, she died of the plague.

Evelyn, in love with another woman, who died of the blood plague. Like Blaze.

And now, her obsession with Slicings make sense, with finding Dreamers and locking us away. I say nothing, even when Zaylam sings after me.

I don't think. I don't know why I'm doing what I'm doing.

I just know that I finally know how to reconcile the girl I met in the Forest and the mask that has been the Controller. And I'm not sure why—maybe because I'm nauseous now, for accusing her of not caring that Blaze was dying, not caring about any of the plague deaths. Maybe because I need to apologize.

Whatever it is, I just start flying.

I think of Evelyn's agonized yell; her repeated declarations of love, like her words could save Fiora from death itself; her broken fist, like a small, wounded creature she had to cradle to her body; the music box she brought to Blaze from the land she missed so much, the way she wiped blood away from quer mouth; her nails, digging into her arms as she listened to Blaze's rattled breath. Tears sting my eyes again.

I fly faster.

Chapter Twenty

IT FEELS GOOD to have some sort of purpose again, even if I can't figure out exactly what that purpose is. But that listlessness, that hopelessness, it's all been carved out of me now, replaced with the burning need to get to Evelyn.

Because Fiora died, and Blaze is dead, and I can't get her scream when Fiora breathed the last time out of my ears, and I can't get the look on her face when I accused her of not caring about any plague deaths out of my eyes.

As I approach the Lunavic River, which I know has been guarded at night since the uprising after Rada's arrest, I slip above the Forest canopy, too high up for them to make out my form. Too high up, normally, for me to breathe easily, but tonight is not like other nights.

Tonight, I need to slip into the Controller's dwelling undetected.

Lerian's voice in the back of my head screams that that's exactly what nights like tonight call for. *You don't know*, I tell her, even though she's not here. *Fiora was legitimately friends with the horses in the stables—she cuddled close to one of them as she died. You think Evelyn could love someone like that and not be at least sympathetic to us?*

Oh, so she's Evelyn now, not the Controller? Lerian's sarcastic tones play in my head.

I'm not a traitor, I insist. *Maybe I can just see things you're too stubborn to accept.*

The imagined conversation only goes downhill from there. I try to shush my own mind. My own guilt.

It doesn't work well until I start my descent into the small restricted area of the southern Forest, slightly back from the Lethean border, where the Controller's dwelling sits a few stone throws away from the rest of the clustered Hand dwellings.

I swerve low enough to look down on the configuration of Hands guarding their homes, the Controller's home, below the trees. I trace their patterns, their concentrations, and it leads me straight to her dwelling. I weave my way carefully through the thick mass of branches, of budding leaves, until I'm staring down at what must be her dwelling, separated from the others, in a tiny clearing close enough to the river to hear its soft roar. Guards are only posted at the borders of the clearing, and half of them are sleeping on the job. It's too easy to slip past them.

Non dwellings, like the Lethean Inn, are usually constructed from dead trees, like the ones we dismember at labor. But the Controller's dwelling is different. It's constructed of stones, mostly gray, mostly smooth, looking like they came from the river bottom. The angular roof is made of thatched faye glass, and a wide, tall window that serves as the entire top half of a wall faces the river itself.

That window's been thrown open all the way, probably—based on what Os and Kashat have been telling me—by Iema, and I fly up to it cautiously, tentatively, the sounds of the river at night rushing through my ears.

My eyes sweep around the inside of the place. Next to the unlit fireplace—which I notice headily is only full of shed branches, rather than chopped body parts—there's a desk with a rolling top that dominates most of the single room. Littered with parchment, berry ink, and quills though it is, it's still elegant enough to make me think she brought it here directly from whatever fancy Highland dwelling she was running through in Kashat's—my—Dream. Some faintly flickering lamps hang from the faye-glass ceiling, and though there aren't too many other personal things lying around, there are books lining each corner, and scattered across the elegant chest of drawers, topped with paint for her lips, with a large non-glass mirror. Like the one she'd broken in the Highlands, but smaller. Simpler. With a design around the edges that reminds me of the Flowing-like patterns on the music box she gave Blaze.

Blaze.

My eyes inevitably are drawn to Evelyn herself. She's asleep on a simple cot, a book resting near her head, which is wrapped in a silky purple scarf. The softly crackling light of her lanterns reveal the faded words on the golden binding. It's a human Highlander to Underlander word and gesture guide.

I smile before I realize with a jolt how repulsive I would be to Lerian right now. Not to mention how repulsive I'd be to Evelyn, sneaking into her dwelling when she's sleeping, vulnerable, her nightgown riding up quite high on her exposed thighs. I avert my eyes, ignoring the heat pooling in my core.

Though it's a warm night, I pull at the Energies and spark the fireplace with my fingertips. I say her name firmly as the light grows, wanting to wake her as gently as I can.

She gives a muffled scream when she opens her eyes and sees me. I toss my hands up and fly backward as she sits up quickly, the backs of my knees colliding with her desk chair painfully.

Her eyes still wide but her face adjusting itself into a cautious glare, Evelyn flicks her wrists and my gut lurches as she pulls the Energies into a purple haze of smoke around her. When it fades, her nightgown is nearly folded on the edge of her cot, and she's fully dressed in her usual Controller attire. She's left the scarf on her hair, though, and touches its edges with ginger fingertips to make sure it's still properly in place.

Her swollen eyes rake up and down my body, demanding an explanation. I swallow. "I'm sorry, I just…" I stop and try to control my stuttering. "I'm sorry I woke you. And scared you." I look away from her. "And violated your space." I stop, not knowing what to say next, humiliated by how right Lerian was about my impulsiveness. Evelyn could punish all of us for my violation.

But that's just the point. I trust that she won't, and Lerian doesn't.

I shake my head like I'm trying to get water out of my ears.

"Has something else happened?" Evelyn demands, and her voice is full of gravel, like she hasn't used it in days. If her last few sunups were anything like mine, she probably hasn't.

I shake my head in the human fashion. Her body relaxes, but only slightly. I take a deep breath and land softly, reminding myself that she's the Controller and I need to show due respect. If I have any hope of maneuvering out of this situation without Lerian's fears coming true.

"I hear you haven't been out, since…"

The deep breath Evelyn takes pushes out her chest slightly and I lick my lips involuntarily. "I hear you haven't been either." My brow must furrow, because her voice becomes more clipped, more like the Controller. "It's my duty to keep track of suspected dissidents." My heart sinks.

She chews on the bottom of her lip. "How's your brother? Iema says you and he were nowhere to be found." Her voice is different now; still loaded with gravel, but traced with something more like the sweetness and concern I overheard when she asked Aon how Blaze was, and earlier, when Aon and Blaze—Blaze—ran into her.

When Blaze was still alive.

I shrug and shuffle off my left foot. She notices and inclines her hand toward her desk chair behind me. I pull it out and sit gratefully, my elbows on my wide spread knees.

"He's...I don't know how he is. P'Tal came to get him today, said he and Zeel and Aora wanted to swap stories with him about..." But quer name catches on my lips, and I stare at the space between us, a space that, the night we met, was full of snow, of Iema's blood. I wonder if she's thinking of that night too.

"Did you come here to talk about Blaze?" She looks confused, but there's a vaguely hopeful lilt to her voice.

I wish Kashat hadn't given me his Dream memory. But I came to tell her the truth, but I'm not sure why. So she doesn't retaliate against Dreamers, maybe, because she's watched too many young people die of the plague? So she doesn't break another mirror? I don't know.

But I have to tell her. I don't know why.

"Evelyn..." I start but then correct myself. "Controller, do you know that faeries can sometimes remember Dreams they had before Slici— before *Initiations*?" It's not entirely untrue. Kashat had to twist the Energies with medical experiments to help him remember, but some of us do remember naturally. The little lie boils my insides, but it feels necessary. Like somehow, I'm still being loyal to Lerian, even if she'd hate me for just being here.

Evelyn nods, her brow furrowed. Her fingers toy with the edges of her scarf again, and I get the urge to undo her hair for her. I look away.

"My friend Kashat, you know him, he did the accounting performance..." She bristles, and I know she's remembering the image he'd produced of Fiora.

"He didn't—"

I swallow in affirmation. "Before he was Sliced"—I emphasize the *before* carefully—"he Dreamed you, at the time of her death, and he showed me just now, because he thought..."

I hear his voice ringing in my head, saying that I'm in love with the woman in front of me, with the woman who could destroy us all with a single command.

I squirm and don't meet her eyes. "He thought you might be extra upset about Blaze. Because of Fio—because of her. So I wanted to..."

She mutters something in Izlanian non, and I wait, eyes downcast.

"How much did you see? In this...Dream memory?" She sounds panicked.

I wrap my left wing around my arm and fiddle with its tensile tip. "You running to get her journal, but she didn't have time to write in it...and then the mirror."

I look up enough to see her left hand smooth over her right in her lap, thumb swiping over the spot that took the most damage, the knuckle of the littlest finger.

"Sadie." Her voice is ragged, but not impatient. I raise my head and meet her eyes. She's regarding me silently, and she stays that way for a long moment.

She takes a slow, ragged breath, and absently continues to stroke her right hand. When she speaks, it's softly, like she's somewhere else.

"Kashat had no right to share that with you. It wasn't acceptable for him to tell you anything, let alone share the images with you. It's private. I..." Her eyes flutter closed and it looks like she's counting in her head. Guilt digs at my insides and crawls all over my skin. I shouldn't have let him tell me. "I fail to understand why you people find Dreams so compelling. In Izla, Dreams are so...exposing."

I consider her, weighing her words in my hands like I weigh my axe before taking a swing. My voice is low and creaky when I open my mouth. "You're right. It wasn't his story to tell. And I'm sorry. I really am. Evelyn." She meets my eyes and my chest threatens to cave in. "But vulnerability is only as painful as you make it. It can also be beautiful. Powerful, even." I'm not sure why I'm whispering.

There's a long silence in which I hear nothing but the crackling of the fire and the rush of the River from outside.

"Perhaps you're right," she tells me evenly. "But perhaps sometimes our vulnerabilities are what can be used most easily against us."

I furrow my brow. She stops breathing, then, and cocks her head to listen intently. She gestures that I should do the same. I hear nothing. Neither, apparently, does she. Seeming satisfied that no one is listening nearby, her eyes come back to lock with mine.

"Fiora didn't happen to catch the blood plague. Nobody happens to catch it anymore, not with the Initiations." She holds up her hand to stop my protest. "You might not like them, Sadie, but they do effectively prevent the plague. Perhaps there are other ways, but that's not what I'm talking about right now. What I was trying to explain to you, is that Fiora heard lots of things, being a stable girl. She heard of a plan to attack the dragons, before the massacre. She told me she was going to try to warn your people, but she…" Her voice cracks.

"Got the plague instead? And you think we gave it to her?"

A single tear tracks down her face as she shakes her head. I lean forward, putting my hand out to wipe it away. She puts her fingers on the underside of my wrist, and her touch crackles like the flame behind me.

"I was told she was exposed to a rebel who had not been Initiated, that they exposed her to the plague through their resistance to Initiations, and that's how she got sick. I was told she was killed by your little rebellion."

Evelyn squeezes my hand slightly, and I withdraw it unwillingly.

"Why are you telling me this?"

She lets out a rueful laugh and tilts her head to the side, staring at me through gleaming eyes, every bit composed. "You haven't figured it out yet?" I blink.

She laughs ruefully again, and then the shake of laughter becomes the shake of a sob. "It's my fault, Sadie, don't you see? It's my…my…" And then her flesh racks with sobs, and I look around the dwelling like I'm looking for someone else to tell me how to comfort her. Or to do it for me.

I lean forward awkwardly, having no clue what to do with my hands, with my body.

"Evelyn…" I'm about to say that the plague is its own creature, that its creation, its existence, is no one's fault, and certainly not hers.

But I bite down my words, because Lerian's are still strong in my head. Because the plague hadn't existed until the palace started contaminating our waters, our air, eating flesh and spreading their *development* everywhere. The plague is the fault of the government she works for, the soldiers in that stone dwelling she ran through the day Fiora died.

And yet the plague struck the workers in the Izlanian mines even earlier than it struck here, and what do I know about Evelyn's family? She could have people in those mines; she might be a non, but nons aren't all born with equal footing. Fiora's death in the stable is testament to that.

"Evelyn." I almost touch her arm, so close to me. My hands tremble in the space between us. "You didn't create the plague."

She sniffles loudly, shaking her head, but somehow, the effect is still graceful.

She smiles sadly as she looks up at me.

"No, Sadie, you misunderstand me. Not abstract guilt. You can't ask me how I know this, not yet, but I am absolutely certain now that Fiora was infected, intentionally, by the king's orders, in attempt to win my obedience. And I am absolutely certain that the same thing happened to Blaze." She takes a deep breath and I almost fall off the chair. "I am absolutely certain that one of my Hands infected Blaze with the plague, on sanction of the king, to exact revenge for protecting the Underland."

I sit bolt upright. "Aora kept saying that Blaze was playing, alone, that your second Hand found quer..." Evelyn nods numbly as I babble on. "He likes trying to hurt the young ones. He was trying to get Blaze and Aon to hunt creatures with his bow, before, he had a fight with Iema. He said he was having fun with them..."

I pause for a long time, during which I'm reasonably certain I can't breathe.

I know she's right. Lerian's distrust be damned, I know her. I believe her.

"Blaze was murdered." Saying it out loud feels heavy, dull, makes my tongue feel so much thicker than it is, so much clumsier. Evelyn blinks as she nods, and tears spill out of both eyes.

Rage sweeps through me.

"Why would they target a young one? Que was just barely Sliced, still learning how to gallop!"

More voice cracks at a higher octave than it ever registers, and both our hands move to caress the spaces on our own bodies where Blaze and Aon's antics left bruises.

I try to choke down a sob. I'm unsuccessful.

I don't know how long I sit there, wailing wordlessly with hot tears streaming down my face, but I know Evelyn's cot rustles as she moves to kneel in front of me, putting her forehead in my lap and drawing soothing circles on the outsides of my thighs with her fingertips.

I don't know how long it is until I realize that I've grasped her left forearm with my hand, that the fingers of my other hand trace what feels like a scar on the back of her neck, normally hidden by her hair.

I don't know how long it is until I register that she is singing softly in a language I don't recognize. I stop crying abruptly and so does her song. Evelyn looks up, surprised and maybe a bit embarrassed. She smiles and backs away from me gingerly, sitting herself back on her cot. My body keens from the loss of warmth.

The loss of her.

"You were singing," I say, and my voice is thick with tears and snot. I wipe my nose with the back of my hand.

She looks away, and now I'm sure she's embarrassed. "It's an Izlanian prayer. For the tears to take your pain out of your body with you, for your grief to be returned to you in its true form."

I wait. She looks back up at me and my breath hitches as her wet, wide eyes sink into mine.

"Grief has a true form?" I croak.

"Love," she breathes.

I blink and she sighs. Clearing her throat a little, she doesn't sing again, but her voice is rhythmic—a poem. She's translating the lyrics for me slowly, deliberately, pausing for long moments when she needs to think of the right word. In the end, the prayer she recites goes like this,

> *Upon the backs of the dragons*
> *And into the depths of Qathram*
> *May your chest keep you rising*
> *Dear one,*
> *For if you sink,*
> *You will swim forever*
> *Breathe forever, but only of the*
> *Water that is your pain*
> *Only of the water that is your*
> *Grief.*
> *So long will you breathe your grief*
> *You will forget what made you*
> *Mourn*
> *What made you cling to*
> *Creatures whose journeys you*
> *Cannot follow.*
> *Dip, swim. Breathe the soured molasses breath of*
> *Grief*

But never forget,
Dear one,
That grief too,
Is Grown.
Grown of loss, grown of
Rage
Grown of futility, yes,
But conjure her face in your mind,
Dear one,
For you would have called
None of these pains to you
If you weren't keening
From the loss of
Love.
May you bathe in ice
Of Qathram
And be warmed by the remembrance that
Grief,
Dear one,
Stripped down,
Is none but,
Precisely,
Love.
Ripened with the agony of knowledge
That bodies fade
But love does not.

Her eyes avoid mine with each "dear one," but when she recites what grief is stripped down to, she finally lifts her gaze to mine, and holds it until she finishes.

Only the fire crackling behind us dares make a sound.

"An Izlanian prayer," I whisper finally.

She nods.

"You've really been practicing your Grovian faeric." She smiles sadly. "We only grieve those we love, Sadie. Without love—"

"Life would be all laughs, all the time."

Zaylam would snort; Jorbam would rumble; Lerian would thwack me upside the head and ask if my ugliness has finally affected my brain.

But Evelyn? Her eyes fly wide open, her mouth following with a soft gasp. For a moment, her lips twitch both up and down. And then she lets out a shaky laugh, like she's afraid that the spirits of Qathram might hear her or something.

"That's not exactly what I was going to say—"

"Thank you."

"What?"

"For reciting the prayer. Maybe one day you could actually sing the whole thing, instead of just reciting it. Your voice is nice."

This time, her laugh is easy, but watery.

"Hopefully you don't ever need the Prayer for the Left Behind again."

The crackling of the fire makes us both jump.

"Controller—Evelyn—I know I've got no right to ask, but...who was she?"

She stares at me for so long I don't think she's going to answer. "You already know that her name was Fiora. I was compelled to come to the Highlands Proper from Izla when I was very young. She worked in the stables where I lived in the Highlands. I'm sure you gathered that much. She was...we grew up together. She was my...we grew up together."

"And you can't tell me how you know for sure? About Fiora and Blaze?"

She shakes her head firmly, apologetically. Fearfully.

"I don't even know why I told you that. What are we doing, Sadie? What are you even doing here? You're my enemy, I—"

"Do you really believe that? You just told me that the king—"

"I know what the king's done!"

Her voice rings throughout her dwelling as she jumps to her feet, and even the fire silences in its wake.

Just like that, the glimpses I was getting of the girl behind the Controller mask is gone.

But just as quickly, her face releases with troubled regret and she sits back down heavily. "I don't think you're my enemy. Do you see me as yours?"

Lerian's voice is screaming in my ears and her fists have a tight hold on my insides.

"I mean, you locked my family up. You sent Rada away, and..." I'm about to say Leece and Mara, but I choose my words more carefully than that. "Those Sampians."

Evelyn sighs and lowers her eyes.

"Are they dead too?" I ask.

"No." I'm surprised by how ragged her voice sounds. "You don't know what I had to do for them, Sadie, but, no, they're not dead."

I nod, and a season's worth of knots start unwinding in my stomach.

"Why are you here?" she asks me again.

I heave a sigh. "I have no idea. Most faeries here think I'm their enemy. Lunara, maybe I'm proving that by being here, I don't know. I just I remember watching Idrisim die. Jax's joiner, he died. Was killed. And you, with Fiora... Jax almost died after Id was killed. I don't want you to be in that kind of pain."

A solitary tear tracks out of her open eyes. "She made me promise to date again. When you saved Iema that night, I thought..."

I feel a grin tugging on my lips. Evelyn must notice, because she laughs wryly.

"I was so angry when I saw you in the Gathering with your wings out. The first person to make me smile since Fi, and it was all a lie—"

"But my wings are pretty great, huh?"

"Hush." But her eyes fall to my wing tips and I reach one out for her, using my body to give her my meaning.

"Would you like to touch?"

Her eyes fly wide open.

"Is that all right?"

I flutter my wings insistently, and she gets the meaning. *"Go ahead."*

My breath hitches when her fingertips meet my wingtips. She bites her bottom lip as she shudders slightly, and that shudder echoes back to me at her fingers on the part of me that is most connected to the Energies. Heat swoops down my core, and when I speak, my voice is several registers lower than it usually is.

"Evelyn."

She jump slightly and moved her hand away.

"Sorry." Her voice is a whisper.

"No."

We take deep breaths in sync with each other, and I recover first.

"So is that why you locked up Mama and Aon? You were angry?"

"No!" She looks offended, and I droop slightly. "Artem told me he'd seen you in front of several of my Hands. You haven't the slightest clue how difficult it was for me to convince them not to kill all four of you on the spot."

I shiver.

"I should have fought even harder. Aon was so tiny—"

"He survived." The words feel strange on my lips. Just by being here with her, like this, I'm betraying my whole people.

Evelyn's eyes are cloudy. She's betraying her people too. "I've done evil things, Sadie."

A tiny flare of rage shoots up in me until I look at her eyes. I think of labor and all the times I could have refused to murder the trees. The Hands couldn't kill us all. And if they did, when did we get to decide that our lives are worth more than the trees'?

Evil.

If love is the root of grief, I wonder what the root of evil is.

"Me too," I tell her.

"I want to make it right."

"Me too."

My wings still at being the object of such an intense gaze. All of her attention, usually split between so many things, is focused on me. I wait and try not to wilt.

"I haven't the faintest idea how to proceed," she admits in a voice so low I have to lean in to hear her better.

Her breath is laced with Grovian mint and the tang of skyflower fruit. My heart refuses to beat in a controlled tempo. Her eyes challenge mine.

"But I have some ideas."

We stare at each other. "Come to the Plains with me. Meet the people the king is so eager to kill."

"Will your friends trust me with that?" The fire pops loudly behind us. She means Lerian.

My heart lurches, but I lean in even closer, and I can't tell whose breath hitches first. "Give them a reason to." I breathe her breath a little longer before she pulls back, wiping residue from recent tear tracks off her rounded cheeks.

"Tomorrow, then. Just before sundown. One more sunup in isolation... my absence will be unnoticed."

"That'll work. Faeries aren't usually in the Plains right after labor. But do we have time for that? You said an attack—"

"The rumors Iema's reporting to me suggest next week. And it's almost sunup; we can't very well assemble your people in the middle of the day, hm?"

I nod and she chews on her bottom lip again. I swallow with difficulty, something I'm pretty sure she notes with pleasure.

"Tomorrow, all right. Meet me by the eastern steam pools. The one you took me to, when you arrested me."

She glares at that, and I smirk full on for the first time since…

Blaze.

She catches the flicker of sadness on my face and lowers her eyes, shaking her shoulders back and forth tentatively. I rise, push in her desk chair meticulously, and fly out of her window and straight up into the night.

Chapter Twenty-One

NO ONE EVER sneaks up on me.

Well, maybe sometimes Os can, or Auth when I land near her web. Aon sometimes, when he really tries. But nons? No.

Tonight, though, Evelyn does.

I'm tense, remembering Lerian's scalding words, her at once concerned and infuriated face today at labor, when I actually showed up for the first time since Blaze died and all she had to say was, "Looks like someone finally realized she's not the only one who's mourning."

I'm tense with the knowledge that I am, without a doubt, betraying my people. By trusting a girl who had my best friend shot, who gives labor orders every sunup, who locked up my family, arrested me twice, had Mara and Leece arrested and beaten. A girl who gave a dying young one a music box and looks at me like I could be worth something.

I'm tense thinking of Evelyn, with the idea that she'll be with me tonight, crossing into the Plains at my side. My stomach is knotted with guilt over how much I'm looking forward to that, even though I can't stop replaying the memory of her head in my lap while I cried, her voice, singing, her fingers on the underside of my wrist.

We're going to have to repeat that touch, tonight, to get her through the barrier—something I'd neglected to warn her about. My stomach churns with more guilt.

But I had, at least, warned my friends in the Plains. I told Jorbam about our conversation and had her spread the word to the other Lunavad trees. Jorbam says most of them only said yes when she told them that Evelyn only burns already fallen branches. Zaylam had just sang unhelpful songs about young romance, which made me swipe at her wings and promptly fall out of Jorbam's branches.

I finger the small cut on my forearm from the fall as I wait for her. I stare out at the beach, my toes burying themselves aimlessly in the sand.

A jolt shakes through my body when I feel someone's heat immediately behind me. It's a different kind of heat than the type that's coming from the steam pool next to me. That heat is sun-warmed, built up by long days and trapped in by reflective rocks. The new heat is from the core of someone's stomach, not trapped at all but exuding from the curves under a thin layer of clothing. It sends powerful tingles through my core, and I spin around, facing the source. Facing her.

I wonder for one wild moment what it would be like to always fly around ensconced in the radiant shell of her warmth, to always be by her side. I shake my head roughly, remembering Fiora. I raise my eyebrows at her. *"Ready to go?"*

She gestures out in front of her. *"Lead the way."*

Our journey through the Forest is slow and silent. I walk for her benefit, and hold branches for her so they won't snap back and hit her. Each time I do, she offers me an almost shy smile. Maybe she's remembering when she did the same for me, except back then my hands were chained behind my back. This time, our hands brush each other on occasion, and my blood sizzles.

It's a long trip on foot, and I can't walk quickly or without pain. She never seems impatient when I have to stop to massage and stretch my foot, and she even offers to walk while I fly. I choose to limp instead, being sure to always offer my hand when she's hiking up her skirt to climb over some fallen tree or other. She always chuckles and shrugs away my hand, never taking it. I offer it anyway.

I wonder if she's as relieved as I am to be focusing on something other than Blaze's death.

I pause when we reach the invisible barrier of the Plains.

"I'll need your hand. We'll, uh... We need to be touching so you can get in. If that's all right." My face burns.

"Excuse me?" Her eyebrows are raised, but the corners of her mouth are twitching. "Did you orchestrate this whole excursion because you couldn't find a smoother way to ask if you could hold my hand? We were alone in my dwelling last night. Surely there were simpler methods you could have tried, Sadie." Her eyes dance.

I sputter. She laughs, then, a soft, rich sound like bathing in a stream on a hot morning, and takes my hand without warning. She laces our fingers together, and I swallow with difficulty. Her eyes are steady now, and the ghosts of guilt for laughing when Blaze is dead flicker in her eyes.

"I saw you give quer and Aon candy once. I think que would have liked seeing you like this more. Relaxed and not so Controller-y."

"Controller-y." The corners of her lips twitch, but her eyes are dark with my mention of Blaze.

"Listen."

"I'm sorry—"

"No, it's fine. It's strange for me. Talking with you about quer. All of this. I'm betraying my people." Her eyes are fixed on the spot where our fingers are interwoven.

"So am I."

She says nothing, and I can't think of anything else to say, so I limp forward with her, through the Barrier that separates the Plains from the rest of the Forest. As we walk through, her eyes squeeze shut, unaccustomed as she is to the tight pull of the Energies that going into the barrier puts you through. I look at her as we emerge into the Plains, my heart pounding hard.

It isn't until this moment that I fully realize the change in Evelyn's attire from her usual uniform dress. The moonlight shines down on her body, highlighting the pleated top that layers down her chest in sky blue waves, curving down her ample stomach into a fitted skirt with material that flows perfectly with her body. It clings to her curves but is slit all the way up to her thighs.

I stop breathing.

One of Jorbam's far extended roots shuffles teasingly beneath my feet and jerks me out of my stupor. Thankfully, Evelyn hasn't noticed my distraction. She's too busy taking in the Plains.

Dragon bulbs are hanging from the lowest canopy branches of a few trees. There are fewer now than there used to be, but there are still some, including the surviving one on Aon's hatchling tree, Banion. They're glowing, and different hues of purples and greens are reflecting in her eyes. The air is tingling with dragon songs, and Evelyn shivers.

I wait in silence. For her, so used to the calls and songs of birds in her ears, to adjust to the calls and songs of dragons, with their shadows swooping over us in intricate patterns, all their different colors and forms daring her to look away.

The sun is just disappearing over the northernmost section of the Plains, and since we've come in from the south, the fire oranges and passion reds glow in her eyes. Her lips are open slightly, and for a moment, I forget the beauty of the sunset making the few remaining dragon bulbs glow. I notice only the way that the glowing is interacting with the dying sunlight in Evelyn's eyes.

When they realize we're here, the dragon songs drop off gradually, and a wordless hum falls over the Plains. Zaylam slips into view, unwreathing herself from Jorbam's branches, and flies toward us hesitantly. By unsung agreement, everyone else stays back. Taking flight, Gimla beats his wings steadily, staring at Zaylam. Harlenikal's golden back spikes—so much like the short, spiny leaves that coat her hatchling tree's canopy—are all erect, at attention. Ready. But she remains still, hovering. Watching. Waiting.

I leave the warmth of Evelyn's side and fly up into the ritual embrace of Zaylam's wings. I slip up her body, from tail to neck, with the tips of my fingers, my feet, taking special care to skim gently over her scar. In response, she wraps her wide wings around me, enveloping me in what have always reminded me of stained glass windows in the growing moonlight, and unfurls her tailfin, its massive expanse keeping us afloat as she spins with me one, two, three, four times. Zaylam spins a bit more than is quite traditional, even knowing it tends to make me dizzy, and I grin into her embrace; she's showing off.

When she releases me, I fly back down to Evelyn, whose hands are clasped in front of her like an excited young one, eyes wide, almost reverent, the ghosts of death for once gone from her face.

"I don't think you two have been properly introduced," I say, and Zay coos, her snout twitching into expansion. "Zaylam tozo," I tell Evelyn, the introduction of a newcomer to a faerie's hatchling mates. Evelyn is still just staring, her eyes now soft and timid under Zaylam's gaze, in a way I've never seen them before. "She's my hatchling mate," I stumble. "We've been—"

"Bonded since before birth, yes," Evelyn interrupts me quietly, eyes still on Zaylam's. "How do you do?"

Zaylam purrs in bemused delight. "You will see," she sings in her best approximation of Highlander non. Harlenikal emits a low groan of displeasure that Zay is singing directly to a non. Gimla sings a reprimanding scale so high I doubt Evelyn can hear it; his green, maple leaf-patterned underbelly is quivering with the effort of holding such a powerful note. I close my eyes and grimace at the frequency.

Evelyn, oblivious to the sound and focused just on Zaylam, shakes her head in the non way and speaks in excellent Grovian faeric. "You don't need to talk to me in a language in which you have little practice. I'm familiar with—"

"Are you saying my Highlander is unworthy?" Zaylam sings, still in an approximation of Highlander, eyes glistening playfully and with a bit of a challenge. "Is this what you want to say, human young one?"

"I—well, no, it's actually quite good, I—"

> *You didn't tell the girl*
> *That dragon humor*
> *Is the best humor,*
> *Did you,*
> *Tiny faerie?*

Zaylam sings loudly to me before flying off. I shake my head in the human fashion and motion for Evelyn to follow. Harlenikal flies low, cutting off my path, with a swarm of disapproving dragons in formation behind her.

> *Has anyone informed*
> *The human near that her people*
> *Are destroying dragonkind by*
> *Destroying the fayes'*
> *Dreaming?*

As other dragons harmonize their agreement, Zaylam interjects her own melody, Gimla on her tailfin.

> *Has anyone informed*
> *The overly judgmental dragon*
> *That the human near put her tiny body*
> *Between this dragon and*
> *An entire army,*
> *Protecting this dragon and this dragon's*
> *Hatchling faye,*
> *Not to mention the entire*
> *Underland*
> *From the fire and the*
> *Sword?*

There's a hum of approval at that, and Harlenikal's snout retreats into her face as even she can't argue with that. She speeds off in a huff, the others behind her.

I sigh and start flying too, then stop and turn around.

"This ground is hard on your feet." I hold my hand out to a hesitating Evelyn.

She glances down at her own body after tearing her gaze away from the dragons. "I don't think you can lift me." Her voice is full of promise.

I scoff and flex my arm muscles, truly happy for the first time that I spend most of my days swinging an axe. I grin as she puckers her lips in amusement and shakes her head with a soft, tinkling chuckle. I memorize the sound. And the heady look in her eyes.

I flutter my wings at her. "And these are stronger than they look."

I beckon to her again. *"Come."* She takes my hand.

We rise. Toward the mushroom canopy of Jorbam's branches. Toward the sky.

She's right. She is heavy. And I revel in it. My wings strain slightly against my solid back and my forearms bulge as they grasp her soft hands. We rise higher and higher. The stars are coming out, and we are soaring.

All attention is on us. Her eyes seek only mine.

"I'm flying," she breaths, her open mouth curved into a shocked smile. She looks beneath us and pulls me closer to her, grasping my hands tighter. The wind our flight is creating billows her skirt out, and it flows away from her body. Her exposed legs flutter kick softly, absently.

"I'm flying," she keeps whispering.

"You're flying," I confirm, wondering if the starlight has ever lit up anyone's face the way it's lighting up hers.

I almost kiss her, then, almost bend at the elbows to propel her into my arms. But I'm not sure it's what she wants. We fly on.

Her weight pulls strongly on even my arms and wings, but I know enchantments for flying that most nons—I guess I should say most humans—don't. I blow softly toward her so that our hands can stop grasping each other quite so tightly, the enchanted wind from my lungs twisting the Energies beneath her, lifting us higher.

Laughter bubbles from deep in her chest the more we rise, and the more we rise, the more my cheeks burn from all the smiling. More confident with each new height we reach—and soon even the tallest Lunavad trees are beneath us, and even Harlenikal looks small—Evelyn rotates her hips and spins me around, tossing her head back toward the growing starlight, the growing moonlight. She laughs with a delight that dances with the fireflies that have risen to witness this curiosity of human and human-faye holding hands and soaring together above the Plains. A brave soul lands on Evelyn's bare forearm and lights up; Evelyn laughs again, and the fireflies look like tiny stars. Their flickering lights frame her face, her hair, her body. Her lips slightly parted, her awed smile.

I know in that moment that Kashat and Lerian are right.

I know in that moment that I love her.

Still spinning us around and around, Evelyn pulls her arms in toward her waist, bringing the rest of me with them so I am flush against her body. Her eyes sparkle with the brightest stars just barely above our heads. I breathe in her breath.

She glances down at my lips, her radiant, young-one-like smile now one of soft, intimate pleasure. Her eyes shift rapidly between both of mine.

"Evelyn," I breathe. I swallow hard, which makes her smile deeper. "Would it make you happy if I kissed you?" I ask in what little Izlanian language that I know. I let my eyes tell her how much I want to.

"Yes," she whispers as she closes the space between our mouths, her full lips moist and soft and powerful and gentle all at once. One of her hands finds my short hair and the other, my wing sprouts, as one of my hands cups her face, neck, and lower ear and the other sinks into the gloriously abundant flesh of her waist. She moans softly as she parts her lips for my tongue, and I decide that I will always be happy if I can coax that magnificent sound from her whenever she wants me to.

I don't know how long we stay there, floating in the starlight, firefly flickers surrounding us and the glow of growing dragon bulbs beneath us, kissing like we can prevent the sun from ever rising again. Kissing like it's all we need to permanently unsettle the power of the palace government. Maybe it is.

When we finally part, she pushes off away from me, but still holds my hands. Bewildered, I'm terrified I've done something she didn't want, but she's beaming.

"*Can I try on my own?*" She gestures with her head to the air around us, and I laugh at the eagerness in her question. So when she is just herself—Evelyn, not the Controller—she is playful, curious, eager. I wonder again how she became Controller so young. I save the questions for later and let my smile widen.

I draw another deep breath and blow out toward her. It won't work permanently, and I'll have to watch her closely, but I can't imagine being anywhere else. So I squeeze her hands once for reassurance before letting go, but her face betrays no fear. She screams with laughter when she finds herself afloat, unsupported, in midair. I belly laugh for the first time in I don't know how long when she makes a swimming motion with her arms and legs. She joins in too, but still manages to pout, asking, "*Well, how do I move, then?*" with her tossed-up arms. For the first time, I truly see her as my age-mate, as a fellow near.

I spin rapidly with my wings, unable to resist showing off.

"Just believe you can," I tell her. She squints at me slightly, pouting some more. I want to take her bottom lip, jutting out now, back between my own, but she lets out a laugh, and then she soars.

As graceful as though she's been flying since birth, and as enthusiastic as though she's heading for an old friend she hasn't seen in too many harvests, she tears across the Plains, laughter tinkling out of her very pores the entire time. I catch a glimpse of Zaylam's extended snout as she flies up to us, and watch happily as she challenges Evelyn to a race around the circumference of the Plains.

Zay's wing wind will help keep her in the air, so I settle down with Jorbam to watch them with glee. Evelyn refuses to take a head start, but she is, unsurprisingly, not a graceful loser. After demanding a third rematch, still refusing a head start, and promptly losing again, Evelyn rides on Zaylam's tailfin, back to Jorbam and me.

"Jorbam tozo," I say as I take her hand, helping her settle onto Jor's branches. "My other hatchling mate."

Evelyn looks at me inquiringly, and I nod. She reaches her fingers out to Jorbam's bark, stroking her greeting. Jorbam rumbles her hellos, and Evelyn's eyes widen like they did when we first rose in flight.

"Thank you," she murmurs to Jorbam, and I wonder what she'd said. And how Evelyn understood her rumbles.

Zaylam perches smugly beneath us. Evelyn glares down at her. "I don't even have wings, and you didn't win by that much," Evelyn huffs, but the twitching of her lips gives her away.

"This one you keep, Sadie, Controller or no. A fighter," Jorbam rumbles, tickling Evelyn with a spiney leaf as she does so.

I glance at Evelyn. "Or maybe not, maybe she's just too stubborn to accept advantages when they're offered to her!" I tease. Evelyn pretends to scoff.

"Yes, dear, you've discovered a pattern in my life. Fleeing a life of luxury in the Highlands to be Controller of this place, and forsaking even that to revolt against the palace with a motley crew of overly smug Grovian young ones."

We all laugh. I've never seen this part of Evelyn, and I love it. Love. I want to learn so much more. And to kiss her. Again and again and again.

But after the laughter dies down, the truth of Evelyn's comment sinks into us all, and we grow quiet. Not unpleasantly so. We just know we have to transition, somehow, from kissing and racing and laughing into making decisions that can mean life, death, or torture for so many. I've never felt so ready and so overwhelmed at the same time.

Evelyn must be feeling similarly, because she takes my hand.

"I'm uncertain what my function is on this visit," she offers up to no one in particular. "Are you going to interrogate me? Evaluate whether Sadie has behaved ridiculously by deciding to trust me? Or will that come later, when her growns join us?" My thumb strokes the back of her hand, where she punched the mirror.

Zaylam looks up from her perch under us, then sings softly, relishing her chance to practice human Highlander. "You think the only way for learning us about you is with interrogation?"

Jorbam leaks some sap near my neck. "Taste it," I encourage Evelyn. She does. The sight of her licking her fingers is exquisite.

But then her eyes fill with tears. I swipe my own finger through Jorbam's sap and lick my finger roughly. It tastes like labor, like the Plains becoming an isolated hideaway instead of a hub of Grovian life. Like the smoke that's rising from the factories near the Highlands, into our water and our veins. Like the Slicings, like the withering of so many potential dragon bulbs because of the loss of Dreaming, without which most of us can't form hatchling bonds with the Lunavad trees who reach out to us. Like how hard Jorbam and some others had to work to make sure no one sounded the alarm about Evelyn's presence here tonight.

"I'm sorry," the Controller whispers, shaking her head side to side, her eyes down. "Not that it matters, of course. But I am sorry." Her eyes fly around the Plains before returning to us, and the dragons that are hovering at the level of Jorbam's canopy to get a glimpse of her scatter. "I'm willing to work with you in whatever ways I can."

There's a silence, and I break it with a shaking voice. I have to.

"Why did you become Controller, Evelyn? Why help us now? Why not before you all arrested Rada? Or the Sampians? Why betray your people, now?"

She swallows and holds my eyes with hers. The dragon sons around us go soft, like the entire Plains needs to know.

"I thought you all ranged somewhere between reckless and murderous after Fi died, I..." She takes a shuddering sigh. "I'm not betraying my people. My people aren't the king's. I'm not a traitor, I'm just...I'm trying to live my life as I see it, as it needs to be lived. They murdered Fi, they murdered Blaze. I'm just trying to do what needs to be done."

> *The humans execute*
> *The human*
> *Dissidents,*

Zay sings softly. Evelyn straightens.

"Like Fiora. I know. I should have fulfilled her work earlier instead of letting myself be deluded by their lies. I should have been stronger."

"They might kill you, Evelyn."

She meets my eyes.

"I'll be in good company, then."

I put my hand on hers, rub my thumb gently over the knuckles she broke when she put her fist through that mirror. Her eyes mist over, and I know, beyond a shadow of a doubt, that trusting her isn't betraying my people, either; it's fighting for them.

For us all.

"What do you have in mind?" I ask her, and she visibly relaxes now that we've moved from feelings to planning.

Evelyn shakes her shoulders back and forth. "I can't tell you how to fight violence I'm responsible for inflicting. But my Hands don't expect my presence right now; I've locked myself away since..." There's a silence in which we all think of Blaze.

"I can use this time to tell you what I know about the king's plans, and do whatever you think it is I should to throw them off course."

> *And dragonkind will ever know*
> *Whether the human*
> *Is trapping the rest—*

"You won't, especially if you don't care to listen when I explain myself," Evelyn deadpans, trying to look directly into Harlenikal's eyes as she hovers nearby. Zaylam stretches her long neck into Evelyn's line of sight, blocking her view to Harlenikal. They lock eyes, and I cock an eyebrow. Zay's only ever made eye contact with me, and sometimes Os and Lerian. After a few long moments, Zaylam must see what she wants to, because she wrenches her crystal orbs away from Evelyn's to grin at me, her elongated snout grazing my nose. Harlenikal snorts angrily and swoops away.

"I like the *joiner* you have, Sade," she sings in Highlander.

"Oh, no, she's not—we're not—" I can't speak.

"Aren't we?" Evelyn asks me with big eyes and a slight pout. I know her mind is on my lips, and I almost fall out of Jorbam's humming branches.

I sputter. My stomach has fallen out of my body and crashed onto the ground beneath us. The corners of Evelyn's mouth twitch.

Zaylam finally takes pity on me. "Come," she sings to Evelyn in Highlander, flying out so that her broad back is underneath Evelyn's seated body. "Let me show you the more of the Plains. No for the racing this time. Maybe by we will be done time, the *joiner* you have will remember how to speak, yes?"

I stammer some more, trying to protest. It's no use. Evelyn is laughing, squeezing my hand before she lets go, then slipping her long fingers into the short, thin magenta fur lining the front of Zaylam's long neck. And off they go.

Jorbam curls her branches tighter around my body. *"What just happened?"* I want to know.

My friend just rumbles softly and holds me closer. I sigh into her soft leaves, as the unlikely pair of my hatchling dragon and the human Controller soar above us.

As the night grows deeper, Zaylam roars softly across the Plains to me. I dislodge myself from Jorbam's embrace and fly toward Zaylam, dodging the disapproving glances of some dragons and the curious glances of others. I meet Zay and a windswept, shaking Evelyn at the northernmost point of the Plains. This spot is the only one that is completely covered in grass, continuing from a field on the other side of the Barrier, and it is here that Zaylam sets Evelyn down.

"Thank you," she bows deeply as she slips off of Zaylam's back and stumbles slightly to my side.

"My pleasure, my dear," Zaylam sings warmly, and I wonder what they'd discussed together. "We'll be watching," she adds teasingly to me before flying off with another singsong roar.

Evelyn laughs softly as Zaylam flies off. She's shaking pretty hard. — Flight is cold at night. I slip my cloak off and put it tentatively around her shoulders. "You don't need to do that," she tells me, but wraps it tighter around herself nonetheless.

"I know. But flying can be—"

"Freezing!" she laughs. She looks out at the Plains and shakes her head. She looks to me uncertainly, and I bend to ask permission from the grasses beneath us to sit down. Not receiving it, I gesture Evelyn toward a different part of the patch, asking them. Receiving an affirmative response this time, I fold my legs in midair and nervously land on my backside next to her. She collapses elegantly next to me, running her hand gently over the grass, offering her thanks. "It's magnificent, isn't it? And you see the world like that at every moment." Her fingers are working to separate her windswept curls, but her eyes are still fixed on the Plains.

I don't know what to say, so I stay quiet. She doesn't seem to mind. She even puts her head on my shoulder after a few more moments of untangling her hair, the two of us just staring out at the Plains. "It's so beautiful," she whispers eventually.

"You think it's beautiful now? Imagine, Evelyn, this whole place with huge cocoon-like bulbs hanging down from the branches, two or three a tree. Dragon bulbs. There are a few now, one even on Aon's hatchling tree, right there—" I point Banion out to her—"but not nearly as many as there used to be, because…" I trail off. She knows. "And they light up, what's the word…" My tongue sticks out of the side of my mouth as I concentrate. Evelyn looks distracted, staring at my lips. I remember the word and swallow heavily before I forget it. "Iridescence, right? Yeah. They glow, like iridescence. See? Just to the right of where Zay's flying. That blue glow. They all have a slightly separate color, all unique. Used to be that you could see newly hatched dragons' paws and tails through the branches of almost every tree, because they were so bright and sometimes you'd see a little face... And then there was us, flying all around and tending to the bulbs, nuzzling with the little ones, learning..."

Her eyes are full of tears and her face contorts for a moment, like she's going to sob. But then she shifts her body to be flush against mine. I stiffen, surprised. Then I relax, content, and let a subtle pressure from her hand on my arm bring me down to lie next to her, the songs of my friends and the embrace of the grass beneath us pulling me into relaxation.

Chapter Twenty-Two

I WAKE, WITH the moon directly overhead and my arm draped across Evelyn's waist. I blink into the moonlight, spotted with dragon shadows. She is already awake, her eyes on mine. Her fingers are stroking slow patterns across my wingtips. She smiles when she sees me stirring. I've never seen anything like it. Moonlight reflected in her eyes.

"Hi," she whispers, pebbles in her voice.

I grin. My hand reaches up to stroke her cheek. I stop before touching her to ask, and she brings her own hand to complete our connection. Her skin is warm. She licks her lips and I lean forward.

A loud faeric clearing of the throat startles us both up and away from each other.

"So," Mom begins lazily, eyebrow raised in tandem with Mama's. "This is what you meant when you said you had something important to show us tonight." Her eyes swivel to Evelyn. "I see you've gotten involved with one of your lowly faeric subjects."

"I wouldn't phrase it that way," Evelyn counters softly but evenly, disentangling our limbs and rising to her feet with infinitely more poise than I could ever aspire to. She's different here, somehow. Her voice is smaller. Like she's not trying to be the Controller. Like maybe she's just Evelyn.

"How would you phrase it then?" Mom asks coolly, and I stand too, looking down at Osley, who's peeking out from under Aon's feet, who's in turn peeking out from behind Mom's back. Os's ears twitch.

Evelyn doesn't respond.

"Won't your soldiers be wondering where you are?" Mom continues.

"I've been grieving, and my Hands know this. Iema is taking care of everything in my absence, and my other Hands are none the wiser."

"We've all been grieving," Mom tells her, her hand shifting back to touch Aon protectively. "Why would you bring her here, Sadie?"

"She saved the Underland, Mom. She helped Blaze." Mom's eyes soften, and she looks away.

I meet Mama's eyes. *"Please."* She sighs and puts her hand on Mom's back underneath her wing sprouts.

Mom ignores her and takes a flutter toward Evelyn.

"I don't want know sort of sadistic fantasy you're playing out, toying with my daughter like this, but it needs to end."

"Faye—"

"You locked up my joiner, you've arrested both of our young ones—"

"Not a young one anymore, Mom—"

"Shush, Sadie."

"Ow! What do you do, sharpen your elbows before slamming into my ribs? This some Sampian thing you haven't told me about yet?"

"Sadie."

This time, my name comes from three different mouths: one angry, one at once irritated and amused, and one softer, pleading, rich with humility.

I lower my head, but can't erase my smirk.

"Is there a single reason I should trust you? And don't say because the Lunavad trees granted you entry. Sadie's the last faerie with hatchling mates thanks to you and your government, they're overly fond of her—"

"The king is planning an attack on the Plains. He thinks he's found a way to penetrate the barrier, and I'm going to help you stop them. Just like I protected the Underland from my people, just like I stopped the crackdown on your uprising, just like I tried to help Blaze—"

Her voice, usually so steady and cold,, wavers now, cracking like it'll shatter into tiny irreparable pieces if she keeps talking. I reach for her hand and she takes it.

When Evelyn speaks again, it's so softly we all lean in slightly.

"Blaze didn't deserve to die. And que wouldn't have if it weren't for my government." She raises her eyes to meet Mom's, which is more than I can manage. "No apology can ever make up for what I've done."

"Evelyn—"

"But I won't let anything happen to your daughter. Or your son. Any of you. Not if I can help it."

I glance up at Mama, who's staring at Mom, whose eyes are locked in some sort of battle with Evelyn. I almost back away from the energy passing between them. Mama and Aon exchange a glance while Osley and I gulp.

"We've got a lot to do tonight, then. Let's talk somewhere more private, shall we?" Mom offers finally.

Evelyn nods once, deeply, almost a bow. Mom flies off and we follow, me holding Evelyn's hand and Aon with a disgruntled but willing Osley in his arms. Zaylam meets us above Jorbam's canopy, where Evelyn sits on her neck and we form an enclosed circle in the sky around her.

I take Aon's hand. He keeps glancing furtively at Evelyn, like he doesn't know what to make of her presence. I know he has two things on his mind: her secret kindnesses to him and Blaze, and the cage she put him in.

"Well?" Mama says. "You said they were planning another attack."

Evelyn nods. "King Xavier is planning to raid the Plains." She holds up her hands before we can interrupt her. "I'm not sure when, but the rumors Iema has been able to gather suggest some time next week. He believes he's found a way to penetrate the shield—you all call it the barrier, yes?—around this place."

"And let's play a guessing game. Your little trip here is going to help him along."

"Aon," I whisper, but honestly it's so good to hear his voice, which has been pretty absent since Blaze died, that my reprimand is only halfhearted. He looks at me with pained sorrow, but there's Evelyn with her hands again.

"The only thing I've learned that would be of any help to the king is that I needed to be touched by a hatched faerie to enter, but if you honestly think the king hasn't surmised that already, you haven't been spending nearly enough time thinking as your enemy does." She pauses, regarding Aon with sadness in her eyes. He looks down toward Banion and his dangling, swollen dragon bulb.

"No, the king and his advisers think in terms of blood." A longer pause this time.

And then it hits me, and it feels like an axe to my stomach. "He thinks by using hatched faerie blood, they'll be able to cross the barrier without Jorbam and the others being able to control it, doesn't he?" Pause. "Doesn't he?"

"But Ler and Os can get in. And all the fae who aren't hatched yet. Or who'll never be hatched, now with Dreaming—" Aon cuts off his own objection, consuming himself with stroking Osley's ears, eyes downcast.

"By the trees' choosing," I counter. "Hatched faeries can get in anyway."

Evelyn nods thoughtfully. "That's why you had so much trouble combating the rebels who killed Jax's joiner, isn't it? Tacon and his followers? They continued to have access to the Plains because they had hatchling mates."

"Yeah." A pause.

"Wait, though. Wouldn't we know if the king was collecting blood from us?" Aon's voice is steady, but there's fear in his brown eyes.

The humans have been
Collecting the fae's blood
For time and time
Unless the truth
Is cloudier.
The Head Slicers, correct?
They
Inject the blood of dragonkind
Into the brains of the faye
In the Slicings.
And in the process
The Slicers have also been
Harvesting faee blood
From Slicings
Is that not right?
Sing that it
Is not,

Zaylam offers softly, her melody sad, slow, and tentative. Grave.

Evelyn's head rises and falls again.

"Oh, Lunara," Mama mutters as Aon runs his fingers under his hair, over his Slicing scar.

"Indeed," Evelyn responds in kind, her eyes finding my scar, easily visible because of my close cut hair.

"Why now?" Osley's feet tap onto Aon's curled arm. I verbalize the question for Evelyn's sake.

"I fear that I am no longer in Xavier's highest favor. He seems... he seems to believe that my interference with the Underland's destruction was motivated more by loyalty to Grovians than loyalty to the letter of his law."

Tears sting my eyes, and Evelyn meets them briefly. I say nothing, and neither does she; this is not the time to tell my little brother that Blaze didn't just die. That que was murdered, in retaliation.

"And was it?" Mom asks, her voice clipped and tense. Mama glances wide-eyed between Mom, Aon, and Evelyn.

She sighs. "I have always borne great discomfort with the wanton destruction of lives."

"So you became a Controller," Mom cuts in. "And let me guess, you didn't realize that the wanton destruction of lives is literally the task of Controllers."

Evelyn's eyes widen and she looks somewhat panicked. Her words spill out in a rush. "The circumstances under which I became Controller were not—"

There's a rustling of faeric wings beneath us, and Zaylam's neck tenses. We all look down. Kashat.

"You started without me," he says mildly. At the sight of him, Evelyn goes rigid. I think of Fiora and I look between them nervously.

Kashat lowers his eyes, hovering in front of her. "I can't help what I Dreamed, I—"

"You used it to manipulate me in your performance. I didn't know it then, but now I understand that you knew who she was the whole time—"

"No, I didn't realize at the time—"

The skin behind Mama's eyes crinkles. "What are we on about, there, you two?"

Silence.

It occurs to me that this is exactly why we need Dreaming. Kashat Dreamed a piece of Evelyn's life; he can't hate her now, not really, because—if only fleetingly—he felt what it was to be her. So here he is, worried about hurting Evelyn while my moms are still ready to hate her.

Dreaming binds us. And we need it if we're going to do this.

Mama interrupts my thoughts. "Sadie?"

I wave my hands up noncommittally as Kashat and Evelyn continue to stare each other down. *"It's not my place to say."*

More silence, as the defiant apology in Kashat's eyes battles the hurt anger in Evelyn's. Without breaking eye contact with him, she says, "The fact remains that I don't know exactly when Xavier plans to send the Mach to attack the Plains, but as I said, perhaps as early as next week. I could try to find out directly, but I think that would be too dange—"

"Wait, the palace is attacking the Plains?" Kashat interjects.

"Keep up, Kash. Maybe don't fall asleep next time I tell you to meet us somewhere," Aon teases, touching his forearm. Mama waggles her eyebrows at Mom at their touch. Osley squirms uncomfortably until Aon secures both arms back around quer. Zaylam hums in amusement but Mom just rolls her eyes and twists the fabric of her flowing trousers between her fingers.

I widen my eyes briefly at Evelyn, who smirks.

And then the entire Plains quakes, and she falls off of Zaylam's neck, plummeting toward Jorbam's canopy.

I speed down after her, but Zaylam's wings are bigger—she gets there first, and swoops her tailfin under Evelyn right before she's crushed on Jorbam's branches.

With her safe, I spin in midair, trying to locate the source of the massive quake. Something is rocking the Energies themselves, all throughout the Plains.

"Sadie!" I take Evelyn's hand and weave with her through the thick mass of dragons, following Aon's panicked voice down, down.

"I thought you said they wouldn't attack until next week!" Mom's voice follows us.

"That's what I thought!" Evelyn calls back, harried.

We land roughly, Zaylam hovering low above us. Aon crashes down next to us and sets a quaking Osley down gently. I bend to put my hand on quer trembling fur before looking up to see what the others are staring at, transfixed.

When I see it, I am quaking as much as Osley.

"It can't be this soon, this is too soon," Evelyn mutters next to me.

Squadrons of Mach soldiers are in an attack formation just outside the Plains, slamming dozens of spells at a time into the invisible barrier, which is the only thing separating us from fighting a battle we just aren't ready for.

Chapter Twenty-Three

MY HANDS ON her waistline and hers clutching at my forearms, Evelyn and I stand together on the edge of the Plains, staring out of the barrier into the Forest where we first locked eyes.

It is all about to burn.

Another series of earthquake-causing thuds erupts as the air in front of us shudders with a sickening yellow explosion. The barrier flickers.

"They can't get in," I tell Evelyn, trying to keep my voice steady and failing miserably. She nods, but her eyes aren't on mine. She's staring at the Commander of the Mach, just a flutter away from us. The barrier hasn't been penetrated. He can't see us yet. But he is so close to us. I can see the sweat gathering on his temples and the vicious gleam in his eyes. My stomach rolls over.

Reve.

I guide Evelyn away from the border, my hands still on her waist.

There is a reprieve, a moment where all I hear is our breath and Mom and Mama fighting with Aon, all but shoving him out into the Forest, away from the Mach, with Osley. Away from the attack zone. To tell the others what is happening, if they don't already know. If they haven't already been killed trying to stop the invasion.

Aon is screaming that he's not a young one anymore, but he's losing the fight. I tune out his screams because they sound too much like Blaze's death. Mom and Mama will get him away, to safety.

Evelyn's chest is rising and falling in time with mine, her nails digging into my forearms. Zaylam's shadow over us comforts me. But not for long.

Because the next moment, the ground itself is rent open. I fly up instinctively, pulling Evelyn with me. We look down, and the earth itself is coming undone. Root after agonized root is breaking free of the ground, writhing like massive, solid worms. Zaylam, Gimla, and the rest of the dragons roar like their scaled throats are on fire. The sound makes it hard for my wings to keep holding Evelyn out of the way of the flailing roots.

I've never seen trees in pain so intense that they uproot themselves, but I can't see what's causing it. "What—" I start to shout at Kashat, who's dodging roots and looking terrified a few flutterdrops from us.

In answer to my question, Evelyn points below quickly before grabbing hold of me again. I renew my grip on her and look in the direction she pointed to.

The Mach have abandoned their spell work. They're split up now into two groups. One is several flutters back, in attack formation, swords and axes drawn. The other, farther group is shooting arrows into the barrier. When they hit, their tips burst into thick, pink droplets.

Faerie blood.

The barrier is flickering. They'll be inside soon.

"Zay!" I shout. My body contracts with fear, and I can't see what's in front of me. But then she's at my side. She, too, is shaking so violently she keeps knocking Evelyn and me almost out of the air. But when Zay sings, her voice is steady, rising so all the Plains can hear.

> *The Mach will break through*
> *Swords in flesh soon*
> *But dragonkind has friends with magic*
> *Too*
> *The Mach burn the Plains*
> *The faye shoot water from their veins*
> *Dragonkind must circle now*
> *All in formation*
> *How*
> *The Mach will break through*
> *Swords in flesh soon.*

Gimla and the others take it up like a soothing battle cry, full of determined serenity instead of the ferocity that nons go to battle with. Harlenikal joins in with more verses, on and on until the Plains is full to the brink with dragon songs, most of the singers revolving in a circle above our heads, ready to dive when the Mach come through.

"They look like birds of prey," Evelyn shouts over the din, flexing her fingers, preparing to unleash battle magic.

"They're not," Kashat yells back, though he looks equally mesmerized. "They won't kill any of them on purpose. That's what your people don't understand about dragons. They're more peaceful than we are, usually."

We dodge more flailing roots. Kashat draws his labor axe, and there are tears mixed with the sweat on his face as he looks back down at the Mach.

He grabs my forearm. "If I die, tell your brother—"

But I can only imagine what message he wants me to send, because there is a throaty shout under us. The Mach have broken through.

Evelyn starts to speed down toward them, pulling me along, but I yank back against the wind current the passing dragons are creating.

"Please don't," I beg her, shouting to be heard amidst the clashes of metal on metal, metal on flesh. Amidst the screaming.

"Are you fighting?" she shouts impatiently, putting both hands in mine.

"This is my family," I choke out, tears streaking my cheeks.

Her trembling hands move to frame my face as I clutch at her waist.

"Then we'll protect each other, Sadie. We'll get through this, you understand me?"

I can't answer. I hear my moms shouting as they twist the Energies below us, and Zaylam's battle song thuds in my ears.

Evelyn kisses my lips fiercely. I forget how to breathe. Her wet eyes meet mine.

"We'll protect each other," I agree.

She gives me a quick, small smile and touches her forehead to mine.

She looks down briefly, screws up her face like she's calculating something, and wills me to let her free fall out of the sky.

I yell, but she lands, as she planned, on Zaylam's back. Zay arches her tailfin around to swoop her off and safely deposits her onto the ground. I'm about to fly down to where Evelyn is, but then Zaylam, above her, screams.

She's thrown herself in front of Jorbam as a wave of fire sparked by four soldiers working as one cascades toward Jorbam's trunk. Her shrieks rent the air as her chest and underbelly blister open and burst into flames. Evelyn, Mama, and I send cooling water her way out of our own bodies, extinguishing the flames, but there are so few of us and so many of them, and there is only so much bending the Energies can take before they snap. Mama is yelling something I can't understand, but I make out one word—Xamamlee. The name of her hatchling dragon. Who died the last time they attacked the Plains.

Gimla yanks Zaylam away, dragging her by her tailfin with his teeth, and I fly up to Mama and shake her by the shoulders. Her face is streaked with dirt, Zaylam's blood, and tears. I don't want to know what my face looks like.

She nods at me and kisses me briefly on the forehead. "You keep yourself safe, Sadie, you understand me?"

I nod and turn as Kashat shouts my name. He tosses me a fae glass sword. I don't know where he got it from, and I can't stop to ask. I don't ask, either, when Aora got here, because she's at Kashat's side, the two of them fighting off three soldiers together. That must mean Aon's flown with Osley to safety, spread the word. Relief pools in my stomach even as I catch the sword and swing my eyes around, desperately seeking Evelyn amidst the rising smoke. I vaguely register Ezrae, a deer elder who often brings us information from Lethe, who is dodging arrows to run for more help. I wrench the Energies into a shield around him as he gallops and I spend a satisfied moment as arrows deflect off of him and speed back to their shocked and scattered senders.

The moment I take is too much. I hear Evelyn's scream and I speed toward the sound. On the way, I feel the pull of Energies caused by my growns fighting near me, above Aon.

Aon's back. Mama is yelling something at him as she raises protective spells around him with her wiry arms. Aon. In battle. My baby brother.

He's never looked so small.

But Mama's protecting him. She has to. I keep flying, coughing in the smoke, toward the sound of Evelyn's scream.

Armed only with magic against soldiers with both metal weapons and magic, Evelyn is holding her own well. But she's surrounded.

I shout her name and tug the Energies into a gust of wind directed at the soldier nearest her, knocking him over. I keep speeding toward them, but they keep coming. They slash at her with spells and with sharp metal.

Nothing else exists.

I will be too late.

I yank the Energies into spells. They are not falling properly. Everyone is moving too fast, faster than our training prepared us for, faster than I can think. One of the soldiers is bringing down his sword, slashing toward Evelyn's chest.

She doesn't see him—she's busy sending waves of water toward the tree nearest her, coughing in all the smoke. She doesn't hear me shouting.

THE GRATING SQUEAK of non metal on faye glass slams into my ears, and the world speeds up to regular time again. The soldier's sword is not buried in Evelyn's flesh. It is swinging down, down. Unsuccessfully.

Because his sword is being held off by Lerian's axe.

My heart soars, almost bursting out of my chest.

"Sadie, either get her another weapon or get her out of her," Lerian shouts as she thrusts his sword away and launches her axe at him. He cowers; with her powerful centaur lower body, she is much, much bigger than he is.

Lerian whinnies and rears up on her hind legs, brandishing her front hooves at him. "More of us are on the way, horse-killer! Not so much fun when we're not chained down, huh?" But more Mach are approaching, beginning to surround even Lerian, who is now reared back to back with Evelyn.

"Hey, faerie! Might wanna wipe that smirk off your face and come help us out here!" Ler yells as she swings her axe wildly at the jumpy non soldiers around her.

I realize with a jolt that I'm frozen, smiling on a battlefield that was home mere moments ago.

"On three!" I shout as I speed toward them. Evelyn nods and Lerian whoops. I shout the countdown, flying up and forward, and on three, Lerian rears up wildly. Evelyn and I take advantage of the Mach's distraction to knock a few of them unconscious with an enchanted gust of noxious wind aimed at them from either side.

I laugh with our temporary triumph, and then I am doubled over, free-wheeling out of the sky.

Chapter Twenty-Four

I SEE, AS though I'm observing if distantly as someone else, an arrow, soaked with my blood, tearing clean through my skin. I hear my flesh skewer open. Smoke stings my eyes and I struggle to regain control of my wings. I hear Mama shouting as she yanks the Energies at whoever shot at me, her voice cracked and terrified. I don't look down at my wound. I don't even know where I've been hit.

I look up at Evelyn as I careen to the ground. Her lips are moving soundlessly as she sends streams of water at my burning friends while she runs toward me. Mom and Jax are tending to fallen dragons. Zaylam is among them.

I roll over and wretch.

Lerian is galloping toward me, my name on her lips, coughing though she is with the smoke rising thickly through the entire Plains.

Almost all the Lunavads are on fire. I send a weak rush of wet wind Lerian's way, clearing the air around her and pushing smoke away from her lungs. The effort of bending the Energies keeps me pinned to the hard, hot ground. A pair of thick roots tears out of the ground and lifts me away, planting me under my Mom before smacking three oncoming soldiers aside. I try dimly to figure out whose roots saved me, but the pain is getting too much.

"Sadie!" Mom screams above the chaos, focused only on me. Her eyes are vivid in the haze, desperate. Her hands run all over my body, tears streaking tracks through the ash and blood on her face.

"Mom," I groan, but stop when I realize how much my mouth tastes like vomit.

"Chew on this." She shows something minty in my mouth, and I don't question her, even as she ducks under the cascading roots that are wrenching themselves near apart to keep us safe. I try to turn my head again to see who is protecting us, but Mom puts a firm hand on my forehead to stop me from moving. She's craning her neck every which way for a better view, her fingers testing the area around the arrow in me. She takes a deep breath and looks at me sternly.

"Sadie, I need to take this arrow out of you. It's not going to be—"

She tightens her fist over the arrow and yanks. A sick squelching sound shoots through my veins as pain, worse than actually getting shot to begin with, wracks my entire body.

"Pleasant," she says grimly when I finally stop screaming.

"A little warning next time," I pant as she sutures my side with a prominently veined, wrinkled hand, the Energies contorting to help her around me.

"Anticipation makes it worse." Her voice is casual, but her brown eyes are pure agony.

"No point in telling you to get yourself somewhere safe, is there?" she asks me. I just stare up at her face, streaked with my blood.

"One day, you two will listen to your mother and me," she mutters as she pulls me up, half carrying me through the air, toward Jax and Aora and Kashat. We converge with Mama, surrounding Lerian, Aon, and Evelyn, away from the flailing bodies of the dragons Semad, Archa, Kamid. And Zaylam.

I scream her name but Mom won't let me go. Her hand grazes my still bloodied side, and I gasp with the renewed pain.

"She'll be all right, Sadie, the burns aren't—"

"Zay!"

She's just lying there, sprawled all wrong.

"She can't hear you, Sade, but the burns aren't deep—"

"She'll suffocate!"

"I twisted the Energies around her face, all of their faces, she'll be fine—"

I stop struggling and stare at Mom's blood and soot-streaked face as her viselike grip on me tightens.

"Then why are you keeping me from her?"

"You just got shot, Sadie. If you—" I'm struggling again, and she shoves my back into Banion's trunk as a spell from a Mach soldier burns into the Energies where I was just hovering. "If you're going to insist on staying and fighting, I need to know you're—" She and I nod at each other before sending a strong blast of Energies-twisting wind around the other side of Banion's trunk at two advancing Mach soldiers. "—protected."

I turn my eyes back across the Plains to Zaylam's resting form. I squint through the haze. Her underbelly is rising, falling. Too weakly for my liking, but significantly. Jorbam's trunk is scorch free. Thanks to her. I swallow vomit, nod, and shake my hands out.

"Do we have a plan?"

Gimla shrieks a warning above us and we speed up to him, combining our wing winds to quell flames heading toward a younger Lunavad sapling.

"I need your other mother—we can freeze everything!"

Relief floods through me. A plan. Maybe with a plan, the rest of my life won't look like flames and smell like flesh.

My eyes water and Mom tugs me down. "Try to stay low—the smoke goes up."

"Faye!"

Mama. We fly in the direction of her voice below us, and I almost choke when a wall of smoke clears and reveals her. She's surrounded by three Mach soldiers, hovering protectively above Aon.

"What are you doing back?" Mom shouts at him as she and I both pick a soldier to get away from them.

"Now's not a great time to scold me!" my little brother calls, and my laughter ignites the pain in my side but gives my spell the extra push I need to make the soldier I'm facing turn back. Away from Aon. He will not die like Blaze. I won't allow it.

Mom doesn't laugh. She spins to round on Aon, not seeing the Mach soldier she's facing take advantage and pull his fingers back to yank the Energies into a spell at her. Before I can even call to her, the soldier drops down, unconscious.

Evelyn steps out of the smoke behind him, her forehead streaked with a thin gash of blood, her face set, steely.

"Thank you." Mom's voice is shocked, humbled. Numb.

Evelyn's eyes meet mine. "You don't leave people to die."

She holds my eyes for a moment longer and then, without warning, she speeds off, away. Back toward the breach in the barrier.

"Told you it was a bad time to scold me," Aon is saying as Mom scoops him behind her. I pull her into my arms, put my forehead against hers.

"I love you."

And I take off after Evelyn.

Mom's face is stricken, but she can't object. She spins to send a gust of water at the nearest trees, at the nearest fire-wielding Hands.

I don't look back.

When I catch up with her, Evelyn glances at me between sword swipes—someone must have passed her the weapon in the chaos—and her eyes linger too long on my bloodied side.

Then the Energies tug strangely around us. Not like a spell, not like something deliberate. It feels like a Dream, the way the Energies twist around someone when we Dream. But who could be sleeping right now?

The Commander of the Mach steps out from the smoke and raises his sword to meet Evelyn's neck. Fast. The feeling of that Energy twisting intensifies. I ignore it and shout Evelyn's name so she'll pay attention to Reve. Their swords lock just above her forehead, her fleshy and powerful arms trembling but holding.

That sensation of Energy tugging redoubles, and I realize with a jolt that I've felt it each time Reve has been near me. Now; when he tried to invade the Underland; when Iema was bleeding in the snow.

"I was hoping you wouldn't choose the wrong side to fight for, Your Majesty." His lips curl menacingly.

I almost fall out of the air. *Her Majesty?*

Lerian's eyes flash as she whips her face, gashed and bloodied, away from the scene.

"You got something you want to tell me about your friend over there?" she shouts.

"I have no idea," I yell back. *Her Majesty?*

A few whistled notes rise above the fray, from the spot where I'd left my family. Its distinct pattern, lilting up on the last note, signals us all to rush toward it. Like young ones entering a racing game.

Lerian jerks her head toward the noise, and I tug on Evelyn's arm, encouraging her to run with us. Toward my growns. Toward their plans to unlease a freeze spell on the Plains.

I lose my breath halfway there, and Lerian practically tosses me onto her back. She glares over her shoulder when I struggle, and she only lets go of me when we've joined a circle made up of Zeel, my growns, Jax, Aon, Kashat, a few others whose names I don't know.

Mama lets loose the whistle signal again, and on the last note, we lock hands. With the next breath, each of us who can twist the Energies send everything buried inside of us, locked in our bones, out into the Plains. We unhinge ourselves momentarily from the primary Energies flying through us, and we send them out into the world.

An azure thread goes out from our joined, bloodied hands and weaves its way out from our bodies, stilling almost everything and everyone it touches.

We are freezing the Plains, as Mama and Mom did to that clearing the night we raided the weapons caravan.

The night I met the woman fighting for us nearby.

A small gap of silence, of stillness, rises around us.

I look back to where we left Evelyn, to where I thought she was following us.

Reve is only slowed by the spell, his sword in slow motion, midswing, slowed in time with the rest of his body. Some small fires near us stop flickering, their growth halted by the freeze. But the azure thread flails and stops the freeze, too weak, too small; the Plains are enormous, and the rest of it is still at full speed, smoking, crackling sickeningly, full of agonized yells, of the nauseating scent of burning flesh, of vomit, of decay.

We need to freeze flame and force all across the Plains, not just the part immediately surrounding us. We need more power.

Evelyn, disentangling herself finally from her now slowed sword fight, runs toward us. Her entire body is shaking with the effort, but she holds a gentle, trembling hand out to my bloodied side.

When her skin touches mine, three explosions occur at once.

Chapter Twenty-Five

THE FIRST, A great wind tears across the whole Plains, freezing in its wake every flame, every invader, exactly as my growns had planned.

The second, an enormous wave of water emanates out from the spot where her fingers touch my skin, drenching and extinguishing the stilled flames and thoroughly soaking and jostling all of us in its wake.

The third, a tremendous boom inside my chest, my heart screaming with the impact of her touch.

Shocked silence fills the Plains. It lasts until the groans of the injured and the cries of the deads' loved ones start rising up along with the falling boughs of friends that had, an hour before, stood healthy and unharmed.

The fluttering of wings and the treading of hooves of other Grovians who've come into the fighting start converging on us. P'Tal and Zeel gallop straight into Aora's embrace, and Tamzel tosses an arm around Mama. Kashat flies into the open arms of his growns, knocking them back a few flutters with the force of his embrace. Other faeries and centaurs I don't know so well find each other, embrace. Lerian, who's settled in next to me, is looking everywhere at once, trying to account for everyone she knows, everyone she saw in the fighting. I know because I'm doing the same thing. She glances down at me and curls her fingers around mine. I squeeze back.

No one comes up to Evelyn, grateful to find her alive. Then again, no one's coming up to me, either. She stands alone next to me, one hand on her thigh, breathing hard. Her other hand is still on my body. She looks up at me, curly hair plastered by water around her face. My heart swells and she smiles slightly.

We're alive. And she's touching me like she'll never stop.

Osley—I don't know when que slipped back into the fray—is beating out a message to my moms. I can't catch it, too busy wondering whether the blood on quer coat is quer's or someone else's. I don't know which possibility terrifies me more. But Mom agrees to whatever que's saying, raising her voice to repeat it to all of us while her hands comb Osley's body to check for wounds.

"The freeze won't last long. Those of you who can, carry the Mach away. Take them to the edge of the Forest, scatter them. Distort their memories so they think they recall that they couldn't get through the barrier, that their mission failed. Get the impression of the spell from someone if you need to." A pause. "Go!"

The centaurs glance at Tamzel, who stares at Mama for a moment before nodding. "Do as she says," she orders, her rank as leader of the Centauric Council carrying immediate impact, as centaurs pair up with faeries all across the Plains to gather the soldiers and take them away.

Lerian nudges her head against mine and looks me square in the face, her hand roughly falling on my cheek. "Got your back."

I nod, tears stinging my eyes. "Got yours too, Ler."

She scoffs and backs away, bending to toss two limp soldiers on her back. "No need to get all sentimental, faerie. Makes you even uglier."

I grin and she returns it before tossing her head at E'rix, who follows her out of the Plains at a rapid pace. In twos, threes, and fours, every faerie and centaur that is able follows their example. I stay behind with Evelyn, my growns, and Jax, an odd tugging in my side reminding me that I got shot.

There's a low, melodic groan off toward the side, and I start flying immediately.

"Zaylam."

I speed to where she's lying under Jorbam's trunk, Evelyn's footsteps behind me. Zaylam's underbelly is ripe with silver blisters, and her eyes are closed. I collapse next to her face, slipping my forehead onto one of Jorbam's bigger roots.

Jor starts rumbling immediately, a lot shakier than normal.

"She protected me. That's how your Mama's hatchling died. Xamamlee. Protecting. He dove into fire. Sadie, she protected me."

"I know, Jorbam. I know. Mom says she'll be fine, she'll be..." I turn wildly to Evelyn, who's hanging back, her face stricken. "She'll be all right, right?"

She just stares, her eyes riveted on Zaylam's angry blisters, her slack pose.

"Zay. Zay, it's me." I grip Jorbam's root, hard, until my knuckles are nearly purple. She rumbles wordlessly now, because there aren't any words for her terror. "Zaylam!"

I shove the top of her wings, wrapped around her lower belly like a shroud.

> *No need to shout so,*
> *Sadie.*
> *And quit rumbling so,*
> *Jorbam.*
> *One hatchling feels like an*
> *Earthquake,*
> *And the other sounds like an*
> *Explosion.*

I half hit at her, and half try to throw my arms around her. "You scared us, Zay!"

> *The hatchlings would slip*
> *In and out of*
> *Consciousness too, if the hatchlings*
> *Were all burn-covered.*
> *But I think Faye*
> *Stemmed the worst of the damage.*
> *Gimla, Harlenikal, Banion, the*
> *Others?*
> *Who lived?*

I look around shakily. Smoke is still clearing across the Plains. I look back at Evelyn, and her eyes are brimming with tears. We don't know who lived, not yet. But I know what Mom would do in the infirmary. Evelyn nods at me slightly.

"Everybody lived, Zay. It's gonna be all right."

Her snout twitches outward slightly, and I burl into an unburned length of her neck, keeping my face, my hand, rested on Jorbam's root.

> *Good then. I think it's time*
> *To go back to sleep*
> *Then.*

"Sleep, Zay, yeah. I'll heal you more while you rest."

"Sadie," Jorbam rumbles warningly as Zaylam droops back to painless unconsciousness. *"Something's wrong. With Banion. Sadie."*

A scream—one that rents my chest open and threatens never to let it close again—tears out of my mom's throat, then. Evelyn jumps and grabs at my hand tightly. I look without wanting to. Back by my growns, Jax is bent over a faerie's still body.

The body's chest isn't rising or falling.

I recognize it.

The dead body is Aon's.

Chapter Twenty-Six

EVELYN CHECKS VAGUELY to make sure I haven't broken anything, and then she runs again, this time away from Aon and Mom. I try not to feel betrayed that she's left me at this moment.

I try not to feel anything at all.

Maybe he's happy. Maybe he's met Blaze, scattered in the Energies.

I doubt it.

I don't register much until she returns. Jax trying to coax life back into my brother. Mama holding a screaming Mom while her own shrieks of agony tear into my soul.

Their screams are familiar. The way their bodies writhe, the way they're reaching out, touching his body, screaming his name, like saying it with enough despair, with enough love, will be enough to bring him back.

Their grief is familiar.

Blaze's growns.

I feel nothing.

I don't even know what happened. I can't see too much blood on his body.

Mama is screaming. About how it must have been while we were trying to cast the Freeze spell. Surrounded by his family and no one noticed. No one noticed our little boy dying right next to us.

He must have been so scared.

There is so much screaming.

I am immobilized.

Why haven't the Plains exploded?

Why are my growns still yelling his name? Why is Jax is even trying? Why am I breathing?

Evelyn steps back in front of me and I want to scream at her for leaving my side when Aon is dead. When the world is over.

But she passes me and approaches where my moms and Jax are splayed over Aon. She kneels next to Jax smoothly, and I dimly register that her body starts...glowing. A soft golden hue, tinted with green.

I want to scream, ask what she thinks she's doing. I want to tell them all to leave his body alone, to let him rest.

He just wants to be with Blaze.

They should let him. They should stop messing with his body; they should let him be with Blaze; they should let me go next.

I don't understand why Evelyn is glowing, why golden threads are now streaming from her fingertips into Aon's chest and back again, forming a double loop between them, back and forth, back and forth, the golden threads getting thicker and thicker, brighter and brighter, the longer she stays bent over him.

Mom and Mama's eyes widen, and Jax backs his away on his hands. My growns, too, back away from their dead son, like they're in a trance. The grief is retreating from their eyes, being replaced by something that looks like hope.

My wings, of their own accord, drag me off the ground and fly me forward, toward the strange scene.

"Evelyn, what..." But she doesn't answer me. No one does. Her eyes are glowing solid golden, the amber ring sometimes visible around her pupils replacing her usual brown color entirely. She places both of her hands on Aon's glistening chest, bringing the double looping golden threads with her, before sliding them underneath him to stroke his wings. A deep red glow, like the sunset color of his wings, slips out of his body and moves into hers.

"Mom, what..." I try again. But it's Jax's voice that answers me.

"This is soul keeping magic, Sadie. The Controller's a soul keeper. She's trying to save your brother."

Dull recognition courses through me. Her Healing magic is that same golden, soul keeping color. She'd spoken so kindly, but so warningly, to Blaze and Aon, when Aon told her they wanted to learn to be soul keepers.

Heat swirls through my core as I stare at her, openmouthed.

She's a soul keeper. I can Dream.

The glow is filling her now, and I've never seen anything so beautiful.

Evelyn smiles softly, like she can feel me watching her, feel me understanding. Her eyes roll into the back of her head and she licks her lips absently, arching her chest up toward the sky. Her arms float up, seemingly of their own accord. For a bizarre moment, I imagine that she is about to take flight.

Silence. Only breathing.

And then a small, high-pitched moan comes from her lips, and the golden glow leaves her, undulating ethereally toward the other side of the Plains, where Banion, Aon's hatchling tree, is rooted. The reddish glow Evelyn coaxed from Aon's still body swims soundlessly through the destruction-ridden Plains until it reaches Banion's roots. It seeps into the ground and weaves through each root up into the ropelike tendrils of Banion's trunk. The reddish hue of Aon's glow—of Aon's soul, I realize numbly—melts effortlessly into the golden-brown, green-tinged waves of Banion's.

Close by me, Evelyn gasps, and she's sweating, glowing golden, one arm out toward Banion, one toward Aon's limp body, her head lolled back, guiding the flow of their souls. She looks like she's unconscious, like she'll crumple at any moment. I start forward to touch her, but Jax holds out his hands to stop me.

I pause only a flutter from her, ready to catch her if she wavers.

She doesn't. A low roar reaches us from Banion, and the dragon bulb that hangs, never to hatch, on his branches glows so bright for a moment that we all have to turn away. But it only lasts for a moment. When I look back, each one of Banion's spiney leaves is the wildest, most brilliant green I have ever seen, ever could have imagined. They're greener than the healthiest grass on the sunniest day; richer than the sight of entire communities of vibrant coral under the Flowing on the purest Highland beaches. I didn't know colors could be that bright, didn't know anything could be so full; Banion's canopy looks ready to lift his entire body, roots and all, into flight, into the depths of the bluest sky.

Until abruptly, it stops. All that green; the golden-brown tint of Banion's soul; everything fades back into Aon's red one, and their waves seep back down Banion's trunk, back through his roots, back through the air.

Back to this side of the Plains. Back into Aon's dead body.

The Plains seem extremely dark, even though by now, the sun is starting to peek over the treetops.

More silence.

"Come on, Aon."

My brother gasps loudly, his chest rising for the first time in too long. His face bathes in a deep golden glow inflected with green that's started to shine out through the haze across the Plains. A sob wracks through my chest.

Five pairs of hands swarm forward to hold Aon steady as he tries to sit, struggling to haul himself up onto his elbows.

"What... did I die?" His voice is creaky and both my moms draw him into their embrace, heads buried on his chest. My hands are all over his wings, his hair, and Jax's hands are covering his own face as he rocks back and forth softly. Evelyn leans back on her haunches, a small smile on her lips, tears streaking her face, back to its regular, smooth brown.

"You said you wanted to be a soul keeper," she whispers to him. "I'm afraid this doesn't make you one, but it does mean you and your hatchling tree were brought back to life by one."

Aon blinks rapidly, staring at Evelyn like she just sprouted a third arm and a pair of dragon wings.

"You...you're a..."

She nods, that smile growing bigger, and I wonder if she's ever told anyone before, ever shown anyone what she could do.

"I've known since I was a young one. Kept it very hidden, of course. I've never soul kept for someone with a hatchling mate, so when I realized you'd... I'm sorry, that you'd..."

"Died," Aon supplies, and he sounds excited now. Mom and Mama laugh until they're sobbing again into his side.

"Right. I reached out to your hatchling tree—Sadie pointed him out last night—and of course he gave consent. I facilitated the melding of your souls, in my body and in his, to help me heal your body. To bring you back with your body. You... you're both fine now, I think. I mean, you seem to be. Do you feel all right?"

Aon flexes his wings and his eyes well up. Evelyn looks concerned, but he shakes his head. "I wish Blaze was here," he says, and I squeeze his shoulder before standing up and crossing over him to get to Evelyn.

She takes my hand and rises too, backing a little away from the others.

"That was the most beautiful thing I've ever seen. A soul keeper."

"You can imagine why I didn't tell anyone."

"You saved his life, Evelyn, I... I can never repay you for that."

She turns toward my growns, toward Aon. That smile comes back to her face. "That's all I'll ever need."

"How long have you known?"

"There was a lightning storm in Izla, when I was a young one. I was outside alone, and one of the trees was struck, and she spoke to me, with her soul... I've never known how to describe it. And I hosted her." She meets my eyes, licks her lips.

"That's not what you wanted to ask me about."

I shift uncomfortably. Now that Aon's alive and safe, the battle has returned to the front of my mind. The battle, the arrow in my flesh, Zaylam's screams... Reve's voice.

"Evelyn." I take her hands. "Reve called you *Your Majesty*. Why?"

"Sadie..."

"What did he mean, Evelyn?"

"Sadie, I can't. Aon's safe, I need to leave, and I can't, I won't... It won't matter if they wipe Reve's memories successfully. Xavier cast a spell over them both, so that he Dreams whatever Reve sees. The perfect spy. I felt the Energies twist—didn't you?—the taste of Dreaming, whenever he was close to me."

I scratch roughly at my ear. "So the king Dreams what Reve sees? And he doesn't think that's a bit hypocritical, that he's gonna bring the plague down on everyone? But wait, Reve's a spy? Like me? Or like, for the king? And you're not answering me, Evelyn, he called you..."

"Shush, I'm getting to it, but there isn't a lot of time. Sadie, Xavier sent him here to test me, and he did, when they tried to attack the Underland. And Xavier didn't like what he saw, so they had Blaze killed, they attacked tonight..." She starts rocking, and her voice cracks with guilt. I put my hands on her shoulders. "And whatever Reve sees, Xavier sees in those controlled Dreams, so by now Xavier must know..."

"Whose side you were fighting on, yeah. But—" I shiver slightly, my mind spinning, as even in her own panic, she reaches over to my side and soothes my hastily sealed wound with golden threads twirling out of her fingertips. "But why did he call you *Your Majesty*, Evelyn? And the king! Why would the king spy on you, why are you suddenly calling him Xavier like you're on first-name basis with him?"

She looks up at me, and the tears in her eyes make my heart stop.

"Because I am his wife."

Chapter Twenty-Seven

I'VE BEEN HOVERING in front of her and unceremoniously fall out of the air, my foot collapsing beneath me as it touches down first. I feel her try to catch me, but I don't want to be caught. My face hits the parched, hard dirt of the Plains, but I don't lift my head. Until I hear the soft crack of her knees as she squats next to me, her hand stroking my wing tentatively. I drag my head up.

"You're...the queen."

"I never meant to deceive you," she breathes. I blink, and I'm dimly away of my eyes hardening, my lips slightly parted in disbelief.

"Never meant to deceive me? A soul keeper, the...the queen, Evelyn, and you never meant to—"

"Oh, spare me, Sadie, we're not in one of your ethics learning pods. It's not as if you wouldn't have built a relationship with me that wasn't built on lies."

"Evelyn, I—"

"Were you going to meet me for dinner the night after you saved Iema, if I hadn't turned up in the Gathering the next sunup as Controller?" Her eyes are blazing, and I gulp.

"Evelyn, what—"

"Were you planning on meeting me at the Lethean Inn for a date—"

"So it was a date—" She's not amused.

"Sadie—"

I toss up my hands. "Yes, all right, yes."

"And I imagine you wouldn't have let me see these beautiful wings of yours, would you? You would have kept them hidden away, lying about your entire life, your history, your people—" She's almost crying now, her eyes wide and not matching the anger of her voice.

"All right, yeah, but that didn't happen—"

"Sadie, I'm sorry. I can't say anything else. I'm sorry I lied to you. But you can't insist on taking this so personally when I needed...I needed... you don't know what it's like to... Sadie, I never wanted to be his wife."

Mom puts her hand on my wing sprouts, and I jump at her presence. But her eyes are soft, on Evelyn.

"I know what that feels like, Contro—Evelyn. I do. Listen to her, Sadie. Hear her out." Her voice is soft, and I look over her shoulder at Mama, who nods over Aon's head, nuzzled into her torso, before turning back to the dragons and trees she's trying to help Jax heal.

I take a shaky breath. "All right. Tell me."

Evelyn stands as Mom backs away again, nodding her confused thanks. I brace my hands on the ground for leverage and fly up toward Evelyn, but she holds up her hands and steps back like she thinks I'm about to hit her.

My heart breaks.

I hold up my hands, palms first, and approach more cautiously. I touch her waist as gently as my shaking hands allow. Her body relaxes and she clears her throat.

"I was born a duchess in Ilza, and when Xavier's father began the occupation there, he had my mother killed for insubordination. He brought me back to marry his son as a symbol of what he called the peace between our peoples." Her voice is soft, steady. Bitter.

My brow furrows. "But he took over Izla so many harvests ago. You must have been..."

Evelyn smiles softly as my arm muscles tense under her hands.

"Young? I was. Xavier, Fiora, and I grew up together." Her gaze is distant now, and she looks idly at Aon over my shoulder, like she's seeing her past burn behind me.

"Does he know you're a soul keeper?" My voice is cracking.

There's gravel in hers. "No. My mother died keeping the secret, and my father never would have... It's a long story, we don't have time—" She changes the topic, speaking quickly now. "Fiora had just died and I begged him to let me leave the grounds that were so full of our memories. He was the one who told me the Grovian rebels did it, murdered her through exposing her to a young one who hadn't been Initiated, and I was broken, Sadie, angry, so I believed him. He sent me to the Grove as Controller to give me a taste of real power, of hurting the people who'd taken Fiora from me. And then I met you, and I—"

Her voice cracks. Our eyes meet. "But really, he ordered Fiora's death," I offer.

She nods. "Reve saw Fi and I together the night before she fell ill; we weren't joiners, not exactly, but what we thought of ourselves together wouldn't have mattered to him, so it's no coincidence. Nor is it a coincidence that Blaze fell ill right after I denied Reve and the Mach access to the Underlands." She blinks tears out of her eyes, and I catch them with my lips.

"They must have chosen quer because a young one would hurt me most and would be easiest to target. If they chose one who was just Initiated—Sliced—they could make it look like it was the rebels' fault, that you all had sabotaged quer Slicing, but that's not what happened. Que was murdered like Fi was, and all of it because of me, my fault…"

Her voice breaks, but she presses on before I can protest. I run my hands up and down her shoulders, shaking my head uselessly.

"And now you must hate me, you must—"

"No, no. You can't help your past." I stare off at Mom, my brow furrowed, my mind spinning. "You're not the only one with a secret, Evelyn. I have to—"

I stop, flinching, when a voice calling her name makes her jump out of my grasp.

Jealousy flits through my stomach as Evelyn spins and puts her hands all over Iema's face, sides, shoulders, face again.

"Iema, where have you been?" The agony in her voice makes my insecurity curl up before it disintegrates into shame.

"Helping the Grovians defend the Gathering, the Underland. They've set up defense perimeters, but Evy—Reve is with them. His seal, the Mach. Evy, if he sees you fighting for them—"

"He already has."

"Then you have to leave."

"I will, soon, I promise, never mind that. Did anyone see you?"

Iema grimaces as she reaches under her uniform, rubbing out a stitch in her side. "Had it out with Richard. Called me a traitor, whore, you name it, and he had a word for it. And a blow."

She turns toward me and there's a nasty gash covering her cheek. Crusted blood streaks her face. I inhale sharply and clench my fists, wanting to pummel the man who hurt her like that, who dealt Blaze a death blow with his smooth words and empty heart. Iema's eyes sweep my body, like she's noticing me for the first time, and she breaks out laughing.

"Look at you, Sadie, all stiff and indignant on behalf of a woman you barely know and probably should hate."

A sweaty arm slings over my shoulder above my wing sprouts, and I tug Aon closer—much closer, never close enough now—to me. "Yeah well, my big sister's chivalrous that way," he says, and I wonder, out of nowhere, when his voice started to get so deep.

He could have been dead—he was dead—and I would never have noticed him growing.

I don't care what anyone might think. I let my head sink onto his subtly shaking shoulder and shudder until fresh tears quake out of my body. My little brother envelops me in his fleshy arms, and I hear Iema's confused tone ask what in Lunav she missed. Evelyn is whispering and I'm crying and all that matters is Aon's steady pulse against my skin.

"You did what?" Iema's shout makes both of us jump, and then I'm being wrenched from him and am sprawled flat on my back. Both of my moms yell my name, and pain courses through my wings.

"What are you doing? Let her go!"

"Iema, stop it—"

"Would you die for her, Sadie? Would you? Because you had better be willing to do that rather than spill to anyone—anyone, you hear me?—that she's a—that she saved your brother the way she did, you understand me? If anyone finds out, I will personally—"

"Hunt me down and skin me alive. Yeah, got that part," I wheeze from underneath the tip of her blade. Evelyn and Aon are both yanking and yelling at her still, but she's impervious to their pleas. She must be more powerfully trained with the Energies too, than I thought she was, because I feel Mom and Mama tugging on the Energies to get her blade away from my windpipe. They're unsuccessful, and I'm grateful I've never been up against Iema. Until now. She lifts me by the front of my tunic and slams me back into the ground.

"Sadie!" she growls.

"I'm not gonna give her up, Iema. And if I do, you can kill me all you want."

Maybe it's something in my face, in the way my body is limp, the way I'm not fighting her. Maybe it's the shredded tone of Mama's voice when she yells, "You just betrayed your own people! Do you really want to turn on the only ones who'll protect you now?" Maybe it's that Evelyn's voice cracks, hard, when she says, "Iema, please. I trust her with my life. All of them. Even Lerian saved my life tonight."

Whatever it is, Iema hauls me to my feet, brushes me off and gestures for Evelyn and Mom to heal my cuts and calm my bruises.

"I'm sorry, Sadie. I just had to be sure. She could be killed for being who she is. For doing what she can do." She lowers her voice. "Soul keeping. She'd be killed if anyone knew."

"I know the feeling," I mutter as Mom and Evelyn soothe my scrapes and bruises, Evelyn looking askance at Iema all the while, muttering about overzealousness and ruffians.

"I'm fine, it was just a shove," I squirm.

I clear my throat and pull Evelyn away from the others gently, grimacing ruefully at a now bashful-looking Iema as I do.

"Look, Evelyn. What Iema was saying about having a secret you could die for? You're…" I swallow and she furrows her brow and takes my hands. My heart warms at the casualness of her gesture, and I so want to get used to it.

I hope telling her I can Dream won't utterly destroy any shot we have. But it's the only lie that I still have between us. And it needs to be done. So we can really begin.

"Evelyn, I have to tell you something. I can—"

There's a rustling, a loud rustling, near the breach in the barrier. With a glance at Evelyn, Iema sprints off toward it.

We both stare after her as she skids to a halt and dashes back toward us.

"Reve!" she mouths, speeding toward us. "He's coming!"

Chapter Twenty-Eight

THE QUEEN AND I lock eyes, and when she speaks, her voice is steel.

"You know he's coming back for me, Sadie. The king knows that I fought alongside you, because Reve saw." She looks toward the barrier; we can't see anything yet, but the rustling through the Forest outside is getting louder.

"Mom! The Hands are coming back!" Aon is shouting. Jax is swearing and Mom is singing up to Gimla to round up whatever dragons are left flying. The ground is rumbling like the aftershock of an earthquake, and the trees prepare themselves for another battle.

"Mama, does that mean they hurt our people? The ones who took them out of the Plains? Kashat and Lerian, Mama!"

We both stare at Aon and take a simultaneous deep breath.

"Sadie, if you want to keep your people safe, I have to return to mine,—to the king. Now, and lead him off of your trail, make him believe that you died in a struggle with the Mach, that I've been loyal to him all along..."

"No." I cut her off, my voice thick with fluid. "Stay. Evelyn, we can protect each other, like you said we could."

"I couldn't protect Fiora, what makes you think I can protect you?"

Her shout is sudden, anguished, her voice torn, so unexpected that I jump back from her.

"Evelyn—"

"Sadie, he murdered Fiora because he saw her with me. He murdered Blaze because I defied him in front of his enemies. What do you think he'll do to you? To your family? Now that he's seen me fight alongside you?"

I look around wildly, at the Grovians streaming in from the Forest, all bearing warnings that the Mach have awoken from the Freeze, that they're heading back to the Plains. We don't have much time. The Energies are too strained to try another freeze spell so soon.

"You don't have to protect us, Evelyn, we've always protected ourselves, and we can protect you. And Iema, we—"

"Sadie, Xavier's never ever going to stop, not until he's satisfied that you are no longer a threat to him." Her eyes bore into mine, and I almost drown. "Not until he's satisfied that I'm no longer yours."

My breath hitches. I lick my lips. I taste like my own blood, and soot. "Mom and Mama will think of something."

"No. Sadie, go into hiding. I still have people in Izla, they'll keep you safe, you and Zaylam, and Aon. Go on Zaylam's back, my people will find you on the coast, above Qathram. You can't protect me, Sadie, but I'm still the queen; I can protect you."

Her head is tilted slightly to the side, tears streaming down her face but her mouth slipped into a sad smile, a broken smile. Her eyes refuse to leave mine.

Our faces are just flutters apart. My hands find her waist, and her fingertips, my face. I am about to say something, anything, to object, to come up with a brilliant plan so she won't have to go back to him.

But then we hear them. Storming through the breach in the barrier.

The soldiers.

Led by Reve. So the shouts are true. They must have woken and escaped from those who'd been carrying them away. Lerian, Kashat. Aora, P'Tal, Zeel. Tamzel. E'rix. Are they all dead?

Because here, now, are people there shouldn't be. Mach soldiers.

Speeding through the Plains. Toward us. I hear Aon, barely with life back in his body, trying to twist the Energies defensively as Jax and my moms encircle him and curve the Energies into spells that send two of the Mach spiraling off their feet. My growns call my name, Iema screams Evelyn's. They're forming a wall between the soldiers and us, blocking us from their view, from their spells. The soldiers can't see us yet, but my family can't keep this wall up for long. Even with help from whoever's come back from the Forest, Aon's still weak, and there are so many injured to protect—Zaylam, Zaylam among them—that's more than they can take at once.

Evelyn's eyes widen and hold mine harder than they ever have, blazing deeply.

She pulls my face forward. Touches her forehead to mine. I feel like we're being caught up in one of those massive waves of water our touch created earlier. Are we doing that again? We might be.

And then her lips meet mine.

I taste sorrow and I taste promise. I taste the first moment I laid eyes on her, and I taste last night. Last night? Wasn't it eons ago?

I flutter my wings so our bodies are flush against each other, and she wraps her arms around my neck. I deepen our kiss. I feel her smile softly. A tear drips from her face onto mine.

"Sadie. I'm not going to grieve. Because I'm not losing you. Not for good."

"Evelyn, stay, we can—"

She shakes her head, her hands framing my face, the amber ring in her eyes glowing.

"But if I did ever lose you, Sadie?"

The shouts get louder, Iema is calling for Evelyn to leave, to leave now.

"I would grieve."

She's kissing me again, and I forget everything but her lips, the smooth warmth of her skin, the skyflower tang of her breath.

"I would grieve you too," I hope my body tells her. I hope it tells her, because now I'm stumbling on empty air as the Energies rent through me. Painful, but not enough to really hurt me.

She's gone.

Reve, Iema, the other soldiers are gone too.

"What in Lunav happened?" Aon's shouting. "Where'd they all go?"

"Evelyn," I call out.

Mama reaches her fingers into the air, into the Energies, around us. They've bent so hard the entire Plains smells metallic, now. No magic will come to the Plains for quite some time. "Feels like a snap spell. She must have snapped them all away."

Snapped them all away, and absorbed most of the pain of such an immense job into her own body.

"She saved us, then. All of us, not just me."

No one responds to Aon. Everyone just stares at me.

Her snap spell, so strong I double over like I've been hit in the gut, must have saved us all. With that snap spell, taking herself and all the Mach away, she used our last moment together to kiss me, to say goodbye, because she's saved the Plains, like Aon said. But at the cost of giving herself up to a life with a man she didn't choose. She doesn't love the king, but she loves…

Me.

A pair of solid hands catch me before I stumble to the ground. Lerian's.

I sink into her torso and she curls her arm under my drooping wings.

A soft wind blows across the Plains, and gentle humming from where Zaylam lies sweetens our ears.

Aon's arm meets Lerian's on the other side of my body, and they hoist me up between them.

"Come on, faerie. You can cry all those lovesick tears about your *joiner* later. We've got a lot of healing to do right now."

"You getting all metaphorical on me now, Ler?" My voice sounds like I haven't used it in harvests.

Aon snorts and Lerian rolls her eyes as we set off toward Zaylam. "Maybe I am. I'm full of surprises."

The sound of her axe clinking above a sword aimed at Evelyn's body rings in my memory. Evelyn.

That wind flutters past again, and it's laced, somehow, amidst the metallic musk, with the tang of skyflower fruit. Evelyn.

"Yeah. Yeah, I guess we all are, huh?"

I don't hear what Aon and Ler carry on about as we trudge through the still-smoking Plains. I glance toward the Forest, in the direction of the Highlands.

In the direction of the biggest surprise I've ever had, the one I know I'll see whenever I close my eyes.

Until, one day, she's in front of my open eyes again.

Glossary

Age-mate: A Grovian faeric term that indicates when people are of the same age; this gets complicated because faeries age faster than humans during childhood, but their growth evens out in teenage years.

Dream: In Lunav, Dreams are real; when one magical creature is asleep, their Energies can lock with another creature's that is awake, and the Dreamer will experience the other creature's waking perspective.

Energies: The threads of magical potential that enables spell-creation in Lunav.

The Flowing: The Lunavic ocean, consisting of several provinces, including Qathram, where Plains dragons swam to each year before the Kinzemna massacre.

The Gathering: The central community space in the Grovian Forest.

Grove: A Lunavic province consisting of the Forest, the Plains, and the Underland.

Grown (food): Food that has never been alive, but rather is magicked into existence by centaur and faerie Growers.

Growns (people): A Lunavic term for parents.

Hands: A term for human soldiers that work for the human monarch.

Hatchling mates: Before Slicings destroyed faeries' ability to Dream, a Lunavad tree from the Plains would have two hatchling mates: one faerie and one dragon. The faerie would Dream the dragon as que was being developed from the tree's sap, in a bulb on the tree's branches; this bond will remain between the three of the hatchling mates (the tree, the dragon, and the faerie) throughout their lives.

Highland: A province of Lunav in which mostly humans (now) live; the seat of the monarchy's power is in the Highlands.

Izla: A Grovian province located across the Flowing from the Grove, the Samp, and the Highlands.

Joiners: A Lunavic term for romantic partners.

Kinzemna: A Grovian celebration for the dragons that live in the Plains; this holiday marks the departure of the dragons into the Flowing for two seasons each year, where they journey to Qathram (a province in the Flowing).

Kinzemna massacre: An attack orchestrated by the human monarchy designed to destroy dragons' ability to live both in the Flowing and in the air/on land; its other motive was to bleed the dragons for their valued blood.

Lunamez: A Grovian holiday celebrating Lunavic history and origin stories.

Lunav: A land full of magical creatures and humans, which includes five major provinces: the Highlands, the Flowing, the Grove, the Samp, and Izla.

Lunavic blood plague: A plague that infects humans, faeries, and centaurs alike; it began after the human monarchy started development projects across Lunav. The plague is only contagious after death, and is allegedly prevented by Slicings.

Nears: A Lunavic term for teenagers.

Non: A faeric term for human (has negative connotations).

The Plains: The most sacred part of the Grove, where Lunavad trees live and where dragons are hatched; since the human monarchy began attacking dragons, the Lunavad trees erected an invisible magical barrier to protect the Plains from invasion.

The Pits: An underground prison network in the Highlands, notorious in the Grove for disappearing dissidents like Dreamers and soul keepers.

Que/quer/quer's: Genderqueer/nonbinary pronouns used in Lunav.

Soul keepers: Magical creatures (most often, humans, but sometimes faeries or centaurs as well) who can temporarily host the souls of other Lunavic creatures, combining their Energies with the other's, often to heal them, even bring them back to life, or transfer their soul to another consent-giving body.

Slicing: A surgical procedure forced on magical newly borns (faeric, human, and centaur) that destroys the ability to Dream. The human government calls Slicings "Initiations" and claims that they eliminate susceptibility to the Lunavic blood plague.

Tread: A path in the Forest that winds through the Grove, out into the provinces of the Samp, as well as into the human-populated province of Lethe.

Underland: A Grovian province bordering the Flowing; the major magical creatures that live in the Underland are centaurs.

Acknowledgements

Girls who love girls deserve faerie tales about girls who love girls (who will live their happy endings together, even if it takes some obstacle-laden middles). Also dragons. You, reading this, deserve to be friends with dragons. The entire world of this novel springs from that need, from the kinds of stories that we don't get enough of. But I promise, you deserve them. All of them. So my first thank-you is to LGBTQA+ fandom, to those who have the courage to create and read pieces of the worlds we want to live in. Keep being you, always.

Jason Bradley, my editor at NineStar: you know the drill by now. You make me a better writer, etcetera. But you also did something so profound: you believed in Sadie and her adventures and love story. You took a chance on singing dragons, and on me, and I will never be able to thank you enough for that. And Beth Phelan, with your #DVpit amazingness: you make publishing—and therefore the world—so much better every day. Thank you doesn't cover it.

Marcos, you've read pretty much every draft of this thing. You've listened to me cry about it, and you've been the best cheerleader that Sunnydale High has ever seen (sorry, Cordelia). This time, it's NOT a trap!! Katie, you enthusiastically endured Sadie's rambling notes, tied together and called a first draft. Your unwavering support—for my gay disaster characters and my gay disaster self—is something that will glow in my heart forever. Jason, my Nemo, if I'd never FOUND you, I'd have never found enough of myself to write this book. Thank you. Kaysi, Josh, James: from bitmojis and hand-holding to first-times-coming-out and panic-attack-talk-downs, I am so much better because you exist and because (for some reason), you always love me.

Mom, for library trips, bedtime cuddles, and unwavering love. Dad, for storytelling and memories while looking out over Ostego Lake (and getting soaked while searching for deer). Sis, for feeding ants chocolate and showing me how beautiful spiders are. Aunt Jamie, for telling me that thing about looking at my own eyes in the mirror and one day loving who I see (I remember things!).

And my angel: I was going to propose to you with the dedication of this book, but alas, the timing was off (and our engagement was still pretty great, huh?). Erika, you are my soul keeper and you are my first kiss amongst the fireflies. You are dragon flights and life-giving tree sap. You are, my darling, everything. Truly: thank you.

About the Author

Jenn Polish is the author of two young adult books, *Lunav* and *Lost Boy, Found Boy*. Their debut novella, *Lost Boy, Found Boy*, is a scifi re-telling of *Peter Pan* in which Neverland is a holomatrix, Hook is a bisexual cyborg, and Tink is an asexual lesbian computer interface. Their debut novel, *Lunav*, a lesbian faerie tale, features dragons that grow on trees and friendship amongst rebellion. They teach Theater and English in the CUNY system, where they are also a doctoral candidate in English. They live in New York with their fiancée and their fantasies of having multiple puppies.

Twitter: @jpolishwrites

Website: www.jpolish.com

Other books by this author

Lost Boy, Found Boy

Also Available from NineStar Press

Connect with NineStar Press

www.ninestarpress.com

www.facebook.com/ninestarpress

www.facebook.com/groups/NineStarNiche

www.twitter.com/ninestarpress

www.tumblr.com/blog/ninestarpress

CPSIA information can be obtained
at www.ICGtesting.com
Printed in the USA
BVOW08s0832220318
511248BV00001B/34/P

9 781948 608336

My Great-Grandpa Collins

by Jimmy Keating

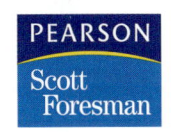

PEARSON
Scott Foresman

Editorial Offices: Glenview, Illinois • Parsippany, New Jersey • New York, New York
Sales Offices: Needham, Massachusetts • Duluth, Georgia • Glenview, Illinois
Coppell, Texas • Sacramento, California • Mesa, Arizona

Boston

New York City

This is Great-Grandpa Collins as a boy. He grew up in a small town in Ireland.

For my History Day project, I researched the life of my great-grandfather. This is what I learned about him. My family called him Great-Grandpa Collins. His name was James Patrick Collins. He was born in a small town in Ireland in 1888. He died in 1977. He was eighty-nine years old. I never met him, but my Grandma says I look just like him.

Great-Grandpa Collins was from a family of eight boys and girls. He was the youngest child in the family. His father was a farmer. His mother worked very hard taking care of the children.

Great-Grandpa Collins was a tall man. He loved to laugh. He loved to tell stories and jokes. My daddy loved to visit him when he was a little boy. I wish I could have met Great-Grandpa.

Great-Grandpa Collins must have seen lots of interesting things through his spectacles. He was very proud to be a policeman.

On my tenth birthday, my dad gave me a special present. He gave me my Great-Grandpa Collins's spectacles. Dad remembers when Great-Grandpa Collins would read him the Sunday comics. Great-Grandpa always wore the spectacles when he was reading. He would laugh so hard that the spectacles would fall halfway down his nose.

Dad also gave me Great-Grandpa Collins's police badge and hat. Great-Grandpa was a policeman. When I was a little boy, I pretended that I was a policeman. Sometimes Daddy let me wear Great-Grandpa's hat as a special treat.

3

Statue of Liberty

Great-Grandpa Collins came to America in 1915. Two of his brothers had already immigrated to America. He lived with them at first. He came on a ship to Ellis Island, which is near the Statue of Liberty in New York Harbor. Great-Grandpa Collins loved to tell how the Statue of Liberty was the first "person" he saw when he arrived in America.

Great-Grandpa and his brothers lived in Boston, Massachusetts. After a few months in Boston, he met a young woman he liked. Her name was Claire. She was also from Ireland. She was a nurse. They both loved to dance and sing. They got married two years after they met. Dad says they used to sing and dance in their living room even when they were old.

Did You Know? Ellis Island

Ellis Island is located in New York Harbor, New York. Between 1892 and 1954, Ellis Island was the fist stop in America for immigrants who came across the Atlantic Ocean. Ellis Island is now an immigration museum.

---

immigrated: moved into a country

In this wedding picture, Great-Grandpa and Great-Grandma are standing with many friends. They were married in Boston.

Great-Grandpa and Great-Grandma Collins lived in Boston all of their lives. They had three children. One of them was my Grandma Nancy.

My Grandma Nancy says all her friends loved Great-Grandpa. He built the best snowmen in the neighborhood. Every Sunday the children came to hear him read the comics. They loved to watch his glasses fall down his nose.

Great-Grandpa was a brave policeman. He saved three children from drowning. He caught at least four bank robbers. Grandma Nancy says that every night when she was a girl, she whispered to her father that he was the best policeman in Boston.

Our Collins family reunion

Great-Grandpa and Great-Grandma Collins were proud of being Irish. They were proud of being American citizens too.

They had fourteen grandchildren and thirty-six great-grandchildren, including me. Last summer we had a huge family reunion. We had a picnic at a park.

Everyone brought American food and Irish food. I made Irish soda bread from our family recipe. Lots of relatives brought family photos.

There were so many people having fun. We sang Irish songs. Some of the children did Irish step dancing.

If Great-Grandpa and Great-Grandma Collins hadn't come to America and gotten married, none of their family would have been born.

---

reunion: special party that brings together a family or old friends

step dancing: a special type of dancing

Here are photos of the town where Great-Grandpa Collins was born.

Great-Grandpa and Great-Grandma left Ireland when they were young. They only went back to Ireland for visits two times. In those days, people didn't travel as much as they do now. They didn't talk on the telephone as often either. They could not e-mail each other. Instead, they wrote lots of letters. I think Great-Grandpa and Great-Grandma were very homesick for their family and country.

My dad has researched our Irish relatives. Many still live in the town where Great-Grandpa Collins was born. Six months ago, I wrote to one of my cousins in Ireland. Now I have a new pen pal. His name is Jimmy Collins. That is my name too, except Collins is my middle name. My pen pal Jimmy Collins lives in Great-Grandpa Collins's town.

This summer my family and I are going to Ireland. I cannot wait to meet Jimmy. Jimmy promised to show me the farmhouse where Great-Grandpa Collins grew up. He sent me a picture of the house. His aunt and uncle live there now.

Jimmy also sent a picture of himself. Grandma Nancy says we look like twins. She says it's eerie. She says we both look exactly like Great-Grandpa Collins!

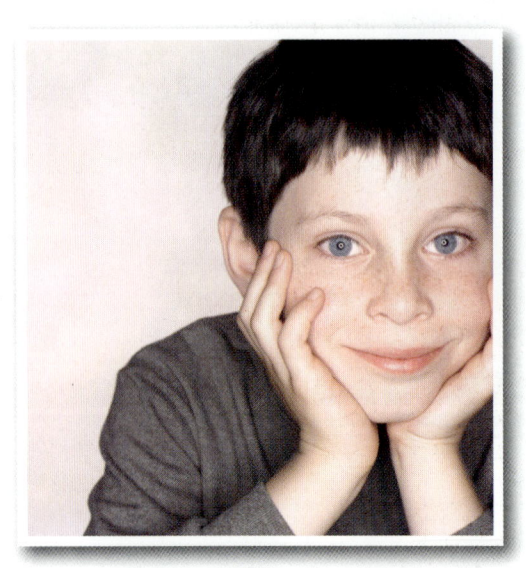

Jimmy Collins from Ireland

Jimmy Collins from Massachusetts